John Galsworthy was born on August 14, [...] the son of John and Blanche Galsworthy [...] John Galsworthy senior, whose family came from Devon, was a successful solicitor in London and a man of 'new money', determined to provide privilege and security for his family. They idolised him. By contrast, their mother Blanche was a more difficult woman, strict and distant. Galsworthy commented, 'My father really predominated in me from the start . . . I was so truly and deeply fond of him that I seemed not to have a fair share of love left to give my mother'.

Young Johnny enjoyed the happy, secure childhood of a Victorian, upper-middle-class family. Educated at Harrow, he was popular at school and a good sportsman. Holidays were spent with family and friends, moving between their country houses. After finishing school, John went up to New College, Oxford to read law. There he enjoyed the carefree life of a privileged student, not working particularly hard, gambling and becoming known as 'the best dressed man in College'. But he could also be quiet and serious, a contemporary describing how 'He moved among us somewhat withdrawn . . . a sensitive, amused, somewhat cynical spectator of the human scene'.

The period after university was one of indecision for Galsworthy. Although his father wanted him to become a barrister, the law held little appeal. So he decided to get away from it all and travel. It was on a voyage in the South Seas in 1893 that he met Joseph Conrad, and the two became close friends. It was a crucial friendship in Galsworthy's life. Conrad encouraged his love of writing, but Galsworthy attributes his final inspiration to the woman he was falling in love with: Ada.

Ada Nemesis Pearson Cooper married Major Arthur Galsworthy, John's cousin, in 1891. But the marriage was a tragic mistake. Embraced by the entire family, Ada became close friends with John's beloved sisters, Lilian and Mabel, and through them John heard of her increasing misery, fixing in his imagination the pain of an unhappy marriage. Thrown together more and more, John and Ada eventually became lovers in September 1895. They were unafraid of declaring their relationship and facing the consequences, but the only person they couldn't bear to hurt was John's adored father, with his traditional values. And so they endured ten years of secrecy until Galsworthy's father died in December 1904. By September 1905 Ada's divorce had come through and they were finally able to marry.

It was around this time, in 1906, that Galsworthy's writing career flourished. During the previous decade he had been a man 'in chains', emotionally and professionally, having finally abandoned law in 1894. He struggled to establish himself as an author. But after many false starts and battling a lifelong insecurity about his writing, Galsworthy turned an affectionately satirical eye on the world he knew best and created the indomitable Forsytes, a mirror image of his own relations – old Jolyon: his father; Irene: his beloved Ada, to name but a few. On reading the manuscript, his sister Lilian was alarmed that he could so expose their private lives, but John dismissed her fears saying only herself, Mabel and their mother, 'who perhaps had better not read the book', knew enough to draw comparisons. *The Man of Property*, the first book in *The Forsyte Saga*, was published to instant acclaim; Galsworthy's fame as an author was now sealed.

By the time the first Forsyte trilogy had been completed, with *In Chancery* (1920) and *To Let* (1921), sales of *The Forsyte Saga* had reached one million on both sides of the Atlantic. With the public clambering for more, Galsworthy followed these with six more Forsyte novels, the last of which, *Over The River*, was completed just before his death in 1933. And their appeal endures, immortalised on screen in much-loved adaptations such as the film *That Forsyte Woman* (1949), starring Errol Flynn. The celebrated BBC drama in 1967 with Kenneth Moore and Eric Porter was a phenomenal success, emptying the pubs and churches of Britain on a Sunday evening, and reaching an estimated worldwide audience of 160 million. The recent popular 2002 production starred Damien Lewis, Rupert Graves and Ioan Gruffudd and won a Bafta TV award.

Undoubtedly *The Forsyte Saga* is Galsworthy's most distinguished work, but he was well known, if not more successful in his time, as a dramatist. His inherent compassion meant Galsworthy was always involved in one cause or another, from women's suffrage to a ban on ponies in mines, and his plays very much focus on the social injustices of his day. *The Silver Box* (1906) was his first major success, but *Justice* (1910), a stark depiction of prison life, had an even bigger impact. Winston Churchill was so impressed by it that he immediately arranged for prison reform, reducing the hours of solitary confinement. *The Skin Game* (1920) was another big hit and later adapted into a film, under the same title, by Alfred Hitchcock.

Despite Galsworthy's literary success, his personal life was still troubled. Although he and Ada were deeply in love, the years of uncertainty had taken their toll. They never had children and their marriage reached a crisis in 1910 when Galsworthy formed a close friendship with a young dancer called Margaret Morris while working on one of his plays with her. But John, confused and tortured by the thought of betraying Ada, broke off all contact with Margaret in 1912 and went abroad with his wife. The rest of their lives were spent constantly on the move; travelling in America, Europe, or at home in London, Dartmoor and later Sussex. Numerous trips were made in connection with PEN, the international writers club, after Galsworthy was elected its first president in 1921. Many people have seen the constant travelling as unsettling for Galsworthy and destructive to his writing, but being with Ada was all that mattered to him: 'This is what comes of giving yourself to a woman body and soul. A. paralyses and has always paralysed me. I have never been able to face the idea of being cut off from her.'

By the end of his life, Galsworthy, the man who had railed against poverty and injustice, had become an established, reputable figure in privileged society. Having earlier refused a knighthood, he was presented with an Order of Merit in 1929. And in 1932 he was awarded the Nobel Prize for literature. Although it was fashionable for younger writers to mock the traditional Edwardian authors, Virginia Woolf dismissing Galsworthy as a 'stuffed shirt', J.M. Barrie perceived his contradictory nature: 'A queer fish, like the rest of us. So sincerely weighed down by the out-of-jointness of things socially . . . but outwardly a man-about-town, so neat, so correct – he would go to the stake for his opinions but he would go courteously raising his hat.'

John Galsworthy died on January 31, 1933, at the age of sixty-five, at Grove Lodge in Hampstead, with Ada by his side. At his request, his ashes were scattered over Bury Hill in Sussex. *The Times* hailed him as the 'mouthpiece' of his age, 'the interpreter in drama, and in fiction of a definite phase in English social history'.

*Other Forsyte novels by John Galsworthy and available from
Headline Review*

The Man Of Property
In Chancery
To Let
The White Monkey
Swan Song
Maid In Waiting
Flowering Wilderness
Over The River

The Forsyte Saga
The Silver Spoon

John Galsworthy

headline
review

First published in Great Britain in 1926

This paperback edition published in 2007 by HEADLINE REVIEW
An imprint of HEADLINE PUBLISHING GROUP

1

ISBN 978 0 7553 4089 7

Typeset in Sabon by Palimpsest Book Production Limited,
Grangemouth, Stirlingshire

Printed and bound in Great Britain by
Clays Ltd, St Ives plc

Headline's policy is to use papers that are natural, renewable
and recyclable products and made from wood grown in
sustainable forests. The logging and manufacturing processes
are expected to conform to the environmental regulations
of the country of origin.

HEADLINE PUBLISHING GROUP
A division of Hachette Livre UK Ltd
338 Euston Road
London NW1 3BH

www.reviewbooks.co.uk
www.headline.co.uk

To John Fortescue

FORSYTE FA

b. 1741, JOLYON FORSYTE (Farmer, of Hays, D[

b. 1770, Jolyon 'Superior Dossett' (Builder),   Edgar
d. 1850 *m.* 1798, Ann Pierce, daughter   (In Jute)
of Country Solicitor

(1)   (2)

b. 1799, Ann,   *b.* 1806; Jolyon 'Old Jolyon' *d.* 1892
d. 1886   (Tea Merchant 'Forsyte and Treffry'   (Soli
'Aunt Ann'   Chairman of Companies), Stanhope Gate,   ar
m. 1846, Edith Moor, *d.* 1874, daughter of Barrister

b. 1847, Jolyon, *d.* 1920,
'Young Jolyon' (Underwriter and Artist),
St John's Wood and Robin Hill, *m.* 1880

m. 1868 (1), Frances Crisson (2), Helene Hilmer *d.* 1894 (Austro-English)   *m.* 1901 (3), Irene,   *m.* 1[
d. 1880, daughter   daughter of   daugh[
of Colonel   Professor Heron   He
and divorced wife   di[

b. 1869, June   *b.* 1879, Jolly,   *b.* 1881, Holly,   of Soames Forsyte
(Engaged to Philip Bosinney,   *d.* in Transvaal,   *m.* 1900,
never married)   1900   Val Dartie   *b.* 1901, Joylon,
'Jon', *m.* 1924,   m
Anne Wilmot
b.

*   (5)   (6)   (7)

b. 1813, Roger, *d.* 1899 (Collector   *b.* 1814, Julia, *d.* 1905 'Aunt Juley' *m.* Septimus   *b.* 1815, Heste[
of House Property), Prince's   Small, of weak constitution, who died   *d.* 1907 'Aunt He
Gardens, *m.* 1853, Mary Monk   of it. Reverted to Bayswater Road   Bayswater Ro[

b. 1853, Roger   *b.* 1856,   *b.* 1858, Francie   *b.* 1860,   *b.* 1862,   *b.* 1849, Nicholas 'Youn[
'Young Roger'   George,   (Composer   Eustace   Thomas   Nicholas' (Insurances)
m. Muriel Wake   *d.* 1922   and poetess)   *m.* No Offspring   *m.* No Offspring   *m.* 1877, Dorothy Boxto[
Widower before   *b.* 1879, Nicholas   *b.* 1880,   *b.* 1[
b. 1890, Roger   the War   'Very Young Nicholas',   Blanche
'Very Young Roger',   (Barrister, O.B.E.) *m.*
Wounded in the War

encombe, Dorset), *d.* 1812, *m.* 1768, Julia Hayter

Nicholas
(Mayor of Bosport)

Julia
m. Nightingale

Roger
(Merchant Service)

(3)   (4)   *

b. 1811, James, *d.* 1901
icitor. Founder of firm 'Forsyte, Bustard,
id Forsyte'), Park Lane, *m.* 1852, Emily
Golding, *b.* 1831, 'Emily'

b. 1811, Swithin, *d.* 1891
(Estate and Land Agent)
'Four-in-hand Forsyte',
Hyde Park Mansions

b. 1855, Soames
(Solicitor and Connoisseur)
Montpelier Square and
883 (1), Irene,   Mapledurham, *m.* 1901
iter of Professor (2), Annette, *b.* 1880, daughter
:ron, *b.* 1863,   of Mme. Lamotte
vorced 1900

b. 1858, Winifred,   *b.* 1861,   *b.* 1865,
m. 1879,   Rachel   Cicely
Montague Dartic
'Man of the World',
Green Street

b. 1880, Val, *m.* 1900,   *b.* 1882, Imogen   *b.* 1884,   *b.* 1886, Benedict
Holly, daughter of   *m.* 1906, Jack Cardigan   Maud
'Young Jolyon'

b. 1901, Fleur
. 1920, Michael Mont

1923, Christopher 'Kit'

b. 1910, John   *b.* 1912, James

(8)   (9)   (10)

·r,   *b.* 1817, Nicholas *d.* 1908 (Mines, Railways,
·ster'   and House Property), Ladbroke Grove,
ıd   *m.* 1848, Elizabeth Blaine, 'Fanny'

b. 1819, Timothy
(Publisher, in Consols),
Bayswater Road

b. 1821, Susan, *d.* 189:
Campden Hill,
m. Hayman

ıg *b.* 1853, *b.* 1857, *b.* 1859, *b.* 1861, *b.* 1862,
ı   Ernest   Archibald Marian   Florence Euphemia
ın

St. John   Augustus   Annabel   Giles   Jesse
m.   *m.*   *m.* Spender   'The Dromios'

881, Christopher   *b.* 1884, Violet   *b.* 1886,   *b.* 1894,
(Inclining to   (Artistic Pastels) Gladys Patrick (In the War)
the stage)

Offspring,
One killed in the War

'But O, the thorns we stand upon!'

The Winter's Tale, William Shakespeare

Part I

Chapter One

A Stranger

The young man, who, at the end of September, 1924, dismounted from a taxicab in South Square, Westminster, was so unobtrusively American that his driver had some hesitation in asking for double his fare. The young man had no hesitation in refusing it.

'Are you unable to read?' he said, softly. 'Here's four shillings.'

With that he turned his back and looked at the house before which he had descended. This, the first private English house he had ever proposed to enter, inspired him with a certain uneasiness, as of a man who expects to part with a family ghost. Comparing a letter with the number chased in pale brass on the door, he murmured: 'It surely is,' and rang the bell.

While waiting for the door to be opened, he was conscious of extreme quietude, broken by a clock chiming four as if with the voice of Time itself. When the last boom died, the door yawned inward, and a man, almost hairless, said:

'Yes, sir?'

The young man removed a soft hat from a dark head.

'This is Mrs Michael Mont's house?'

'Correct, sir.'

'Will you give her my card, and this letter?'

'"Mr Francis Wilmot, Naseby, S.C." Will you wait in here, sir?'

Ushered through the doorway of a room on the right, Francis Wilmot was conscious of a commotion close to the ground, and some teeth grazing the calf of his leg.

'Dandie!' said the voice of the hairless man, 'you little devil! That dog is a proper little brute with strangers, sir. Stand still! I've known him bite clean through a lady's stockings.'

Francis Wilmot saw with interest a silver-grey dog nine inches high and nearly as broad, looking up at him with lustrous eyes above teeth of extreme beauty.

'It's the baby, sir,' said the hairless man, pointing to a sort of nest on the floor before the fireless hearth; 'he *will* go for people when he's with the baby. But once he gets to smelling your trousers, he's all right. Better not touch the baby, though. Mrs Mont was here a minute ago; I'll take your card up to her.'

Francis Wilmot sat down on a settee in the middle of the room; and the dog lay between him and the baby.

And while the young man sat he gazed around him. The room was painted in panels of a sub-golden hue, with a silver-coloured ceiling. A clavichord, little golden ghost of a piano, stood at one end. Glass lustres, pictures of flowers and of a silvery-necked lady swinging a skirt and her golden slippers, adorned the walls. The curtains were of gold and silver. The silver-coloured carpet felt wonderfully soft beneath his feet, the furniture was of a golden wood.

The young man felt suddenly quite homesick. He was back in the living-room of an old 'Colonial' house, in the bend of a lonely South Carolina river, reddish in hue. He was staring at the effigy of his high-collared, red-coated great-grandfather, Francis Wilmot, Royalist major in the War of Independence. They always said it was like the effigy he saw when shaving every morning; the smooth dark hair drooping across his right temple, the narrow nose and lips, the narrow dark hand on the sword-hilt or the razor, the slits of dark eyes gazing steadily out. Young Francis was seeing the darkies working in the cotton-fields under a sun that he did not seem to have seen since he came over here; he was walking with his setter along the swamp edge, where Florida moss festooned the tall dolorous trees; he was thinking of the Wilmot inheritance, ruined in the Civil War, still decayed yet precious, and whether to struggle on with it, or to sell it to the Yank who wanted a weekend run-to from his Charleston dock job, and would improve it out of recognition. It would be lonely there, now that Anne had married that young Britisher, Jon Forsyte, and gone away north, to Southern Pines. And he thought of his sister, thus lost to him, dark, pale, vivid, 'full of sand'. Yes! this room made him homesick, with its perfection, such as he had never beheld, where the only object out of keeping was that dog, lying on its side now, and so thick through that all its little legs were in the air. Softly he said:

'It's the prettiest room I ever was in.'

'What a perfectly charming thing to overhear!'

A young woman, with crinkly chestnut hair above a creamy face, with smiling lips, a short straight nose, and very white dark-lashed eyelids active over dark hazel eyes, stood near the door. She came towards him, and held out her hand.

Francis Wilmot bowed over it, and said, gravely:

'Mrs Michael Mont?'

'So Jon's married your sister. Is she pretty?'

'She is.'

'Very?'

'Yes, indeed.'

'I hope baby has been entertaining you.'

'He's just great.'

'He is, rather. I hear Dandie bit you?'

'I reckon he didn't break the cuticle.'

'Haven't you looked? But he's quite healthy. Sit down, and tell me all about your sister and Jon. Is it a marriage of true minds?'

Francis Wilmot sat down.

'It certainly is. Young Jon is a pretty white man, and Anne—'

He heard a sigh.

'I'm very glad. He says in his letter that he's awfully happy. You must come and stay here. You can be as free as you like. Look on us as an hotel.'

The young man's dark eyes smiled.

'That's too good of you! I've never been on this side before. They got through the war too soon.'

Fleur took the baby out of its nest.

'*This* creature doesn't bite. Look – two teeth, but they don't antagonise – isn't that how you put it?'

'What is its name?'

'Kit – for Christopher. We agreed about its name, luckily. Michael
– my husband – will be in directly. He's in Parliament, you know.
They're not sitting till Monday – Ireland, of course. We only came back
for it from Italy yesterday. Italy's so wonderful – you must see it.'

'Pardon me, but is that the Parliament clock that chimes so loud?'

'Big Ben – yes. He marks time for them. Michael says Parliament
is the best drag on Progress ever invented. With our first Labour
Government, it's been specially interesting this year. Don't you think
it's rather touching the way this dog watches my baby? He's got the
most terrific jaw!'

'What kind of dog is he?'

'A Dandie Dinmont. We did have a Peke. It was a terrible tragedy.
He *would* go after cats; and one day he struck a fighting Tom, and
got clawed over both eyes – quite blinded – and so—'

The young man saw her eyes suddenly too bright. He made a soft
noise, and said gently: 'That was too bad.'

'I had to change this room completely. It used to be Chinese. It
reminded me too much.'

'This little fellow would chaw any cat.'

'Luckily he was brought up with kittens. We got him for his legs
– they're so bowed in front that he can hardly run, so he just suits
the pram. Dan, show your legs!'

The Dandie looked up with a negative sound.

'He's a terrible little "character". Do tell me, what's Jon like now?
Is he still English?'

The young man was conscious that she had uttered at last something really in her mind.

'He is; but he's a dandy fellow.'

'And his mother? She used to be beautiful.'

'And is to this day.'

'She would be. Grey, I suppose, by now?'

'Yes. You don't like her?'

'Well, I hope she won't be jealous of your sister!'

'I think, perhaps, you're unjust.'

'I think, perhaps, I am.'

She sat very still, her face hard above the baby's. And the young man, aware of thoughts beyond his reach, got up.

'When you write to Jon,' she said, suddenly, 'tell him that I'm awfully glad, and that I wish him luck. I shan't write to him myself. May I call you Francis?'

Francis Wilmot bowed. 'I shall be proud, ma'am.'

'Yes; but you must call me Fleur. We're sort of related, you know.'

The young man smiled, and touched the name with his lips.

'Fleur! It's a beautiful name!'

'Your room will be ready when you come back. You'll have a bathroom to yourself, of course.'

He put his lips to the hand held out.

'It's wonderful,' he said. 'I was feeling kind of homesick; I miss the sun over here.'

In going out, he looked back. Fleur had put her baby back in its nest, and was staring straight before her.

Chapter Two

Change

But more than the death of a dog had caused the regarnishing of Fleur's Chinese room. On the evening of her twenty-second birthday Michael had come home saying:

'Well, my child, I've chucked publishing. With old Danby always in the right – it isn't a career.'

'Oh! Michael, you'll be bored to death.'

'I'll go into Parliament. It's quite usual, and about the same screw.'

He had spoken in jest. Six days later it became apparent that she had listened in earnest.

'You were absolutely right, Michael. It's the very thing for you. You've got ideas.'

'Other people's.'

'And the gift of the gab. We're frightfully handy for the House, here.'

'It costs money, Fleur.'

'Yes; I've spoken to Father. It was rather funny – there's never been a Forsyte, you know, anywhere near Parliament. But he thinks it'll be good for me; and that it's all baronets are fit for.'

'One has to have a Seat, unfortunately.'

'Well, I've sounded your father, too. He'll speak to people. They want young men.'

'Ah! And what are my politics?'

'My dear boy, you must know – at thirty.'

'I'm not a Liberal. But am I Labour or Tory?'

'You can think it out before the next election!'

Next day, while he was shaving, and she was in her bath, he cut himself slightly and said:

'The land and this unemployment is what I really care about. I'm a Foggartist.'

'What?'

'Old Sir James Foggart's book, that he published after all. You read it.'

'No.'

'Well, you said so.'

'So did others.'

'Never mind – his eyes are fixed on 1944, and his policy's according. Safety in the Air, the Land, and Child Emigration; adjustment of Supply and Demand within the Empire; cut our losses in Europe; and endure a worse Present for the sake of a better Future. Everything, in fact, that's unpopular, and said to be impossible.'

'Well, you could keep all that to yourself till you get in. You'll have to stand as a Tory.'

'How lovely you look!'

'If you get in, you can disagree with everybody. That'll give you a position from the start.'

'Some scheme!' murmured Michael.

'You can initiate this – this Foggartism. He isn't mad, is he?'

'No, only too sane, which is much the same thing, of course. You see we've got a higher wage-scale than any other country except America and the Dominions; and it isn't coming down again; we really group in with the new countries. He's for growing as much of our food as we can, and pumping British town children, before they're spoiled, into the Colonies, till Colonial demand for goods equals our supply. It's no earthly, of course, without whole-hearted co-operation between the Governments within the Empire.'

'It sounds very sensible.'

'We published him, you know, but at his own expense. It's a "faith and the mountain" stunt. He's got the faith all right, but the mountain shows no signs of moving up to now.'

Fleur stood up. 'Well,' she said, 'that's settled. Your father says

he can get you a nomination as a Tory, and you can keep your own
views to yourself. You'll get in on the human touch, Michael.'

'Thank you, ducky. Can I help dry you?' . . .

Before redecorating her Chinese room, however, Fleur had waited
till after Michael was comfortably seated for a division which
professed to be interested in agriculture. She chose a blend between
Adam and Louis Quinze. Michael called it the 'bimetallic parlour';
and carried off 'The White Monkey' to his study. The creature's
pessimism was not, he felt, suited to political life.

Fleur had initiated her 'salon' with a gathering in February. The
soul of society had passed away since the Liberal débâcle and Lady
Alison's politico-legal coterie no longer counted. Plainer people were
in the ascendant. Her Wednesday evenings were youthful, with age
represented by her father-in-law, two minor ambassadors, and
Pevensey Blythe, editor of *The Outpost*. So unlike his literary style
that he was usually mistaken for a Colonial Prime Minister, Blythe
was a tall man with a beard, and grey bloodshot eyes, who expressed
knowledge in paragraphs that few could really understand. 'What
Blythe thinks today, the Conservative Party will not think tomorrow,'
was said of him. He spoke in a small voice, and constantly used the
impersonal pronoun.

'One is walking in one's sleep,' he would say of the political situation, 'and will wake up without any clothes on.'

A warm supporter of Sir James Foggart's book, characterising it
as 'the masterpiece of a blind archangel', he had a passion for listening
to the clavichord, and was invaluable in Fleur's 'salon'.

Freed from poetry and modern music, from Sibley Swan, Walter
Nazing and Hugo Solstis, Fleur was finding time for her son – the
eleventh baronet. He represented for her the reality of things. Michael
might have posthumous theories, and Labour predatory hopes, but
for her the year 1944 would see the eleventh baronet come of age.
That Kit should inherit an England worth living in was of more
intrinsic importance than anything they proposed in the Commons
and were unable to perform. All those houses they were going to
build, for instance – very proper, but a little unnecessary if Kit still
had Lippinghall Manor and South Square, Westminster, to dwell in.

Not that Fleur voiced such cynical convictions, or admitted them even to herself. She did orthodox lip-service to the great god Progress.

The Peace of the World, Hygiene, Trade, and the End of Unemployment, preoccupied all, irrespective of Party, and Fleur was in the fashion; but instinct, rather than Michael and Sir James Foggart, told her that the time-honoured motto: 'Eat your cake and have it', which underlay the platforms of all Parties, was not 'too frightfully' sound. So long as Kit had cake, it was no good bothering too deeply about the rest; though, of course, one must seem to. Fluttering about her 'salon' – this to that person, and that to the other, and to all so pretty, she charmed by her grace, her common sense, her pliancy. Not infrequently she attended at the House, and sat, not listening too much to the speeches, yet picking up, as it were, by a sort of seventh sense (if women in Society all had six, surely Fleur had seven) what was necessary to the conduct of that 'salon' – the rise and fall of the Governmental barometer, the catchwords and clichés of policy; and, more valuable, impressions of personality, of the residuary man within the Member. She watched Michael's career, with the fostering eye of a godmother who has given her godchild a blue morocco prayer-book, in the hope that some day he may remember its existence. Although a sedulous attendant at the House all through the spring and summer, Michael had not yet opened his mouth, and so far she had approved of his silence, while nurturing his desire to know his own mind by listening to his wanderings in Foggartism. If it were indeed the only permanent cure for Unemployment, as he said, she too was a Foggartist; common sense assuring her that the only real danger to Kit's future lay in that national malady. Eliminate Unemployment, and nobody would have time to make a fuss. But her criticisms were often pertinent:

'My dear boy, does a country ever sacrifice the present for the sake of the future?' or: 'Do you really think country life is better than town life?' or: 'Can you imagine sending Kit out of England at fourteen to some Godforsaken end of the world?' or: 'Do you suppose the towns will have it?' And they roused Michael to such persistence and fluency that she felt he would really catch on in time – like old Sir Giles Snoreham, whom they would soon be making a peer, because he had always worn low-crowned hats and advocated a return to hansom cabs. Hats, buttonholes, an eyeglass – she turned over in her mind all such little realities as help a political career.

'Plain glass doesn't harm the sight; and it really has a focusing value, Michael.'

'My child, it's never done my dad a bit of good; I doubt, if it's sold three copies of any of his books. No! If I get on, it'll be by talking.'

But still she encouraged him to keep his mouth shut.

'It's no good starting wrong, Michael. These Labour people aren't going to last out the year.'

'Why not?'

'Their heads are swelling, and their tempers going. They're only on sufferance; people on sufferance have got to be pleasant or they won't be suffered. When they go out, the Tories will get in again and probably last. You'll have several years to be eccentric in, and by the time they're out again, you'll have your licence. Just go on working the human touch in your constituency; I'm sure it's a mistake to forget you've got constituents.'

Michael spent most week-ends that summer working the human touch in mid-Bucks; and Fleur spent most weekends with the eleventh baronet at her father's house near Mapledurham.

Since wiping the dust of the city off his feet, after that affair of Elderson and the P.P.R.S., Soames had become almost too countrified for a Forsyte. He had bought the meadows on the far side of the river and several Jersey cows. Not that he was going in for farming or nonsense of that sort, but it gave him an interest to punt himself over and see them milked. He had put up a good deal of glass, too, and was laying down melons. The English melon was superior to any other, and every year's connection with a French wife made him more and more inclined to eat what he grew himself. After Michael was returned for Parliament, Fleur had sent him Sir James Foggart's book, *The Parlous State of England*. When it came, he said to Annette:

'I don't know what she thinks I want with this great thing!'

'To read it, Soames, I suppose.'

Soames sniffed, turning the pages.

'I can't tell what it's all about.'

'I will sell it at my bazaar, Soames. It will do for some good man who can read English.'

From that moment Soames began almost unconsciously to read the book. He found it a peculiar affair, which gave most people some good hard knocks. He began to enjoy them, especially the chapter deprecating the workman's dislike of parting with his children at a reasonable age. Having never been outside Europe, he had a somewhat sketchy idea of places like South Africa, Australia, Canada, and New Zealand; but this old fellow Foggart, it appeared, had been there, and knew what he was talking about. What he said about their development seemed quite sensible. Children who went out there put on weight at once, and became owners of property at an age when in England they were still delivering parcels, popping in and out of jobs, hanging about street corners, and qualifying for unemployment and Communism. Get them out of England! There was a startling attraction in the idea for one who was English to a degree. He was in favour, too, of what was said about growing food and making England safe in the air. And then, slowly, he turned against it. The fellow was too much of a Jeremiah altogether. He complained to Fleur that the book dealt with nothing but birds in the bush; it was unpractical. What did 'Old Mont' say?

'He won't read it; he says he knows old Foggart.'

'H'm!' said Soames, 'I shouldn't be surprised if there were something in it, then.' That little-headed baronet was old fashioned! 'Anyway it shows that Michael's given up those Labour fellows.'

'Michael says Foggartism will be Labour's policy when they understand all it means.'

'How's that?'

'He thinks it's going to do them much more good than anybody else. He says one or two of their leaders are beginning to smell it out, and that the rest of the leaders are bound to follow in time.'

'In that case,' said Soames, 'it'll never go down with their rank and file.' And for two minutes he sat in a sort of trance. Had he said something profound, or had he not?

Fleur's presence at weekends with the eleventh baronet was extremely agreeable to him. Though at first he had felt a sort of disappointment that his grandchild was not a girl – an eleventh baronet belonged too definitely to the Monts – he began, as the months wore on, to find him 'an engaging little chap', and in any case, to have him down at Mapledurham kept him away from Lippinghall. It tried him at times, of course, to see how the women hung about the baby – there was something very excessive about motherhood. He had noticed it with Annette; he noticed it now with Fleur. French – perhaps! He had not remembered his own mother making such a fuss; indeed, he could not remember anything that happened when he was one. A weekend, when Madame Lamotte, Annette and Fleur were all hanging over his grandson, three generations of maternity concentrated on that pudgy morsel, reduced him to a punt, fishing for what he felt sure nobody would eat.

By the time he had finished Sir James Foggart's book, the disagreeable summer of 1924 was over, and a more disagreeable September had set in. The mellow golden days that glow up out of a haze which stars with dewdrops every cobweb on a gate, simply did not come. It rained, and the river was so unnaturally full, that the newspapers were at first unnaturally empty – there was literally no news of drought; they filled up again slowly with reports of the wettest summer 'for thirty years'. Calm, greenish with weed and tree shadow, the river flowed unendingly between Soames's damp lawn and his damp meadows. There were no mushrooms. Blackberries tasted of rain. Soames made a point of eating one every year, and, by the flavour, could tell what sort of year it had been. There was a good deal of 'old-man's-beard'. In spite of all this, however, he was more cheerful than he had been for ages. Labour had been 'in', if not in real power, for months, and the heavens had only lowered. Forced by Labour-in-office to take some notice of politics, he would utter prophecies at the breakfast-table. They varied somewhat, according to the news; and, since he always forgot those which did not come true, he was constantly able to tell Annette that he had told her so. She took no interest, however, occupied, like a woman, with her bazaars and jam-making, running about in the car, shopping in London, attending garden-parties; and, in spite of her tendency to put on flesh, still remarkably handsome. Jack Cardigan, his niece Imogen's husband, had made him a sixty-ninth-birthday present of a set of golf-clubs. This was more puzzling to Soames than anything that had ever happened to him. What on earth was he to do with them? Annette, with that French quickness which so often annoyed him, suggested that he should use them. She was uncomfortable! At his age—! And then, one weekend in May the fellow himself had come down with Imogen, and, teeing a ball up on half a molehill, had driven it across the river.

'I'll bet you a box of cigars, Uncle Soames, that you don't do that before we leave on Monday.'

'I never bet,' said Soames, 'and I don't smoke.'

'Time you began both. Look here, we'll spend tomorrow learning to knock the ball!'

'Absurd!' said Soames.

But in his room that night he had stood in his pyjamas swinging his arms in imitation of Jack Cardigan. The next day he sent the women out in the car with their lunch; he was not going to have them grinning at him. He had seldom spent more annoying hours than those which followed. They culminated in a moment when at last he hit the ball, and it fell into the river three yards from the near bank. He was so stiff next morning in arms and ribs, that Annette had to rub him till he said:

'Look out! you're taking the skin off!'

He had, however, become infected. After destroying some further portions of his lawn, he joined the nearest Golf Club, and began to go round by himself during the luncheon-hour, accompanied by a little boy. He kept at it with characteristic tenacity, till by July he had attained a certain proficiency; and he began to say to Annette that it would do her all the good in the world to take it up, and keep her weight down.

'*Merci*, Soames,' she would reply; 'I have no wish to be the figure of your English Misses, flat as a board before and behind.' She was reactionary, 'like her nation'; and Soames, who at heart had a certain sympathy with curves, did not seriously press the point. He found that the exercise jogged both his liver and his temper. He began to have colour in his cheeks. The day after his first nine-hole round with Jack Cardigan, who had given him three strokes a hole and beaten him by nine holes, he received a package which, to his dismay, contained a box of cigars. What the fellow was about, he could not imagine! He only discovered when, one evening a few days later, sitting at the window of his picture gallery, he found that he had one in his mouth. Curiously enough, it did not make him sick. It produced rather something of the feeling he used to enjoy after 'doing Coué' – now comparatively out of fashion, since an American, so his sister Winifred said, had found a shorter cut. A suspicion, however, that the family had set Jack Cardigan on, prevented him from indulging his new sensation anywhere but in his picture gallery; so that cigars gathered the halo of a secret vice. He renewed his store stealthily. Only when he found that Annette, Fleur, and others had known for weeks, did he relax his rule, and say openly that the vice of the present day was cigarettes.

'My dear boy,' said Winifred, when she next saw him, 'everybody's saying you're a different man!'

Soames raised his eyebrows. He was not conscious of any change.

'That chap Cardigan,' he said, 'is a funny fellow! . . . I'm going to dine and sleep at Fleur's; they're just back from Italy. The House sits on Monday.'

'Yes,' said Winifred; 'very fussy of them – sitting in the Long Vacation.'

'Ireland!' said Soames, deeply. 'A pretty pair of shoes again!' Always had been; always would be!

Chapter Three

Michael Takes 'a Lunar'

*M*ichael had returned from Italy with the longing to 'get on with it', which results from Southern holidays. Countryman by upbringing, still deeply absorbed by the unemployment problem, and committed to Foggartism, as its remedy, he had taken up no other hobby in the House, and was eating the country's bread, if somewhat unbuttered, and doing nothing for it. He desired, therefore, to know where he stood, and how long he was going to stand there.

Bent on 'taking this lunar' – as 'Old Forsyte' would call it – at his own position, he walked away from the House that same day, after dealing with an accumulated correspondence. He walked towards Pevensey Blythe, in the office of that self-sufficing weekly: *The Outpost*. Sunburnt from his Italian holiday and thinned by Italian cookery, he moved briskly, and thought of many things. Passing down on to the Embankment, where a number of unemployed birds on a number of trees were also wondering, it seemed, where they stood and how long they were going to stand there, he took a letter from his pocket to read a second time.

'12 SAPPER'S ROW, CAMDEN TOWN.

'HONOURABLE SIR,

'Being young in "Who's Who", you will not be hard, I think, to those in suffering. I am an Austrian woman who married a German eleven years ago. He was an actor on the English stage,

for his father and mother, who are no more living, brought him
to England quite young. Interned he was, and his health broken
up. He has the neurasthenie very bad so he cannot be trusted
for any work. Before the war he was always in a part, and we
had some good money; but this went partly when I was left
with my child alone, and the rest was taken by the P.T., and
we got very little back, neither of us being English. What we
did get has all been to the doctor, and for our debts, and for
burying our little child, which died happily, for though I loved
it much this life which we have is not fit for a child to live.
We live on my needle, and that is not earning much, a pound
a week and sometimes nothing. The managers will not look at
my husband all these years, because he shakes suddenly, so they
think he drinks, but, Sir, he has not the money to buy it. We
do not know where to turn, or what to do. So I thought, dear
Sir, whether you could do anything for us with the P.T.; they
have been quite sympatical; but they say they administrate an
order and cannot do more. Or if you could get my husband
some work where he will be in open air – the doctor say that
is what he want. We have nowhere to go in Germany or in
Austria, our well-loved families being no more alive. I think
we are like many, but I cannot help asking you, Sir, because
we want to keep living if we can, and now we are hardly having
any food. Please to forgive me my writing, and to believe your
very anxious and humble

'ANNA BERGFELD.'

'God help them!' thought Michael, under a plane-tree close to
Cleopatra's Needle, but without conviction. For in his view God was
not so much interested in the fate of individual aliens as the Governor
of the Bank of England in the fate of a pound of sugar bought with
the fraction of a Bradbury; He would not arbitrarily interfere with
a ripple of the tides set loose by His arrangement of the Spheres.
God, to Michael, was a monarch strictly limited by His own
Constitution. He restored the letter to his pocket. Poor creatures!

But really, with 1,200,000 and more English unemployed, mostly due to that confounded Kaiser and his Navy stunt—! If that fellow and his gang had not started their Naval rivalry in 1899, England would have been out of the whole mess, or, perhaps, there never would have been a mess!

He turned up from the Temple station towards the offices of *The Outpost*. He had 'taken' that Weekly for some years now. It knew everything, and managed to convey a slight impression that nobody else knew anything; so that it seemed more weighty than any other Weekly. Having no particular Party to patronise, it could patronise the lot. Without Imperial bias, it professed a special knowledge of the Empire. Not literary, it made a point of reducing the heads of literary men – Michael, in his publishing days, had enjoyed every opportunity of noticing that. Professing respect for Church and the Law, it was an adept at giving them 'what-for'. It fancied itself on Drama, striking a somewhat Irish attitude towards it. But, perhaps above all, it excelled in neat detraction from political reputations, keeping them in their place, and that place a little lower than *The Outpost*'s. Moreover, from its editorials emanated that 'holy ghost' of inspired knowledge in periods just a little beyond average comprehension, without which no such periodical had real importance.

Michael went up the stairs two at a time, and entered a large square room, where Mr Blythe, back to the door, was pointing with a rule to a circle drawn on a map.

'This is a bee map,' said Mr Blythe to himself. 'Quite the bee-est map I ever saw.'

Michael could not contain a gurgle, and the eyes of Mr Blythe came round, prominent, epileptic, richly encircled by pouches.

'Hallo!' he said defiantly: 'You? The Colonial Office prepared this map specially to show the best spots for Settlement schemes. And they've left out Baggersfontein – the very hub.'

Michael seated himself on the table.

'I've come in to ask what you think of the situation? My wife says Labour will be out in no time.'

'Our charming little lady!' said Mr Blythe; 'Labour will survive

Ireland; they will survive Russia; they will linger on in their precarious way. One hesitates to predict their decease. Fear of their Budget may bring them down in February. After the smell of Russian fat has died away – say in November, Mont – one may make a start.'

'This first speech,' said Michael, 'is a nightmare to me. How, exactly, am I to start Foggartism?'

'One will have achieved the impression of a body of opinion before then.'

'But will there be one?'

'No,' said Mr Blythe.

'Oh!' said Michael. 'And, by the way, what about Free Trade?'

'One will profess Free Trade, and put on duties.'

'God and Mammon.'

'Necessary in England, before any new departure, Mont. Witness Liberal-Unionism, Tory-Socialism, and—'

'Other ramps,' said Michael, gently.

'One will glide, deprecate Protection till there is more Protection than Free Trade, then deprecate Free Trade. Foggartism is an end, not a means; Free Trade and Protection are means, not the ends politicians have made them.'

Roused by the word politician, Michael got off the table; he was coming to have a certain sympathy with those poor devils. They were supposed to have no feeling for the country, and to be wise only after the event. But, really, who could tell what was good for the country, among the mists of talk? Not even old Foggart, Michael sometimes thought.

'You know, Blythe,' he said, 'that we politicians don't think ahead, simply because we know it's no earthly. Every elector thinks his own immediate good is the good of the country. Only their own shoes pinching will change electors' views. If Foggartism means adding to the price of living now, and taking wage-earning children away from workmen's families for the sake of benefit – ten or twenty years hence – who's going to stand for it?'

'My dear young man,' said Mr Blythe, 'conversion is our job. At present our trade-unionists despise the outside world. They've never seen it. Their philosophy is bounded by their smoky little streets. But five million pounds spent on the organised travel of a hundred thousand working men would do the trick in five years. It would infect the working class with a feverish desire for a place in the sun. The world is their children's for the taking. But who can blame them, when they know nothing of it?'

'Some thought!' said Michael: 'Only – what Government will think it? Can I take those maps? . . . By the way,' he said at the door, 'there are Societies, you know, for sending out children.'

Mr Blythe grunted. 'Yes. Excellent little affairs! A few hundred children doing well – concrete example of what might be. Multiply it a hundredfold, and you've got a beginning. You can't fill pails with a teaspoon. Good-bye!'

Out on the Embankment Michael wondered if one could love one's country with a passion for getting people to leave it. But this over-bloated town condition, with its blight and smoky ugliness; the children without a chance from birth; these swarms of poor devils without work, who dragged about and hadn't an earthly, and never would, on present lines; this unbalanced, hand-to-mouth, dependent state of things – surely that wasn't to be for ever the state of the country one loved! He stared at the towers of Westminster, with the setting sun behind them. And there started up before him the thousand familiars of his past – trees, fields and streams, towers, churches, bridges; the English breeds of beasts, the singing birds, the owls, the jays and rooks at Lippinghall, the little differences from foreign sorts in shrub, flower, lichen, and winged life; the English scents, the English haze, the English grass; the eggs and bacon; the slow good humour, the moderation and the pluck; the smell of rain; the apple-blossom, the heather, and the sea. His country, and his breed – unspoilable at heart! He passed the Clock Tower. The House looked lacy and imposing, more beautiful than fashion granted. Did they spin the web of England's future in that House? Or were they painting camouflage – a screen, over old England?

A familiar voice said: 'This is a monstrous great thing!'

And Michael saw his father-in-law staring up at the Lincoln statue. 'What did they want to put it here for?' said Soames. 'It's not English.' He walked along at Michael's side. 'Fleur well?'

'Splendid. Italy suited her like everything.'

Soames sniffed. 'They're a theatrical lot,' he said. 'Did you see Milan cathedral!'

'Yes, sir. It's about the only thing we didn't take to.'

'H'm! Their cooking gave me the collywobbles in '79. I dare say it's better now. How's the boy?'

'A1, sir.'

Soames made a sound of gratification, and they turned the corner into South Square.

'What's this?' said Soames.

Outside the front door were two battered-looking trunks, a young man, grasping a bag, and ringing the bell, and a taxicab turning away.

'I can't tell you, sir,' murmured Michael. 'Unless it's the angel Gabriel.'

'He's got the wrong house,' said Soames, moving forward.

But just then the young man disappeared within.

Soames walked up to the trunks. 'Francis Wilmot,' he read out. '"S.S. Amphibian." There's some mistake!'

Chapter Four

Mere Conversation

*W*hen they came in, Fleur was returning downstairs from showing the young man to his room. Already fully dressed for the evening, she had but little on, and her hair was shingled . . .

'My dear girl,' Michael had said, when shingling came in, 'to please me, don't! Your *nuque* will be too bristly for kisses.'

'My dear boy,' she had answered, 'as if one could help it! You're always the same with any new fashion!'

She had been one of the first twelve to shingle, and was just feeling that without care she would miss being one of the first twelve to grow some hair again. Marjorie Ferrar, 'the Pet of the Panjoys', as Michael called her, already had more than an inch. Somehow, one hated being distanced by Marjorie Ferrar . . .

Advancing to her father, she said:

'I've asked a young American to stay, Dad; Jon Forsyte has married his sister, out there. You're quite brown, darling. How's Mother?'

Soames only gazed at her.

And Fleur passed through one of those shamed moments, when the dumb quality of his love for her seemed accusing the glib quality of her love for him. It was not fair – she felt – that he should look at her like that; as if she had not suffered in that old business with Jon more than he; if she could take it lightly now, surely he could! As for Michael – not a word! – not even a joke! She bit her lips, shook her shingled head, and passed into the 'bimetallic parlour'.

Dinner began with soup and Soames deprecating his own cows

for not being Herefords. He supposed that in America they had plenty of Herefords?

Francis Wilmot believed that they were going in for Holsteins now.

'Holsteins!' repeated Soames. 'They're new since my young days. What's their colour?'

'Parti-coloured,' said Francis Wilmot. 'The English grass is just wonderful.'

'Too damp, with us,' said Soames. 'We're on the river.'

'The river Thames? What size will that be, where it hasn't a tide?'

'Just there – not more than a hundred yards.'

'Will it have fish?'

'Plenty.'

'And it'll run clear – not red; our Southern rivers have a red colour. And your trees will be willows, and poplars, and elms.'

Soames was a good deal puzzled. He had never been in America. The inhabitants were human, of course, but peculiar and all alike, with more face than feature, heads fastened upright on their backs, and shoulders too square to be real. Their voices clanged in their mouths; they pronounced the words 'very' and 'America' in a way that he had tried to imitate without success; their dollar was too high, and they all had motor-cars; they despised Europe, came over in great quantities, and took back all they could; they talked all the time, and were not allowed to drink. This young man cut across all these preconceptions. He drank sherry and only spoke when he was spoken to. His shoulders looked natural; he had more feature than face; and his voice was soft. Perhaps, at least, he despised Europe.

'I suppose,' he said, 'you find England very small.'

'No, sir. I find London very large; and you certainly have the loveliest kind of a countryside.'

Soames looked down one side of his nose. 'Pretty enough!' he said.

Then came turbot and a silence, broken, low down, behind his chair.

'That dog!' said Soames, impaling a morsel of fish he had set aside as uneatable.

'No, no, Dad! He just wants to know you've seen him!'

Soames stretched down a finger, and the Dandie fell on his side.

'He never eats,' said Fleur; 'but he has to be noticed.'

A small covey of partridges came in, cooked.

'Is there any particular thing you want to see over here, Mr Wilmot?' said Michael.

'There's nothing very un-American left. You're just too late for Regent Street.'

'I want to see the Beefeaters; and Cruft's Dog Show; and your blood horses; and the Derby.'

'Darby!' Soames corrected. 'You can't stay for that – it's not till next June.'

'My cousin Val will show you race-horses,' said Fleur. 'He married Jon's sister, you know.'

A 'bombe' appeared. 'You have more of this in America, I believe,' said Soames.

'We don't have much ice cream in the South, sir; but we have special cooking – very tasty.'

'I've heard of terrapin.'

'Well, *I* don't get frills like that. I live away back, and have to work pretty hard. My place is kind of homey; but I've got some mighty nice darkies that can cook fine – old folk that knew my grannies. The old-time darky is getting scarce, but he's the real thing.'

A Southerner!

Soames had been told that the Southerner was a gentleman. He remembered the 'Alabama', too; and his father, James, saying: 'I told you so' when the Government ate humble pie over that business.

In the savoury silence that accompanied soft roes on toast, the patter of the Dandie's feet on the parquet floor could be plainly heard.

'This is the only thing he likes,' said Fleur. 'Dan! go to your master. Give him a little bit, Michael.' And she stole a look at Michael, but he did not answer it.

On their Italian holiday, with Fleur in the throes of novelty, sun and wine warmed, disposed to junketing, amenable to his caresses, he had been having his real honeymoon, enjoying, for the first time since his marriage, a sense of being the chosen companion of his adored. And now had come this stranger, bringing reminder that one played but second fiddle to that young second cousin and first lover; and he couldn't help feeling the cup withdrawn again from his lips. She had invited this young man because he came from that past of hers whose tune one could not play. And, without looking up, he fed the Dandie with tidbits of his favourite edible.

Soames broke the silence.

'Take some nutmeg, Mr Wilmot. Melon without nutmeg – beats ginger hollow.'

When Fleur rose, Soames followed her to the drawing room; while Michael led the young American to his study.

'You knew Jon?' said Francis Wilmot.

'No; I never met him.'

'He's a great little fellow; and some poet. He's growing dandy peaches.'

'Is he going on with that, now he's married?'

'Surely.'

'Not coming to England?'

'Not this year. They have a nice home – horses and dogs. They have some hunting there, too. Perhaps he'll bring my sister over for a trip, next fall.'

'Oh!' said Michael. 'And are you staying long, yourself?'

'Why! I'll go back for Christmas. I'd like to see Rome and Seville; and I want to visit the old home of my people, down in Worcestershire.'

'When did they go over?'

'William and Mary. Catholics – they were. Is it a nice part, Worcestershire?'

'Very; especially in the spring. It grows a lot of fruit.'

'Oh! You still grow things in this country?'

'Not many.'

'I thought that was so, coming on the cars, from Liverpool. I saw a lot of grass and one or two sheep, but I didn't see anybody working. The people all live in the towns, then?'

'Except a few unconsidered trifles. You must come down to my father's; they still grow a turnip or two thereabouts.'

'It's sad,' said Francis Wilmot.

'It is. We began to grow wheat again in the war; but they've let it all slip back – and worse.'

'Why was that?'

Michael shrugged his shoulders: 'No accounting for statesmanship. It lets the Land go to blazes when in office; and beats the drum of it when in opposition. At the end of the war we had the best air force in the world, and agriculture was well on its way to recovery. And what did they do? Dropped them both like hot potatoes. It was tragic. What do you grow in Carolina?'

'Just cotton, on my place. But it's mighty hard to make cotton pay nowadays. Labour's high.'

'High with you, too?'

'Yes, sir. Do they let strangers into your Parliament?'

'Rather. Would you like to hear the Irish debate? I can get you a seat in the Distinguished Strangers' gallery.'

'I thought the English were stiff; but it's wonderful the way you make me feel at home. Is that your father-in-law – the old gentleman?'

'Yes.'

'He seems kind of rarefied. Is he a banker?'

'No. But now you mention it – he ought to be.'

Francis Wilmot's eyes roved round the room and came to rest on 'The White Monkey'.

'Well, now,' he said, softly, 'that, surely, is a wonderful picture. Could I get a picture painted by that man, for Jon and my sister?'

'I'm afraid not,' said Michael. 'You see, he was a Chink – not quite of the best period; but he must have gone West five hundred years ago at least.'

'Ah! Well, he had a great sense of animals.'

'We think he had a great sense of human beings.'

Francis Wilmot stared.

There was something, Michael decided, in this young man unresponsive to satire.

'So you want to see Cruft's Dog Show?' he said. 'You're keen on dogs, then?'

'I'll be taking a bloodhound back for Jon, and two for myself. I want to raise bloodhounds.'

Michael leaned back, and blew out smoke. To Francis Wilmot, he felt, the world was young, and life running on good tyres to some desirable destination. In England—!

'What is it you Americans want out of life?' he said abruptly.

'Well, I suppose you might say we want success – in the North at all events.'

'*We* wanted that in 1824,' said Michael.

'Oh! And nowadays?'

'We've had success, and now we're wondering whether it hasn't cooked our goose.'

'Well,' said Francis Wilmot, 'we're sort of thinly populated, compared with you.'

'That's it,' said Michael. 'Every seat here is booked in advance; and a good many sit on their own knees. Will you have another cigar, or shall we join the lady?'

Chapter Five

Side-Slips

If Providence was completely satisfied with Sapper's Row, Camden Town, Michael was not. What could justify those twin dismal rows of three-storeyed houses, so begrimed that they might have been collars washed in Italy? What possible attention to business could make these little ground-floor shops do anything but lose money? From the thronged and tram-lined thoroughfare so pregnantly scented with fried fish, petrol and old clothes, who would turn into this small backwater for sweetness or for profit? Even the children, made with heroic constancy on its second and third floors, sought the sweets of life outside its precincts; for in Sapper's Row they could neither be run over nor stare at the outside of Cinemas. Hand-carts, bicycles, light vans which had lost their nerve and taxicabs which had lost their way, provided all the traffic; potted geraniums and spotted cats supplied all the beauty. Sapper's Row drooped and dithered.

Michael entered from its west end, and against his principles. Here was overcrowded England, at its most dismal, and here was he, who advocated a reduction of its population, about to visit some broken-down aliens with the view of keeping them alive. He looked into three of the little shops. Not a soul! Which was worst? Such little shops frequented, or – deserted? He came to No. 12, and, looking up, saw a face looking down. It was wax white, movingly listless, above a pair of hands sewing at a garment. 'That,' he thought, 'is my "obedient humble" and her needle.' He entered the shop below, a hairdresser's, containing a dirty basin below a dusty mirror, suspicious towels, bottles, and two dingy chairs. In his shirt-sleeves, astride

one of them, reading the *Daily Mail*, sat a shadowy fellow with pale
hollow cheeks, twisted moustache, lank hair, and the eyes, at once
knowing and tragic, of a philosopher.

'Hair cut, sir?'

Michael shook his head.

'Do Mr and Mrs Bergfeld live here?'

'Upstairs, top floor.'

'How do I get up?'

'Through there.'

Passing through a curtained aperture, Michael found a stairway,
and at its top, stood, hesitating. His conscience was echoing Fleur's
comment on Anna Bergfeld's letter: 'Yes, I dare say; but what's the
good?' when the door was opened, and it seemed to him almost as
if a corpse were standing there, with a face as though someone had
come knocking on its grave, so eager and so white.

'Mrs Bergfeld? My name's Mont. You wrote to me.'

The woman trembled so, that Michael thought she was going to
faint.

'Will you excuse me, sir, that I sit down?' And she dropped on
to the end of the bed. The room was spotless, but, besides the bed,
held only a small deal wash-stand, a pot of geranium, a tin trunk
with a pair of trousers folded on it, a woman's hat on a peg, and a
chair in the window covered with her sewing.

The woman stood up again. She seemed not more than thirty, thin
but prettily formed; and her oval face, without colour except in her
dark eyes, suggested Rafael rather than Sapper's Row.

'It is like seeing an angel,' she said. 'Excuse me, sir.'

'Queer angel, Mrs Bergfeld. Your husband not in?'

'No, sir. Fritz has gone to walk.'

'Tell me, Mrs Bergfeld. If I pay your passages to Germany, will
you go?'

'We cannot hope from that now, Fritz has been here twenty years,
and never back; he has lost his German nationality, sir; they do not
want people like us, you know.'

Michael stivered up his hair.

'Where are you from yourself?'

'From Salzburg.'

'What about going back there?'

'I would like to, but what would we do? In Austria every one is poor now, and I have no relative left. Here at least we have my sewing.'

'How much is that a week?'

'Sometimes a pound; sometimes fifteen shillings. It is bread and the rent.'

'Don't you get the dole?'

'No, sir. We are not registered.'

Michael took out a five-pound note and laid it with his card on the wash-stand. 'I've got to think this over, Mrs Bergfeld. Perhaps your husband will come and see me.' He went out quickly, for the ghostly woman had flushed pink.

Repassing through the curtained aperture, he caught the hairdresser wiping out the basin.

'Find 'em in, sir?'

'The lady.'

'Ah! Seen better days, I should say. The 'usband's a queer customer; 'alf off his nut. Wanted to come in here with me, but I've got to give this job up.'

'Oh! How's that?'

'I've got to have fresh air – only got one lung, and that's not very gaudy. I'll have to find something else.'

'That's bad, in these days.'

The hairdresser shrugged his bony shoulders. 'Ah!' he said. 'I've been a hairdresser from a boy, except for the war. Funny place this, to fetch up in after where I've been. The war knocked me out.' He twisted his little thin moustache.

'No pension?' said Michael.

'Not a bob. What I want to keep me alive is something in the open.'

Michael took him in from head to foot. Shadowy, narrow-headed, with one lung.

'But do you know anything about country life?'

'Not a blessed thing. Still, I've got to find something, or peg out.'

His tragic and knowing eyes searched Michael's face.

'I'm awfully sorry,' said Michael. 'Good-bye!'

The hairdresser made a queer jerky little movement.

Emerging from Sapper's Row into the crowded, roaring thoroughfare, Michael thought of a speech in a play he had seen a year or two before. 'The condition of the people leaves much to be desired. I shall make a point of taking up the cudgels in the House. I shall move—!' The condition of the people! What a remote thing! The sportive nightmare of a few dreaming nights, the skeleton in a well-locked cupboard, the discomforting rare howl of a hungry dog! And probably no folk in England less disturbed by it than the gallant six hundred odd who sat with him in 'that House'. For to improve the condition of the people was their job, and that relieved them of a sense of nightmare. Since Oliver Cromwell some sixteen thousand, perhaps, had sat there before them, to the same end. And was the trick done – not bee likely! Still *they* were really working for it, and other people were only looking on and telling them how to do it!

Thus was he thinking when a voice said:

'Not got a job about you, sir?'

Michael quickened his steps, then stood still. He saw that the man who had spoken, having cast his eyes down again, had missed this sign of weakness; and he went back to him. They were black eyes in a face round and pasty like a mince pie. Decent and shabby, quiet and forlorn, he wore an ex-Serviceman's badge.

'You spoke to me?' said Michael.

'I'm sure I don't know why, sir; it just hopped out of me.'

'No work?'

'No; and pretty low.'

'Married?'

'Widower, sir; two children.'

'Dole?'

'Yes; and fair sick of it.'

'In the war, I see?'

'Yes, Mespot.'

'What sort of job do you want?'

'Any mortal thing.'

'Give me your name and address.'

'Henry Boddick, 94 Waltham Buildings, Gunnersbury.'

Michael took it down.

'Can't promise anything,' he said.

'No, sir.'

'Good luck, anyway. Have a cigar?'

'Thank you, and good luck to you, sir.'

Michael saluted, and resumed his progress; once out of sight of Henry Boddick, he took a taxi. A little more of this, and he would lose the sweet reasonableness without which one could not sit in 'that House'!

'For Sale or to Let' recorded recurrently in Portland Place, somewhat restored his sense of balance.

That same afternoon he took Francis Wilmot with him to the House, and leaving him at the foot of the Distinguished Strangers' stairway, made his way on to the floor.

He had never been in Ireland, so that the debate had for him little relation to reality. It seemed to illustrate, however, the obstacles in the way of agreement on any mortal subject. Almost every speech emphasized the paramount need for a settlement, but declared the impossibility of 'going back' on this, that, or the other factor which precluded such settlement. Still, for a debate on Ireland it seemed good tempered; and presently they would all go out and record the votes they had determined on before it all began. He remembered the thrill with which he had listened to the first debates after his election; the impression each speech had given him that somebody must certainly be converted to something; and the reluctance with which he had discovered that nobody ever was. Some force was at work far stronger than any eloquence, however striking or sincere. The clothes were washed elsewhere; in here they were but aired before being put on. Still, until people put thoughts into words, they didn't know what they thought, and sometimes they didn't know afterwards. And for the hundredth time Michael was seized by a weak feeling in his legs. In a few weeks he himself must rise on them. Would the House accord him its 'customary indulgence'; or would it say: 'Young fellow – teaching your grandmother to suck eggs – shut up!'

He looked around him.

His fellow members were sitting in all shapes. Chosen of the people, they confirmed the doctrine that human nature did not change, or so slowly that one could not see the process – he had seen their prototypes in Roman statues, in mediaeval pictures . . . 'Plain but pleasant,' he thought, unconsciously reproducing George Forsyte's description of himself in his palmy days. But did they take themselves seriously, as under Burke, as under Gladstone even?

The words 'customary indulgence' roused him from reverie; for they meant a maiden speech. Ha! yes! The member for Cornmarket. He composed himself to listen. Delivering himself with restraint and clarity, the speaker seemed suggesting that the doctrine 'Do unto others as you would they should do unto you' need not be entirely neglected, even in Ireland; but it was long – too long – Michael watched the House grow restive. 'Alas! poor brother!' he thought, as the speaker somewhat hastily sat down. A very handsome man rose in his place. He congratulated his honourable friend on his able and well-delivered effort, he only regretted that it had nothing to do with the business in hand. Exactly! Michael slipped out. Recovering his 'distinguished stranger', he walked away with him to South Square.

Francis Wilmot was in a state of some enthusiasm.

'That was fine,' he said. 'Who was the gentleman under the curtains?'

'The Speaker?'

'No; I mean the one who didn't speak.'

'Exactly; he's the dignity of the House.'

'They ought to feed him oxygen; it must be sleepy under there. I liked the delegate who spoke last but one. He would "go" in America; he had big ideas.'

'The idealism which keeps you out of the League of Nations, eh?' said Michael with a grin.

Francis Wilmot turned his head rather sharply.

'Well,' he said, 'we're like any other people when it comes down to bed-rock.'

'Quite so,' said Michael. 'Idealism is just a by-product of geography – it's the haze that lies in the middle distance. The farther you are from bed-rock, the less quick you need be to see it. We're twenty sea-miles more idealistic about the European situation than the French are. And you're three thousand sea-miles more idealistic than we are. But when it's a matter of niggers, we're three thousand sea-miles more idealistic than you; isn't that so?'

Francis Wilmot narrowed his dark eyes.

'It is,' he said. 'The farther North we go in the States, the more idealistic we get about the negro. Anne and I've lived all our life with darkies, and never had trouble; we love them, and they love us; but I wouldn't trust myself not to join in lynching one that laid his hands on her. I've talked that over many times with Jon. He doesn't see it that way; he says a darky should be tried like a white man; but he doesn't know the real South. His mind is still three thousand sea-miles away.'

Michael was silent. Something within him always closed up at mention of a name which he still spelt mentally with an h.

Francis Wilmot added ruminatively: 'There are a few saints in every country proof against your theory; but the rest of us, I reckon, aren't above human nature.'

'Talking of human nature,' said Michael, 'here's my father-in-law!'

Chapter Six

Soames Keeps his Eyes Open

Soames, having prolonged his week-end visit, had been spending the afternoon at the Zoological Gardens, removing his great-nephews, the little Cardigans, from the too close proximity of monkeys and cats. After standing them once more in Imogen's hall, he had roosted at his Club till, idly turning his evening paper, he had come on this paragraph, in the 'Chiff-chaff' column:

'A surprise for the coming Session is being confectioned at the Wednesday gatherings of a young hostess not a hundred miles from Westminster. Her husband, a prospective baronet lately connected with literature, is to be entrusted with the launching in Parliament of a policy which enjoys the peculiar label of Foggartism, derived from Sir James Foggart's book called *The Parlous State of England*. This amusing alarum is attributed to the somewhat fantastic brain which guides a well-known weekly. We shall see what comes of it. In the meantime the enterprising little lady in question is losing no chance of building up her "salon" on the curiosity which ever surrounds any buccaneering in politics.'

Soames rubbed his eyes; then read it again with rising anger. 'Enterprising little lady is losing no chance of building up her "salon".' Who had written that? He put the paper in his pocket – almost the first theft he had ever committed – and all the way across St James's Park in the gathering twilight he brooded on that anonymous paragraph. The allusion seemed to him unmistakable, and malicious into the bargain. 'Lion-hunter' would not have been plainer. Unfortunately, in a primary sense 'lion-hunter' was a compliment, and Soames doubted whether its secondary sense had ever been 'laid down' as libellous. He was still brooding deeply, when the young men ranged alongside.

'Well, sir?'

'Ah!' said Soames. 'I want to speak to you. You've got a traitor in the camp.' And, without meaning to at all, he looked angrily at Francis Wilmot.

'Now, sir?' said Michael, when they were in his study.

Soames held out the folded paper.

Michael read the paragraph and made a face.

'Whoever wrote that comes to your evenings,' said Soames; 'that's clear. Who is he?'

'Very likely a she.'

'D'you mean to say they print such things by women?'

Michael did not answer. Old Forsyte was behind the times.

'Will they tell me who it is, if I go down to them?' asked Soames.

'No, fortunately.'

'How d'you mean "fortunately"?'

'Well, sir, the Press is a sensitive plant. I'm afraid you might make it curl up. Besides, it's always saying nice things that aren't deserved.'

'But this—' began Soames; he stopped in time, and substituted: 'Do you mean that we've got to sit down under it?'

'To lie down, I'm afraid.'

'Fleur has an evening tomorrow.'

'Yes.'

'I shall stay up for it, and keep my eyes open.'

Michael had a vision of his father-in-law, like a plainclothes man in the neighbourhood of wedding-presents.

But in spite of assumed levity, Michael had been hit. The knowledge that his adored one had the collector's habit, and flitted, alluring, among the profitable, had, so far, caused him only indulgent wonder. But now it seemed more than an amusing foible. The swiftness with which she turned her smile off and on as though controlled by a switch under her shingled hair; the quick turns of her neck, so charming and exposed; the clever roving, disguised so well but not quite well enough, of the pretty eyes; the droop and flutter of their white lids; the expressive hands grasping, if one could so call such slim and dainty apprehensions, her career – all this suddenly caused Michael pain. Still she was doing it for him and Kit! French women, they said, co-operated with their husbands in the family career. It was the French blood in her. Or perhaps just idealism, the desire to have and be the best of whatever bunch there was about! Thus Michael, loyally. But his uneasy eyes roved from face to face of the Wednesday gathering, trying to detect signs of quizzicality.

Soames followed another method. His mind, indeed, was uncomplicated by the currents awash in that of one who goes to bed with the object of his criticism. For him there was no reason why Fleur should not know as many aristocrats, Labour members, painters, ambassadors, young fools, and even writing fellows, as might flutter her fancy. The higher up they were, the less likely, he thought with a certain naïveté, would they be to borrow money or get her into a mess. His daughter was as good or better than any of them, and his deep pride was stung to the quick by the notion that people should think she had to claw and scrape to get them round her. It was not she who was after them, but they who were after her! Standing under the Fragonard which he had given her, grizzled, neatly moustached, close-faced, chinny, with a gaze concentrated on nothing in particular, as of one who has looked over much and found little in it, he might have been one of her ambassadors.

A young woman, with red-gold hair, about an inch long on her de-shingled neck, came and stood with her back to him, beside a soft man, who kept washing his hands. Soames could hear every word of their talk.

'Isn't the little Mont amusing? Look at her now, with "Don Fernando" – you'd think he was her only joy. Ah! There's young Rashly! Off she goes. She's a born little snob. But that doesn't make this a "salon", as she thinks. To found a "salon" you want personality, and wit, and the "don't care a damn" spirit. She hasn't got a scrap. Besides, who is she?'

'Money?' said the soft man.

'Not so very much. Michael's such dead nuts on her that he's getting dull; though it's partly Parliament, of course. Have you heard them talk this Foggartism? All food, children, and the future – the very dregs of dullness.'

'Novelty,' purred the soft man, 'is the vice of our age.'

'One resents a nobody like her climbing in on piffle like this Foggartism. Did you read the book?'

'Hardly. Did you?'

'No jolly fear! I'm sorry for Michael. He's being exploited by that little snob.'

Penned without an outlet, Soames had begun breathing hard. Feeling a draught, perhaps, the young woman turned to encounter a pair of eyes so grey, so cold, in a face so concentrated, that she moved away. 'Who was that old buffer?' she asked of the soft man; 'he gave me "the jim-jams".'

The soft man thought it might be a poor relation – he didn't seem to know anybody.

But Soames had already gone across to Michael.

'Who's that young woman with the red hair?'

'Marjorie Ferrar.'

'She's the traitress – turn her out!'

Michael stared.

'But we know her quite well – she's a daughter of Lord Charles Ferrar, and—'

'Turn her out!' said Soames again.

'How do you know that she's the traitress, sir?'

'I've just heard her use the very words of that paragraph, and worse.'

'But she's our guest.'

'Pretty guest!' growled Soames through his teeth.

'One can't turn a guest out. Besides, she's the granddaughter of a marquess and the pet of the Panjoys – it would make the deuce of a scandal.'

'Make it, then!'

'We won't ask her again; but really, that's all one can do.'

'Is it?' said Soames; and walking past his son-in-law, he went towards the object of his denunciation. Michael followed, much perturbed. He had never yet seen his father-in-law with his teeth bared. He arrived in time to hear him say in a low but quite audible voice:

'You were good enough, madam, to call my daughter a snob in her own house.'

Michael saw the de-shingled neck turn and rear, the hard blue eyes stare with a sort of outraged impudence; he heard her laugh, then Soames saying:

'You are a traitress; be so kind as to withdraw.'

Of the half-dozen people round, not a soul was missing it! Oh, hell! And he the master of the house! Stepping forward, he put his arm through that of Soames:

'That'll do, sir,' he said, quietly; 'this is not a Peace Conference.'

There was a horrid hush; and in all the group only the soft man's white hands, washing each other, moved.

Marjorie Ferrar took a step towards the door.

'I don't know who this person is,' she said; 'but he's a liar.'

'I reckon not.'

At the edge of the little group was a dark young man. His eyes were fixed on Marjorie Ferrar's, whose eyes in turn were fixed on his.

And, suddenly, Michael saw Fleur, very pale, standing just behind him. She must have heard it all! She smiled, waved her hand, and said:

'Madame Carelli's going to play.'

Marjorie Ferrar walked on towards the door, and the soft man followed her, still washing those hands, as if trying to rid them of the incident. Soames, like a slow dog making sure, walked after them; Michael walked after him. The words 'How amusing!' floated back, and a soft echoing snigger. Slam! Both outer door and incident were closed.

Michael wiped his forehead. One half of the brain behind admired his father-in-law; the other thought: 'Well, the old man *has* gone and done it!' He went back into the drawing room. Fleur was standing near the clavichord, as if nothing had happened. But Michael could see her fingers crisping at her dress; and his heart felt sore. He waited, quivering, for the last chord.

Soames had gone upstairs. Before 'The White Monkey' in Michael's study, he reviewed his own conduct. He regretted nothing. Red-headed cat! 'Born snob!' 'Money? Not very much.' Ha! 'A nobody like her!' Grand-daughter of a marquess, was she? Well, he had shown the insolent baggage the door. All that was sturdy in his fibre, all that was acrid in his blood, all that resented patronage and privilege, the inherited spirit of his forefathers, moved within him. Who were the aristocracy, to give themselves airs? Jackanapes! Half of 'em descendants of those who had got what they had by robbery or jobbery! That one of them should call his daughter, *his* daughter, a snob! He wouldn't lift a finger, wouldn't cross a road, to meet the Duke of Seven Dials himself! If Fleur liked to amuse herself by having people round her, why shouldn't she? His blood ran suddenly a little cold. Would she say that he had spoiled her 'salon'? Well! He couldn't help it if she did; better to have had the thing out, and got rid of that cat, and know where they all were. 'I shan't wait up for her,' he thought. 'Storm in a teacup!'

The thin strumming of the clavichord came up to him out on the landing, waiting to climb to his room. He wondered if these evenings woke the baby. A gruff sound at his feet made him jump. That dog lying outside the baby's door! He wished the little beggar had been downstairs just now – he would have known how to put his teeth through that red-haired cat's nude stockings. He passed on up, looking at Francis Wilmot's door, which was opposite his own.

That young American chap must have overheard something too; but he shouldn't allude to the matter with him; not dignified. And, shutting his door on the strumming of the clavichord, Soames closed his eyes again as best he could.

Chapter Seven

Sounds in the Night

*M*ichael had never heard Fleur cry, and to see her, flung down across the bed, smothering her sobs in the quilt, gave him a feeling akin to panic. She stopped at his touch on her hair, and lay still.

'Buck up, darling!' he said, gently. 'If you aren't one, what does it matter?'

She struggled up, and sat cross-legged, her flushed face smudged with tears, her hair disordered.

'Who cares what one is? It's what one's labelled.'

'Well, we've labelled her "Traitress".'

'As if that made it better! We all talk behind people's backs. Who minds that? But how can I go on when everybody is sniggering and thinking me a lion-hunting snob? She'll cry it all over London in revenge. How can I have any more evenings?'

Was it for her career, or his, that she was sorrowing? Michael went round to the other side of the bed and put his arms about her from behind.

'Never mind what people think, my child. Sooner or later one's got to face that anyway.'

'It's you who aren't facing it. If I'm not thought nice, I can't *be* nice.'

'Only the people who really know one matter.'

'Nobody knows one,' said Fleur, sullenly. 'The fonder they are, the less they know, and the less it matters what they think.'

Michael withdrew his arms.

She sat silent for so long that he went back to the other side of the bed to see if he could tell anything from her face resting moodily on her hands. The grace of her body thus cramped was such that his senses ached. And since caresses would only worry her, they ached the more.

'I hate her,' she said, at last; 'and if I can hurt her, I will.'

He would have liked to hurt the 'pet of the Panjoys' himself, but it did not console him to hear Fleur utter that sentiment; it meant more from her than from himself, who, when it came to the point, was a poor hand at hurting people.

'Well, darling,' he said, 'shall we sleep on it?'

'I said I wouldn't have any more evenings; but I shall.'

'Good!' said Michael; 'that's the spirit.'

She laughed. It was a funny hard little sound in the night. And with it Michael had to remain discontented.

All through the house it was a wakeful night. Soames had the three o'clock tremors, which cigars and the fresh air wherein he was obliged to play his golf had subdued for some time past. He was disturbed, too, by that confounded great clock from hour to hour, and by a stealthy noise between three and four, as of someone at large in the house.

This was, in fact, Francis Wilmot. Ever since his impulsive denial that Soames was a liar, the young man had been in a peculiar state of mind. As Soames surmised, he too had overheard Marjorie Ferrar slandering her hostess; but in the very moment of his refutation, like Saul setting forth to attack the Christians, he had been smitten by blindness. Those blue eyes, pouring into his the light of defiance, had finished with a gleam which seemed to say: 'Young man, you please me!' And it haunted him. That lissome nymph – with her white skin and red-gold hair, her blue eyes full of insolence, her red lips full of joy, her white neck fragrant as a pine-wood in sunshine – the vision was abiding. He had been watching her all through the evening; but it was uncanny the way she had left her image on his senses in that one long moment, so that now he got no sleep. Though he had not been introduced, he knew her name to be Marjorie Ferrar, and he thought it 'fine'. Countryman that he was and with little knowledge of women – she was unlike any woman he had known.

And he had given her the lie direct! This made him so restless that he drank the contents of his water-bottle, put on his clothes, and stole downstairs. Passing the Dandie, who stirred as though muttering: 'Unusual! But I know those legs!' he reached the hall, where a milky glimmer came in through the fanlight. Lighting a cigarette, he sat down on the marble coat-sarcophagus. It cooled his anatomy, so that he got off it, turned up the light, saw a telephone directory resting beside him, and mechanically sought the letter 'F'. There she was! 'Ferrar, Marjorie, 3, River Studios, Wren Street.' Switching off the light, he slipped back the door-chain, and stole out. He knew his way to the river, and went towards it.

It was the hour when sound, exhausted, has trailed away, and one can hear a moth pass. London, in clear air, with no smoke going up, slept beneath the moon. Bridges, towers, water, all silvered, had a look as if withdrawn from man. Even the houses and the trees enjoyed their moony hour apart, and seemed to breathe out with Francis Wilmot a stanza from 'The Ancient Mariner':

> 'O Sleep, it is a gentle thing,
> Beloved from pole to pole!
> To Mary Queen the praise be given,
> She sent the gentle sleep from heaven
> That slid into my soul!'

He turned at random to the right along the river. Never in his life had he walked through a great city at the dead hour. Not a passion alive, nor a thought of gain; haste asleep, and terrors dreaming; here and there would be one turning on his bed: perchance a soul passing. Down on the water lighters and barges lay shadowy and abandoned, with red lights burning; the lamps along the Embankment shone without purpose, as if they had been freed. Man was away. In the whole town only himself up and doing – what? Natively shrewd and resourceful in all active situations, the young Southerner had little power of diagnosis, and certainly did not consider himself ridiculous wandering about like this at night, not even when he suddenly felt that if he could 'locate' her windows, he could go home and sleep. He passed the Tate Gallery and saw a human being with moonlit buttons.

'Pardon me, officer,' he said, 'but where is Wren Street?'

'Straight on and fifth to the right.'

Francis Wilmot resumed his march. The 'moving' moon was heeling down, the stars were gaining light, the trees had begun to shiver. He found the fifth turning, walked down 'the block', and was no wiser; it was too dark to read names or numbers. He passed another buttoned human effigy and said:

'Pardon me, officer, but where are River Studios?'

'Comin' away from them; last house on the right.'

Francis Wilmot retraced his steps. There it was, then – by itself, back from the street. He stood before it and gazed at dark windows. She might be behind any one of them! Well! He had 'located' her; and, in the rising wind, he turned and walked home. He went up-stairs stealthily as he had come down, past the Dandie, who again raised his head, muttered: 'Still more unusual, but the same legs!' entered his room, lay down, and fell asleep like a baby.

Chapter Eight

Round and About

 $\mathcal{G}$ eneral reticence at breakfast concerning the incident of the night before, made little impression on Soames, because the young American was present, before whom, naturally, one would not discuss it; but he noted that Fleur was pale. In his early-morning vigil legal misgivings had assailed him. Could one call even a red-haired baggage 'traitress' in the hearing of some half-dozen persons with impunity? He went off to his sister Winifred's after breakfast, and told her the whole story.

'Quite right, my dear boy,' was her comment. 'They tell me that young woman is as fast as they're made. Her father, you know, owned the horse that didn't beat the French horse – I never can remember its name – in that race, the Something Stakes, at – dear me! what was the meeting?'

'I know nothing about racing,' said Soames.

But that afternoon at 'The Connoisseurs Club' a card was brought to him:

LORD CHARLES FERRAR
High Marshes,
Nr Newmarket. Burton's Club.

For a moment his knees felt a little weak; but the word 'snob' coming to his assistance, he said drily: 'Show him into the strangers' room.' He was not going to hurry himself for this fellow, and finished his tea before repairing to that forlorn corner.

A tallish man was standing in the middle of the little room, thin and upright, with a moustache brushed arrogantly off his lips, and a single eyeglass which seemed to have grown over the right eye, so unaided was it. There were corrugations in his thin weathered cheeks, and in his thick hair flecked at the sides with grey. Soames had no difficulty in disliking him at sight.

'Mr Forsyte, I believe?'

Soames inclined his head.

'You made use of an insulting word to my daughter last night in the presence of several people.'

'Yes; it was richly deserved.'

'You were not drunk, then?'

'Not at all,' said Soames.

His dry precision seemed to disconcert the visitor, who twisted his moustache, frowned his eyeglass closer to his eye, and said:

'I have the names of those who overheard it. You will be good enough to write to each of them separately withdrawing your expression unreservedly.'

'I shall do nothing of the kind.'

A moment's silence ensued.

'You are an attorney, I believe?'

'A solicitor.'

'Then you know the consequences of refusal.'

'If your daughter likes to go into Court, I shall be happy to meet her there.'

'You refuse to withdraw?'

'Absolutely.'

'Good evening, then!'

'Good evening!'

For two pins he would have walked round the fellow, the bristles rising on his back, but, instead, he stood a little to one side to let him out. Insolent brute! He could so easily hear again the voice of old Uncle Jolyon, characterising some person of the 'eighties as 'a pettifogging little attorney'. And he felt that, somehow or other, he must relieve his mind. 'Old Mont' would know about this fellow – he would go across and ask him.

At 'The Aeroplane' he found not only Sir Lawrence Mont, looking almost grave, but Michael, who had evidently been detailing to his father last evening's incident. This was a relief to Soames, who felt the insults to his daughter too bitterly to talk of them. Describing the visit he had just received, he ended with the words:

'This fellow – Ferrar – what's his standing?'

'Charlie Ferrar? He owes money everywhere, has some useful horses, and is a very good shot.'

'He didn't strike me as a gentleman,' said Soames.

Sir Lawrence cocked his eyebrow, as if debating whether he ought to answer this remark about one who had ancestors, from one who had none.

'And his daughter,' said Soames, 'isn't a lady.'

Sir Lawrence wagged his head.

'Single-minded, Forsyte, single-minded; but you're right; there's a queer streak in that blood. Old Shropshire's a dear old man; it skipped his generation, but it's there – it's there. His aunt—'

'He called me an attorney,' said Soames with a grim smile, 'and she called me a liar. I don't know which is worse.'

Sir Lawrence got up and looked into St James's Street. Soames had the feeling that the narrow head perched up on that straight thin back counted for more than his own, in this affair. One was dealing here with people who said and did what they liked and damned the consequences; this baronet chap had been brought up in that way himself, no doubt, he ought to know how their minds worked.

Sir Lawrence turned.

'She may bring an action, Forsyte; it was very public. What evidence have you?'

'My own ears.'

Sir Lawrence looked at the ears, as if to gauge their length.

'M'm! Anything else?'

'That paragraph.'

'She'll get at the paper. Yes?'

'The man she was talking to.'

Michael ejaculated: 'Philip Quinsey – put not your trust in Gath!'

'What more?'

'Well,' said Soames, 'there's what that young American overheard, whatever it was.'

'Ah!' said Sir Lawrence: 'Take care she doesn't get at *him*. Is that all?'

Soames nodded. It didn't seem much, now he came to think of it!

'You say she called you a liar. How would it be to take the offensive?'

There was a silence; then Soames said. 'Women? No!'

'Quite right, Forsyte! They have their privileges still. There's nothing for it but to wait and see how the cat jumps. Traitress! I suppose you know how much the word costs?'

'The cost,' said Soames, 'is nothing; it's the publicity!'

His imagination was playing streets ahead of him. He saw himself already in 'the box', retailing the spiteful purrings of that cat, casting forth to the public and the papers the word 'snob', of his own daughter; for if he didn't, he would have no defence. Too painful!

'What does Fleur say?' he asked, suddenly, of Michael.

'War to the knife.'

Soames jumped in his chair.

'Ah!' he said: 'That's a woman all over – no imagination!'

'That's what I thought at first, sir, but I'm not so sure. She says if Marjorie Ferrar is not taken by the short hairs, she'll put it across everybody – and that the more public the thing is, the less harm she can do.'

'I think,' said Sir Lawrence, coming back to his chair, 'I'll go and see old Shropshire. My father and his shot woodcock together in Albania in 'fifty-four.'

Soames could not see the connection, but did not snub the proposal. A marquess was a sort of gone-off duke; even in this democratic age, he would have some influence, one supposed.

'He's eighty,' went on Sir Lawrence, 'and gets gout in the stomach, but he's as brisk as a bee.'

Soames could not be sure whether it was a comfort.

'The grass shall not grow, Forsyte. I'll go there now.'

They parted in the street, Sir Lawrence moving north – towards Mayfair.

The Marquess of Shropshire was dictating to his secretary a letter to his County Council, urging on them an item of his lifelong programme for the electrification of everything. One of the very first to take up electricity, he had remained faithful to it all his brisk and optimistic days. A short, bird-like old man, in shaggy Lovat tweeds, with a blue tie of knitted silk passed through a ring, bright cheeks and well-trimmed white beard and moustache, he was standing in his favourite attitude, with one foot on a chair, his elbow on his knee, and his chin on his hand.

'Ah! young Mont!' he said: 'Sit down.'

Sir Lawrence took a chair, crossed his knees, and threaded his finger-tips. He found it pleasing to be called 'young Mont', at sixty-six or so.

'Have you brought me another of your excellent books?'

'No, Marquess; I've come for your advice.'

'Ah! Go on, Mr Mersey: "In this way, gentlemen, you will save at least three thousand a year to your rate-payers; confer a blessing on the countryside by abolishing the smoke of four filthy chimneys; and make me your obliged servant,

"SHROPSHIRE."

'Thank you, Mr Mersey. Now, my dear young Mont?'

Having watched the back of the secretary till it vanished, and the old peer pivot his bright eyes, with their expression of one who means to see more every day, on the face of his visitor, Sir Lawrence took his eyeglass between thumb and finger, and said:

'Your granddaughter, sir, and my daughter-in-law want to fight like billy-o.'

'Marjorie?' said the old man, and his head fell to one side like a bird's. 'I draw the line – a charming young woman to look at, but I draw the line. What has she done now?'

'Called my daughter-in-law a snob and a lion-hunter; and my daughter-in-law's father has called your granddaughter a traitress to her face.'

'Bold man,' said the marquess; 'bold man! Who is he?'

'His name is Forsyte.'

'Forsyte?' repeated the old peer; 'Forsyte? The name's familiar – now where would that be? Ah! Forsyte and Treffry – the big tea men. My father had his tea from them direct – real caravan; no such tea now. Is that the—?'

'Some relation, perhaps. This man is a solicitor – retired; chiefly renowned for his pictures. A man of some substance, and probity.'

'Indeed! And *is* his daughter a – a lion-hunter?'

Sir Lawrence smiled.

'She's a charmer. Likes to have people about her. Very pretty. Excellent little mother, some French blood.'

'Ah!' said the marquess: 'the French! Better built round the middle than our people. What do you want me to do?'

'Speak to your son Charles.'

The old man took his foot off the chair, and stood nearly upright. His head moved sideways with a slight continuous motion.

'I never speak to Charlie,' he said, gravely. 'We haven't spoken for six years.'

'I beg your pardon, sir. Didn't know. Sorry to have bothered you.'

'No, no; pleasure to see you. If I run across Marjorie, I'll see – I'll see. But, my dear Mont, what shall we do with these young women – no sense of service; no continuity; no hair; no figures? By the way, do you know this Power Scheme on the Severn?' He held up a pamphlet: 'I've been at them to do it for years. My Colliery among others could be made to pay with electricity; but they won't move. We want some Americans over here.'

Sir Lawrence had risen; the old man's sense of service had so clearly taken the bit between its teeth again. He held out his hand.

'Good-bye, Marquess; delighted to see you looking so well.'

'Good-bye, my dear young Mont; command me at any time, and let me have another of your nice books.'

They shook hands; and from the Lovat clothes was disengaged a strong whiff of peat. Sir Lawrence, looking back, saw the old man back in his favourite attitude, foot on chair and chin on hand, already reading the pamphlet. 'Some boy!' he thought; 'as Michael would say. But what has Charlie Ferrar done not to be spoken to for six years? Old Forsyte ought to be told about that.' . . .

In the meantime 'Old Forsyte' and Michael were walking home-ward across St James's Park.

'That young American,' said Soames; 'what do you suppose made him put his oar in?'

'I don't know, sir; and I don't like to ask.'

'Exactly,' said Soames, glumly. There was, indeed, something repulsive to him in treating with an American over a matter of personal dignity.

'Do they use the word "snob" over there?'

'I'm not sure; but, in the States to hunt lions is a form of idealism. They want to associate with what they think better than themselves. It's rather fine.'

Soames did not agree; but found difficulty in explaining why. Not to recognise anyone as better than himself or his daughter had been a sort of guiding principle, and guiding principles were not talked about. In fact, it was so deep in him that he hadn't known of it.

'I shan't mention it,' he said, 'unless he does. What more can this young woman do? She's in a set, I suppose?'

'The Panjoys—'

'Panjoys!'

'Yes, sir; out for a good time at any cost – they don't really count, of course. But Marjorie Ferrar is frightfully in the limelight. She paints a bit; she's got some standing with the Press; she dances; she hunts; she's something of an actress; she goes everywhere week-ending. It's the weekends that matter, where people have nothing to do but talk. Were you ever at a weekend party, sir?'

'I?' said Soames: 'Good Lord – no!'

Michael smiled – incongruity, indeed, could go no farther.

'We must get one up for you at Lippinghall.'

'No, thank you.'

'You're right, sir, nothing more boring. But they're the *coulisses* of politics. Fleur thinks they're good for me. And Marjorie Ferrar knows all the people we know, and lots more. It *is* awkward.'

'I should go on as if nothing had happened,' said Soames: 'But about that paper? They ought to be warned that this woman is venomous.'

Michael regarded his father-in-law quizzically.

On entering, they found the man-servant in the hall.

'There's a man to see you, sir, by the name of Bugfill.'

'Oh! Ah! Where have you put him, Coaker?'

'Well, I didn't know what to make of him, sir, he shakes all over. I've stood him in the dining room.'

'Excuse me, sir,' said Michael.

Soames passed into the 'parlour', where he found his daughter and Francis Wilmot.

'Mr Wilmot is leaving us, Father. You're just in time to say good-bye.'

If there were moments when Soames felt cordial, they were such as these. He had nothing against the young man; indeed, he rather liked the look of him; but to see the last of almost anybody was in a sense a relief, besides, there was this question of what he had over-heard, and to have him about the place without knowing would be a continual temptation to compromise with one's dignity and ask him what it was.

'Good-bye, Mr Wilmot,' he said; 'if you're interested in pictures –' he paused, and, holding out, his hand, added, 'you should look in at the British Museum.'

Francis Wilmot shook the hand deferentially.

'I will. It's been a privilege to know you, sir.'

Soames was wondering why, when the young man turned to Fleur.

'I'll be writing to Jon from Paris, and I'll surely send your love. You've been perfectly wonderful to me. I'll be glad to have you and Michael visit me at any time you come across to the States; and if you bring the little dog, why – I'll just be honoured to let him bite me again.'

He bowed over Fleur's hand and was gone, leaving Soames staring at the back of his daughter's neck.

'That's rather sudden,' he said, when the door was closed; 'anything upset him?'

She turned on him, and said coldly:

'Why did you make that fuss last night, Father?'

The injustice of her attack was so palpable, that Soames bit his moustache in silence. As if he could help himself, when she was insulted in his hearing!

'What good do you think you've done?'

Soames, who had no notion, made no attempt to enlighten her. He only felt sore inside.

'You've made me feel as if I couldn't look anybody in the face. But I'm going to, all the same. If I'm a lion-hunter and a snob, I'll do it thoroughly. Only I do wish you wouldn't go on thinking I'm a child and can't defend myself.'

And still Soames was silent, sore to the soles of his boots.

Fleur flashed a look at him, and said:

'I'm sorry, but I can't help it; everything's queered;' and she too went out of the room.

Soames moved blindly to the window and stood looking out. He saw a cab with luggage drive away; saw some pigeons alight, peck at the pavement, and fly off again; he saw a man kissing a woman in the dusk; a policeman light his pipe and go off duty. He saw many human and interesting things; he heard Big Ben chime. Nothing in it all! He was staring at a silver spoon. He himself had put it in her mouth at birth.

Chapter Nine

Poultry and Cats

He who had been stood in the dining room, under the name of Bugfill, was still upright. Rather older than Michael, with an inclination to side-whisker, darkish hair, and a pale face stamped with that look of schooled quickness common to so many actors but unfamiliar to Michael, he was grasping the edge of the dining table with one hand, and a wide-brimmed black hat with the other. The expression of his large, dark-circled eyes was such that Michael smiled and said:

'It's all right, Mr Bergfeld, I'm not a Manager. Do sit down, and smoke.'

The visitor silently took the proffered chair and cigarette with an attempt at a fixed smile. Michael sat on the table.

'I gather from Mrs Bergfeld that you're on the rocks.'

'Fast,' said the shaking lips.

'Your health, and your name, I suppose?'

'Yes.'

'You want an open-air job, I believe? I haven't been able to think of anything very gaudy, but an idea did strike me last night in the stilly watches. How about raising poultry – everybody's doing it.'

'If I had my savings.'

'Yes, Mrs Bergfeld told me about them. I can inquire, but I'm afraid—'

'It's robbery.' The chattered sound let Michael at once into the confidence of the many Managers who had refused to employ him who uttered it.

'I know,' he said, soothingly, 'robbing Peter to pay Paul. That clause in the Treaty was a bit of rank barbarism, of course, camouflage it as they like. Still, it's no good to let it prey on your mind, is it?'

But his visitor had risen. 'To take from civilian to pay civilian! Then why not take civilian life for civilian life? What is the difference? And England does it – the leading nation to respect the individual. It is abominable.'

Michael began to feel that he was overdoing it.

'You forget,' he said, 'that the war made us all into barbarians, for the time being; we haven't quite got over it yet. And your country dropped the spark into the powder magazine, you know. But what about this poultry stunt?'

Bergfeld seemed to make a violent effort to control himself.

'For my wife's sake,' he said, 'I will do anything; but unless I get my savings back, how can I start?'

'I can't promise; but perhaps I could start you. That hairdresser below you wants an open-air job, too. What's his name, by the way?'

'Swain.'

'How do you get on with him?'

'He is an opinionated man, but we are good friends enough.'

Michael got off the table. 'Well, leave it to me to think it out. We shall be able to do something, I hope;' and he held out his hand.

Bergfeld took it silently, and his eyes resumed the expression with which they had first looked at Michael.

'That man,' thought Michael, 'will be committing suicide some day, if he doesn't look out.' And he showed him to the door. He stood there some minutes gazing after the German actor's vanishing form, with a feeling as if the dusk were formed out of the dark stories of such as he and the hairdresser and the man who had whispered to him to stand and deliver a job. Well, Bart must lend him that bit of land beyond the coppice at Lippinghall. He would buy a War hut if there were any left and some poultry stock, and start a colony – the Bergfelds, the hairdresser, and Henry Boddick. They could cut the timber in the coppice, and put up the fowl-houses for themselves. It would be growing food – a practical experiment in

Foggartism! Fleur would laugh at him. But was there anything one could do nowadays that somebody couldn't laugh at? He turned back into the house. Fleur was in the hall.

'Francis Wilmot has gone,' she said.

'Why?'

'He's off to Paris.'

'What was it he overheard last night?'

'Do you suppose I asked?'

'Well, no,' said Michael, humbly. 'Let's go up and look at Kit, it's about his bath time.'

The eleventh baronet, indeed, was already in his bath.

'All right, nurse,' said Fleur, 'I'll finish him.'

'He's been in three minutes, ma'am.'

'Lightly boiled,' said Michael.

For one aged only fourteen months this naked infant had incredible vigour – from lips to feet he was all sound and motion. He seemed to lend a meaning to life. His vitality was absolute, not relative. His kicks and crows and splashings had the joy of a gnat's dance, or a jackdaw's gambols in the air. They gave thanks not for what he was about to receive, but for what he was receiving. White as a turtle-dove, with pink toes, darker in eyes and hair than he would be presently, he grabbed at the soap, at his mother, at the bath-towelling – he seemed only to need a tail. Michael watched him, musing. This manikin, born with all that he could possibly wish for within his reach – how were they to bring him up? Were they fit to bring him up, they who had been born – like all their generation in the richer classes – emancipated, to parents properly broken-in to worship the fetish – Liberty? Born to everything they wanted, so that they were at wits' end to invent something they could not get; driven to restive searching by having their own way? The war had deprived one of one's own way, but the war had overdone it, and left one grasping at licence. And for those, like Fleur, born a little late for the war, the tale of it had only lowered what respect they could have for anything. With veneration killed, and self-denial 'off', with atavism buried, sentiment derided, and the future in the air, hardly a wonder that modernity should be a dance of gnats, taking itself damned seriously! Such were the reflections of Michael, sitting there above the steam, and frowning at his progeny. Without faith was one fit to be a parent? Well, people were looking for faith again. Only they were bound to hatch the egg of it so hard that it would be addled long before it was a chicken. 'Too self-conscious!' he thought. 'That's our trouble!'

Fleur had finished drying the eleventh baronet, and was dabbing powder over him; her eyes seemed penetrating his skin, as if to gauge the state of health behind it. He watched her take the feet and hands one by one and examine each nail, lost in her scrutiny, unselfconscious in her momentary devotion! And oppressed by the difficulty, as a Member of Parliament, of being devoted, Michael snapped his fingers at the baby and left the nursery. He went to his study and took down a volume of the Encyclopaedia Britannica containing the word Poultry. He read about Leghorns, Orpingtons, White Sussex, Bramaputras, and was little the wiser. He remembered that if you drew a chalk-line to the beak of a hen, the hen thought it was tied up. He wished somebody would draw a chalk-line to his beak. Was Foggartism a chalk-line? A voice said:

'Tell Fleur I'm going to her aunt's.'

'Leaving us, sir?'

'Yes, I'm not wanted.'

What had happened?

'You'll see her before you go, sir?'

'No,' said Soames.

Had somebody rubbed out the chalk-line to Old Forsyte's nose?

'Is there any money in poultry-farming, sir?'

'There's no money in anything nowadays.'

'And yet the Income Tax returns continue to rise.'

'Yes,' said Soames; 'there's something wrong there.'

'You don't think people make their incomes out more than they are?'

Soames blinked. Pessimistic though he felt at the moment, he could not take quite that low view of human nature.

'You'd better see that Fleur doesn't go about abusing that red-haired baggage,' he said. 'She was born with a silver spoon in her mouth; she thinks she can do what she likes.' And he shut Michael in again.

Silver spoon in her mouth! How apropos! . . .

After putting her baby into its cot Fleur had gone to the marque-terie bureau in the little sanctuary that would have been called a boudoir in old days. She sat there brooding. How could her father have made it all glaringly public? Couldn't he have seen that it was nothing so long as it was not public, but everything the moment it was? She longed to pour out her heart, and tell people her opinion of Marjorie Ferrar.

She wrote three letters – one to Lady Alison, and two to women in the group who had overheard it all last night. She concluded her third letter with the words: 'A woman like that, who pretends to be a friend and sneaks into one's house to sting one behind one's back, is a snake of the first water. How Society can stick her, I can't think; she hasn't a moral about her nor a decent impulse. As for her charm – Good Lord!' Yes! And there was Francis Wilmot! She had not said all she wanted to say to him.

'My Dear Francis,' she wrote:

'I am so sorry you have to run away like this. I wanted to thank you for standing up for me last night. Marjorie Ferrar is just about the limit. But in London society one doesn't pay attention to backbiting. It has been so jolly to know you. Don't forget us; and do come and see me again when you come back from Paris.

'Your very good friend,

'Fleur Mont.'

In future she would have nothing but men at her evenings! But would they come if there were no women? And men like Philip Quinsey were just as snakelike. Besides, it would look as if she were really hurt. No! She would have to go on as before, just dropping people who were 'catty'. But who wasn't? Except Alison, and heavyweights like Mr Blythe, the minor Ambassadors, and three or four earnest politicians, she couldn't be sure about any of them. It was the thing to be 'catty'. They all scratched other people's backs, and their faces too when they weren't looking. Who in Society was exempt from scratches, and who didn't scratch? Not to scratch a little was so dreadfully dull. She could not imagine a scratchless life except perhaps in Italy. Those Fra Angelico frescoes in the San Marco monastery! *There* was a man who did not scratch. St Francis, too, talking to his birds, among his little flowers, with the sun and the moon and the stars for near relations. St Claire! St Fleur – little sister of St Francis! To be unworldly and quite good! To be one who lived to make other people happy! How new! How exciting, even – for about a week; and how dull afterwards! She drew aside the curtains and looked out into the Square. Two cats were standing in the light of a lamp – narrow, marvellously graceful, with their heads turned towards each other. Suddenly they began uttering horrible noises, and became all claws. Fleur dropped the curtain.

Chapter Ten

Francis Wilmot Reverses

About that moment Francis Wilmot sat down in the lounge of the Cosmopolis Hotel, and as suddenly sat up. In the middle of the parquet floor, sliding and lunging, backing and filling, twisting and turning in the arms of a man with a face like a mask, was she, to avoid whom, out of loyalty to Fleur and Michael, he had decided to go to Paris. Fate! For he could hardly know that she came there most afternoons during the dancing hours. She and her partner were easily the show couple; and, fond of dancing, Francis Wilmot knew he was looking at something special. When they stopped, quite close to him, he said in his soft drawl:

'That was beautiful.'

'How do you do, Mr Wilmot?'

Why! She knew his name! This was the moment to exhibit loyalty! But she had sunk into a chair next his.

'And so you thought me a traitress last night?'

'I did.'

'Why?'

'Because I heard you call your hostess a snob.'

Marjorie Ferrar uttered an amused sound.

'My dear young man, if one never called one's friends anything worse than that—! I didn't mean you to hear, or that poptious old person with the chin!'

'He was her father,' said Francis Wilmot, gravely. 'It hurt him.'

'Well! I'm sorry!'

A hand without a glove, warm but dry, was put into his. When it was withdrawn the whole of his hand and arm were tingling.

'Do you dance?'

'Yes, indeed, but I wouldn't presume to dance with you.'

'Oh! but you must.'

Francis Wilmot's head went round, and his body began going round too.

'You dance better than an Englishman, unless he's professional,' said her lips six inches from his own.

'I'm proud to hear you say so, ma'am.'

'Don't you know my name? or do you always call women ma'am? It's ever so pretty.'

'Certainly I know your name and where you live. I wasn't six yards from you this morning at four o'clock.'

'What were you doing there?'

'I just thought I'd like to be near you.'

Marjorie Ferrar said, as if to herself:

'The prettiest speech I ever heard. Come and have tea with me there tomorrow.'

Reversing, side-stepping, doing all he knew, Francis Wilmot said, slowly:

'I have to be in Paris.'

'Don't be afraid, I won't hurt you.'

'I'm not afraid, but—'

'Well, I shall expect you.' And, transferring herself again to her mask-faced partner, she looked back at him over her shoulder.

Francis Wilmot wiped his brow. An astonishing experience, another blow to his preconception of a stiff and formal race! If he had not known she was the daughter of a lord, he would have thought her an American. Would she ask him to dance with her again? But she left the lounge without another glance.

An up-to-date young man, a typical young man, would have felt the more jaunty. But he was neither. Six months' training for the Air Service in 1918, one visit to New York, and a few trips to Charleston and Savannah, had left him still a countryman, with a tradition of good manners, work, and simple living. Women, of whom he had known few, were to him worthy of considerable respect. He judged them by his sister, or by the friends of his dead mother, in Savannah, who were all of a certain age. A Northern lady on the boat had told him that Southern girls measured life by the number of men they could attract; she had given him an amusing take-off of a Southern girl. It had been a surprise to this young Southerner. Anne was not like that; she had never had the chance to be, anyway, having married at nineteen the first young man who had asked her!

By the morning's post he received Fleur's little letter. 'Limit!' Limit of what? He felt indignant. He did not go to Paris, and at four o'clock he was at Wren Street.

In her studio Marjorie Ferrar, clad in a flax-blue overall, was scraping at a picture with a little knife. An hour later he was her slave. Cruft's Dog Show, the Beefeaters, the Derby – he could not even remember his desire to see them; he only desired to see one English thing – Marjorie Ferrar. He hardly remembered which way the river flowed, and by mere accident walked East instead of West. Her hair, her eyes, her voice – he 'had fallen for her'! He knew himself for a fool, and did not mind; farther man cannot go. She passed him in a little open car, driving it herself, on her way to a rehearsal. She waved her hand. Blood rushed to his heart and rushed away; he trembled and went pale. And, as the car vanished, he felt lost, as if in a world of shadows, grey and dreary! Ah! There was Parliament! And, near by, the one spot in London where he could go and talk of Marjorie Ferrar, and that was where she had misbehaved herself! He itched to defend her from the charge of being 'the limit'. He could perceive the inappropriateness of going back there to talk to Fleur of her enemy, but anything was better than not talking of her. So, turning into South Square, he rang the bell.

Fleur was in her 'parlour', if not precisely eating bread and honey, at least having tea.

'Not in Paris? How nice! Tea?'

'I've had it,' said Francis Wilmot, colouring. 'I had it with *her*.'

Fleur stared.

'Oh!' she said, with a laugh. 'How interesting! Where did she pick you up?'

Without taking in the implication of the words, Francis Wilmot was conscious of something deadly in them.

'She was at the "the dansant" at my hotel yesterday. She's a wonderful dancer. I think she's a wonderful person altogether; I'd like to have you tell me what you mean by calling her "the limit"?'

'I'd like to have you tell me why this *volte face* since Wednesday night?'

Francis Wilmot smiled: 'You people have been ever so kind to me, and I want you to be friends with her again. I'm sure she didn't mean what she said that night.'

'Indeed! Did she tell you that?'

'Why – not exactly! She said she didn't mean us to hear them.'

'No?'

He looked at her smiling face, conscious, perhaps, of deep waters, but youthfully, Americanly, unconscious of serious obstacle to his desire to smooth things out.

'I just hate to think you two are out after each other. Won't you come and meet her at my hotel, and shake hands?'

Fleur's eyes moved slowly over him from head to toe.

'You look as if you might have some French blood in you. Have you?'

'Yes. My grandmother was of French stock.'

'Well, I have more. The French, you know, don't forgive easily. And they don't persuade themselves into believing what they want to.'

Francis Wilmot rose, and spoke with a kind of masterfulness.

'You're going to tell me what you meant in your letter.'

'Am I? My dear young man, the limit of perfection, of course. Aren't you a living proof?'

Aware that he was being mocked, and mixed in his feelings, Francis Wilmot made for the door.

'Good-bye,' he said. 'I suppose you'll have no use for me in future.'

'Good-bye!' said Fleur.

He went out rueful, puzzled, lonelier even than when he went in.

He was guideless, with no one to 'put him wise'! No directness and simplicity in this town. People did not say what they meant; and his goddess – as enigmatic and twisting as the rest! More so – more so – for what did the rest matter?

Chapter Eleven

Soames Visits the Press

*S*oames had gone off to his sister's in Green Street thoroughly upset. That Fleur should have a declared enemy, powerful in Society, filled him with uneasiness; that she should hold him accountable for it, seemed the more unjust, because in fact he was.

An evening spent under the calming influence of Winifred Dartie's common sense, and Turkish coffee, which, though 'liverish stuff', he always drank with relish, restored in him something of the feeling that it was a storm in a teacup.

'But that paper paragraph,' he said, 'sticks in my gizzard.'

'Very tiresome, Soames, the whole thing; but I shouldn't bother. People skim those "chiff-chaff" little notes and forget them the next moment. They're just put in for fun.'

'Pretty sort of fun! That paper says it has a million readers.'

'There's no name mentioned.'

'These political people and whipper-snappers in Society all know each other,' said Soames.

'Yes, my dear boy,' said Winifred in her comfortable voice, so cosy, and above disturbance, 'but nobody takes anything seriously nowadays.'

She was sensible. He went up to bed in more cheerful mood.

But retirement from affairs had effected in Soames a deeper change than he was at all aware of. Lacking professional issues to anchor the faculty for worrying he had inherited from James Forsyte, he was inclined to pet any trouble that came along. The more he thought of that paragraph, the more he felt inclined for a friendly talk with the editor. If he could go to Fleur and say: 'I've made it all right with those fellows, anyway. There'll be no more of that sort of thing,' he would wipe out her vexation. If you couldn't make people in private think well of your daughter, you could surely check public expression of the opposite opinion.

Except that he did not like to get into them, Soames took on the whole a favourable view of 'the papers'. He read *The Times*; his father had read it before him, and he had been brought up on its crackle. It had news – more news for his money than he could get through. He respected its leading articles; and if its great supplements had at times appeared to him too much of a good thing, still it was a gentleman's paper. Annette and Winifred took the *Morning Post*. That also was a gentleman's paper, but it had bees in its bonnet. Bees in bonnets were respectable things, but personally Soames did not care for them. He knew little of the other papers except that those he saw about had bigger headlines and seemed cut up into little bits. Of the Press as a whole he took the English view: it was an institution. It had its virtues and its vices – anyway you had to put up with it.

About eleven o'clock he was walking towards Fleet Street.

At the office of the *Evening Sun* he handed in his card and asked to see the Editor. After a moment's inspection of his top-hat, he was taken down a corridor and deposited in a small room. It seemed a 'wandering great place'. Someone would see him!

'Someone?' said Soames: 'I want the Editor.'

The Editor was very busy; could he come again when the rush was over?

'No,' said Soames.

Would he state his business? Soames wouldn't.

The attendant again looked at his top-hat and went away.

Soames waited a quarter of an hour, and was then taken to an even smaller room, where a cheery-looking man in eyeglasses was turning over a book of filed cuttings. He glanced up as Soames entered, took his card from the table, and read from it:

'Mr Soames Forsyte? Yes?'

'Are you the Editor?' asked Soames.

'One of them. Take a seat. What can I do for you?'

Impressed by a certain speed in the air, and desirous of making a good impression, Soames did not sit down, but took from his pocket-book the paragraph.

'I've come about this in your issue of last Thursday.'

The cheery man put it up to his eyes, seemed to chew the sense of it a little with his mouth, and said: 'Yes?'

'Would you kindly tell me who wrote it?'

'We never disclose the names of correspondents, sir.'

'Well, as a matter of fact, I know.'

The cheery man's mouth opened, as if to emit the words: 'Then why did you ask?' but closed in a smile instead.

'You'll forgive me,' said Soames; 'it quite clearly refers to my daughter, Mrs Michael Mont, and her husband.'

'Indeed! You have the advantage of me; but what's the matter with it? Seems rather a harmless piece of gossip.'

Soames looked at him. He was too cheery!

'You think so?' he said, drily. 'May I ask if you would like to have your daughter alluded to as an enterprising little lady?'

'Why not? It's quite a pleasant word. Besides, there's no name mentioned.'

'Do you put things in,' asked Soames, shrewdly, 'in order that they may be Greek to all your readers?'

The cheery man laughed: 'Well,' he said, 'hardly. But really, sir, aren't you rather thin-skinned?'

This was an aspect of the affair that Soames had not foreseen. Before he could ask this Editor chap not to repeat his offence, he had apparently to convince him that it *was* an offence; but to do that he must expose the real meaning of the paragraph.

'Well,' he said, 'if you can't see that the tone of the thing's unpleasant, I can't make you. But I beg you won't let any more such paragraphs appear. I happen to know that your correspondent is actuated by malevolence.'

The cheery man again ran his eye over the cutting.

'I shouldn't have judged that. People in politics are taking and giving knocks all the time – they're not mealy-mouthed. This seems perfectly innocuous as gossip goes.'

Thus backhanded by the words 'thin-skinned' and 'mealy-mouthed', Soames said testily:

'The whole thing's extremely petty.'

'Well, sir, you know, I rather agree. Good morning!' and the cheery man blandly returned to his file.

The fellow was like an india-rubber ball! Soames clenched his top-hat. Now or never he must make him bound.

'If your correspondent thinks she can vent her spleen in print with impunity, she will find herself very much mistaken.' He waited for the effect. There was absolutely none. 'Good morning!' he said, and turned on his heel.

Somehow it had not been so friendly as he had expected. Michael's words 'The Press is a sensitive plant' came into his mind. He shouldn't mention his visit.

Two days later, picking up the *Evening Sun* at The Connoisseurs, he saw the word 'Foggartism'. H'm! A leader!

'Of the panaceas rife among the young hopefuls in politics, perhaps the most absurd is one which goes by the name of Foggartism. We are in a position to explain the nature of this patent remedy for what is supposed to be the national ill-health before it has been put on the market. Based on Sir James Foggart's book, *The Parlous State of England*, the main article of faith in this crazy creed would appear to be the depletion of British man-power. According to its prophets, we are to despatch to the ends of the Empire hundreds of thousands of our boys and girls as soon as they leave school. Quite apart from the rank impossibility of absorbing them into the life of the slowly developing Dominions, we are to lose this vital stream of labour and defensive material, in order that twenty years hence the demand from our Dominions may equal the supplying power of Great Britain. A crazier proposition was never conceived in woolly brains. Well does the word Foggartism characterise such a proposition. Alongside this emigration "stunt" – for there is no other term which suits its sensational character – rises a feeble back-to-the-land propaganda. The keystone of the whole professes to be the doctrine that the standard of British wages and living now preclude us from any attempt to rival German production, or to recover our trade with Europe. Such

a turning of the tail on our industrial supremacy has probably never
before been mooted in this country. The sooner these cheap-jack
gerrymanders of British policy realise that the British voter will have
nothing to do with so crack-brained a scheme, the sooner it will
come to the stillbirth which is its inevitable fate.'

Whatever attention Soames had given to *The Parlous State of
England*, he could not be accused of anything so rash as a faith in
Foggartism. If Foggartism were killed tomorrow, he, with his inherent
distrust of theories and ideas, his truly English pragmatism, could
not help feeling that Michael would be well rid of a white elephant.
What disquieted him, however, was the suspicion that he himself had
inspired this article. Was this that too-cheery fellow's retort?

Decidedly, he should not mention his visit when he dined in South
Square that evening.

The presence of a strange hat on the sarcophagus warned him of
a fourth party. Mr Blythe, in fact, with a cocktail in his hand, and
an olive in his mouth, was talking to Fleur, who was curled up on
a cushion by the fire.

'You know Mr Blythe, Dad?'

Another Editor! Soames extended his hand with caution.

Mr Blythe swallowed the olive. 'It's of no importance,' he said.

'Well,' said Fleur, '*I* think you ought to put it all off, and let them
feel they've made fools of themselves.'

'Does Michael think that, Mrs Mont?'

'No; Michael's got his shirt out!' And they all looked round at
Michael, who was coming in.

He certainly had a somewhat headstrong air.

According to Michael, they must take it by the short hairs and
give as good as they got, or they might as well put up the shutters.
They were sent to Parliament to hold their own opinions, not those
stuck into them by Fleet Street. If they genuinely believed the Foggart
policy to be the only way to cure unemployment, and stem the steady
drain into the towns, they must say so, and not be stampeded by
every little newspaper attack that came along. Common sense was
on their side, and common sense, if you aired it enough, won through
in the end. The opposition to Foggartism was really based on an

intention to force lower wages and longer hours on Labour, only they daren't say so in so many words. Let the papers jump through their hoops as much as they liked. He would bet that when Foggartism had been six months before the public, they would be eating half their words with an air of eating someone else's! And suddenly he turned to Soames:

'I suppose, sir, you didn't go down about that paragraph?'

Soames, privately, and as a business man, had always so conducted himself that, if cornered, he need never tell a direct untruth. Lies were not English, not even good form. Looking down his nose, he said slowly:

'Well, I let them know that I knew that woman's name.'

Fleur frowned; Mr Blythe reached out and took some salted almonds.

'What did I tell you, sir?' said Michael. 'They always get back on you. The Press has a tremendous sense of dignity; and corns on both feet; eh, Mr Blythe?'

Mr Blythe said weightily: 'It's a very human institution, young man. It prefers to criticise rather than to be criticised.'

'I thought,' said Fleur, icily, 'that I was to be left to my own cudgels.'

The discussion broke back to Foggartism, but Soames sat brooding. He would never again interfere in what didn't concern himself. Then, like all who love, he perceived the bitterness of his fate. He had only meddled with what *did* concern himself – her name, her happiness; and she resented it. Basket in which were all his eggs, to the end of his days he must go on walking gingerly, balancing her so that she was not upset, spilling his only treasure.

She left them over the wine that only Mr Blythe was drinking. Soames heard an odd word now and then, gathered that this great frog-chap was going to burst next week in *The Outpost*, gathered that Michael was to get on to his hind legs in the House at the first opportunity. It was all a muzz of words to him. When they rose, he said to Michael:

'I'll take myself off.'

'We're going down to the House, sir: won't you stay with Fleur?'

'No,' said Soames: 'I must be getting back.'

Michael looked at him closely.

'I'll just tell her you're going.'

Soames had wrapped himself into his coat, and was opening the door when he smelled violet soap. A bare arm had come round his neck. He felt soft pressure against his back. 'Sorry, Dad, for being such a pig.'

Soames shook his head.

'No,' said her voice; 'you're not going like that.'

She slipped between him and the door. Her clear eyes looked into his; her teeth gleamed, very white. 'Say you forgive me!'

'There's no end to it,' said Soames.

She thrust her lips against his nose. 'There! Good night, ducky! I know I'm spoiled!'

Soames gave her body a convulsive little squeeze, opened the door and went out without a word.

Under Big Ben boys were calling – political news, he supposed. Those Labour chaps were going to fall – some Editor had got them into trouble. He would! Well – one down, t'other come on! It was all remote to him. She alone – she alone mattered.

Chapter Twelve

Michael Muses

*M*ichael and Mr Blythe sought the Mother of Parliaments and found her in commotion. Liberalism had refused, and Labour was falling from its back. A considerable number of people were in Parliament Square contemplating Big Ben and hoping for sensation.

'I'm not going in,' said Michael. 'There won't be a division to-night. General Election's a foregone conclusion, now. I want to think.'

'One will go up for a bit,' said Mr Blythe; and they parted, Michael returning to the streets. The night was clear, and he had a longing to hear the voice of his country. But – where? For his countrymen would be discussing this pro and that con, would be mentioning each his personal 'grief' – here the Income Tax, there the dole, the names of leaders, the word Communism. Nowhere would he catch the echo of the uneasiness in the hearts of all. The Tories – as Fleur had predicted – would come in now. The country would catch at the anodyne of 'strong stable government'. But could strong stable government remove the inherent canker, the lack of balance in the top-heavy realm? Could it still the gnawing ache which everybody felt, and nobody would express?

'Spoiled', thought Michael, 'by our past prosperity. We shall never admit it,' he thought, 'never! And yet in our bones we feel it!'

England with the silver spoon in her mouth and no longer the teeth to hold it there, or the will to part with it! And her very qualities – the latent 'grit', the power to take things smiling, the lack of nerves and imagination! Almost vices, now, perpetuating the rash belief that England could still 'muddle through' without special effort, although with every year there was less chance of recovering from shock, less time in which to exercise the British 'virtues'. 'Slow in the uptak',' thought Michael, 'it's a bad fault in 1924.'

Thus musing, he turned East. Mid-theatre-hour, and the 'Great Parasite' – as Sir James Foggart called it – was lying inert, and bright. He walked the length of wakeful Fleet Street into the City so delirious by day, so dead by night. Here England's wealth was snoozing off the day's debauch. Here were all the frame and filaments of English credit. And based on – what? On food and raw material from which England, undefended in the air, might be cut off by a fresh war; on Labour, too big for European boots. And yet that credit stood high still, soothing all with its 'panache' – save, perhaps, receivers of the dole. With her promise to pay, England could still purchase anything, except a quiet heart.

And Michael walked on – through Whitechapel, busy still and coloured – into Mile End. The houses had become low, as if to give the dwellers a better view of stars they couldn't reach. He had crossed a frontier. Here was a different race almost; another England, but as happy-go-lucky and as hand-to-mouth as the England of Fleet Street and the City. Aye, and more! For the England in Mile End knew that whatever she felt could have no effect on policy. Mile on mile, without an end, the low grey streets stretched towards the ultimate deserted grass. Michael did not follow them, but coming to a cinema, turned in.

The show was far advanced. Bound and seated in front of the bad cowboy on a bronco, the heroine was crossing what Michael shrewdly suspected to be the film company's pet paddock. Every ten seconds she gave way to John T. Bronson, Manager of the Tucsonville Copper Mine, devouring the road in his 60-h.p. Packard, to cut her off before she reached the Pima river. Michael contemplated his fellow gazers. Lapping it up! Strong stable government – not much! This was their anodyne and they could not have enough of it. He saw the bronco fall, dropped by a shot from John T. Bronson, and the screen disclose the words: 'Hairy Pete grows desperate . . . "You shall not have her, Bronson."' Quite! He was throwing her into the river instead, to the words: 'John T. Bronson dives.' There he goes! He has her by her flowing hair! But Hairy Pete is kneeling on the bank. The bullets chip the water. Through the heroine's fair perforated shoulder the landscape is almost visible. What is that sound? Yes! John T. Bronson is setting his teeth! He lands, he drags her out. From his cap he takes his automatic. Still dry – thank God!

'Look to yourself, Hairy Pete!' A puff of smoke. Pete squirms and bites the sand – he seems almost to absorb the desert. 'Hairy Pete gets it for keeps!' Slow music, slower! John T. Bronson raises the reviving form. Upon the bank of the Pima river they stand embraced, and the sun sets. 'At last, my dinky love!'

'Pom, pom! that's the stuff!' thought Michael, returning to the light of night: 'Back to the Land! "Plough the fields and scatter" – when they can get this? Not much!' And he turned West again, taking a seat on the top of a 'bus beside a man with grease-stains on his clothes. They travelled in silence till Michael said:

'What do you make of the political situation, sir?'

The possible plumber replied, without turning his head:

'I should say they've overreached theirselves.'

'Ought to have fought on Russia – oughtn't they?'

'Russia – that cock won't fight either. Nao – ought to 'ave 'eld on to the spring, an' fought on a good stiff Budget.'

'Real class issue?'

'Yus!'

'But do you think class politics can wipe out unemployment?'

The man's mouth moved under his moustache as if mumbling a new idea.

'Ah! I'm fed up with politics; in work today and out tomorrow – what's the good of politics that can't give you a permanent job?'

'That's it.'

'Reparations,' said his neighbour; '*we're* not goin' to benefit by reparations. The workin' classes ought to stand together in every country.' And he looked at Michael to see how he liked *that*.

'A good many people thought so before the war; and see what happened.'

'Ah!' said the man, 'and what good's it done us?'

'Have you thought of emigrating to the Dominions?'

The man shook his head.

'Don't like what I see of the Austrylians and Canydians.'

'Confirmed Englishman – like myself.'

'That's right,' said the man. 'So long, Mister,' and he got off.

Michael travelled till the 'bus put him down under Big Ben, and it was nearly twelve. Another election! Could he stand a second time without showing his true colours? Not the faintest hope of making Foggartism clear to a rural constituency in three weeks! If he spoke from now till the day of the election, they would merely think he held rather extreme views on Imperial Preference, which, by the way, he did. He could never tell the electorate that he thought England was on the wrong tack – one might just as well not stand. He could never buttonhole the ordinary voter, and say to him: 'Look here, you know, there's no earthly hope of any real improvement for another ten years; in the meantime we must face the music, and pay more for everything, so that twenty years hence we may be safe from possible starvation, and self-supporting within the Empire.' It wasn't done. Nor could he say to his Committee: 'My friends, I represent a policy that no one else does, so far.'

No! If he meant to stand again, he must just get the old wheezes off his chest. But did he mean to stand again? Few people had less conceit than Michael – he knew himself for a lightweight. But he had got this bee into his bonnet; the longer he lived the more it buzzed, the more its buzz seemed the voice of one crying in the wilderness, and that wilderness his country. To stop up that buzzing in his ears; to turn his back on old Blythe; to stifle his convictions, and yet remain in Parliament – he could not! It was like the war over again. Once in, you couldn't get out. And he was 'in' – committed to something deeper far than the top dressings of Party politics. Foggartism had a definite solution of England's troubles to work towards – an independent, balanced Empire; an England safe in the air, and free from unemployment – with Town and Country once more in some sort of due proportion! Was it such a hopeless dream? Apparently!

'Well,' thought Michael, putting his latchkey in his door, 'they may call me what kind of a bee fool they like – I shan't budge.' He went up to his dressing room and, opening the window, leaned out.

The rumourous town still hummed; the sky was faintly coloured by reflection from its million lights. A spire was visible, some stars; the tree foliage in the Square hung flat, unstirred by wind. Peaceful and almost warm – the night. Michael remembered a certain evening – the last London air raid of the war. From his convalescent hospital he had watched it for three hours.

'What fools we all are not to drop fighting in the air,' he thought: 'Well, if we don't, I shall go all out for a great air force – all hangs, for us, on safety from air attack. Even the wise can understand that.'

Two men had stopped beneath his window, talking. One was his next-door neighbour.

'Mark my words,' said his neighbour, 'the election'll see a big turnover.'

'Yes; and what are you going to do with it?' said the other.

'Let things alone; they'll right themselves. I'm sick of all this depressing twaddle. A shilling off the Income Tax, and you'll see.'

'How are you going to deal with the Land?'

'Oh! damn the Land! Leave it to itself, that's all the farmers really want. The more you touch it, the worse it gets.'

'Let the grass grow under your feet?'

The neighbour laughed. 'That's about it. Well, what else *can* you do – the Country won't have it. Good night!'

Sounds of a door, of footsteps. A car drove by; a moth flew in Michael's face. 'The Country won't have it!' Policies! What but mental yawns, long shrugs of the shoulders, trustings to Luck! What else could they be? *The country wouldn't have it*! And Big Ben struck twelve.

Chapter Thirteen

Inception of the Case

*T*here are people in every human hive born to focus talk; perhaps their magnetism draws the human tongue, or their lives are lived at an acute angle. Of such was Marjorie Ferrar – one of the most talked-of young women in London. Whatever happened to her was rumoured at once in that collection of the busy and the idle called Society. That she had been ejected from a drawing room was swiftly known. Fleur's letters about her became current gossip. The reasons for ejectment varied from truth to a legend that she had lifted Michael from the arms of his wife.

The origins of lawsuits are seldom simple. And when Soames called it all 'a storm in a teacup', he might have been right if Lord Charles Ferrar had not been so heavily in debt that he had withdrawn his daughter's allowance; if, too, a Member for a Scottish borough, Sir Alexander MacGown, had not for some time past been pursuing her with the idea of marriage. Wealth made out of jute, a rising Parliamentary repute, powerful physique, and a determined character, had not advanced Sir Alexander's claims in twelve months so much as the withdrawal of her allowance advanced them in a single night. Marjorie Ferrar was, indeed, of those who can always get money at a pinch, but even to such come moments when they have seriously to consider what kind of pinch. In proportion to her age and sex, she was 'dipped' as badly as her father, and the withdrawal of her allowance was in the nature of a last straw. In a moment of discouragement she consented to an engagement, not yet to be made public. When the incident at Fleur's came to

Sir Alexander's ears, he went to his betrothed flaming. What could he do?

'Nothing, of course; don't be silly, Alec! Who cares?'

'The thing's monstrous. Let me go and exact an apology from this old blackguard.'

'Father's been, and he wouldn't give it. He's got a chin you could hang a kettle on.'

'Now, look here, Marjorie, you've got to make our engagement public, and let me get to work on him. I won't have this story going about.'

Marjorie Ferrar shook her head.

'Oh! no, my dear. You're still on probation. I don't care a tuppenny ice about the story.'

'Well, I do, and I'm going to that fellow tomorrow.'

Marjorie Ferrar studied his face – its brown, burning eyes, its black, stiff hair, its jaw – shivered slightly, and had a brainwave.

'You will do nothing of the kind, Alec, or you'll spill your ink. My father wants me to bring an action. He says I shall get swinging damages.'

The Scotsman in MacGown applauded, the lover quailed.

'That may be very unpleasant for you,' he muttered, 'unless the brute settles out of Court.'

'Of course he'll settle. I've got all his evidence in my vanity-bag.'

MacGown gripped her by the shoulders and gave her a fierce kiss.

'If he doesn't, I'll break every bone in his body.'

'My dear! He's nearly seventy, I should think.'

'H'm! Isn't there a young man in the same boat with him?'

'Michael? Oh! Michael's a dear. I couldn't have his bones broken.'

'Indeed!' said MacGown. 'Wait till he launches this precious Foggartism they talk of – dreary rot! I'll eat him!'

'Poor little Michael!'

'I heard something about an American boy, too.'

'Oh!' said Marjorie Ferrar, releasing herself from his grip. 'A bird of passage – don't bother about him.'

'Have you got a lawyer?'

'Not yet.'

'I'll send you mine. He'll make them sit up!'

She remained pensive after he had left her, distrusting her own brainwave. If only she weren't so hard up! She had learned during this month of secret engagement that 'Nothing for nothing and only fair value for sixpence' ruled North of the Tweed as well as South. He had taken a good many kisses and given her one trinket which she dared not take to 'her Uncle's'. It began to look as if she would have to marry him. The prospect was in some ways not repulsive – he was emphatically a man; her father would take care that she only married him on terms as liberal as his politics; and perhaps her motto 'Live dangerously' could be even better carried out with him than without. Resting inert in a long chair, she thought of Francis Wilmot. Hopeless as husband, he might be charming as lover, naïve, fresh, unknown in London, absurdly devoted, oddly attractive, with his lithe form, dark eyes, engaging smile. Too old fashioned for words, he had made it clear already that he wanted to marry her. He was a baby. But until she was beyond his reach, she had begun to feel that he was beyond hers. After? Well, who knew? She lived in advance, dangerously, with Francis Wilmot. In the meantime this action for slander was a bore! And shaking the idea out of her head, she ordered her horse, changed her clothes, and repaired to the Row. After that she again changed her clothes, went to the Cosmopolis Hotel, and danced with her mask-faced partner, and Francis Wilmot. After that she changed her clothes once more, went to a first night, partook of supper afterwards with the principal actor and his party, and was in bed by two o'clock.

Like most reputations, that of Marjorie Ferrar received more than its deserts. If you avow a creed of indulgence, you will be indulged by the credulous. In truth she had only had two love-affairs passing the limits of decorum; had smoked opium once, and been sick over it; and had sniffed cocaine just to see what it was like. She gambled only with discretion, and chiefly on race-horses; drank with strict moderation and a good head; smoked of course, but the purest cigarettes she could get, and through a holder. If she had learned suggestive forms of dancing, she danced them but once in a blue moon. She rarely rode at a five-barred gate, and that only on horses whose powers she knew.

To be in the know she read, of course, anything 'extreme', but would not go out of her way to do so. She had flown, but just to Paris. She drove a car well, and of course fast, but, never to the danger of herself, and seldom to the real danger of the public. She had splendid health, and took care of it in private. She could always sleep at ten minutes' notice, and when she sat up half the night, slept half the day. She was 'in' with the advanced theatre, but took it as it came. Her book of poems, which had received praise because they emanated from one of a class supposed to be unpoetic, was remarkable not so much for irregularity of thought as for irregularity of metre. She was, in sum, credited with a too strict observance of her expressed creed: 'Take life in both hands, and eat it.'

This was why Sir Alexander MacGown's lawyer sat on the edge of his chair in her studio the following morning, and gazed at her intently. He knew her renown better than Sir Alexander. Messrs. Settlewhite and Stark liked to be on the right side of a matter before they took it up. How far would this young lady, with her very attractive appearance and her fast reputation, stand fire? For costs – they had Sir Alexander's guarantee and the word 'traitress' was a good enough beginning; but in cases of word against word, it was ill predicting.

Her physiognomy impressed Mr Settlewhite favourably. She would not 'get rattled' in Court, if he were any judge; nor had she the Aubrey Beardsley cast of feature he had been afraid of, that might alienate a Jury. No! an upstanding young woman with a good blue eye and popular hair. She would do, if her story were all right.

Marjorie Ferrar, in turn, scrutinised one who looked as if he might take things out of her hands. Long-faced, with grey deep eyes under long dark lashes, with all his hair, and good clothes, he was as well preserved a man of sixty as she had ever seen.

'What do you want me to tell you, Mr Settlewhite?'

'The truth.'

'Oh! but naturally. Well, I was just saying to Mr Quinsey that Mrs Mont was very eager to form a "salon", and had none of the right qualities, and the old person who overheard me thought I was insulting her—'

'That all?'

'Well, I may have said she was fond of lions; and so she is.'

'Yes; but why did he call you a traitress?'

'Because she was his daughter and my hostess, I suppose.'

'Will this Mr Quinsey confirm you?'

'Philip Quinsey? – oh! rather! He's in my pocket.'

'Did anybody else overhear you running her down?'

She hesitated a second. 'No.'

'First lie!' thought Mr Settlewhite, with his peculiar sweet-sarcastic smile. 'What about an American?'

Marjorie Ferrar laughed. 'He won't say so, anyway.'

'An admirer?'

'No. He's going back to America.'

'Second lie!' thought Mr Settlewhite. 'But she tells them well.'

'You want an apology you can show to those who overheard the insult; and what we can get, I suppose?'

'Yes. The more the better.'

'Speaking the truth there,' thought Mr Settlewhite. 'Are you hard up?'

'Couldn't well be harder.'

Mr Settlewhite put one hand on each knee, and reared his slim body.

'You don't want it to come into Court?'

'No; though I suppose it might be rather fun.'

Mr Settlewhite smiled again.

'That entirely depends on how many skeletons you have in your cupboard.'

Marjorie Ferrar also smiled.

'I shall put everything in your hands,' she said.

'Not the skeletons, my dear young lady. Well, we'll serve him and see how the cat jumps; but he's a man of means and a lawyer.'

'I think he'll hate having anything about his daughter brought out in Court.'

'Yes,' said Mr Settlewhite, drily. 'So should I.'

'And she *is* a little snob, you know.'

'Ah! Did you happen to use that word?'

'N-no; I'm pretty sure I didn't.'

'Third lie!' thought Mr Settlewhite: 'not so well told.'

'It makes a difference. Quite sure?'

'Not quite.'

'He says you did?'

'Well, I told him he was a liar.'

'Oh! did you? And they heard you?'

'Rather!'

'That may be important.'

'I don't believe he'll say I called her a snob, in Court, anyway.'

'That's very shrewd, Miss Ferrar,' said Mr Settlewhite. 'I think we shall do.'

And with a final look at her from under his long lashes, he stalked, thin and contained, to the door.

Three days later Soames received a legal letter. It demanded a formal apology, and concluded with the words 'failing it, action will be taken'. Twice in his life he had brought actions himself; once for breach of contract, once for divorce; and now to be sued for slander! In every case he had been the injured party, in his own opinion. He was certainly not going to apologise. Under the direct threat he felt much calmer. He had nothing to be ashamed of. He would call that 'baggage' a traitress to her face again tomorrow, and pay for the luxury, if need be. His mind roved back to when, in the early 'eighties, as a very young lawyer, he had handled his Uncle Swithin's defence against a fellow member of the Walpole Club. Swithin had called him in public 'a little touting whipper-snapper of a parson'. He remembered how he had whittled the charge down to the word 'whipper-snapper', by proving the plaintiff's height to be five feet four, his profession the church, his habit the collection of money for the purpose of small-clothing the Fiji islanders. The Jury had assessed 'whipper-snapper' at ten pounds – Soames always believed the small clothes had done it. His Counsel had made great game of them – Bobstay, Q.C. There *were* Counsel in those days; the Q.C.'s had been better than the K.C.'s were. Bobstay would have gone clean through this 'baggage' and come out on the other side. Uncle Swithin had asked him to dinner afterwards and given him York ham with Madeira sauce, and his special Heidsieck. He had never given anybody anything else. Well! There must still be cross-examiners who could tear a reputation to tatters, especially if there wasn't one to tear. And one could always settle at the last moment if one wished. There was no possibility anyway of Fleur being dragged in as witness or anything of that sort.

He was thunder-struck, a week later, when Michael rang him up at Mapledurham to say that Fleur had been served with a writ for libel in letters containing among others the expressions 'a snake of the first water' and 'she hasn't a moral about her'.

Soames went cold all over. 'I told you not to let her go about abusing that woman.'

'I know; but she doesn't consult me every time she writes a letter to a friend.'

'Pretty friend!' said Soames into the mouthpiece. 'This is a nice pair of shoes!'

'Yes, sir; I'm very worried. She's absolutely spoiling for a fight – won't hear of an apology.'

Soames grunted so deeply that Michael's ear tingled forty miles away.

'In the meantime, what shall we do?'

'Leave it to me,' said Soames. 'I'll come up tonight. Has she any evidence, to support those words?'

'Well, she says—'

'No,' said Soames, abruptly, 'don't tell me over the phone.' And he rang off. He went out on to the lawn. Women! Petted and spoiled – thought they could say what they liked! And so they could till they came up against another woman. He stopped by the boat-house and gazed at the river. The water was nice and clean, and there it was – flowing down to London to get all dirty! That feverish, quarrelsome business up there! Now he would have to set to and rake up all he could against this Ferrar woman, and frighten her off. It was distasteful. But nothing else for it, if Fleur was to be kept out of Court! Terribly petty. Society lawsuits – who ever got anything out of them, save heart-burning and degradation? Like the war, you might win and regret it ever afterwards, or lose and regret it more. All temper! Jealousy and temper!

In the quiet autumn light, with the savour of smoke in his nostrils from his gardener's first leaf bonfire, Soames felt moral. Here was his son-in-law, wanting to do some useful work in Parliament, and make a name for the baby, and Fleur beginning to settle down and take a position; and now this had come along, and all the chatterers and busy mockers in Society would be gnashing on them with their teeth – if they had any! He looked at his shadow on the bank, grotesquely slanting towards the water as if wanting to drink. Everything was grotesque, if it came to that! In Society, England, Europe – shadows scrimmaging and sprawling; scuffling and posturing; the world just marking time before another Flood! H'm! He moved towards the river. There went his shadow, plunging in before him! They would all plunge into that mess of cold water if they didn't stop their squabblings. And, turning abruptly, he entered his kitchen-garden. Nothing unreal there, and most things running to seed – stalks, and so on! How to set about raking up the past of this young woman? Where was it? These young sparks and fly-by-nights! They all had pasts, no doubt; but the definite, the concrete bit of immorality alone was of use, and when it came to the point, was unobtainable, he shouldn't wonder. People didn't like giving chapter and verse! It was risky, and not the thing! Tales out of school!

And, among his artichokes, approving of those who did not tell tales, disapproving of anyone who wanted them told, Soames resolved grimly that told they must be. The leaf-fire smouldered, and the artichokes smelled rank, the sun went down behind the high brick wall mellowed by fifty years of weather; all was peaceful and chilly, except in his heart. Often now, morning or evening, he would walk among his vegetables – they were real and restful, and you could eat them. They had better flavour than the greengrocer's and saved his bill – middlemen's profiteering and all that. Perhaps they represented atavistic instincts in this great-grandson of 'Superior Dosset's' father, that last of a long line of Forsyte 'agriculturists'. He set more and more store by vegetables the older he grew. When Fleur was a little bit of a thing, he would find her when he came back from the City, seated among the sunflowers or blackcurrants, nursing her doll. He had once taken a bee out of her hair, and the little brute had stung him. Best years he ever had, before she grew up and took to this gadabout Society business, associating with women who went behind her back. Apology! So she wouldn't hear of one? She was in the right. But to be in the right and have to go into Court because of it, was one of the most painful experiences that could be undergone. The Courts existed to penalise people who were in the right – in divorce, breach of promise, libel and the rest of it. Those who were in the wrong went to the South of France, or if they did appear, defaulted afterwards and left you to pay your costs. Had he not himself had to pay them in his action against Bosinney? And in his divorce suit had not Young Jolyon and Irene been in Italy when he brought it? And yet, he couldn't bear to think of Fleur eating humble-pie to that red-haired cat. Among the gathering shadows, his resolve hardened. Secure evidence that would frighten the baggage into dropping the whole thing like a hot potato – it was the only way!

Chapter Fourteen

Further Consideration

he Government had 'taken their toss' over the Editor – no one could say precisely why – and Michael sat down to compose his Address. How say enough without saying anything? And, having impetuously written: 'Electors of Mid-Bucks', he remained for many moments still as a man who has had too good a dinner. 'If' – he traced words slowly – 'if you again return me as your representative, I shall do my best for the Country according to my lights. I consider the limitation of armaments, and, failing that, the security of Britain through the enlargement of our Air defences; the development of home agriculture; the elimination of unemployment through increased emigration to the Dominions; and the improvement of the national health particularly through the abatement of slums and smoke, to be the most pressing and immediate concerns of British policy. If I am returned, I shall endeavour to foster these ends with determination and coherence; and try not to abuse those whose opinions differ from my own. At my meetings I shall seek to give you some concrete idea of what is in my mind, and submit myself to your questioning.'

Dared he leave it at that? Could one issue an address containing no disparagement of the other side, no panegyric of his own? Would his Committee allow it? Would the electors swallow it? Well, if his Committee didn't like it – they could turn it down, and himself with it; only – they wouldn't have time to get another candidate!

The Committee, indeed, did not like it, but they lumped it; and the Address went out with an effigy on it of Michael, looking, as he said, like a hairdresser. Thereon he plunged into a fray, which, like every other, began in the general and ended in the particular.

During the first Sunday lull at Lippinghall, he developed his poultry scheme – by marking out sites, and deciding how water could be laid on. The bailiff was sulky. In his view it was throwing away money. 'Fellers like that!' Who was going to teach them the job? He had no time, himself. It would run into hundreds, and might just as well be poured down the gutter. 'The townsman's no mortal use on the land, Master Michael.'

'So everybody says. But, look here, Tutfield, here are three "down and outs", two of them ex-Service, and you've got to help me put this through. You say yourself this land's all right for poultry – well, it's doing no good now. Bowman knows every last thing about chickens; set him on to it until these chaps get the hang. Be a good fellow and put your heart into it; you wouldn't like being "down and out" yourself.'

The bailiff had a weakness for Michael, whom he had known from his bottle up. He knew the result, but if Master Michael liked to throw his father's money away, it was no business of his. He even went so far as to mention that he knew 'a feller' who had a hut for sale not ten miles away; and that there was 'plenty of wood in the copse for the cuttin''.

On the Tuesday after the Government had fallen Michael went up to town and summoned a meeting of his 'down and outs'. They came at three the following day, and he placed them in chairs round the dining table. Standing under the Goya, like a general about to detail a plan of attack which others would have to execute, he developed his proposal. The three faces expressed little, and that without conviction. Only Bergfeld had known anything of it, before, and his face was the most doubting.

'I don't know in the least,' went on Michael, 'what you think of it; but you all want jobs – two of you in the open, and you, Boddick, don't mind what it is, I think.'

'That's right, sir,' said Boddick, 'I'm on.'

Michael instantly put him down as the best man of the three. The other two were silent till Bergfeld said:

'If I had my savings—'

Michael interrupted quickly:

'I'm putting in the capital; you three put in the brains and labour. It's probably not more than a bare living, but I hope it'll be a healthy one. What do *you* say, Mr Swain?'

The hairdresser, more shadow-stricken than ever, in the glow of Fleur's Spanish room, smiled.

'I'm sure it's very kind of you. I don't mind havin' a try – only, who's goin' to boss the show?'

'Co-operation, Mr Swain.'

'Ah!' said the hairdresser; 'thought so. But I've seen a lot of tries at that, and it always ends in one bloke swallerin' the rest.'

'Very well,' said Michael, suddenly, 'I'll boss it. But if any of you crane at the job, say so at once, and have done with it. Otherwise I'll get that hut delivered and set up, and we'll start this day month.'

Boddick got up, and said: 'Right, sir. What about my children?'

'How old, Boddick?'

'Two little girls, four and five.'

'Oh! yes!' Michael had forgotten this item. 'We must see about that.'

Boddick touched his forelock, shook Michael's hand, and went out. The other two remained standing.

'Good-bye, Mr Bergfeld; good-bye, Mr Swain!'

'If I might—'

'Could I speak to you for a minute?'

'Anything you have to say,' said Michael, astutely, 'had better be said in each other's presence.'

'I've always been used to hair.'

'Pity,' thought Michael, 'that Life didn't drop that "h" for him – poor beggar!' 'Well, we'll get you a breed of birds that can be shingled,' he said. The hairdresser smiled down one side of his face. 'Beggars can't be choosers,' he remarked.

'*I* wished to ask you,' said Bergfeld, 'what system we shall adopt?'

'That's got to be worked out. Here are two books on poultry-keeping; you'd better read one each, and swop.'

He noted that Bergfeld took both without remonstrance on the part of Swain.

Seeing them out into the Square, he thought: 'Rum team! It won't work, but they've got their chance.'

A young man who had been standing on the pavement came forward.

'Mr Michael Mont, M.P.?'

'Yes.'

'Mrs Michael Mont at home?'

'I think so. What do you want?'

'I must see her personally, please.'

'Who are you from?'

'Messrs. Settlewhite and Stark – a suit.'

'Dressmakers?'

The young man smiled.

'Come in,' said Michael. 'I'll see if she's at home.'

Fleur was in the 'parlour'.

'A young man from some dressmaker's for you, dear.'

'Mrs Michael Mont? In the suit of Ferrar against Mont – libel. Good day, madam.'

Between those hours of four and eight, when Soames arrived from Mapledurham, Michael suffered more than Fleur. To sit and see a legal operation performed on her with all the scientific skill of the British Bar, it was an appalling prospect; and there would be no satisfaction in Marjorie Ferrar's also being on the table, with her inside exposed to the gaze of all! He was only disconcerted, therefore, when Fleur said:

'All right; if she wants to be opened up, she shall be. I know she flew to Paris with Walter Nazing last November; and I've always been told she was Bertie Curfew's mistress for a year.'

A Society case – cream for all the cats in Society, muck for all the blow-flies in the streets – and Fleur the hub of it! He waited for Soames with impatience. Though 'Old Forsyte's' indignation had started this, Michael turned to him now, as to an anchor let go off a lee shore. The 'old man' had experience, judgement, and a chin; he would know what, except bearing it with a grin, could be done.

Gazing at a square foot of study wall which had escaped a framed caricature, he reflected on the underlying savagery of life. He would be eating a lobster tonight that had been slowly boiled alive! This study had been cleaned out by a charwoman whose mother was dying of cancer, whose son had lost a leg in the war, and who looked so jolly tired that he felt quite bad whenever he thought of her. The Bergfelds, Swains and Boddicks of the world – the Camden Towns, and Mile Ends – the devastated regions of France, the rock villages of Italy! Over it all what a thin crust of gentility! Members of Parliament, and ladies of fashion, like himself and Fleur, simpering and sucking silver spoons, and now and then dropping spoons and simper, and going for each other like Kilkenny cats!

'What evidence has she got to support those words?' Michael racked his memory. This was going to be a game of bluff. That Walter Nazing and Marjorie Ferrar had flown to Paris together appeared to him of next to no importance. People could still fly in couples with impunity; and as to what had happened afterwards in the great rabbit-warren *Outre Manche* – Pff! The Bertie Curfew affair was different. Smoke of a year's duration probably had fire behind it. He knew Bertie Curfew, the enterprising Director of the 'Ne Plus Ultra' Play Society, whose device was a stork swallowing a frog – a long young man, with long young hair that shone and was brushed back, and a long young record; a strange mixture of enthusiasm and contempt, from one to the other of which he passed with extreme suddenness. His sister, of whom he always spoke as 'Poor Norah', in Michael's opinion was worth ten of him. She ran a Children's House in Bethnal Green, and had eyes from which meanness and evil shrank away.

Big Ben thumped out eight strokes; the Dandie barked, and Michael knew that Soames had come.

Very silent during dinner, Soames opened the discussion over a bottle of Lippinghall Madeira by asking to see the writ.

When Fleur had brought it, he seemed to go into a trance.

'The old boy', thought Michael, 'is thinking of his past. Wish he'd come to!'

'Well, Father?' said Fleur at last.

As if from long scrutiny of a ghostly Court of Justice, Soames turned his eyes on his daughter's face.

'You won't eat your words, I suppose?'

Fleur tossed her now de-shingled head. 'Do you want me to?'

'Can you substantiate them? You mustn't rely on what was told you – that isn't evidence.'

'I know that Amabel Nazing came here and said that she didn't mind Walter flying to Paris with Majorie Ferrar, but that she did object to not having been told beforehand, so that she herself could have flown to Paris with somebody else.'

'We could subpoena that young woman,' said Soames.

Fleur shook her head. 'She'd never give Walter away in Court.'

'H'm! What else about this Miss Ferrar?'

'Everybody knows of her relationship with Bertie Curfew.'

'Yes,' Michael put in, 'and between "everybody knows" and "somebody tells" is a great gap fixed.'

Soames nodded.

'She just wants money out of us,' cried Fleur; 'she's always hard up. As if she cared whether people thought her moral or not! She despises morality – all her set do.'

'Ah! Her view of morality!' said Soames, deeply; he was suddenly seeing a British Jury confronted by a barrister describing the modern view of morals: 'No need, perhaps, to go into personal details.'

Michael started up.

'By Jove, sir, you've hit it! If you can get her to admit that she's read certain books, seen or acted in certain plays, danced certain dances, worn certain clothes—' He fell back again into his chair; what if the other side started asking Fleur the same questions? Was it not the fashion to keep abreast of certain things, however moral one might really be? Who could stand up and profess to be shocked, today?

'Well?' said Soames.

'Only that one's own point of view isn't quite a British Jury's, sir. Even yours and ours, I expect, don't precisely tally.'

Soames looked at his daughter. He understood. Loose talk – afraid of being out of the fashion – evil communications corrupting all profession of good manners! Still, no Jury could look at her face without – who could resist the sudden raising of those white lids? Besides, she was a mother, and the other woman wasn't; or if she was – she shouldn't be! No, he held to his idea. A clever fellow at the Bar could turn the whole thing into an indictment of the fast set and modern morality, and save all the invidiousness of exposing a woman's private life.

'You give me the names of her set and those books and plays and dancing clubs and things,' he said. 'I'll have the best man at the Bar.'

Michael rose from the little conference somewhat eased in mind. If the matter could be shifted from the particular to the general; if, instead of attacking Marjorie Ferrar's practice, the defence could attack her theory, it would not be so dreadful. Soames took him apart in the hall.

'I shall want all the information I can get about that young man and her.'

Michael's face fell.

'You can't get it from me, sir, I haven't got it.'

'She must be frightened,' said Soames. 'If I can frighten her, I can probably settle it out of Court without an apology.'

'I see; use the information out of Court, but not in.'

Soames nodded. 'I shall tell them that we shall justify. Give me the young man's address.'

'Macbeth Chambers, Bloomsbury. It's close to the British Museum. But do remember, sir, that to air Miss Ferrar's linen in Court will be as bad for us as for her.'

Again Soames nodded.

When Fleur and her father had gone up, Michael lit a cigarette, and passed back into the 'parlour'. He sat down at the clavichord. The instrument made very little noise so he could strum on it without fear of waking the eleventh baronet. From a Spanish tune picked up three years ago on his honeymoon, whose savagery always soothed him, his fingers wandered on: 'I got a crown, you got a crown – all God's children got a crown! Eb'ryone dat talk 'bout 'Eaben ain't goin' dere. All God's children got a crown.'

Glass lustres on the walls gleamed out at him. As a child he had loved the colours of his aunt Pamela's glass chandeliers in the panelled rooms at Brook Street; but when he knew what was what, he and everyone had laughed at them. And now lustres had come in again; and Aunt Pamela had gone out! 'She had a crown – he had a crown –' 'Confound that tune! *'Auprès de ma blonde – il fait bon – fait bon – fait bon; Auprès de ma blonde, il fait bon dormir.'*

His 'blonde' – not so very blonde, either – would be in bed by now. Time to go up! But still he strummed on, and his mind wandered in and out – of poultry and politics, Old Forsyte, Fleur, Foggartism, and the Ferrar girl – like a man in a maelstrom whirling round with his head just above water. Who was it said the landing-place for modernity was a change of heart; the re-birth of a belief that life was worthwhile, and better life attainable? 'Better life?' Prerogative of priests? Not now. Humanity had got to save itself! To save itself – what was that, after all, but expression of 'the will to live'? But did humanity will to live as much as it used? That was the point. Michael stopped strumming and listened to the silence. Not even a clock ticking – time was inhospitable in 'parlours'; and England asleep outside. Was the English 'will to live' as strong as ever; or had they all become so spoiled, so sensitive to life, that they had weakened on it? Had they sucked their silver spoon so long that, threatened with a spoon of bone, they preferred to get down from table? 'I don't believe it,' thought Michael, 'I won't believe it. Only where are we going? Where am I going? Where are all God's children going?' To bed, it seemed! And Big Ben struck: One.

Part II

Chapter One

Michael Makes his Speech

W—hen in the new Parliament Michael rose to deliver his maiden effort towards the close of the debate on the King's Speech, he had some notes in his hand and not an idea in his head. His heart was beating and his knees felt weak. The policy he was charged to express, if not precisely new in concept, was in reach and method so much beyond current opinion, that he awaited nothing but laughter. His would be a stray wind carrying the seed of a new herb into a garden, so serried and so full that no corner would welcome its growth. There was a plant called Chinese weed which having got hold never let go, and spread till it covered everything. Michael desired for Foggartism the career of Chinese weed; but all he expected was the like of what he had seen at Monterey on his tour round the world after the war. Chance had once brought to that Californian shore the seeds of the Japanese yew. In thick formation the little dark trees had fought their way inland to a distance of some miles. That battalion would never get farther now that native vegetation had been consciously roused against it; but its thicket stood – a curious and strong invader.

His first period had been so rehearsed that neither vacant mind nor dry mouth could quite prevent delivery. Straightening his waistcoat, and jerking his head back, he regretted that the Speech from the throne foreshadowed no coherent and substantial policy such as might hope to free the country from its present plague of under-employment, and over-population. Economically speaking, any foreseeing interpretation of the course of affairs must now place Britain definitely in the orbit of the overseas world . . . (*'Oh! oh!'*) Ironical laughter so soon and sudden cleared Michael's mind, and relaxed his lips; and, with the grin that gave his face a certain charm, he resumed:

Speakers on all sides of the House, dwelling on the grave nature of the Unemployment problem, had pinned their faith to the full recapture of European trade, some in one way, some in another. August as they were, he wished very humbly to remark that they could not eat cake and have it. (*Laughter.*) Did they contend that wages in Britain must come down and working hours be lengthened; or did they assert that European wages must go up, and European working hours be shortened? No, they had not had the temerity. Britain, which was to rid itself of unemployment in the ways suggested, was the only important country in the world which had to buy about seven-tenths of its food, and of whose population well-nigh six-sevenths lived in Towns. It employed those six-sevenths in producing articles in some cases too dearly for European countries to buy, and yet it had to sell a sufficient surplus above the normal exchanges of trade, to pay for seven-tenths of the wherewithal to keep its producers alive. (*A laugh.*) If this was a joke, it was a grim one. (*A voice: 'You have forgotten the carrying trade.'*) He accepted the honourable Member's correction, and hoped that he felt happy about the future of that trade. It was, he feared, a somewhat shrinking asset.

At this moment in his speech Michael himself became a some-what shrinking asset, overwhelmed by a sudden desire to drop Foggartism, and sit down. The cool attention, the faint smiles, the expression on the face of a past Prime Minister, seemed conspiring towards his subsidence. 'How young – oh! how young you are!' they seemed to say. 'We sat here before you were breeched.' And he agreed with them completely. Still there was nothing for it but to go on – with Fleur in the Ladies' Gallery, old Blythe in the Distinguished Strangers'; yes, and something stubborn in his heart! Clenching the notes in his hand, therefore, he proceeded:

In spite of the war, and because of the war, the population of their Island had increased by 2,000,000. Emigration had fallen from 300,000 to 100,000. And this state of things was to be remedied by the mere process of recapturing to the full European trade which, quite obviously, had no intention of being so recaptured. What alternative, then, was there? Some honourable Members, he was afraid not many, would be familiar with the treatise of Sir James Foggart, entitled *The Parlous State of England*. (*'Hear, hear!' from a back Labour bench*.) He remembered to have read in a certain organ, or perhaps he should say harmonium, of the Press, for it was not a very deep-voiced instrument – (*laughter*) – that no such crack-brained policy had ever been devised for British consumption. (*'Hear, hear!'*) Certainly Foggartism was mad enough to look ahead, to be fundamental, and to ask the country to face its own position and the music into the bargain . . .

About to go over 'the top' – with public confession of his faith trembling behind his lips – Michael was choked by the sudden thought: 'Is it all right – is it what I think it, or am I an ignorant fool?' He swallowed vigorously, and staring straight before him, went on:

'Foggartism deprecates surface measures for a people in our position; it asks the country to fix its mind on a date – say twenty years hence – a minute in a nation's life – and to work steadily and coherently up to that date. It demands recognition of the need to make the British Empire, with its immense resources mostly latent, a self-sufficing unit. Imperialists will ask: What is there new in that? The novelty lies in degree and in method. Foggartism urges that the British people should be familiarised with the Empire by organised tours and propaganda on a great scale. It urges a vast increase – based on this familiarisation – of controlled and equipped emigration from these shores. But it has been found impossible, as honourable members well know, to send out suitable grown folk in any adequate quantity, because confirmed town-dwellers with their town tastes and habits, and their physique already impaired by town life, are of little use in the Dominions, while the few still on the English land cannot be spared. Foggartism, therefore, would send out boys and girls, between the ages of fourteen, or perhaps fifteen, and eighteen, in great numbers. The House is aware that experiments in this direction have already been made, with conspicuous success, but such experiments are but a drop in the bucket. This is a matter which can only be tackled in the way that things were tackled during the war. Development of child emigration is wanted, in fact, on the same scale and with the same energy as was manifested in Munitions after a certain most honourable Member had put his shoulder to that wheel – multiplication a hundredfold. Although the idea must naturally prove abortive without the utmost goodwill and co-operating energy on the part of the Dominions, I submit that this co-operation is not beyond the bounds of hope. The present hostility of people in the Dominions towards British immigrants is due to their very reasonable distrust of the usefulness of adult immigrants from this country. Once they have malleable youth to deal with, that drawback vanishes. In fact, the opening up of these vast new countries is like the progress of a rolling snowball, each little bit of "all right" – I beg the House's pardon – picks up another little bit; and there is no limit to the cumulative possibilities if a start is made at the right end and the scheme pushed and controlled by the right people.' Someone behind him said: 'Talking through his hat.' Michael paused, disconcerted; then, snatching at his bit, went on: 'A job of this sort half done is better left alone, but in the war, when something was found necessary, it *was* done, and men were always available for the doing of it. I put it to the House that the condition of our country now demands efforts almost as great as then.'

He could see that some members were actually listening to him with attention, and, taking a deep breath, he went on:

'Leaving out Ireland—' (*A voice: 'Why?'*) 'I prefer not to touch on anything that does not like to be touched—' (*laughter*) 'the present ratio of white population between Britain and the rest of the Empire is roughly in the nature of five to two. Child Emigration on a great scale will go far to equalise this ratio within twenty years; the British character of the British Empire will be established for ever, and supply and demand between the Mother Country and the Dominions will be levelled up.' (*A voice: 'The Dominions will then supply themselves.'*) 'The honourable Member will forgive me if I doubt that, for some time to come. We have the start in the machinery of manufacture. It may, of course, be five, seven, ten years before unemployment here comes down even to the pre-war rate, but can you point to any other plan which will really decrease it? I am all for good wages and moderate working hours. I believe the standard in Britain and the new countries, though so much higher than the European, is only a decent minimum, and in some cases does not reach it; I want better wages, even more moderate working hours; and the want is common among working men wherever the British flag flies.' (*'Hear, hear!'*) 'They are not going back on that want; and it is no good supposing that they are!' (*'Hear, hear!' 'Oh! oh!'*) 'The equalisation of demand and supply *within the empire* is the only way of preserving and improving the standards of life, which are now recognised as necessary on British soil. The world has so changed that the old maxim 'buy in the cheapest, sell in the dearest market' is standing on its head so far as England is concerned. Free Trade was never a principle—' (*'Oh! oh!' 'Hear, hear!' and laughter.*) 'Oh! well, it was born twins with expediency, and the twins have got mixed, and are both looking uncommonly peeky.' (*Laughter.*) 'But I won't go into that . . .' (*A voice: 'Better not!'*) Michael could see the mouth it came from below a clipped moustache in a red, black-haired face turned round at him from a Liberal bench. He could not put a name to it, but he did not like the unpolitical expression it wore. Where was he? Oh! yes . . . 'There is another point in the Foggart programme: England, as she now is, insufficiently protected in the air, and lamentably devoid of food-producing power, is an abiding temptation to the aggressive feelings of other nations. And here I must beg the House's pardon for a brief reference to Cinderella – in other words, the Land. The Speech from the throne gave no lead in reference to that vexed question, beyond implying that a Conference of all interested will be called. Well, without a definite intention in the minds of all the political Parties to join in some fixed and long-lasting policy for rehabilitation, such a Conference is bound to fail. Here again Foggartism—' (*'Ho! ho!'*) 'Here again Foggartism steps in. Foggartism says: Lay down your Land policy *and don't change it.* Let it be as sacred as the Prohibition Law in America.' (*A voice: 'And as damned!'* *Laughter.*) 'The sacred and damned – it sounds like a novel by Dostoievski.' (*Laughter.*) 'Well, we shall get nowhere without this damned sanctity. On our Land policy depends not only the prosperity of farmers, landlords, and labourers, desirable and important though that is, but the very existence of England, if unhappily there should come another war under the new conditions. Yes, and in a

fixed land policy lies the only hope of preventing the permanent de-
terioration of the British type. Foggartism requires that we lay down
our land policy, so that within ten years we may be growing up to
seventy per cent. of our food. Estimates made during the war showed
that as much as eighty-two per cent. could be grown at a pinch; and
the measures then adopted went a long way to prove that this estimate was no more than truth. Why were those measures allowed to
drop? Why was all that great improvement allowed to run to seed
and grass? What is wanted is complete confidence in every branch
of home agriculture; and nothing but a policy guaranteed over a long
period can ever produce that confidence.' Michael paused. Close by,
a member yawned; he heard a shuffle of feet; another old Prime
Minister came in; several members were going out. There was nothing
new about 'the Land'. Dared he tackle the air – that third plank in
the Foggart programme? There was nothing new about the air either!
Besides, he would have to preface it by a plea for the abolition of
air fighting, or at least for the reduction of armaments. It would take
too long! Better leave well alone! He hurried on:

'Emigration! The Land! Foggartism demands for both the same
sweeping attention as was given to vital measures during the war. I
feel honoured in having been permitted to draw the attention of all
Parties to this – I will brave an honourable Member's disposition to
say "Ho, ho!" – great treatise of Sir James Foggart. And I beg the
House's pardon for having been so long in fulfilling my task.'

He sat down, after speaking for thirteen minutes. Off his chest!
An honourable Member rose.

'I must congratulate the Member for Mid-Bucks on what, despite
its acquaintanceship with the clouds, and its Lewis Carrollian appeal
for less bread, more taxes, we must all admit to be a lively and well-
delivered first effort. The Member for Tyne and Tees, earlier in the
Debate, made an allusion to the Party to which I have the honour
to belong, which – er—'

'Exactly!' thought Michael, and after waiting for the next speech,
which contained no allusion whatever to his own, he left the House.

Chapter Two

Results

He walked home, lighter in head and heart. That was the trouble – a light weight! No serious attention would be paid to him. He recollected the maiden speech of the Member for Cornmarket. At least he had stopped, today, as soon as the House began to fidget. He felt hot, and hungry. Opera-singers grew fat through their voices, Members of Parliament thin. He would have a bath.

He was half clothed again when Fleur came in.

'You did splendidly, Michael. That beast!'

'Which?'

'His name's MacGown.'

'Sir Alexander MacGown? What about him?'

'You'll see tomorrow. He insinuated that you were interested in the sale of the Foggart book, as one of its publishers.'

'That's rather the limit.'

'And all the rest of his speech was a cut-up; horrid tone about the whole thing. Do you know him?'

'MacGown? No. He's Member for some Scottish borough.'

'Well, he's an enemy. Blythe is awfully pleased with you, and wild about MacGown; and so is Bart. I've never seen him so angry. You'll have to write to *The Times* and explain that you've had no interest in Danby & Winter's since before you were elected. Bart and your mother are coming to dinner. Did you know she was with me?'

'Mother? She abhors politics.'

'All she said was: "I wish dear Michael would brush his hair back before speaking. I like to see his forehead." And when MacGown sat down, she said: "My dear, the back of that man's head is perfectly straight. D'you think he's a Prussian? And he's got thick lobes to his ears. I shouldn't like to be married to him!" She had her opera-glasses.'

Sir Lawrence and Lady Mont were already in the 'parlour' when they went down, standing opposite each other like two storks, if not precisely on one leg, still very distinguished. Pushing Michael's hair up, Lady Mont pecked his forehead, and her dove-like eyes gazed at the top of his head from under their arched brows. She was altogether a little Norman in her curves; she even arched her words. She was considered 'a deah; but not too frightfully all there'.

'How did you manage to stick it, Mother?'

'My dear boy, I was thrilled; except for that person in jute. I thought the shape of his head insufferable. Where did you get all that knowledge? It was so sensible.'

Michael grinned. 'How did it strike you, sir?'

Sir Lawrence grimaced.

'You played the *enfant terrible*, my dear. Half the party won't like it because they've never thought of it; and the other half won't like it because they *have*.'

'What! Foggartists at heart?'

'Of course; but in Office. You mustn't support your real convictions in Office – it's not done.'

'This nice room,' murmured Lady Mont. 'When I was last here it was Chinese. And where's the monkey?'

'In Michael's study, Mother. We got tired of him. Would you like to see Kit before dinner?'

Left alone, Michael and his father stared at the same object, a Louis Quinze snuff-box picked up by Soames.

'Would you take any notice of MacGown's insinuation, Dad?'

'Is that his name – the hairy haberdasher! I should.'

'How?'

'Give him the lie.'

'In private, in the Press, or in the House?'

'All three. In private I should merely call him a liar. In the Press you should use the words: "Reckless disregard for truth." And in Parliament – that you regret he "should have been so misinformed".'

To complete the crescendo you might add that men's noses have been pulled for less.'

'But you don't suppose,' said Michael, 'that people would believe a thing like that?'

'They will believe anything, my dear, that suggests corruption in public life. It's one of the strongest traits in human nature. Anxiety about the integrity of public men would be admirable, if it wasn't so usually felt by those who have so little integrity themselves that they can't give others credit for it.' Sir Lawrence grimaced, thinking of the P.P.R.S. 'And talking of that – why wasn't Old Forsyte in the House today?'

'I offered him a seat, but he said he hadn't been in the House since Gladstone moved the Home Rule Bill, and then only because he was afraid his father would have a fit.'

Sir Lawrence screwed his eyeglass in.

'That's not clear to me,' he said.

'His father had a pass, and didn't like to waste it.'

'I see. That was noble of Old Forsyte.'

'He said that Gladstone had been very windy.'

'Ah! They were even longer in those days. You covered your ground very quickly, Michael. I should say with practice you would do. I've a bit of news for Old Forsyte. Shropshire doesn't speak to Charlie Ferrar because the third time the old man paid his debts to prevent his being posted, he made that a condition, for fear of being asked again. It's not so lurid as I'd hoped. How's the action?'

'The last I heard was something about administering what they call interrogatories.'

'Ah! I know. They answer you in a way nobody can make head or tail of, and that without prejudice. Then they administer them to you, and you answer in the same way; it all helps the lawyers. What is there for dinner?'

'Fleur said we'd kill the fatted calf when I'd got my speech off.'

Sir Lawrence sighed.

'I'm glad. Your mother has Vitamins again rather badly; we eat little but carrots, generally raw. French blood in a family is an excellent thing – prevents faddiness about food. Ah! here they come! . . .'

It has often been remarked that the breakfast tables of people who avow themselves indifferent to what the Press may say of them are garnished by all the newspapers on the morning when there is anything to say. In Michael's case this was a waste of almost a shilling. The only allusions to his speech were contained in four out of thirteen dailies. *The Times* reported it (including the laughter) with condensed and considered accuracy. The *Morning Post* picked out three imperial bits, prefaced by the words: 'In a promising speech.' The *Daily Telegraph* remarked: 'Among the other speakers were Mr Michael Mont.' And the *Manchester Guardian* observed: 'The Member for Mid-Bucks in a maiden speech advocated the introduction of children into the Dominions.'

Sir Alexander MacGown's speech received the added attention demanded by his extra years of Parliamentary service, but there was no allusion to the insinuation. Michael turned to Hansard. His own speech seemed more coherent than he had hoped. When Fleur came down he was still reading MacGown's.

'Give me some coffee, old thing.'

Fleur gave him the coffee and leaned over his shoulder.

'This MacGown is after Marjorie Ferrar,' she said; 'I remember now.'

Michael stirred his cup. 'Dash it all! The House is free from that sort of pettiness.'

'No. I remember Alison telling me – I didn't connect him up yesterday. Isn't it a disgusting speech?'

'Might be worse,' said Michael, with a grin.

'"As a member of the firm who published this singular production, he is doubtless interested in pressing it on the public, so that we may safely discount the enthusiasm displayed." Doesn't that make your blood boil?'

Michael shrugged his shoulders.

'Don't you ever feel angry, Michael?'

'My dear, I was through the war. Now for *The Times*. What shall I say?

'SIR,

'May I trespass upon your valuable space (that's quite safe), in the interests of public life— (that keeps it impersonal) to— er – Well?'

'To say that Sir Alexander MacGown in his speech yesterday told a lie when he suggested that I was interested in the sale of Sir James Foggart's book.'

'Straight,' said Michael, 'but they wouldn't put it in. How's this?

'To draw attention to a misstatement in Sir Alexander MacGown's speech of yesterday afternoon. As a matter of fact (always useful) I ceased to have any interest whatever in the firm which published Sir James Foggart's book, *The Parlous State of England*, even before I became a member of the late Parliament; and am therefore in no way interested, as Sir Alexander MacGown suggested, in pressing it on the Public. I hesitate to assume that he meant to impugn my honour (must get in "honour") but his words might bear that construction. My interest in the book is simply my interest in what is truly the "parlous state of England".

Faithfully, etc.

That do?'

'Much too mild. Besides, I shouldn't say that you really believe the state of England is parlous. It's all nonsense, you know. I mean it's exaggerated.'

'Very well,' said Michael, 'I'll put the state of the Country, instead. In the House I suppose I rise to a point of order. And in the Lobby to a point of disorder, probably. I wonder what the *Evening Sun* will say?'

The *Evening Sun*, which Michael bought on his way to the House, gave him a leader, headed: 'Foggartism again', beginning as follows: 'Young Hopeful, in the person of the Member for Mid-Bucks, roused the laughter of the House yesterday by his championship of the insane policy called Foggartism, to which we have already alluded in these columns'; and so on for twenty lines of vivid disparagement. Michael gave it to the door-keeper.

In the House, after noting that MacGown was present, he rose at the first possible moment.

'Mr Speaker, I rise to correct a statement in yesterday's debate reflecting on my personal honour. The honourable Member for

Greengow, in his speech said –' He then read the paragraph from Hansard. 'It is true that I was a member of the firm which published Sir James Foggart's book in August, 1923, but I retired from all connection with that firm in October, 1923, before ever I entered this House. I have therefore no pecuniary or other interest whatever in pressing the claims of the book, beyond my great desire to see its principles adopted.'

He sat down to some applause; and Sir Alexander MacGown rose. Michael recognised the face with the unpolitical expression he had noticed during his speech.

'I believe,' he said, 'that the honourable Member for Mid-Bucks was not sufficiently interested in his own speech to be present when I made my reply to it yesterday. I cannot admit that my words bear the construction which he has put on them. I said, and I still say, that one of the publishers of a book must necessarily be interested in having the judgement which induced him to publish it vindicated by the Public. The honourable Member has placed on his head a cap which I did not intend for it.' His face came round towards Michael, grim, red, provocative.

Michael rose again.

'I am glad the honourable Member has removed a construction which others besides myself had put on his words.'

A few minutes later, with a certain unanimity, both left the House.

The papers not infrequently contain accounts of how Mr Swash, the honourable Member for Topcliffe, called Mr Buckler, the honourable Member for Footing, something unparliamentary. ('Order!') And of how Mr Buckler retorted that Mr Swash was something worse. ('Hear, hear!' and 'Order!') And of how Mr Swash waved his fists (uproar), and Mr Buckler threw himself upon the Chair, or threw some papers. ('Order! order! order!') And of how there was great confusion, and Mr Swash, or Mr Buckler, was suspended, and led vociferous out of the Mother of Parliaments by the Serjeant-at-Arms, with other edifying details. The little affair between Michael and Sir Alexander went off in other wise. With an instinct of common decency, they both made for the lavatory; nor till they reached those marble halls did either take the slightest notice of the other. In front of a roller towel Michael said:

'Now, sir, perhaps you'll tell me why you behaved like a dirty dog. You knew perfectly well the construction that would be placed on your words.'

Sir Alexander turned from a hairbrush.

'Take that!' he said, and gave Michael a swinging box on the ear. Staggering, Michael came up wildly with his right, and caught Sir Alexander on the nose. Their movements then became intensive. Michael was limber, Sir Alexander stocky; neither was over proficient with his fists. The affair was cut short by the honourable Member for Washbason, who had been in retirement. Coming hastily out of a door, he received simultaneously a black eye, and a blow on the diaphragm, which caused him to collapse. The speaker, now, was the Member for Washbason, in language stronger than those who knew the honourable gentleman would have supposed possible.

'I'm frightfully sorry, sir,' said Michael. 'It's always the innocent party who comes off worst.'

'I'll dam' well have you both suspended,' gasped the Member for Washbason.

Michael grinned, and Sir Alexander said: 'To hell!'

'You're a couple of brawling cads!' said the Member for Washbason. 'How the devil am I to speak this afternoon?'

'If you went in bandaged,' said Michael, dabbing the damaged eye with cold water, 'and apologised for a motor accident, you would get special hearing, and a good Press. Shall I take the silver lining out of my tie for a bandage?'

'Leave my eye alone,' bellowed the Member for Washbason, 'and get out, before I lose my temper!'

Michael buttoned the top of his waistcoat, loosened by Sir Alexander's grip, observed in the glass that his ear was very red, his cuff bloodstained, and his opponent still bleeding from the nose, and went out.

'Some scrap!' he thought, entering the fresher air of Westminster. 'Jolly lucky we were tucked away in there! I don't think I'll mention it!' His ear was singing, and he felt rather sick, physically and mentally. The salvational splendour of Foggartism already reduced to a brawl in a lavatory! It made one doubt one's vocation. Not even the Member for Washbason, however, had come off with dignity, so that the affair was not likely to get into the papers.

Crossing the road towards home, he sighted Francis Wilmot walking West.

'Hallo!'

Francis Wilmot looked up, and seemed to hesitate. His face was thinner, his eyes deeper set; he had lost his smile.

'How is Mrs Mont?'

'Very well, thanks. And you?'

'Fine,' said Francis Wilmot. 'Will you tell her I've had a letter from her cousin Jon. They're in great shape. He was mighty glad to hear I'd seen her, and sent his love.'

'Thanks,' said Michael, drily. 'Come and have tea with us.'

The young man shook his head.

'Have you cut your hand?'

Michael laughed. 'No, somebody's nose.'

Francis Wilmot smiled wanly. 'I'm wanting to do that all the time. Whose was it?'

'A man called MacGown's.'

Francis Wilmot seized Michael's hand. 'It's the very nose!' Then, apparently disconcerted by his frankness, he turned on his heel and made off, leaving Michael putting one and one together.

Next morning's papers contained no allusion to the blood-letting of the day before, except a paragraph to the effect that the Member for Washbason was confined to his house by a bad cold. The Tory journals preserved a discreet silence about Foggartism; but in two organs – one Liberal and one Labour – were little leaders, which Michael read with some attention.

The Liberal screed ran thus: 'The debate on the King's speech produced one effort which at least merits passing notice. The policy alluded to by the Member for Mid-Bucks under the label of Foggartism, because it emanates from that veteran Sir James Foggart, has a certain speciousness in these unsettled times, when everyone is looking for quack specifics. Nothing which departs so fundamentally from all that Liberalism stands for will command for a moment the support of any truly Liberal vote. The risk lies in its appeal to backwoodism in the Tory ranks. Loose thought and talk of a pessimistic nature always attracts a certain type of mind. The state of England is not really parlous. It in no way justifies any unsound or hysterical departure from our traditional policy. But there is no disguising the fact that certain so-called thinkers have been playing for some time past with the idea of reviving a "splendid isolation", based (whether they admit it or not) on the destruction of Free Trade. The young Member for Mid-Bucks in his speech handled for a moment that corner-stone of Liberalism, and then let it drop; perhaps he thought it too weighty for him. But reduced to its elements, Foggartism is a plea for the abandonment of Free Trade, and a blow in the face of the League of Nations.'

Michael sighed and turned to the Labour article, which was signed, and struck a more human note:

'And so we are to have our children carted off to the Antipodes as soon as they can read and write, in order that the capitalist class may be relieved of the menace lurking in Unemployment. I know nothing of Sir James Foggart, but if he was correctly quoted in Parliament yesterday by a member for an agricultural constituency, I smell Prussianism about that old gentleman. I wonder what the working man is saying over his breakfast-table? I fear the words: "To hell!" are not altogether absent from his discourse. No, Sir James Foggart, English Labour intends to call its own hand; and with all the old country's drawbacks, still prefers it for itself and its children. We are not taking any, Sir James Foggart.'

'There it is, naked,' thought Michael. 'The policy ought never to have been entrusted to me. Blythe ought to have found a Labour townsman.'

Foggartism, whittled to a ghost by jealousy and class-hatred, by shibboleth, section and Party – he had a vision of it slinking through the purlieus of the House and the corridors of the Press, never admitted to the Presence, nor accepted as flesh and blood!

'Never mind,' he muttered; 'I'll stick it. If one's a fool, one may as well be a blazing fool. Eh, Dan?'

The Dandie, raising his head from his paws, gave him a lustrous glance.

Chapter Three

Marjorie Ferrar at Home

*F*rancis Wilmot went on his way to Chelsea. He had a rendezvous with Life. Over head and ears in love, and old fashioned to the point of marriage, he spent his days at the tail of a petticoat as often absent as not. His simple fervour had wrung from Marjorie Ferrar confession of her engagement. She had put it bluntly: she was in debt, she wanted shekels and she could not live in the backwoods. He had promptly offered her all his shekels. She had refused them with the words:

'My poor dear, I'm not so far gone as that.' Often on the point of saying 'Wait until I'm married', the look on his face had always deterred her. He was primitive; would never understand her ideal: perfection, as wife, mistress, and mother, all at once. She kept him only by dangling the hope that she would throw MacGown over; taking care to have him present when MacGown was absent, and absent when MacGown was present. She had failed to keep them apart on two occasions, painful and productive of more lying than she was at all accustomed to. For she was really taken with this young man; he was a new flavour. She 'loved' his dark 'slinky' eyes, his grace, the way his 'back-chat' grew, dark and fine, on his slim comely neck. She 'loved' his voice and his old-fashioned way of talking. And, rather oddly, she 'loved' his loyalty. Twice she had urged him to find out whether Fleur wasn't going to 'climb down' and 'pay up'. Twice he had refused, saying: 'They were mighty nice to me; and I'd never tell you what they said, even if I did go and find out.'

She was painting his portrait, so that a prepared canvas with a little paint on it chaperoned their almost daily interviews, which took place between three and four when the light had already failed. It was an hour devoted by MacGown to duty in the House. A low and open collar suited Francis Wilmot's looks. She liked him to sit lissom on a divan with his eyes following her; she liked to come close to him, and see the tremor of his fingers touching her skirt or sleeve, the glow in his eyes, the change in his face when she moved away. His faith in her was inconvenient. P's and Q's were letters she despised. And yet, to have to mind them before him gave her a sort of pleasure, made her feel good. One did not shock children!

That day, since she expected MacGown at five, she had become uneasy before the young man came in, saying:

'I met Michael Mont; his cuff was bloody. Guess whose blood!'

'Not Alec's?'

Francis Wilmot dropped her hands.

'Don't call that man "Alec" to me.'

'My dear child, you're too sensitive. I thought they'd have a row – I read their speeches. Hadn't Michael a black eye? No? Tt – tt! Al– er – "that man" will be awfully upset. Was the blood fresh?'

'Yes,' said Francis Wilmot, grimly.

'Then he won't come. Sit down, and let's do some serious work for once.'

But throwing himself on his knees, he clasped his hands behind her waist.

'Marjorie, Marjorie!'

Disciple of Joy, in the forefront of modern mockery, she was yet conscious of pity, for him and for herself. It was hard not to be able to tell him to run out, get licence and ring, or whatever he set store by, and have done with it! Not even that she was ready to have done with it without ring or licence! For one must keep one's head. She had watched one lover growing tired, kept her head, and dismissed him before he knew it; grown tired of another, kept her head, and gone on till he was tired too. She had watched favourites she had backed go down, kept her head and backed one that didn't; had seen cards turn against her, and left off playing before her pile was gone. Time and again she had earned the good mark of Modernity.

So she kissed the top of his head, unclasped his hands, and told him to be good; and, in murmuring it, felt that she had passed her prime.

'Amuse me while I paint,' she said. 'I feel rotten.'

And Francis Wilmot, like a dark ghost, amused her.

Some believe that a nose from which blood has been drawn by a blow swells less in the first hour that it does later. This was why Sir Alexander MacGown arrived at half-past four to say that he could not come at five. He had driven straight from the House with a little bag of ice held to it. Having been led to understand that the young American was 'now in Paris', he stood stock still, staring at one whose tie was off and whose collar was unbuttoned. Francis Wilmot rose from the divan, no less silent. Marjorie Ferrar put a touch on the canvas.

'Come and look, Alec; it's only just begun.'

'No, thanks,' said MacGown.

Crumpling his tie into his pocket, Francis Wilmot bowed and moved towards the door.

'Won't you stay for tea, Mr Wilmot?'

'I believe not, thank you.'

When he was gone Marjorie Ferrar fixed her eyes on the nose of her betrothed. Strong and hard, it was as yet, little differentiated from the normal.

'Now,' said MacGown, 'why did you lie about that young blighter? You said he was in Paris. Are you playing fast and loose with me, Marjorie?'

'Of course! Why not?'

MacGown advanced to within reach of her.

'Put down that brush.'

Marjorie Ferrar raised it; and suddenly it hit the wall opposite.

'You'll stop that picture, and you'll not see that fellow again; he's in love with you.'

He had taken her wrists.

Her face, quite as angry as his own, reined back.

'Let go! I don't know if you call yourself a gentleman?'

'No, a plain man.'

'Strong and silent – out of a dull novel. Sit down, and don't be unpleasant.'

The duel of their eyes, brown and burning, blue and icy, endured for quite a minute. Then he did let go.

'Pick up that brush and give it to me.'

'I'm damned if I will!'

'Then our engagement is off. If you're old fashioned, I'm not. You want a young woman who'll give you a whip for a wedding-present.'

MacGown put his hands up to his head.

'I want you too badly to be sane.'

'Then pick up the brush.'

MacGown picked it up.

'What have you done to your nose?'

MacGown put his hand to it.

'Ran it against a door.'

Marjorie Ferrar laughed. 'Poor door!'

MacGown gazed at her in genuine astonishment.

'You're the hardest woman I ever came across; and why I love you, I don't know.'

'It hasn't improved your looks or your temper, my dear. You were rash to come here today.'

MacGown uttered a sort of groan. 'I can't keep away, and you know it.'

Marjorie Ferrar turned the canvas face to the wall, and leaned there beside it.

'I don't know what you think of the prospects of our happiness. Alec; but I think they're pretty poor. Will you have a whisky and soda? It's in that cupboard. Tea, then? Nothing? We'd better understand each other. If I marry you, which is very doubtful, I'm not going into purdah. I shall see what friends I choose. And until I marry you, I shall also see them. If you don't like it, you can leave it.'

She watched his clenching hands, and her wrists tingled. To be perfect wife to him would 'take a bit of doing'! If only she knew of

a real 'good thing' instead, and had a 'shirt to put on it'! If only
Francis Wilmot had money and did not live where the cotton came
from, and darkies crooned in the fields; where rivers ran red, Florida
moss festooned the swamps and the sun shone; where grapefruit
grew – or didn't? – and mocking-birds sang sweeter than the nightingale. South Carolina, described to her with such enthusiasm by Francis
Wilmot! A world that was not her world stared straight into the eyes
of Marjorie Ferrar. South Carolina! Impossible! It was like being
asked to be ancient!

MacGown came up to her. 'I'm sorry,' he said. 'Forgive me,
Marjorie.'

On her shrugging shoulders he put his hands, kissed her lips, and
went away.

And she sat down in her favourite chair, listless, swinging her foot.
The sand had run out of her dolly – life was a bore! It was like
driving tandem, when the leader would keep turning round; or the
croquet party in *Alice in Wonderland*, read in the buttercup-fields
at High Marshes not twenty years ago that felt like twenty centuries.

What did she want? Just a rest from men and bills? or that fluffy
something called 'real love'? Whatever it was, she hadn't got it! And
so! Dress, and go out, and dance; and later dress again, and go out
and dine; and the dresses not paid for.

Well, nothing like an egg-nog for 'the hump'!

Ringing for the ingredients, she made one with plenty of brandy,
capped it with nutmeg, and drank it down.

Chapter Four

'Fons Et Origo'

wo mornings later Michael received two letters. The first,
which bore an Australian post-mark, ran thus:

'DEAR SIR,

'I hope you are well and the lady. I thought perhaps you'd like
to know how we are. Well, Sir, we're not much to speak of out
here after a year and a half. I consider there's too much gilt on
the ginger-bread as regards Australia. The climate's all right
when it isn't too dry or too wet – it suits my wife fine, but Sir
when they talk about making your fortune all I can say is tell
it to the marines. The people here are a funny lot they don't
seem to have any use for us and I don't seem to have any use
for them. They call us Pommies and treat us as if we'd took a
liberty in coming to their blooming country. You'd say they
wanted a few more out here, but they don't seem to think so.
I often wish I was back in the old Country. My wife says we're
better off here, but I don't know. Anyway they tell a lot of lies
as regards emigration.

'Well, Sir, I've not forgotten your kindness. My wife says
please to remember her to you and the lady.

'Yours faithfully,

'ANTHONY BICKET.'

With that letter in his hand, Michael, like some psychometric medium, could see again the writer, his thin face, prominent eyes, large ears, a shadowy figure of the London streets behind his coloured balloons. Poor little snipe – square peg in round hole wherever he might be; and all those other pegs – thousands upon thousands, that would never fit in. Pommies! Well! He wasn't recommending emigration for them; he was recommending it for those who could be shaped before their wood had set. Surely they wouldn't put that stigma on to children! He opened the other letter.

'Roll Manor, Nr. Huntingdon.

'MY DEAR SIR,

'The disappointment I have felt since the appearance of my book was somewhat mitigated by your kind allusions to it in Parliament, and your championship of its thesis. I am an old man, and do not come to London now, but it would give me pleasure to meet you. If you are ever in this neighbourhood, I should be happy if you would lunch with me, or stay the night, as suits you best.
    'With kind regards,
    'Faithfully yours,

'JAS: FOGGART.'

He showed it to Fleur.
'If you go, my dear, you'll be bored to tears.'
'I must go,' said Michael; 'Fons et Origo!'
He wrote that he would come to lunch the following day.
He was met at the station by a horse drawing a vehicle of a shape he had never before beheld. The green-liveried man to whose side he climbed introduced it with the words: 'Sir James thought, sir, you'd like to see about you; so 'e sent the T cart.'
It was one of those grey late autumn days, very still, when the few leaves that are left hang listless, waiting to be windswept. The puddled road smelled of rain; rooks rose from the stubbles as if in surprise at

the sound of horses' hoofs; and the turned earth of ploughed fields had the sheen that betokened clay. To the flat landscape poplars gave a certain spirituality; and the russet-tiled farmhouse roofs a certain homeliness.

'That's the manor, sir,' said the driver, pointing with his whip. Between an orchard and a group of elms, where was obviously a rookery, Michael saw a long low house of deeply weathered brick covered by Virginia creeper whose leaves had fallen. At a little distance were barns, outhouses, and the wall of a kitchen-garden. The T cart turned into an avenue of limes and came suddenly on the house unprotected by a gate. Michael pulled an old iron bell. Its lingering clang produced a lingering man, who, puckering his face, said: 'Mr Mont? Sir James is expecting you. This way, sir.'

Through an old low hall smelling pleasantly of wood-smoke, Michael reached a door which the puckered man closed in his face.

Sir James Foggart! Some gaitered old countryman with little grey whiskers, neat, weathered and firm-featured; or one of those short-necked John Bulls, still extant, square and weighty, with a flat top to his head, and a flat white topper on it!

The puckered man reopened the door, and said:

'Sir James will see you, sir.'

Before the fire in a large room with a large hearth and many books was a huge old man, grey-bearded and grey-locked, like a superannuated British lion, in an old velvet coat with whitened seams.

He appeared to be trying to rise.

'Please don't, sir,' said Michael.

'If you'll excuse me, I won't. Pleasant journey?'

'Very.'

'Sit down. Much touched by your speech. First speech, I think?'

Michael bowed.

'Not the last, I hope.'

The voice was deep and booming; the eyes looked up keenly, as if out of thickets, so bushy were the eyebrows, and the beard grew so high on the cheeks. The thick grey hair waved across the forehead and fell on to the coat collar. A primeval old man in a high state of cultivation. Michael was deeply impressed.

'I've looked forward to this honour, sir,' he said, 'ever since we published your book.'

'I'm a recluse – never get out now. Tell you the truth, don't want to – see too many things I dislike. I write, and smoke my pipe. Ring the bell, and we'll have lunch. Who's this Sir Alexander MacGown? – his head wants punching!'

'No longer, sir,' said Michael.

Sir James Foggart leaned back and laughed.

His laugh was long, deep, slightly hollow, like a laugh in a trombone.

'Capital! And how did those fellows take your speech? Used to know a lot of 'em at one time – fathers of these fellows, grand-fathers, perhaps.'

'How do you know so well what England wants, sir,' said Michael, suavely, 'now that you never leave home?'

Sir James Foggart pointed with a large thin hand covered with hair to a table piled with books and magazines.

'Read,' he said; 'read everything – eyes as good as ever – seen a good deal in my day.' And he was silent, as if seeing it again.

'Are you following your book up?'

'M'm! Something for 'em to read when I'm gone. Eighty-four, you know.'

'I wonder,' said Michael, 'that you haven't had the Press down.'

'Have – had 'em yesterday; three by different trains; very polite young men; but I could see they couldn't make head or tail of the old creature – too far gone, eh?'

At this moment the door was opened, and the puckered man came in, followed by a maid and three cats. They put a tray on Sir James's knees and another on a small table before Michael. On each tray was a partridge with chipped potatoes, spinach and bread sauce. The puckered man filled Sir James's glass with barley-water, Michael's with claret, and retired. The three cats, all tortoise-shells, began rubbing themselves against Sir James's trousers, purring loudly.

'Don't mind cats, I hope? No fish today, pussies!'

Michael was hungry and finished his bird. Sir James gave most of his to the cats. They were then served with fruit salad, cheese, coffee and cigars, and everything removed, except the cats, who lay replete before the fire, curled up in a triangle.

Michael gazed through the smoke of two cigars at the fount and origin, eager, but in doubt whether it would stand pumping – it seemed so very old! Well! anyway, he must have a shot!

'You know Blythe, sir, of *The Outpost*? He's your great supporter; I'm only a mouthpiece.'

'Know his paper – best of the weeklies; but too clever by half.'

'Now that I've got the chance,' said Michael, 'would you mind if I asked you one or two questions?'

Sir James Foggart looked at the lighted end of his cigar. 'Fire ahead.'

'Well, sir, can England really stand apart from Europe?'

'Can she stand with Europe? Alliances based on promise of assistance that won't be forthcoming – worse than useless.'

'But suppose Belgium were invaded again, or Holland?'

'The one case, perhaps. Let that be understood. Knowledge in Europe, young man, of what England will or will not do in given cases is most important. And they've never had it. *Perfide Albion*! Heh! We always wait till the last moment to declare our policy. Great mistake. Gives the impression that we serve Time – which, with our democratic system, by the way, we generally do.'

'I like that, sir,' said Michael, who did not. 'About wheat? How would you stabilise the price so as to encourage our growth of it?'

'Ha! My pet lamb. We want a wheat loan, Mr Mont, and Government control. Every year the Government should buy in advance all the surplus we need and store it; then fix a price for the home farmers that gives them a good profit; and sell to the public at the average between the two prices. You'd soon see plenty of wheat grown here, and a general revival of agriculture.'

'But wouldn't it raise the price of bread, sir?'

'Not it.'

'And need an army of officials?'

'No. Use the present machinery properly organised.'

'State trading, sir?' said Michael, with diffidence.

Sir James Foggart's voice boomed out. 'Exceptional case – basic case – why not?'

'I quite agree,' said Michael, hastily. 'I never thought of it, but why not? . . . Now as to the opposition to child emigration in this country. Do you think it comes from the affection of parents for their children?'

'More from dislike of losing the children's wages.'

'Still, you know,' murmured Michael, 'one might well kick against losing one's children for good at fifteen!'

'One might; human nature's selfish, young man. Hang on to 'em and see 'em rot before one's eyes, or grow up to worse chances than one's own – as you say, that's human nature.'

Michael, who had not said it, felt somewhat stunned.

'The child emigration scheme will want an awful lot of money and organisation.'

Sir James stirred the cats with his slippered foot.

'Money! There's still a mint of money – misapplied. Another hundred million loan – four and a half millions a year in the Budget; and a hundred thousand children at least sent out every year. In five years we should save the lot in unemployment dole.' He waved his cigar, and its ash spattered on his velvet coat.

'Thought it would,' said Michael to himself, knocking his own off into a coffee-cup. 'But can children sent out wholesale like that be properly looked after, and given a real chance, sir?'

'Start gradually; where there's a will there's a way.'

'And won't they just swell the big towns out there?'

'Teach 'em to want land, and give it 'em.'

'I don't know if it's enough,' said Michael, boldly; 'the lure of the towns is terrific.'

Sir James nodded. 'A town's no bad thing till it's overdone, as they are here. Those that go to the towns will increase the demand for our supplies.'

'Well,' thought Michael, 'I'm getting on. What shall I ask him next?' And he contemplated the cats, who were stirring uneasily. A peculiar rumbling noise had taken possession of the silence. Michael looked up. Sir James Foggart was asleep! In repose he was more tremendous than ever – perhaps rather too tremendous; for his snoring seemed to shake the room. The cats tucked their heads farther in.

There was a slight smell of burning. Michael picked a fallen cigar from the carpet. What should he do now? Wait for a revival, or clear out? Poor old boy! Foggartism had never seemed to Michael a more forlorn hope than in this sanctum of its fount and origin. Covering his ears, he sat quite still. One by one the cats got up. Michael looked at his watch. 'I shall lose my train,' he thought, and tiptoed to the door, behind a procession of deserting cats. It was as though Foggartism were snoring the little of its life away! 'Good-bye, sir!' he said softly, and went out. He walked to the station very thoughtful. Foggartism! That vast if simple programme seemed based on the supposition that human beings could see two inches before their noses. But was that supposition justified; if so, would England be so town-ridden and over-populated? For one man capable of taking a far and comprehensive view and going to sleep on it, there were nine – if not nine-and-ninety – who could take near and partial views and remain wide awake. Practical politics! The answer to all wisdom, however you might boom it out. 'Oh! Ah! Young Mont – not a practical politician!' It was public death to be so labelled. And Michael, in his railway-carriage, with his eyes on the English grass, felt like a man on whom everyone was heaping earth. Had pelicans crying in the wilderness a sense of humour? If not, their time was poor. Grass, grass, grass! Grass and the towns! And, nestling his chin into his heavy coat, he was soon faster asleep than Sir James Foggart.

Chapter Five

Progress Of The Case

W—hen Soames said 'Leave it to me,' he meant it, of course; but it was really very trying that whenever anything went wrong, he, and not somebody else, had to set it right!

To look more closely into the matter he was staying with his sister Winifred Dartie in Green Street. Finding his nephew Val at dinner there the first night, he took the opportunity of asking him whether he knew anything of Lord Charles Ferrar.

'What do you want to know, Uncle Soames?'

'Anything unsatisfactory. I'm told his father doesn't speak to him.'

'Well,' said Val, 'it's generally thought he'll win the Lincolnshire with a horse that didn't win the Cambridgeshire.'

'I don't see the connection.'

Val Dartie looked at him through his lashes. He was not going to enter for the slander stakes. 'Well, he's got to bring off a coup soon, or go under.'

'Is that all?'

'Except that he's one of those chaps who are pleasant to you when you can be of use, and unpleasant when you can't.'

'So I gathered from his looks,' said Soames. 'Have you had any business dealings with him?'

'Yes; I sold him a yearling by Torpedo out of Banshee.'

'Did he pay you?'

'Yes,' said Val, with a grin; 'and she turned out no good.'

'H'm! I suppose he was unpleasant afterwards? That all you know?'

Val nodded. He knew more, if gossip can be called 'more'; but what was puffed so freely with the smoke of racing-men's cigars was hardly suited to the ears of lawyers.

For so old a man of the world Soames was singularly unaware how in that desirable sphere, called Society, everyone is slandered daily, and no bones broken; slanderers and slandered dining and playing cards together with the utmost good feeling and the intention of reslandering each other the moment they are round the corner. Such genial and hair-raising reports reach no outside ears, and Soames really did not know where to begin investigation.

'Can you ask this Mr Curfew to tea?' he said to Fleur.

'What for, Father?'

'So that I can pump him.'

'I thought there were detectives for all that sort of thing.'

Soames went a special colour. Since his employment of Mr Polteed, who had caught him visiting his own wife's bedroom in Paris, at the beginning of the century, the word detective produced a pain in his diaphragm. He dropped the subject. And yet, without detectives, what was he to do?

One night, Winifred having gone to the theatre, he sat down with a cigar, to think. He had been provided by Michael with a list of 'advanced' books and plays which 'modern' people were reading, attending and discussing. He had even been supplied with one of the books: *Canthar*, by Perceval Calvin. He fetched it from his bedroom, and, turning up a lamp, opened the volume. After reading the first few pages, in which he could see nothing, he turned to the end and read backwards. In this way he could skip better, and each erotic passage, to which he very soon came, led him insensibly on to the one before it. He had reached the middle of the novel, before he had resort in wonder to the title-pages. How was it that the publisher and author were at large? Ah! The imprint was of a foreign nature. Soames breathed more freely. Though sixty-nine, and neither Judge, juryman, nor otherwise professionally compelled to be shocked, he was shaken. If women were reading this sort of thing, then there really was no distinction between men and women nowadays. He took up the book again, and read steadily on to the beginning. The erotic passages alone interested him. The rest seemed rambling, disconnected stuff. He rested again. What was this novel written for? To make money, of course. But was there another purpose? Was the author one of these 'artist' fellows who thought that to give you 'life' – wasn't that the phrase? – they must put down every visit to a bedroom, and some besides? 'Art for Art's sake', 'realism' – what did they call it? In Soames's comparatively bleak experience 'life' did not consist wholly of visiting bedrooms, so that he was unable to admit that this book was life, the whole of life, and nothing but life. 'Calvin's a crank, sir,' Michael had said, when he handed him the novel. 'He thinks people can't become continent except through being excessively incontinent; so he shows his hero and heroine arriving gradually at continence.' 'At Bedlam,' thought Soames. They would see what a British Jury had to say to that, anyway. But how elicit a confession that this woman and her set had read it with gusto? And then an idea occurred to him, so brilliant that he had to ponder deeply before he could feel any confidence in it. These 'advanced' young people had any amount of conceit; every one who didn't share their views was a 'dud', or a 'grundy'. Suppose the book were attacked in the Press, wouldn't it draw their fire? And if their fire could be drawn in print, could it not be used afterwards as evidence of their views on morality?

H'm! This would want very nice handling. And first of all, how was he to prove that Marjorie Ferrar had read this book? Thus casting about him, Soames was rewarded by another brilliant thought: Young Butterfield – who had helped him to prove the guilt of Elderson in that matter of the P.P.R.S. and owed his place at Danby & Winter's, the publishers, to Soames's recommendation! Why not make use of him? Michael always said the young man was grateful. And obscuring the title of the book against his flank, in case he should meet a servant, Soames sought his own bedroom.

His last thought that night was almost diagnostic.

'In my young days we read that sort of book if we could get hold of it, and didn't say so; now, it seems, they make a splash of reading it, and pretend it does them good!'

Next morning from 'The Connoisseurs' he telephoned to Danby & Winter's, and asked to speak to Mr Butterfield.

'Yes?'

'Mr Forsyte speaking. Do you remember me?'

'Yes, indeed, sir.'

'Can you step round to the Connoisseurs' Club this morning some time?'

'Certainly, sir. Will twelve-thirty suit you?'

Secretive and fastidious in matters connected with sex, Soames very much disliked having to speak to a young man about an 'immoral' book. He saw no other way of it, however, and, on his visitor's arrival, shook hands and began at once.

'This is confidential, Mr Butterfield.'

Butterfield, whose dog-like eyes had glowed over the handshake, answered:

'Yes, sir. I've not forgotten what you did for me, sir.'

Soames held out the book.

'Do you know that novel?'

Butterfield smiled slightly.

'Yes, sir. It's printed in Brussels. They're paying five pounds a copy for it.'

'Have you read it?'

The young man shook his head. 'It's not come my way, sir.'

Soames was relieved. 'Well, don't! But just attend a moment. Can you buy ten copies of it, at my expense, and post them to ten people whose names I'll give you? They're all more or less connected with literature. You can put in slips to say the copies are complimentary, or whatever you call it. But mention no names.'

The young man Butterfield said deprecatingly:

'The price is rising all the time, sir. It'll cost you well on sixty pounds.'

'Never mind that.'

'You wish the book boomed, sir?'

'Good Gad – no! I have my reasons, but we needn't go into them.'

'I see, sir. And you want the copies to come – as if – as if from heaven?'

'That's it,' said Soames. 'I take it that publishers often send doubtful books to people they think will support them. There's just one other thing. Can you call a week later on one of the people to whom you've sent the books, and offer to sell another copy as if you were an agent for it? I want to make quite sure it's already reached that person, and been read. You won't give your name, of course. Will you do this for me?'

The eyes of the young man Butterfield again glowed:

'Yes, sir. I owe you a great deal, sir.'

Soames averted his eyes; he disliked all expression of gratitude.

'Here's the list of names, then, with their addresses. I've underlined the one you call on. I'll write you a cheque to go on with; and you can let me know later if there's anything more to pay.'

He sat down, while the young man Butterfield scrutinised the list.

'I see it's a lady, sir, that I'm to call on.'

'Yes; does that make any difference to you?'

'Not at all, sir. Advanced literature is written for ladies nowadays.'

'H'm!' said Soames. 'I hope you're doing well?'

'Splendidly, sir. I was very sorry that Mr Mont left us; we've been doing better ever since.'

Soames lifted an eyebrow. The statement confirmed many an old suspicion. When the young man had gone, he took up *Canthar*. Was he capable of writing an attack on it in the Press, over the signature 'Paterfamilias'? He was not. The job required someone used to that sort of thing. Besides, a real signature would be needed to draw fire. It would not do to ask Michael to suggest one; but Old Mont might know some fogey at the Parthenaeum who carried metal. Sending for a bit of brown paper, he disguised the cover with it, put the volume in his overcoat pocket, and set out for 'Snooks'.

He found Sir Lawrence about to lunch, and they sat down together. Making sure that the waiter was not looking over his shoulder, Soames, who had brought the book in with him, pushed it over, and said:

'Have you read that?'

Sir Lawrence whinnied.

'My dear Forsyte, why this morbid curiosity? Everybody's reading it. They say the thing's unspeakable.'

'Then you haven't?' said Soames, keeping him to the point.

'Not yet, but if you'll lend it me, I will. I'm tired of people who've enjoyed it asking me if I've read "that most disgusting book". It's not fair, Forsyte. Did *you* enjoy it?'

'I skimmed it,' said Soames, looking round his nose. 'I had a reason. When you've read it, I'll tell you.'

Sir Lawrence brought it back to him at 'the Connoisseurs' two days later.

'Here you are, my dear Forsyte,' he said. 'I never was more glad to get rid of a book! I've been in a continual stew for fear of being overseen with it! Perceval Calvin – *quel sale Monsieur*!'

'Exactly!' said Soames. 'Now, I want to get that book attacked.'

'You! Is Saul also among the prophets? Why this sudden zest?'

'It's rather roundabout,' said Soames, sitting on the book. He detailed the reason, and ended with:

'Don't say anything to Michael, or Fleur.'

Sir Lawrence listened with his twisting smile.

'I see,' he said, 'I see. Very cunning, Forsyte. You want me to get someone whose name will act like a red rag. It mustn't be a novelist, or they'll say he's jealous – which he probably is: the book's selling like hot cakes – I believe that's the expression. Ah! I think – I rather think, Forsyte, that I have the woman.'

'Woman!' said Soames. 'They won't pay any attention to that.'

Sir Lawrence cocked his loose eyebrow. 'I believe you're right – the only women they pay attention to nowadays are those who go one better than themselves. Shall I do it myself, and sign "Outraged Parent"?'

'I believe it wants a real name.'

'Again right, Forsyte; it does. I'll drop into the Parthenaeum, and see if any one's alive.'

Two days later Soames received a note.

'The Parthenaeum,
'Friday.

'MY DEAR FORSYTE,

'I've got the man – the Editor of the *Protagonist*; and he'll do it under his own name. What's more, I've put him on to the right line. We had a spirited argument. He wanted to treat it *de haut en bas* as the work of a dirty child. I said: "No. This thing is symptomatic. Treat it seriously; show that it represents a school of thought, a deliberate literary attitude; and make it a plea for censorship." Without the word censorship, Forsyte, they will never rise. So he's leaving his wife and taking it into the country for the weekend. I admire your conduct of the defence, my dear Forsyte; it's very subtle. But if you'll forgive me for saying so, it's more important to prevent the case coming into Court than to get a verdict if it does.

 'Sincerely yours,

'Lawrence Mont.'

With which sentiment Soames so entirely agreed, that he went down to Mapledurham, and spent the next two afternoons going round and round with a man he didn't like, hitting a ball, to quiet his mind.

Chapter Six

Michael Visits Bethnal Green

The feeling of depression with which Michael had come back from the fount and origin was somewhat mitigated by letters he was receiving from people of varying classes, nearly all young. They were so nice and earnest. They made him wonder whether after all practical politicians were not too light-hearted, like the managers of music-halls who protected the Public carefully from their more tasteful selves. They made him feel that there might be a spirit in the country that was not really represented in the House, or even in the Press. Among these letters was one which ran:

'Sunshine House,
'Bethnal Green.

'DEAR MR MONT,

'I was so awfully glad to read your speech in *The Times*. I instantly got Sir James Foggart's book. I think the whole policy is simply splendid. You've no idea how heart-breaking it is for us who try to do things for children, to know that whatever we do is bound to be snowed under by the life they go to when school age ends. We have a good opportunity here of seeing the realities of child life in London. It's wonderful to see the fondness of the mothers for the little ones, in spite of their own hard lives – though not all, of course, by any means; but we often notice, and I think it's common experience, that when the children get beyond ten or twelve, the fondness for them begins to assume another form. I suppose it's really the commercial possibilities of the child making themselves felt. When money comes in at the door, disinterested love seems to move towards the window. I suppose it's natural, but it's awfully sad, because the commercial possibilities are generally so miserable; and the children's after-life is often half ruined for the sake of the few shillings they earn. I do fervently hope something will come of your appeal; only – things move so slowly, don't they? I wish you would come down and see our House here. The children are adorable, and we try to give them sunshine.

'Sincerely yours,

'NORAH CURFEW.'

Bertie Curfew's sister! But surely that case would not really come to anything! Grateful for encouragement, and seeking light on Foggartism, he decided to go. Perhaps Norah Curfew would take the little Boddicks! He suggested to Fleur that she should accompany him, but she was afraid of picking up something unsuitable to the eleventh baronet, so he went alone.

The house, facing the wintry space called Bethnal Green, consisted of three small houses converted into one, with their three small back yards, trellised round and gravelled, for a playground. Over the door were the words: SUNSHINE HOUSE, in gold capitals. The walls were cream-coloured, the woodwork dark, and the curtains of gay chintz. Michael was received in the entrance-lobby by Norah Curfew herself. Tall, slim and straight, with dark hair brushed back from a pale face, she had brown eyes, clear, straight and glowing.

'Gosh!' thought Michael, as she wrung his hand. 'She *is* swept and garnished. No basement in her soul!'

'It *was* good of you to come, Mr Mont. Let me take you over the house. This is the playroom.'

Michael entered a room of spotless character, which had evidently been formed from several knocked into one. Six small children dressed in blue linen were seated on the floor, playing games. They embraced the knees of Norah Curfew when she came within reach. With the exception of one little girl Michael thought them rather ugly.

'These are our residents. The others only come out of school hours. We have to limit them to fifty, and that's a pretty good squeeze. We want funds to take the next two houses.'

'How many of you are working here?'

'Six. Two of us do the cooking; one the accounts; and the rest washing, mending, games, singing, dancing, and general chores. Two of us live in.'

'I don't see your harps and crowns.'

Norah Curfew smiled.

'Pawned,' she said.

'What do you do about religion?' asked Michael, thinking of the eleventh baronet's future.

'Well, on the whole we don't. You see, they're none of them more than twelve; and the religious age, when it begins at all, begins with sex about fourteen. We just try to teach kindness and cheerfulness. I had my brother down the other day. He's always laughed at me; but he's going to do a matinee for us, and give us the proceeds.'

'What play?'

'I think it's called "The Plain Dealer". He says he's always wanted to do it for a good object.'

Michael stared. 'Do you know "The Plain Dealer"?'

'No; it's by one of the Restoration people, isn't it?'

'Wycherley.'

'Oh! yes!' Her eyes remaining clearer than the dawn, Michael thought: 'Poor dear! It's not my business to queer the pitch of her money-getting; but Master Bertie likes his little joke!'

'I must bring my wife down here,' he said; 'she'd love your walls and curtains. And I wanted to ask you. You haven't room, have you, for two more little girls, if we pay for them? Their father's down and out, and I'm starting him in the country – no mother.'

Norah Curfew wrinkled her straight brows, and on her face came the look Michael always connected with haloes, an anxious longing to stretch goodwill beyond power and pocket.

'Oh! we must!' she said. 'I'll manage somehow. What are their names?'

'Boddick – Christian, I don't know. I call them by their ages – Four and Five.'

'Give me the address. I'll go and see them myself; if they haven't got anything catching, they shall come.'

'You really are an angel,' said Michael, simply.

Norah Curfew coloured, and opened a door. 'That's silly,' she said, still more simply. 'This is our mess-room.'

It was not large, and contained a girl working a typewriter, who stopped with her hands on the keys and looked round; another girl beating up eggs in a bowl, who stopped reading a book of poetry; and a third, who seemed practising a physical exercise, and stopped with her arms extended.

'This is Mr Mont,' said Norah Curfew, 'who made that splendid speech in the House. Miss Betts, Miss La Fontaine, Miss Beeston.'

The girls bowed, and the one who continued to beat the eggs, said: 'It was bully.'

Michael also bowed. 'Beating the air, I'm afraid.'

'Oh! but, Mr Mont, it must have an effect. It said what so many people are really thinking.'

'Ah!' said Michael, 'but their thoughts are so deep, you know.'

'Do sit down.'

Michael sat on the end of a peacock-blue divan.

'I was born in South Africa,' said the egg-beater, 'and I know what's waiting.'

'My father was in the House,' said the girl, whose arms had come down to her splendid sides. 'He was very much struck. Anyway, we're jolly grateful.'

Michael looked from one to the other.

'I suppose if you don't all believe in things, you wouldn't be doing this? *You* don't think the shutters are up in England, anyway?'

'Good Lord, no!' said the girl at the typewriter; 'you've only to live among the poor to know that.'

'The poor haven't got every virtue, and the rich haven't got every vice – that's nonsense!' broke in the physical exerciser.

Michael murmured soothingly.

'I wasn't thinking of that. I was wondering whether something doesn't hang over our heads too much?'

'D'you mean poison-gas?'

'Partly; and town blight, and a feeling that Progress has been found out.'

'Well, I don't know,' replied the egg-beater, who was dark and pretty and had a slight engaging stammer, 'I used to think so in the war. But Europe isn't the world. Europe isn't even very important, really. The sun hardly shines there, anyway.'

Michael nodded. 'After all, if the Millennium comes and we do blot each other out, in Europe, it'll only mean another desert about the size of the Sahara, and the loss of a lot of people obviously too ill-conditioned to be fit to live. It'd be a jolly good lesson to the rest of the world, wouldn't it? Luckily the other continents are far off each other.'

'Cheerful!' exclaimed Norah Curfew.

Michael grinned.

'Well, one can't help catching the atmosphere of this place. I admire you all frightfully, you know, giving up everything, to come and do this.'

'That's tosh,' said the girl at the typewriter. 'What is there to give up – bunny-hugging? One got used to doing things, in the war.'

'If it comes to that,' said the egg-beater, 'we admire you much more, for not giving up Parliament.'

Again Michael grinned.

'Miss La Fontaine – wanted in the kitchen!'

The egg-beater went towards the door.

'Can you beat eggs? D'you mind – shan't be a minute.' Handing Michael the bowl and fork, she vanished.

'What a shame!' said Norah Curfew. 'Let me!'

'No,' said Michael; 'I can beat eggs with anybody. What do you all feel about cutting children adrift at fourteen?'

'Well, of course, it'll be bitterly opposed,' said the girl at the typewriter. 'They'll call it inhuman, and all that. It's much more inhuman really to keep them here.'

'The real trouble,' said Norah Curfew, 'apart from the shillings earned, is the class-interference idea. Besides, Imperialism isn't popular.'

'I should jolly well think it isn't,' muttered the physical exerciser.

'Ah!' said the typist, 'but this isn't Imperialism, is it, Mr Mont? It's all on the lines of making the Dominions the equal of the Mother Country.'

Michael nodded. 'Commonwealth.'

'That won't prevent their camouflaging their objection to losing the children's wages,' said the physical exerciser.

A close discussion ensued between the three young women as to the exact effect of children's wages on the working-class budget. Michael beat his eggs and listened. It was, he knew, a point of the utmost importance. The general conclusion seemed to be that children earned on the whole rather more than their keep, but that it was 'very short-sighted in the long run', because it fostered surplus population and unemployment, and a 'great shame' to spoil the children's chances for the sake of the parents.

The re-entrance of the egg-beater put a stop to it.

'They're beginning to come in, Norah.'

The physical exerciser slipped out, and Norah Curfew said:

'Now, Mr Mont, would you like to see them?'

Michael followed her. He was thinking: 'I wish Fleur had come!' These girls seemed really to believe in things.

Downstairs the children were trickling in from school. He stood and watched them. They seemed a queer blend of anaemia and vitality, of effervescence and obedience. Unselfconscious as puppies, but old beyond their years; and yet, looking as if they never thought ahead. Each movement, each action was as if it were their last. They were very quick. Most of them carried something to eat in a paper bag, or a bit of grease-paper. They chattered, and didn't laugh. Their accent struck Michael as deplorable. Six or seven at most were nice to look at; but nearly all looked good-tempered, and none seemed to be selfish. Their movements were jerky. They mobbed Norah Curfew and the physical exerciser; obeyed without question, ate without appetite, and grabbed at the house-cat. Michael was fascinated.

With them came four or five mothers, who had questions to ask, or bottles to fill. They too were on perfect terms with the young women. Class did not exist in this house; only personality was present. He noticed that the children responded to his grin, that the women didn't, though they smiled at Norah Curfew and the physical exerciser; he wondered if they would give him a bit of their minds if they knew of his speech.

Norah Curfew accompanied him to the door.

'Aren't they ducks?'

'I'm afraid if I saw much of them, I should give up Foggartism.'

'Oh! but why?'

'Well, you see it designs to make them men and women of property.'

'You mean that would spoil them?'

Michael grinned. 'There's something dangerous about silver spoons. Here's my initiation fee.' He handed her all his money.

'Oh! Mr Mont, we didn't—!'

'Well, give me back sixpence, otherwise I shall have to walk home.'

'It's frightfully kind of you. Do come again; and please don't give up Foggartism.'

He walked to the train thinking of her eyes; and, on reaching home, said to Fleur:

'You absolutely must come and see that place. It's quite clean, and the spirit's topping. It's bucked me up like anything. Norah Curfew's perfectly splendid.'

Fleur looked at him between her lashes.

'Oh!' she said. 'I will.'

Chapter Seven

Contrasts

*T*he land beyond the coppice at Lippinghall was a ten-acre bit of poor grass, chalk and gravel, fenced round, to show that it was property. Except for one experiment with goats, abandoned because nobody would drink their milk in a country that did not demean itself by growing food, nothing had been done with it. By December this poor relation of Sir Lawrence Mont's estate was being actively exploited. Close to the coppice the hut had been erected, and at least an acre converted into a sea of mud. The coppice itself presented an incised and draggled appearance, owing to the ravages of Henry Boddick and another man, who had cut and stacked a quantity of timber, which a contractor was gradually rejecting for the fowl-house and granary. The incubator-house was at present in the nature of a prophecy. Progress, in fact, was somewhat slow, but it was hoped that fowls might be asked to begin their operations soon after the New Year. In the meantime Michael had decided that the colony had better get the worst over and go into residence. Scraping the Manor House for furniture, and sending in a store of groceries, oil-lamps, and soap, he installed Boddick on the left, earmarked the centre for the Bergfelds, and the right hand for Swain. He was present when the Manor car brought them from the station. The murky day was turning cold, the trees dripped, the car-wheels splashed up the surface water. From the doorway of the hut Michael watched them get out, and thought he had never seen three more untimely creatures. Bergfeld came first; having only one suit, he had put it on, and looked what he was – an actor out of a job. Mrs Bergfeld came second, and having no outdoor coat, looked what she was – nearly frozen. Swain came last. On his shadowy face was nothing quite so spirited as a sneer; but he gazed about him, and seemed to say: 'My hat!'

Boddick, with a sort of prescience, was absent in the coppice. 'He', thought Michael, 'is my only joy!'

Taking them into the kitchen mess-room of the hut, he deployed a Thermos of hot coffee, a cake, and a bottle of rum.

'Awfully sorry things look so dishevelled; but I think the hut's dry, and there are plenty of blankets. These oil-lamps smell rather. You were in the war, Mr Swain; you'll feel at home in no time. Mrs Bergfeld, you look so cold, do put some rum into your coffee; we always do when we go over the top.'

They all put rum into their coffee, which had a marked effect. Mrs Bergfeld's cheeks grew pink, and her eyes darkened. Swain remarked that the hut was a 'bit of all right'; Bergfeld began making a speech. Michael checked him. 'Boddick knows all the ropes. I'm afraid I've got to catch a train; I've only just time to show you round.'

While whirling back to town afterwards he felt that he had, indeed, abandoned his platoon just as it was going over the top. That night he would be dining in Society; there would be light and warmth, jewels and pictures, wine and talk; the dinner would cost the board of his 'down and outs' for a quarter at least; and nobody would give them and their like a thought. If he ventured to draw Fleur's attention to the contrast, she would say:

'My dear boy, that's like a book by Gurdon Minho; you're getting sentimental.' And he would feel a fool. Or would he? Would he not, perhaps, look at her small distinguished head, and think: 'Too easy a way out, my dear; those who take it have little heads!' And, then, his eyes, straying farther down to that white throat and all the dainty loveliness below, would convey a warmth to his blood and a warning to his brain not to give way to blasphemy, lest it end by disturbing bliss. For what with Foggartism, poultry, and the rest of it, Michael had serious thoughts sometimes that Fleur had none; and with wisdom born of love, he knew that if she hadn't, she never would have, and he must get used to it. She was what she was, and could be converted only in popular fiction. Excellent business for the self-centred heroine to turn from interest in her own belongings to interest in people who had none; but in life it wasn't done. Fleur at least camouflaged her self-concentration gracefully; and with Kit—! Ah! but Kit was herself!

So he did not mention his 'down and outs' on their way to dinner in Eaton Square. He took instead a lesson in the royal Personage named on their invitation card, and marvelled at Fleur's knowledge. 'She's interested in social matters. And do remember, Michael, not to sit down till she asks you to, and not to get up before her, and to say "ma'am".'

Michael grinned. 'I suppose they'll all be nobs, or sn— er – why the deuce did they ask us?'

But Fleur was silent, thinking of her curtsey.

Royalty was affable, the dinner short but superb, served and eaten off gold plate, at a rate which suited the impression that there really wasn't a moment to spare. Fleur took a mental note of this new necessity. She knew personally five of the twenty-four diners, and the rest as in an illustrated paper, darkly. She had seen them all there at one time or another, stepping hideously in paddocks, photographed with their offsprings or their dogs, about to reply for the Colonies, or 'taking a lunar' at a flying grouse. Her quick instinct apprehended almost at once the reason why she and Michael had been invited. His speech! Like some new specimen at the Zoo, he was an object of curiosity, a stunt. She saw people nodding in the direction of him, seated opposite her between two ladies covered with flesh and pearls. Excited and very pretty, she flirted with the Admiral on her right, and defended Michael with spirit from the Under-Secretary on her left. The Admiral grew warm, the Under-Secretary, too young for emotion, cold.

'A little knowledge, Mrs Mont,' he said at the end of his short second innings, 'is a dangerous thing.'

'Now where have I heard that?' said Fleur. 'Is it in the Bible?'

The Under-Secretary tilted his chin.

'We who have to work Departments know too much, perhaps; but your husband certainly doesn't know enough. Foggartism is an amusing idea, but there it stops.'

'We shall see!' said Fleur. 'What do you say, Admiral?'

'Foggartism! What's that – new kind of death ray? I saw a fellow yesterday, Mrs Mont – give you my word! – who's got a ray that goes through three bullocks, a nine-inch brick wall, and gives a shock to a donkey on the other side; and only at quarter strength.'

Fleur flashed a look round towards the Under-Secretary, who had turned his shoulder, and, leaning towards the Admiral, murmured:

'I wish you'd give a shock to the donkey on my other side; he wants it, and I'm not nine inches thick.'

But before the Admiral could shoot his death ray, Royalty had risen

In the apartment to which Fleur was withdrawn, she had been saying little for some minutes, and noticing much, when her hostess came up and said:

'My dear, Her Royal Highness –'

Fleur followed, retaining every wit.

A frank and simple hand patted the sofa beside her. Fleur sat down. A frank and simple voice said:

'What an interesting speech your husband made! It was so refreshing, I thought.'

'Yes, ma'am,' said Fleur; 'but there it will stop, I am told.'

A faint smile curled lips guiltless of colouring matter.

'Well, perhaps. Has he been long in Parliament?'

'Only a year.'

'Ah! I liked his taking up the cudgels for the children.'

'Some people think he's proposing a new kind of child slavery.'

'Oh, really! Have you any children?'

'One,' said Fleur, and added honestly: 'And I must say I wouldn't part with him at fourteen.'

'Ah! and have you been long married?'

'Four years.'

At this moment the royal lady saw someone else she wished to speak to, and was compelled to break off the conversation, which she did very graciously, leaving Fleur with the feeling that she had been disappointed with the rate of production.

In the cab trailing its way home through the foggy night, she felt warm and excited, and as if Michael wasn't.

'What's the matter, Michael?'

His hand came down on her knee at once.

'Sorry, old thing! Only, really – when you think of it – eh?'

'Of what? You were quite a li— object of interest.'

'The whole thing's a game. Anything for novelty!'

'The Princess was very nice about you.'

'Ah! Poor thing! But I suppose you get used to anything!'

Fleur laughed. Michael went on:

'Any new idea gets seized and talked out of existence. It never gets farther than the brain, and the brain gets bored; and there it is, already a back number!'

'That can't be true, Michael. What about Free Trade, or Woman Suffrage?'

Michael squeezed her knee. 'All the women say to me: "But how interesting, Mr Mont; I think it's most thrilling!" And the men say: "Good stunt, Mont! But not practical politics, of course." And I've only one answer: "Things as big got done in the war." By George, it's foggy!'

They were going, indeed, at a snail's pace, and through the windows could see nothing but the faint glow of the street-lamps emerging slowly, high up, one by one. Michael let down a window, and leaned out.

'Where are we?'

'Gawd knows, sir.'

Michael coughed, put up the window again, and resumed his clutch of Fleur.

'By the way, Wastwater asked me if I'd read *Canthar*. He says there's a snorting cut-up of it in *The Protagonist*. It'll have the usual effect – send sales up.'

'They say it's very clever.'

'Horribly out of drawing – not fit for children, and tells adults nothing they don't know. I don't see how it can be justified.'

'Genius, my dear. If it's attacked, it'll be defended.'

'Sib Swan won't have it – he says it's muck.'

'Oh! yes; but Sib's getting a back number.'

'That's very true,' said Michael, thoughtfully. 'By Jove! how fast things move, except in politics, and fog.'

Their cab had come to a standstill. Michael let down the window again.

'I'm fair lost, sir,' said the driver's hoarse voice. 'Ought to be near the Embankment, but for the life of me I can't find the turning.' Michael buttoned his coat, put up the window again, and got out on the near side.

The night was smothered, alive only with the continual hootings of creeping cars. The black vapour, acrid and cold, surged into Michael's lungs.

'I'll walk beside you; we're against the kerb; creep on till we strike the river, or a bobby.'

The cab crept on, and Michael walked beside it, feeling with his foot for the kerb.

The refined voice of an invisible man said: 'This is sanguinary!'

'It is,' said Michael. 'Where are we?'

'In the twentieth century, and the heart of civilisation.'

Michael laughed, and regretted it; the fog tasted of filth.

'Think of the police!' said the voice, 'having to be out in this all night!'

'Splendid force, the police!' replied Michael. 'Where are you, sir?'

'Here, sir. Where are you?'

It was the exact position. The blurred moon of a lamp glowed suddenly above Michael's head. The cab ceased to move.

'If I could only smell the 'Ouses of Parliament,' said the cabman. 'They'll be 'avin' supper there be now.'

'Listen!' said Michael – Big Ben was striking. 'That was to our left.'

'At our back,' said the cabman.

'Can't be, or we should be in the river; unless you've turned right round!'

'Gawd knows where I've turned,' said the cabman, sneezing. 'Never saw such a night!'

'There's only one thing for it – drive on until we hit something. Gently does it.'

The cabman started the cab, and Michael, with his hand on it, continued to feel for the kerb with his foot.

'Steady!' he said, suddenly. 'Car in front.' There was a slight bump.

'Nah then!' said a voice. 'Where yer comin'? Cawn't yer see?'

Michael moved up alongside of what seemed to be another taxi. 'Comin' along at that pice!' said its driver; 'and full moon, too!'

'Awfully sorry,' said Michael. 'No harm done. You got any sense of direction left?'

'The pubs are all closed – worse luck! There's a bloomin' car in front o' me that I've hit three times. Can't make any impression on it. The driver's dead, I think. Would yer go and look, Guv'nor?'

Michael moved towards the loom in front. But at that moment it gave way to the more universal blackness. He ran four steps to hail the driver, stumbled off the kerb, fell, picked himself up and spun round. He moved along the kerb to his right, felt he was going wrong, stopped, and called: 'Hallo!' A faint 'Hallo!' replied from – where? He moved what he thought was back, and called again. No answer! Fleur would be frightened! He shouted. Half a dozen faint hallos replied to him; and someone at his elbow said: 'Don't cher know where y'are?'

'No; do you?'

'What do you think? Lost anything?'

'Yes; my cab.'

'Left anything in it?'

'My wife.'

'Lawd! You won't get 'er back tonight.' A hoarse laugh, ghostly and obscene, floated by. A bit of darkness loomed for a moment, and faded out. Michael stood still. 'Keep your head!' he thought. 'Here's the kerb – either they're in front, or they're behind; or else I've turned a corner.' He stepped forward along the kerb. Nothing! He stepped back. Nothing! 'What the blazes have I done?' he muttered: 'or have they moved on?' Sweat poured down him in spite of the cold. Fleur would be really scared! And the words of his election address sprang from his lips. 'Chiefly by the elimination of smoke!'

'Ah!' said a voice, 'got a cigarette, Guv'nor?'

'I'll give you all I've got and half a crown, if you'll find a cab close by with a lady in it. What street's this?'

'Don't arst me! The streets 'ave gone mad, I think.'

'Listen!' said Michael sharply.

'That's right, "Someone callin' so sweet".'

'Hallo!' cried Michael. 'Fleur!'

'Here! Here!'

It sounded to his right, to his left, behind him, in front. Then came the steady blowing of a cab's horn.

'Now we've got 'em,' said the bit of darkness. 'This way, Guv'nor, step slow, and mind my corns!'

Michael yielded to a tugging at his coat.

'It's like No-Man's Land in a smoke barrage!' said his guide.

'You're right. Hallo! Coming!'

The horn sounded a yard off. A voice said: 'Oh! Michael!'

His face touched Fleur's in the window of the cab.

'Just a second, darling. There you are, my friend, and thanks awfully! Hope you'll get home!'

'I've 'ad worse nights out than this. Thank you, Captain! Wish you and the lady luck.' There was a sound of feet shuffling on, and the fog sighed out: 'So long!'

'All right, sir,' said the hoarse voice of Michael's cabman. 'I know where I am now. First on the left, second on the right. I'll bump the kerb till I get there. Thought you was swallered up, sir!'

Michael got into the cab, and clasped Fleur close. She uttered a long sigh, and sat quite still.

'Nothing more scaring than a fog!' he said.

'I thought you'd been run over!'

Michael was profoundly touched.

'Awfully sorry, darling. And you've got all that beastly fog down your throat. We'll drown it out when we get in. The poor chap was an ex-Service man. Wonderful the way the English keep their humour and don't lose their heads.'

'I lost mine!'

'Well, you've got it back,' said Michael, pressing it against his own to hide the emotion he was feeling. 'Fog's our sheet-anchor, after all. So long as we have fog, England will survive.' He felt Fleur's lips against his.

He belonged to her, and she couldn't afford to have him straying about in fogs or Foggartism! Was that the—? And then he yielded to the thrill.

The cabman was standing by the opened door. 'Now, sir, I'm in your Square. P'r'aps you know your own 'ouse.'

Wrenched from the kiss, Michael stammered 'Righto!' The fog was thinner here; he could consult the shape of trees. 'On and to your right, third house.'

There it was – desirable – with its bay-trees in its tubs and its fanlight shining. He put his latchkey in the door.

'A drink?' he said.

The cabman coughed: 'I won't say no, sir.'

Michael brought the drink.

'Far to go?'

'Near Putney Bridge. Your 'ealth, sir!'

Michael watched his pinched face drinking.

'Sorry you've got to plough into that again!'

The cabman handed back the glass.

'Thank'ee, sir; I shall be all right now; keep along the river, and down the Fulham Road. Thought they couldn't lose me in London. Where I went wrong was trying for a short cut instead of takin' the straight road round. 'Ope the young lady's none the worse, sir. She was properly scared while you was out there in the dark. These fogs ain't fit for 'uman bein's. They ought to do somethin' about 'em in Parliament.'

'They ought!' said Michael, handing him a pound note. 'Good night, and good luck!'

'It's an ill wind!' said the cabman, starting his cab. 'Good night, sir, and thank you kindly.'

'Thank *you*!' said Michael.

The cab ground slowly away, and was lost to sight.

Michael went in to the Spanish room. Fleur, beneath the Goya, was boiling a silver kettle, and burning pastilles. What a contrast to the world outside – its black malodorous cold reek, its risk and fear! In this pretty glowing room, with this pretty glowing woman, why think of its tangle, lost shapes, and straying cries?

Lighting his cigarette, he took his drink from her by its silver handle, and put it to his lips.

'I really think we ought to have a car, Michael!'

Chapter Eight
Collecting Evidence

he editor of *The Protagonist* had so evidently enjoyed himself that he caused a number of other people to do the same.

'There's no more popular sight in the East, Forsyte,' said Sir Lawrence, 'than a boy being spanked; and the only difference between East and West is that in the East the boy at once offers himself again at so much a spank. I don't see Mr Perceval Calvin doing that.'

'If he defends himself,' said Soames, gloomily, 'other people won't.'

They waited, reading daily denunciations signed: 'A Mother of Three'; 'Roger: Northampton'; 'Victorian'; 'Alys St Maurice'; 'Plus Fours'; 'Arthur Whiffkin'; 'Sportsman if not Gentleman'; and 'Pro Patria'; which practically all contained the words: 'I cannot say that I have read the book through, but I have read enough to—'

It was five days before the defence fired a shot. But first came a letter above the signature: 'Swishing Block', which, after commenting on the fact that a whole school of so-called literature had been indicted by the Editor of *The Protagonist* in his able letter of the 14th inst., noted with satisfaction that the said school had grace enough to take its swishing without a murmur. Not even an anonymous squeak had been heard from the whole apostolic body.

'Forsyte,' said Sir Lawrence, handing it to Soames, 'that's my very own mite, and if it doesn't draw them – nothing will!'

But it did. The next issue of the interested journal in which the correspondence was appearing contained a letter from the greater novelist L.S.D. which restored everyone to his place. This book might or might not be Art, he hadn't read it; but the Editor of *The Protagonist* wrote like a pedagogue, and there was an end of him. As to the claim that literature must always wear a flannel petticoat, it was 'piffle', and that was that. From under the skirts of this letter the defence, to what of exultation Soames ever permitted himself, moved out in force. Among the defenders were as many as four of the selected ten associates to whom young Butterfield had purveyed copies. They wrote over their own names that *Canthar* was distinctly LITERATURE; they were sorry for people who thought in these days that LITERATURE had any business with morals. The work must be approached aesthetically or not at all. ART was ART, and morality was morality, and never the twain could, would, or should meet. It was monstrous that a work of this sort should have to appear with a foreign imprint. When would England recognise genius when she saw it?

Soames cut the letters out one after the other, and pasted them in a book. He had got what he wanted, and the rest of the discussion interested him no more. He had received, too, a communication from young Butterfield.

'Sir,
'I called on the lady last Monday, and was fortunately able to see her in person. She seemed rather annoyed when I offered her the book. "That book," she said: "I read it weeks ago." "It's exciting a great deal of interest, Madam," I said. "I know," she said. "Then you won't take a copy; the price is rising steadily, it'll be very valuable in time?" "I've got one," she said. That's what you told me to find out, sir; so I didn't pursue the matter. I hope I have done what you wanted. But if there is anything more, I shall be most happy. I consider that I owe my present position entirely to you.'

Soames didn't know about that, but as to his future position – he might have to put the young man into the box. The question of a play remained. He consulted Michael.

'Does that young woman still act in the advanced theatre place you gave me the name of?'

Michael winced. 'I don't know, sir; but I could find out.'

Inquiry revealed that she was cast for the part of Olivia in Bertie Curfew's matinee of 'The Plain Dealer'.

'"The Plain Dealer"?' said Soames. 'Is that an advanced play?'

'Yes, sir, two hundred and fifty years old.'

'Ah!' said Soames; 'they were a coarse lot in those days. How is it she goes on there if she and the young man have split?'

'Oh! well, they're very cool hands. I do hope you're going to keep things out of Court, sir?'

'I can't tell. When's this performance?'

'January the seventh.'

Soames went to his Club library and took down 'Wycherley'. He was disappointed with the early portions of 'The Plain Dealer', but it improved as it went on, and he spent some time making a list of what George Forsyte would have called the 'nubbly bits'. He understood that at that theatre they did not bowdlerise. Excellent! There were passages that should raise hair on any British Jury. Between *Canthar* and this play, he felt as if he had a complete answer to any claim by the young woman and her set to having 'morals about them'. Old professional instincts were rising within him. He had retained Sir James Foskisson, K.C., not because he admired him personally, but because if he didn't, the other side might. As junior he was employing very young Nicholas Forsyte; he had no great opinion of him, but it was as well to keep the matter in the family, especially if it wasn't to come into Court.

A conversation with Fleur that evening contributed to his intention that it should not.

'What's happened to that young American?' he said.

Fleur smiled acidly. 'Francis Wilmot? Oh! he's "fallen for" Marjorie Ferrar.'

'"Fallen for her"?' said Soames. 'What an expression!'

'Yes, dear; it's American.'

'"For" her? It means nothing, so far as I can see.'

'Let's hope not, for his sake! She's going to marry Sir Alexander MacGown, I'm told.'

'Oh!'

'Did Michael tell you that he hit him on the nose?'

'Which – who?' said Soames testily. 'Whose nose?'

'MacGown's, dear, and it bled like anything.'

'Why on earth did he do that?'

'Didn't you read his speech about Michael?'

'Oh!' said Soames. 'Parliamentary fuss – that's nothing. They're always behaving like children, there. And so she's going to marry him. Has he been putting her up to all this?'

'No; *she's* been putting him.'

Soames discounted the information with a sniff; he scented the hostility of woman for woman. Still, chicken and egg – political feeling and social feeling, who could say which first prompted which? In any case, this made a difference. Going to be married – was she? He debated the matter for some time, and then decided that he would go and see Settlewhite and Stark. If they had been a firm of poor repute or the kind always employed in '*causes celebres*', he wouldn't have dreamed of it; but, as a fact, they stood high, were solid family people, with an aristocratic connection and all that.

He did not write, but took his hat and went over from 'The Connoisseurs' to their offices in King Street, St James's. The journey recalled old days – to how many such negotiatory meetings had he not gone or caused his adversaries to come! He had never cared to take things into Court if they could be settled out of it. And always he had approached negotiation with the impersonality of one passionless about to meet another of the same kidney – two calculating machines, making their livings out of human nature. He did not feel like that today; and, aware of this handicap, stopped to stare into the print and picture shop next door. Ah! There were those first proofs of the Roussel engravings of the Prince Consort Exhibition of '51, that Old Mont had spoken of – he had an eye for an engraving, Old Mont. Ah! and there was a Fred Walker, quite a good one! Mason, and Walker – they weren't done for yet by any means. And the sensation that a man feels hearing a blackbird sing on a tree just coming into blossom, stirred beneath Soames's ribs. Long – long since he had bought a picture! Let him but get this confounded case out of the way, and he could enjoy himself again. Riving his glance from the window, he took a deep breath, and walked into Settlewhite and Stark's.

The chief partner's room was on the first floor, and the chief partner standing where chief partners stand.

'How do you do, Mr Forsyte? I've not met you since 'Bobbin against the L. & S.W.' That must have been 1900!'

'1899,' said Soames. 'You were for the Company.'

Mr Settlewhite pointed to a chair.

Soames sat down and glanced up at the figure before the fire. H'm! A long-lipped, long-eyelashed, long-chinned face; a man of his own calibre, education, and probity! He would not beat about the bush.

'This action', he said, 'is a very petty business. What can we do about it?'

Mr Settlewhite frowned.

'That depends, Mr Forsyte, on what you have to propose? My client has been very grossly libelled.'

Soames smiled sourly.

'She began it. And what is she relying on – private letters to personal friends of my daughter's, written in very natural anger! I'm surprised that a firm of your standing—'

Mr Settlewhite smiled.

'Don't trouble to compliment my firm! I'm surprised myself that you're acting for your daughter. You can hardly see all round the matter. Have you come to offer an apology?'

'That!' said Soames. 'I should have thought it was for your client to apologise.'

'If such is your view, I'm afraid it's no use continuing this discussion.'

Soames regarded him fixedly.

'How do you think you're going to prove damage? She belongs to the fast set.'

Mr Settlewhite continued to smile.

'I understand she's going to marry Sir Alexander MacGown,' said Soames.

Mr Settlewhite's lips tightened.

'Really, Mr Forsyte, if you have come to offer an apology and a substantial sum in settlement, we can talk. Otherwise—'

'As a sensible man', said Soames, 'you know that these Society
scandals are always dead sea fruit – nothing but costs and vexation,
and a feast for all the gossips about town. I'm prepared to offer you
a thousand pounds to settle the whole thing, but an apology I can't
look at. A mutual expression of regret – perhaps; but an apology's
out of the question.'

'Fifteen hundred I might accept – the insults have had wide currency.
But an apology is essential.'

Soames sat silent, chewing the injustice of it all. Fifteen hundred!
Monstrous! Still he would pay even that to keep Fleur out of Court.
But humble-pie! She wouldn't eat it, and he couldn't make her, and
he didn't know that he wanted to. He got up.

'Look here, Mr Settlewhite, if you take this into Court, you will find
yourself up against more than you think. But the whole thing is so
offensive to me, that I'm prepared to meet you over the money, though
I tell you frankly I don't believe a Jury would award a penny piece. As
to an apology, a "formula" could be found, perhaps' – why the deuce
was the fellow smiling? – 'something like this: "We regret that we have
said hasty things about each other", to be signed by both parties.'

Mr Settlewhite caressed his chin.

'Well, I'll put your proposition before my client. I join with you
in wishing to see the matter settled, not because I'm afraid of the
result' – 'Oh, no!' thought Soames – 'but because these cases, as you
say, are not edifying.' He held out his hand.

Soames gave it a cold touch.

'You understand that this is entirely "without prejudice",' he said,
and went on. 'She'll take it!' he thought. Fifteen hundred pounds of
his money thrown away on that baggage, just because for once she
had been labelled what she was; and all his trouble to get evidence
wasted! For a moment he resented his devotion to Fleur. Really it
was fatuous to be so fond as that! Then his heart rebounded. Thank
God! He had settled it.

Christmas was at hand. It did not alarm him, therefore, that he
received no answering communication. Fleur and Michael were at
Lippinghall with the ninth and eleventh baronets. He and Annette had
Winifred and the Cardigans down at 'The Shelter'. Not till the 6th of

January did he receive a letter from Messrs. Settlewhite and Stark.

'DEAR SIR,

'In reference to your call of the 17th ultimo, your proposition was duly placed before our client, and we are instructed to say that she will accept the sum of £1,500 – fifteen hundred pounds – and an apology, duly signed by your client, copy of which we enclose.
    'We are, dear Sir,
    'Faithfully yours,

'SETTLEWHITE AND STARK.'

Soames turned to the enclosure. It ran thus:

I, Mrs Michael Mont, withdraw the words concerning Miss Marjorie Ferrar contained in my letters to Mrs Ralph Ppynrryn and Mrs Edward Maltese of October 4th last, and hereby tender a full and free apology for having written them.
    (Signed)

Pushing back the breakfast table, so violently that it groaned, Soames got up.
    'What is it, Soames?' said Annette. 'Have you broken your plate again? You should not bite so hard.'
    'Read that!'
    Annette read.
    'You would give that woman fifteen hundred pounds? I think you are mad, Soames. I would not give her fifteen hundred pence! Pay this woman, and she tells her friends. That is fifteen hundred apologies in all their minds. Really, Soames – I am surprised. A man of business, a clever man! Do you not know the world better than that? With every pound you pay, Fleur eats her words!'
    Soames flushed. It was so French, and yet somehow it was so true. He walked to the window. The French – they had no sense of compromise, and every sense of money!

'Well,' he said, 'that ends it anyway. She won't sign. And I shall withdraw my offer.'

'I should hope so. Fleur has a good head. She will look very pretty in Court. I think that woman will be sorry she ever lived! Why don't you have her what you call shadowed? It is no good to be delicate with women like that.'

In a weak moment he had told Annette about the book and the play; for, unable to speak of them to Fleur and Michael, he had really had to tell someone; indeed, he had shown her *Canthar*, with the words: 'I don't advise you to read it; it's very French.'

Annette had returned it to him two days later, saying: 'It is not French at all; it is disgusting. You English are so coarse. It has no wit. It is only nasty. A serious nasty book – that is the limit. You are so old fashioned, Soames. Why do you say this book is French?'

Soames, who really didn't know why, had muttered:

'Well, they can't get it printed in England.' And with the words: 'Bruxelles, Bruxelles, you call Bruxelles—' buzzing about his ears, had left the room. He had never known any people so touchy as the French!

Her remark about 'shadowing', however, was not easily forgotten. Why be squeamish, when all depended on frightening this woman? And on arriving in London he visited an office that was not Mr Polteed's, and gave instructions for the shadowing of Marjorie Ferrar's past, present, and future.

His answer to Settlewhite and Stark, too, was brief, determined, and written on the paper of his own firm.

'Jan. 6th, 1925.
'DEAR SIRS,

'I have your letter of yesterday's date, and note that your client has rejected my proposition, which, as you know, was made entirely without prejudice, and is now withdrawn *in toto*.
　'Yours faithfully,

'SOAMES FORSTYTE.'

If he did not mistake, they would be sorry. And he gazed at the words '*in toto*'; somehow they looked funny. *In toto*! And now for 'The Plain Dealer'!

The theatre of the 'Ne Plus Ultra' Play-Producing Society had a dingy exterior, a death-mask of Congreve in the hall, a peculiar smell, and an apron stage. There was no music. They hit something three times before the curtain went up. There were no footlights. The scenery was peculiar – Soames could not take his eyes off it till, in the first Entr'acte, its principle was revealed to him by the conversation of two people sitting just behind.

'The point of the scenery here is that no one need look at it, you see. They go farther than anything yet done.'

'They've gone farther in Moscow.'

'I believe not. Curfew went over there. He came back raving about the way they speak their lines.'

'Does he know Russian?'

'No. You don't need to. It's the timbre. I think he's doing pretty well here with that. You couldn't give a play like this if you took the words in.'

Soames, who had been trying to take the words in – it was, indeed, what he had come for – squinted round at the speakers. They were pale and young and went on with a strange unconcern.

'Curfew's doing great work. He's shaking them up.'

'I see they've got Marjorie Ferrar as Olivia.'

'Don't know why he keeps on an amateur like that.'

'Box office, dear boy; she brings the smart people. She's painful, I think.'

'She did one good thing – the dumb girl in that Russian play. But she can't speak for nuts; you're following the sense of her words all the time. She doesn't rhythmatise you a little bit.'

'She's got looks.'

'M'yes.'

At this moment the curtain went up again. Since Marjorie Ferrar had not yet appeared, Soames was obliged to keep awake; indeed, whether because she couldn't 'speak for nuts', or merely from duty, he was always awake while she was on the stage, and whenever she had anything outrageous to say he noted it carefully, otherwise he passed an excellent afternoon, and went away much rested. In his cab he mentally rehearsed Sir James Foskisson in the part of cross-examiner:

'I think, madam, you played Olivia in a production of "The Plain Dealer" by the "Ne Plus Ultra" Play–Producing Society? . . . Would it be correct to say that the part was that of a modest woman? . . . Precisely. And did it contain the following lines? (Quotation of nubbly bits.) . . . Did that convey anything to your mind, madam? . . . I suppose that you would not say it was an immoral passage? . . . No? Nor calculated to offend the ears and debase the morals of a decent-minded audience? . . . No. In fact, you don't take the same view of morality that I, or, I venture to think, the Jury do? . . . No. The dark scene – you did not remonstrate with the producer for not omitting that scene? . . . Quite. Mr Curfew, I think, was the producer? Yes. Are you on such terms with that gentleman as would have made a remonstrance easy? . . . Ah! Now, madam, I put it to you that throughout 1923 you were seeing this gentleman nearly every day . . . Well, say three or four times a week. And yet you say that you were not on such terms as would have made it possible for you to represent to him that no modest young woman should be asked to play a scene like that . . . Indeed! The Jury will form their own opinion of your answer. You are not a professional actress, dependent for your living on doing what you are told to do? . . . No. And yet you have the face to come here and ask for substantial damages because of the allegation in a private letter that you haven't a moral about you? . . . Have you? . . .' And so on, and so on. Oh! no. Damages! She wouldn't get a farthing.

Chapter Nine

'Volte Face'

*K*eeping Sir Alexander MacGown and Francis Wilmot in the air, fulfilling her weekend and other engagements, playing much bridge in the hope of making her daily expenses, getting a day's hunting when she could, and rehearsing the part of Olivia, Marjorie Ferrar had almost forgotten the action, when the offer of fifteen hundred pounds and the formula were put before her by Messrs. Settlewhite and Stark. She almost jumped at it. The money would wipe out her more pressing debts; she would be able to breathe, and reconsider her future.

She received their letter on the Friday before Christmas, just as she was about to go down to her father's, near Newmarket, and wrote hastily to say she would call at their office on her way home on Monday. The following evening she consulted her father. Lord Charles was of opinion that if this attorney fellow would go as far as fifteen hundred, he must be dead keen on settling, and she had only to press for the apology to get it. Anyway she should let them stew in their juice for a bit. On Monday he wanted to show her his yearlings. She did not, therefore, return to Town till the 23rd, and found the office closed for Christmas. It had never occurred to her that solicitors had holidays. On Christmas Eve she herself went away for ten days; so that it was January the 4th before she was again able to call. Mr Settlewhite was still in the South of France, but Mr Stark would see her. Mr Stark knew little about the matter, but thought Lord Charles' advice probably sound; he proposed to write accepting the fifteen hundred pounds if a formal apology were tendered; they could fall back on the formula if necessary, but it was always wise to get as much as you could. With some misgiving Marjorie Ferrar agreed.

Returning from the matinee on January 7th, tired and elated by applause, by Bertie Curfew's words: 'You did quite well, darling,' and almost the old look on his face, she got into a hot bath, and was just out of it when her maid announced Mr Wilmot.

'Keep him, Fanny; say I'll be with him in twenty minutes.'

Feverish and soft, as if approaching a crisis, she dressed hastily, put essence of orange-blossom on her neck and hands, and went to the studio. She entered without noise. The young man, back to the door, in the centre of the room, evidently did not hear her. Approaching within a few feet, she waited for the effect on him of orange-blossom. He was standing like some Eastern donkey, that with drooped ears patiently awaits the fresh burdening of a sore back. And suddenly he spoke: 'I'm all in.'

'Francis!'

The young man turned.

'Oh! Marjorie!' he said, 'I never heard.' And taking her hands, he buried his face in them.

She was hampered at that moment. To convert his mouth from despairing kissing of her hands to triumphal flame upon her lips would have been so easy if he had been modern, if his old-fashioned love had not complimented her so subtly; if, too, she were not feeling for him something more – or was it less? – than passion. Was she to know at last the sensations of the simple – a young girl's idyll – something she had missed? She led him to the divan, sat down by his side, and looked into his eyes. Fabled sweetness, as of a Spring morning – Francis and she, children in the wood, with the world well lost! She surrendered to the innocence of it; deliberately grasped something delicious, new. Poor boy! How delightful to feel him happy at last – to promise marriage and mean to perform it! When? Oh! when he liked – Soon, quite soon; the sooner the better! Almost unconscious that she was 'playing' a young girl, she was carried away by his amazement and his joy. He was on fire, on air; yet he remained delicate – he was wonderful! For an hour they sat – a fragrant hour for memory to sniff – before she remembered that she was dining out at half-past eight. She put her lips to his, and closed her eyes. And thought ran riot. Should she spoil it, and make sure of him in modern fashion? What was his image of her but a phlizz, but a fraud? She saw his eyes grow troubled, felt his hands grow fevered. Something seemed drowning before her eyes. She stood up.

'Now, my darling, you must fly!'

When he had flown, she threw off her dress and brushed out her hair that in the mirror seemed to have more gold than red . . . Some letters on her dressing-table caught her eye. The first was a bill, the second a bill; the third ran thus:

'DEAR MADAM,

'We regret to say that Cuthcott Kingston & Forsyte have refused to give the apology we asked for, and withdrawn their verbal offer *in toto*. We presume, therefore, that the action must go forward. We have every hope, however, that they may reconsider the matter before it comes into Court.

'Your obedient servants,

'SETTLEWHITE & STARK.'

She dropped it and sat very still, staring at a little hard line on the right side of her mouth and a little hard line on the left . . .

Francis Wilmot, flying, thought of steamship-lines and staterooms, of registrars and rings. An hour ago he had despaired; now it seemed he had always known she was 'too fine not to give up this fellow whom she didn't love'. He would make her the queen of South Carolina – he surely would! But if she didn't like it out there, he would sell the 'old home', and they would go and live where she wished – in Venice; he had heard her say Venice was wonderful; or New York, or Sicily; with her he wouldn't care! And London in the cold dry wind seemed beautiful, no longer a grey maze of unreality and shadows, but a city where you could buy rings and steamship passages. The wind cut him like a knife and he did not feel it. That poor devil MacGown! He hated the sight, the thought of him, and yet felt sorry, thinking of him with the cup dashed from his lips. And all the days, weeks, months himself had spent circling round the flame, his wings scorched and drooping, seemed now but the natural progress of the soul towards Paradise. Twenty-four – his age and hers; an eternity of bliss before them! He pictured her on the porch at home. Horses! A better car than the old Ford! The darkies would adore her – kind of grand, and so white! To walk with her among the azaleas in the spring, that he could smell already; no – it was his hands where he had touched her! He shivered, and resumed his flight under the bare trees, well-nigh alone in the East wind; the stars of a bitter night shining.

A card was handed to him as he entered his hotel.

'Mr Wilmot, a gentleman to see you.'

Sir Alexander was seated in a corner of the Lounge, with a crush hat in his hand. He rose and came towards Francis Wilmot, grim and square.

'I've been meaning to call on you for some time, Mr Wilmot.'

'Yes, sir. May I offer you a cocktail, or a glass of sherry?'

'No, thank you. You are aware of my engagement to Miss Ferrar?'

'I was, sir.'

This red aggressive face, with its stiff moustache and burning eyes, revived his hatred; so that he no longer felt sorry.

'You know that I very much object to your constant visits to that young lady. In this country it is not the part of a gentleman to pursue an engaged young woman.'

'That,' said Francis Wilmot, coolly, 'is for Miss Ferrar herself to say.'

MacGown's face grew even redder.

'If you hadn't been an American, I should have warned you to keep clear a long time ago.'

Francis Wilmot bowed.

'Well! Are you going to?'

'Permit me to decline an answer.'

MacGown thrust forward his face.

'I've told you,' he said. 'If you trespass any more, look out for yourself.'

'Thank you; I will,' said Francis Wilmot, softly.

MacGown stood for a moment swaying slightly. Was he going to hit out? Francis Wilmot put his hands into his trouser pockets.

'You've had your warning,' said MacGown, and turned on his heel.

'Good night!' said Francis Wilmot to that square receding back. He had been gentle, he had been polite, but he hated the fellow, yes, indeed! Save for the triumphal glow within him, there might have been a fuss!

Chapter Ten

Photography

*S*ummoned to the annual Christmas covert-shooting at Lippinghall, Michael found there two practical politicians, and one member of the Government.

In the mullion-windowed smoking-room, where men retired, and women too sometimes, into chairs old, soft, leathery, the ball of talk was lightly tossed, and naught so devastating as Foggartism mentioned. But in odd minutes and half-hours Michael gained insight into political realities, and respect for practical politicians. Even on this holiday they sat up late, got up early, wrote letters, examined petitions, dipped into Blue Books. They were robust, ate heartily, took their liquor like men, never seemed fatigued. They shaved clean, looked healthy, and shot badly with enjoyment. The member of the Government played golf instead, and Fleur went round with him. Michael learned the lesson: Have so much on your mind that you have practically nothing in it; no time to pet your schemes, fancies, feelings. Carry on, and be careful that you don't know to what end.

As for Foggartism, they didn't – *à la Evening Sun* – pooh-pooh it; they merely asked, as Michael had often asked himself: 'Yes, but how are you going to work it? Your scheme might be very good, if it didn't hit people's pockets. Any addition to the price of living is out of the question – the country's taxed up to the hilt. Your Foggartism's going to need money in every direction. You may swear till you're blue in the face that ten or twenty years hence it'll bring fivefold return; nobody will listen. You may say: "Without it we're all going to the devil"; but we're accustomed to that – some people think we're there already, and they resent its being said. Others, especially manufacturers, believe what they want to. They can't bear any one who cries "stinking fish", whatever his object. Talk about reviving trade, and less taxation, or offer more wages and talk of a capital levy, and, according to Party, we shall believe you've done the trick – until we find you haven't. But you're talking of less trade and more taxation in the present with a view to a better future. Great Scott! In politics you can shuffle the cards, but you mustn't add or subtract. People only react to immediate benefit, or, as in the war, to imminent danger. You must cut out sensationalism.'

In short, they were intelligent, and completely fatalistic.

After these quiet talks, Michael understood, much better than before, the profession of politics. He was greatly attracted by the member of the Government; his personality was modest, his manner pleasant, he had Departmental ideas, and was doing his best with his own job according to those ideas; if he had others he kept them to himself. He seemed to admire Fleur, and he listened better than the other two. He said, too, some things they hadn't. 'Of course, what we're able to do may be found so inadequate that there'll be a great journalistic outcry, and under cover of it we may bring in some sweeping measures that people will swallow before they know what they're in for.'

'The Press,' said Michael; 'I don't see them helping.'

'Well! It's the only voice there is. If you could get fast hold of the vociferous papers, you might even put your Foggartism over. What you're really up against is the slow town growth of the last hundred and fifty years, an ingrained state of mind which can only see England in terms of industrialism and the carrying trade. And in the town-mind, of course, hope springs eternal. They don't like calamity talk. Some genuinely think we can go on indefinitely on the old lines, and get more and more prosperous into the bargain. Personally, I don't. It's possible that much of what old Foggart advocates may be adopted bit by bit, even child emigration, from sheer practical necessity; but it won't be called Foggartism. Inventor's luck! *He'll* get no credit for being the first to see it. And,' added the Minister, gloomily, 'by the time it's adopted, it'll probably be too late.'

Receiving the same day a request for an interview from a Press Syndicate whose representative would come down to suit his convenience, Michael made the appointment, and prepared an elaborate exposition of his faith. The representative, however, turned out to be a camera, and a photograph entitled: 'The Member for Mid-Bucks expounding Foggartism to our Representative', became the only record of it. The camera was active. It took a family group in front of the porch: 'Right to Left, Mr Michael Mont, M.P., Lady Mont, Mrs Michael Mont, Sir Lawrence Mont, Bt.' It took Fleur: 'Mrs Michael Mont, with Kit and Dandie.' It took the Jacobean wing. It took the Minister, with his pipe, 'enjoying a Christmas rest'. It took a corner of the walled garden: 'In the grounds.' It then had lunch. After lunch it took the whole house-party: 'At Sir Lawrence Mont's, Lippinghall Manor, Bucks'; with the Minister on Lady Mont's right and the Minister's wife on Sir Lawrence's left. This photograph would have turned out better, if the Dandie, inadvertently left out, had not made a sudden onslaught on the camera's legs. It took a photograph of Fleur alone: 'Mrs Michael Mont – a charming young Society hostess.' It understood that Michael was making an interesting practical experiment – could it take Foggartism in action? Michael grinned and said: Yes, if it would take a walk, too.

They departed for the coppice. The colony was in its normal state – Boddick, with two of the contractor's men cheering him on, was working at the construction of the incubator-house; Swain, smoking a cigarette, was reading the *Daily Mail*; Bergfeld was sitting with his head in his hands, and Mrs Bergfeld was washing up.

The camera took three photographs. Michael, who had noted that Bergfeld had begun shaking, suggested to the camera that it would miss its train. It at once took a final photograph of Michael in front of the hut, two cups of tea at the Manor, and its departure.

As Michael was going upstairs that night, the butler came to him.

'The man Boddick's in the pantry, Mr Michael; I'm afraid something's happened, sir.'

'Oh!' said Michael, blankly.

Where Michael had spent many happy hours, when he was young, was Boddick, his pale face running with sweat, and his dark eyes very alive.

'The German's gone, sir.'

'Gone?'

'Hanged hisself. The woman's in an awful state. I cut him down, and sent Swain to the village.'

'Good God! Hanged! But why?'

'He's been very funny these last three days; and that camera upset him properly. Will you come, sir?'

They set out with a lantern, Boddick telling his tale.

'As soon as ever you was gone this afternoon he started to shake and carry on about having been made game of. I told 'im not to be a fool, and went out to get on with it. But when I came in to tea, he was still shakin', and talkin' about his honour and his savin's; Swain had got fed up and was jeerin' at him, and Mrs Bergfeld was as white as a ghost in the corner. I told Swain to shut his head; and Fritz simmered down after a bit, and sat humped up as he does for hours together. Mrs Bergfeld got our tea. I had some chores to finish, so I went out after. When I come in at seven, they was at it again hammer and tongs, and Mrs Bergfeld cryin' fit to bust her heart. "Can't you see," I said, "how you're upsettin' your wife?" "Henry Boddick," he said, "I've nothing against *you*, you've always been decent to me. But this Swain," he said, "'is name is Swine!" and he took up the bread-knife. I got it away from him, and spoke him calm. "Ah!" he said, "but *you've* no pride." Swain was lookin' at him with that sort o' droop in his mouth he's got. "Pride," he says, "you silly blighter, what call 'ave *you* to 'ave any pride?" Well, I see that while we was there he wasn't goin' to get any better, so I took Swain off for a glass at the pub. When we came back at ten o'clock, Swain went straight to bed, and I went into the mess-room, where I found his wife alone. "Has he gone to bed?" I said. "No," she said, "he's gone out to cool his head. Oh! Henry Boddick," she said, "I don't know what to do with him!" We sat there a bit, she tellin' me about 'im brooding, and all that – nice woman she is, too; till suddenly she said: "Henry Boddick," she said, "I'm frightened. Why don't he come?" We went out to look for him, and where d'you think he was, sir? You know that big tree we're just goin' to have down? There's a ladder against it, and the guidin' rope all fixed. He'd climbed up that ladder in the moonlight, put the rope round his neck, and jumped off; and there he was, six feet from the ground, dead as a duck. I roused up Swain, and we got him in, and – Well, we 'ad a proper time! Poor woman, I'm sorry for her, sir – though really I think it's just as well he's gone – he couldn't get upsides with it anyhow. That camera chap would have given something for a shot at what we saw there in the moonlight.'

'Foggartism in action!' thought Michael, bitterly. 'So endeth the First Lesson!'

The hut looked lonely in the threading moonlight and the bitter wind. Inside, Mrs Bergfeld was kneeling beside the body placed on the deal table, with a handkerchief over its face. Michael put a hand on her shoulder. She gave him a wild look, bowed her head again, and her lips began moving. 'Prayer!' thought Michael. 'Catholic – of course!' He took Boddick aside. 'Don't let her see Swain. I'll talk to him.'

When the police and the doctor came in, he buttonholed the hairdresser, whose shadowy face looked ghastly in the moonlight. He seemed much upset.

'You'd better come down to the house for the night, Swain.'

'All right, sir. I never meant to hurt the poor beggar. But he did carry on so, and I've got my own trouble. I couldn't stand 'im monopolisin' misfortune the way he does. When the inquest's over, I'm off. If I can't get some sun soon, I'll be as dead as 'im.'

Michael was relieved. Boddick would be left alone.

When at last he got back to the house with Swain, Fleur was asleep. He did not wake her to tell her the news, but lay a long time trying to get warm, and thinking of that great obstacle to all salvation – the human element. And, mingled with his visions of the woman beside that still, cold body were longings for the warmth of the young body close to him.

The photographs were providential. For three days no paper could be taken up which did not contain some allusion, illustrated, to 'The Tragedy on a Buckinghamshire Estate'; 'German actor hangs himself';

'The drama at Lippinghall'; 'Tragic end of an experiment'; 'Right to Left: Mr Michael Mont, Member for Mid-Bucks; Bergfeld, the German actor who hanged himself; Mrs Bergfeld.'

The *Evening Sun* wrote more in sorrow than in anger:

'The suicide of a German actor on Sir Lawrence Mont's estate at Lippinghall has in it a touch of the grotesquely moral. The unfortunate man seems to have been one of three "out-of-works" selected by the young Member for Mid-Bucks, recently conspicuous for his speech on "Foggartism", for a practical experiment in that peculiar movement. Why he should have chosen a German to assist the English people to return to the Land is not perhaps very clear; but, largely speaking, the incident illustrates the utter unsuitability of all amateur attempts to solve this problem, and the futility of pretending to deal with the unemployment crisis while we still tolerate among us numbers of aliens who take the bread out of the mouths of our own people.' The same issue contained a short leader entitled: 'The Alien in our Midst.' The inquest was well attended. It was common knowledge that three men and one woman lived in the hut, and sensational developments were expected. A good deal of disappointment was felt that the evidence disclosed nothing at all of a sexual character.

Fleur, with the eleventh baronet, returned to town after it was over. Michael remained for the funeral – in a Catholic cemetery some miles away. He walked with Henry Boddick behind Mrs Bergfeld. A little sleet was drifting out of a sky the colour of the gravestones, and against that whitish sky the yew-trees looked very stark. He had ordered a big wreath laid on the grave, and when he saw it thus offered up, he thought: 'First human beings, then rams, now flowers! Progress! I wonder!'

Having arranged that Norah Curfew should take Mrs Bergfeld as cook in Bethnal Green, he drove her up to London in the Manor car. During that long drive he experienced again feelings that he had not had since the war. Human hearts, dressed-up to the nines in circumstance, interests, manners, accents, race, and class, when stripped by grief, by love, by hate, by laughter were one and the same heart. But how seldom were they stripped! Life was a clothed affair! A good thing too, perhaps – the strain of nakedness was too considerable! He was, in fact, infinitely relieved to see the face of Norah Curfew, and hear her cheerful words to Mrs Bergfeld:

'Come in, my dear, and have some tea!' She was the sort who stripped to the heart without strain or shame.

Fleur was in the drawing room when he got home, furred up to her cheeks, which were bright as if she had just come in from the cold.

'Been out, my child?'

'Yes. I—' She stopped, looked at him rather queerly, and said: 'Well, have you finished with that business?'

'Yes; thank God. I've dropped the poor creature on Norah Curfew.'

Fleur smiled. 'Ah! Yes, Norah Curfew! *She* lives for everybody but herself, doesn't she?'

'She does,' said Michael, rather sharply.

'The new woman. One's getting clean out of fashion.'

Michael took her cheeks between his hands.

'What's the matter, Fleur?'

'Nothing.'

'There is.'

'Well, one gets a bit fed up with being left out, as if one were fit for nothing but Kit, and looking appetising.'

Michael dropped his hands, hurt and puzzled. Certainly he had not consulted her about his 'down and outs'; had felt sure it would only bore or make her laugh – No future in it! And had there been?

'Any time you like to go shares in any mortal thing, Fleur, you've only to say so.'

'Oh! I don't want to poke into your affairs. I've got my own. Have you had tea?'

'Do tell me what's the matter?'

'My dear boy, you've already asked me that, and I've already told you – nothing.'

'Won't you kiss me?'

'Of course. And there's Kit's bath – would you like to go up?'

Each short stab went in a little farther. This was a spiritual crisis, and he did not know in the least how to handle it. Didn't she want him to admire her, to desire her? What did she want? Recognition that she was as interested as he in – in the state of the Country? Of course! Only – was she?

'Well,' she said, '*I* want tea, anyway. Is the new woman dramatic?'

Jealousy? The notion was absurd. He said quietly:

'I don't quite follow you.'

Fleur looked up at him with very clear eyes.

'Good God!' said Michael, and left the room.

He went upstairs and sat down before 'The White Monkey'. In that strategic position he better perceived the core of his domestic moment. Fleur had to be first – had to take precedence. No object in her collection must live a life of its own! He was appalled by the bitterness of that thought. No, no! It was only that she had a complex – a silver spoon, and it had become natural in her mouth. She resented his having interests in which she was not first; or rather, perhaps, resented the fact that they were not her interests too. And that was to her credit, when you came to think of it. She was vexed with herself for being egocentric. Poor child! 'I've got to mind my eye,' thought Michael, 'or I shall make some modern-novel mess of this in three parts.' And his mind strayed naturally to the science of dishing up symptoms as if they were roots – ha! He remembered his nursery governess locking him in; he had dreaded being penned up ever since. The psychoanalysts would say that was due to the action of his governess. It wasn't – many small boys wouldn't have cared a hang; it was due to a nature that existed before that action. He took up the photograph of Fleur that stood on his desk. He loved the face, he would always love it. If she had limitations – well! So had he – lots! This was comedy, one mustn't make it into tragedy! Surely she had a sense of humour, too! Had she? Had she not? And Michael searched the face he held in his hands . . .

But, as is usual with husbands, he had diagnosed without knowledge of all the facts.

Fleur had been bored at Lippinghall, even collection of the Minister had tried her. She had concealed her boredom from Michael. But self-sacrifice takes its revenge. She reached home in a mood of definite antagonism to public affairs. Hoping to feel better if she bought a hat or two, she set out for Bond Street. At the corner of Burlington Street, a young man bared his head.

'Fleur!'

Wilfrid Desert! Very lean and very brown!

'You!'

'Yes. I'm just back. How's Michael?'

'Very well. Only he's in Parliament.'

'Great Scott! And how are you?'

'As you see. Did you have a good time?'

'Yes. I'm only perching. The East has got me!'

'Are you coming to see us?'

'I think not. The burnt child, you know.'

'Yes; you *are* brown!'

'Well, good-bye, Fleur! You look just the same, only more so. I'll see Michael somewhere.'

'Good-bye!' She walked on without looking back, and then regretted not having found out whether Wilfrid had done the same.

She had given Wilfrid up for – well, for Michael, who – who had forgotten it! Really she was too self-sacrificing!

And then at three o'clock a note was brought her:

'By hand, ma'am; answer waiting.'

She opened an envelope, stamped 'Cosmopolis Hotel'.

'MADAM,

'We apologise for troubling you, but are in some perplexity. Mr Francis Wilmot, a young American gentleman, who has been staying in this hotel since early October, has, we are sorry to say, contracted pneumonia. The doctor reports unfavourably on his condition. In these circumstances we thought it right to examine his effects, in order that we might communicate with his friends; but the only indication we can find is a card of yours. I venture to ask you if you can help us in the matter.

'Believe me to be, Madam,

'Your faithful servant,

'(for the Management).'

Fleur stared at an illegible signature, and her thoughts were bitter. Jon had dumped Francis on her as a herald of his happiness; her enemy had lifted him! Well, then, why didn't that Cat look after him herself? Oh! well, poor boy! Ill in a great hotel – without a soul!

'Call me a taxi, Coaker.'

On her way to the Hotel she felt slight excitement of the 'ministering angel' order.

Giving her name at the bureau, she was taken up to Room 209. A chambermaid was there. The doctor, she said, had ordered a nurse, who had not yet come.

Francis Wilmot, very flushed, was lying back, propped up; his eyes were closed.

'How long has he been ill like this?'

'I've noticed him looking queer, ma'am; but we didn't know how bad he was until today. I think he's just neglected it. The doctor says he's got to be packed. Poor gentleman, it's very sad. You see, he's hardly there!'

Francis Wilmot's lips were moving; he was evidently on the verge of delirium.

'Go and make some lemon tea in a jug as weak and hot as you can; quick!'

When the maid had gone, she went up and put her cool hand to his forehead.

'It's all right, Francis. Much pain?'

Francis Wilmot's lips ceased to move; he looked up at her and his eyes seemed to burn.

'If you cure me,' he said, 'I'll hate you. I just want to get out, quick!'

She changed her hand on his forehead, whose heat seemed to scorch the skin of her palm. His lips resumed their almost soundless movement. The meaningless, meaningful whispering frightened her, but she stood her ground, constantly changing her hand, till the maid came back with the tea.

'The nurse has come, miss; she'll be up in a minute.'

'Pour out the tea. Now, Francis, drink!'

His lips sucked, chattered, sucked. Fleur handed back the cup, and stood away. His eyes had closed again.

'Oh! ma'am,' whispered the maid, 'he *is* bad! Such a nice young gentleman, too.'

'What was his temperature; do you know?'

'I did hear the doctor say nearly 105. Here is the nurse, ma'am.'

Fleur went to her in the doorway.

'It's not just ordinary, nurse – he *wants* to go. I think a love-affair's gone wrong. Shall I stop and help you pack him?'

When the pneumonia jacket had been put on, she lingered, looking down at him. His eyelashes lay close and dark against his cheeks, long and innocent, like a little boy's.

Outside the door, the maid touched her arm. 'I found this letter, ma'am; ought I to show it to the doctor?'

Fleur read:

'MY POOR DEAR BOY,

'We were crazy yesterday. It isn't any good, you know. Well, I haven't got a breakable heart; nor have you really, though you may think so when you get this. Just go back to your sunshine and your darkies, and put me out of your thoughts. I couldn't stay the course. I couldn't possibly stand being poor. I must just go through it with my Scotsman and travel the appointed road. What is the good of thinking we can play at children in the wood, when one of them is

'Your miserable (at the moment)

'MARJORIE.

'I mean this – I mean it. Don't come and see me any more, and make it worse for yourself. M.'

'Exactly!' said Fleur. 'I've told the nurse. Keep it and give it him back if he gets well. If he doesn't, burn it. I shall come tomorrow.' And, looking at the maid with a faint smile, she added: '*I* am not that lady!'

'Oh! no, ma'am – miss – no, I'm sure! Poor young gentleman! Isn't there nothing to be done?'

'I don't know. I should think not . . .'

She had kept all these facts from Michael with a sudden retaliatory feeling. He couldn't have private – or was it public – life all to himself!

After he had gone out with his 'Good God!' she went to the window. Queer to have seen Wilfrid again! Her heart had not fluttered, but it tantalised her not to know whether she could attract him back. Out in the square it was as dark as when last she had seen him before he fled to the East – a face pressed to this window that she was touching with her fingers. 'The burnt child!' No! She did not want to reduce him to that state again; nor to copy Marjorie Ferrar, who had copied her. If, instead of going East, Wilfrid had chosen to have pneumonia like poor Francis! What would she have done? Let him die for want of her? And what ought she to do about Francis, having seen that letter? Tell Michael? No, he thought her frivolous and irresponsible. Well! She would show him! And that sister – who had married Jon? Ought she to be cabled to? But this would have a rapid crisis, the nurse had said, and to get over from America in time would be impossible! Fleur went back to the fire. What kind of girl was this wife of Jon's? Another in the new fashion – like Norah Curfew; or just one of those Americans out for her own way and the best of everything? But they would have the new kind of woman in America, too – even though it didn't come from Paris. Anne Forsyte! – Fleur gave a little shiver in front of the hot fire.

She went upstairs, took off her hat, and scrutinised her image. Her face was coloured and rounded, her eyes were clear, her brow unlined, her hair rather flattened. She fluffed it out, and went across into the nursery.

The eleventh baronet, asleep, was living his private life with a very determined expression on his face; at the foot of his cot lay the Dandie, with his chin pressed to the floor, and at the table the nurse was sewing. In front of her lay an illustrated paper with the photograph inscribed: 'Mrs Michael Mont, with Kit and Dandie.'

'What do you think of it, nurse?'

'I think it's horrible, ma'am; it makes Kit look as if he hadn't any sense – giving him a stare like that!'

Fleur took up the paper; her quick eyes had seen that it concealed another. There on the table was a second effigy of herself: 'Mrs Michael Mont, the pretty young London hostess, who, rumour says, will shortly be defendant in a Society lawsuit.' And, above, yet another effigy, inscribed: 'Miss Marjorie Ferrar, the brilliant granddaughter of the Marquis of Shropshire, whose engagement to Sir Alexander MacGown, M.P., is announced.'

Fleur dropped paper back on paper.

Chapter Eleven

Shadows

The dinner, which Marjorie Ferrar had so suddenly recollected, was MacGown's, and when she reached the appointed restaurant, he was waiting in the hall.

'Where are the others, Alec?'

'There are no others,' said MacGown.

Marjorie Ferrar reined back. 'I can't dine with you alone in a place like this!'

'I had the Ppynrryns, but they fell through.'

'Then I shall go to my Club.'

'For God's sake, no, Marjorie. We'll have a private room. Go and wait in there, while I arrange it.'

With a shrug she passed into a little 'lounge'. A young woman whose face seemed familiar idled in, looked at her, and idled out again, the ormolu clock ticked, the walls of striped pale grey stared blankly in the brilliant light, and Marjorie Ferrar stared blankly back – she was still seeing Francis Wilmot's ecstatic face.

'Now!' said MacGown. 'Up those stairs, and third on the right. I'll follow in a minute.'

She had acted in a play, she had passed an emotional hour, and she was hungry. At least she could dine before making the necessary scene. And while she drank the best champagne MacGown could buy, she talked and watched the burning eyes of her adorer. That red-brown visage, square, stiff-haired head, and powerful frame – what a contrast to the pale, slim face and form of Francis! This was a man, and when he liked, agreeable. With him she would have everything she wanted except – what Francis could give her. And it was one or the other – not both, as she had thought it might be. She had once crossed the 'striding edge' on Helvellyn, with a precipice on one side and a precipice on the other, and herself, doubting down which to fall, in the middle. She hadn't fallen, and – she supposed – she wouldn't now! One didn't, if one kept one's head!

Coffee was brought; and she sat, smoking, on the sofa. Her knowledge of private rooms taught her that she was now as alone with her betrothed as money could make them. How would he behave?

He threw his cigar away, and sat down by her side. This was the moment to rise and tell him that he was no longer her betrothed. His arm went round her, his lips sought her face. 'Mind my dress; it's the only decent one I've got.'

And, suddenly, not because she heard a noise, but because her senses were not absorbed like his, she perceived a figure in the open doorway. A woman's voice said: 'Oh! I beg your pardon; I thought—' Gone!

Marjorie Ferrar started up.

'Did you see that young woman?'

'Yes. Damn her!'

'She's shadowing me.'

'What?'

'I don't know her, and yet I know her perfectly. She had a good look at me downstairs, when I was waiting.'

MacGown dashed to the door and flung it open. Nobody was there! He shut it, and came back.

'By heaven! Those people, I'll—! Well, that ends it! Marjorie, I shall send our engagement to the papers tomorrow.'

Marjorie Ferrar, leaning her elbows on the mantelpiece, stared at her own face in the glass above it. 'Not a moral about her!' What did it matter? If only she could decide to marry Francis out of hand, slide away from them all – debts, lawyers, Alec! And then the 'You be damned' spirit in her blood revolted. The impudence of it! Shadowing her! No! She was not going to leave Miss Fleur triumphant – the little snob; and that old party with the chin!

MacGown raised her hand to his lips; and, somehow, the caress touched her.

'Oh! well,' she said, 'I suppose you'd better.'

'Thank God!'

'Do you really think that to get me is a cause for gratitude?'

'I would go through Hell to get you.'

'And after? Well, as we're public property, let's go down and dance.'

For an hour she danced. She would not let him take her home, and in her cab she cried. She wrote to Francis when she got in. She went out again to post it. The bitter stars, the bitter wind, the bitter night! At the little slurred thump of her letter dropping, she laughed. To have played at children! It was too funny! So that was done with! 'On with the dance!'

Extraordinary, the effect of a little paragraph in the papers! Credit, like new-struck oil, spurted sky-high. Her post contained, not bills for dresses, but solicitations to feed, frizz, fur, flower, feather, furbelow, and photograph her. London offered itself. To escape that cynical avalanche she borrowed a hundred pounds and flew to Paris. There, every night, she went to the theatre. She had her hair done in a new style, she ordered dresses, ate at places known to the few – living up to Michael's nickname for her; and her heart was heavy.

She returned after a week, and burned the avalanche – fortunately all letters of congratulation contained the phrase 'of course you won't think of answering this'. She didn't. The weather was mild; she rode in the Row; she prepared to hunt. On the eve of departure, she received an anonymous communication.

'Francis Wilmot is very ill with pneumonia at the Cosmopolis Hotel. He is not expected to live.'

Her heart flurried round within her breast and flumped; her knees felt weak; her hand holding the note shook; only her head stayed steady. The handwriting was 'that little snob's'. Had Francis caused this message to be sent? Was it his appeal? Poor boy! And must she go and see him if he were going to die? She so hated death. Did this mean that it was up to her to save him? What did it mean? But indecision was not her strong point. In ten minutes she was in a cab, in twenty at the Hotel. Handing her card, she said:

'You have a Mr Wilmot here – a relative of mine. I've just heard of his serious illness. Can I go up and see the nurse?'

The Management looked at the card, inquisitively at her face, touched a bell, and said:

'Certainly, madam . . . Here, you – take this lady up to Room – er – 209.'

Led by what poor Francis called a 'bell-boy' into the lift, she walked behind his buttons along a pale-grey river of corridor carpet, between pale-grey walls, past cream-coloured after cream-coloured door in the bright electric light, with her head a little down.

The 'bell-boy' knocked ruthlessly on a door.

It was opened, and in the lobby of the suite stood Fleur . . .

Chapter Twelve

Deepening

However untypically American according to Soames, Francis Wilmot seemed to have the national passion for short cuts. In two days from Fleur's first visit he had reached the crisis, hurrying towards it like a man to his bride. Yet, compared with the instinct to live, the human will is limited, so that he failed to die. Fleur, summoned by telephone, went home cheered by the doctor's words: 'He'll do now, if we can coax a little strength into him.' That, however, was the trouble. For three afternoons she watched his exhausted indifference seeming to increase. And she was haunted by cruel anxiety. On the fourth day she had been sitting for more than an hour when his eyes opened.

'Yes, Francis?'

'I'm going to quit all right, after all.'

'Don't talk like that – it's not American. Of course you're not going to quit.'

He smiled, and shut his eyes. She made up her mind then.

Next day he was about the same, more dead than alive. But her mind was at rest; her messenger had brought back word that Miss Ferrar would be in at four o'clock. She would have had the note by now; but would she come? How little one knew of other people, even when they were enemies!

He was drowsing, white and strengthless, when she heard the 'bell-boy's' knock. Passing into the lobby, she closed the door softly behind her, and opened the outer door. So she *had* come!

If this meeting of two declared enemies had in it something

dramatic, neither perceived it at the moment. It was just intensely unpleasant to them both. They stood for a moment looking at each other's chins. Then Fleur said:

'He's extremely weak. Will you sit down while I tell him you're here?'

Having seen her settled where Francis Wilmot put his clothes out to be valeted in days when he had worn them, Fleur passed back into the bedroom, and again closed the door.

'Francis,' she said, 'someone is waiting to see you.'

Francis Wilmot did not stir, but his eyes opened and cleared strangely. To Fleur they seemed suddenly the eyes she had known; as if all these days they had been 'out', and someone had again put a match to them.

'You understand what I mean?'

The words came clear and feeble: 'Yes; but if I wasn't good enough for her before, I surely am not now. Tell her I'm through with that fool business.'

A lump rose in Fleur's throat.

'Thank her for coming!' said Francis Wilmot, and closed his eyes again.

Fleur went back into the lobby. Marjorie Ferrar was standing against the wall with an unlighted cigarette between her lips.

'He thanks you for coming; but he doesn't want to see you. I'm sorry I brought you down.'

Marjorie Ferrar took out the cigarette. Fleur could see her lips quivering. 'Will he get well?'

'I don't know. I think so – now. He says he's "through with that fool business".'

Marjorie Ferrar's lips tightened. She opened the outer door, turned suddenly, and said:

'Will you make it up?'

'No,' said Fleur.

There was a moment of complete stillness; then Marjorie Ferrar gave a little laugh, and slipped out.

Fleur went back. He was asleep. Next day he was stronger. Three days later Fleur ceased her visits; he was on the road to recovery.

She had become conscious, moreover, that she had a little lamb which, wherever Mary went, was sure to go. She was being shadowed! How amusing! And what a bore that she couldn't tell Michael; because she had not yet begun again to tell him anything.

On the day that she ceased her visits he came in while she was dressing for dinner, with 'a weekly' in his hand.

'Listen to this,' he said:

'When to God's fondouk the donkeys are taken –
Donkeys of Africa, Sicily, Spain –
If peradventure the Deity waken,
He shall not easily slumber again.

Where in the sweet of God's straw they have laid them,
Broken and dead of their burdens and sores,
He, for a change, shall remember He made them –
One of the best of His numerous chores –

Order from someone a sigh of repentance –
Donkeys of Araby, Syria, Greece –
Over the fondouk distemper the sentence:
"God's own forsaken – the stable of Peace."'

'Who's that by? It sounds like Wilfrid.'

'It is by Wilfrid,' said Michael, and did not look at her. 'I met him at the "Hotch-Potch".'

'And how is he?'

'Very fit.'

'Have you asked him here?'

'No. He's going East again soon.'

Was he fishing? Did he know that she had seen him? And she said:

'I'm going down to Father's, Michael. He's written twice.'

Michael put her hand to his lips.

'All right, darling.'

Fleur reddened; her strangled confidences seemed knotted in her throat. She went next day with Kit and Dandie. The 'little lamb' would hardly follow to 'The Shelter'.

Annette had gone with her mother to Cannes for a month; and Soames was alone with the English winter. He was paying little attention to it, for the 'case' was in the list, and might be reached in a few weeks' time. Deprived of French influence, he was again wavering towards compromise. The announcement of Marjorie Ferrar's engagement to McGown had materially changed the complexion of affairs. In the eyes of a British Jury, the character of a fast young lady, and the character of the same young lady publicly engaged to a Member of Parliament, with wealth and a handle to his name, would not be at all the same thing. They were now virtually dealing with Lady MacGown, and nothing, Soames knew, was so fierce as a man about to be married. To libel his betrothed was like approaching a mad dog.

He looked very grave when Fleur told him of her 'little lamb'. It was precisely the retaliation he had feared; nor could he tell her that he had 'told her so', because he hadn't. He had certainly urged her to come down to him, but delicacy had forbidden him to give her the reason. So far as he could tell through catechism, there had been nothing 'suspect' in her movements since Lippinghall, except those visits to the Cosmopolis Hotel. But they were bad enough. Who was going to believe that she went to this sick man out of pure kindness? Such a motive was not current in a Court of Law. He was staggered when she told him that Michael didn't know of them. Why not?

'I didn't feel like telling him.'

'Feel? Don't you see what a position you've put yourself in? Here you are, running to a young man's bedside, without your husband's knowledge.'

'Yes, darling; but he was terribly ill.'

'I dare say,' said Soames; 'so are lots of people.'

'Besides, he was over head and ears in love with *her*.'

'D'you think he's going to admit that, even if we could call him?'

Fleur was silent, thinking of Francis Wilmot's face.

'Oh! I don't know,' she said at last. 'How horrid it all is!'

'Of course it's horrid,' said Soames. 'Have you had a quarrel with Michael?'

'No; not a quarrel. Only he doesn't tell *me* things.'

'What things?'

'How should I know, dear?'

Soames grunted. 'Would he have minded your going?'

'Of course not. He'd have minded if I hadn't. He likes that boy.'

'Well, then,' said Soames, 'either you or he, or both, will have to tell a lie, and say that he did know. I shall go up and talk to him. Thank goodness we can prove the illness. If I catch anybody coming down here after you —!'

He went up the following afternoon. Parliament being in recess, he sought the 'Hotch-Potch' Club. He did not like a place always connected in his mind with his dead cousin, that fellow young Jolyon, and said to Michael at once: 'Can we go somewhere else?'

'Yes, sir; where would you like?'

'To your place, if you can put me up for the night. I want to have a talk with you.'

Michael looked at him askance.

'Now,' said Soames, after dinner, 'what's this about Fleur – she says you don't tell her things?'

Michael gazed into his glass of port.

'Well, sir,' he said slowly, 'I'd be only too glad to, of course, but I don't think they really interest her. She doesn't feel that public things matter.'

'Public! I meant private.'

'There aren't any private things. Do you mean that she thinks there are?'

Soames dropped his scrutiny.

'I don't know – she said "things".'

'Well, you can put that out of your head, and hers.'

'H'm! Anyway, the result's been that she's been visiting that young American with pneumonia at the Cosmopolis Hotel, without letting you know. It's a mercy she hasn't picked it up.'

'Francis Wilmot?'

'Yes. He's out of the wood, now. That's not the point. She's been shadowed.'

'Good God!' said Michael.

'Exactly! This is what comes of not talking to your wife. Wives are funny – they don't like it.'

Michael grinned.

'Put yourself in my place, sir. It's my profession, now, to fuss about the state of the Country, and all that; and you know how it is – one gets keen. But to Fleur, it's all a stunt. I quite understand that; but, you see, the keener I get, the more I'm afraid of boring her, and the less I feel I can talk to her about it. In a sort of way she's jealous.'

Soames rubbed his chin. The state of the Country was a curious kind of co-respondent. He himself was often worried by the state of the Country, but as a source of division between husband and wife it seemed to him cold-blooded; he had known other sources in his time!

'Well, you mustn't let it go on,' he said. 'It's trivial.'

Michael got up.

'Trivial! Well, sir, I don't know, but it seems to me very much the sort of thing that happened when the war came. Men had to leave their wives then.'

'Wives put up with that,' said Soames, 'the Country was in danger.'

'Isn't it in danger now?'

With his inveterate distrust of words, it seemed to Soames almost indecent for a young man to talk like that. Michael was a politician, of course; but politicians were there to keep the Country quiet, not to go raising scares and talking through their hats.

'When you've lived a little longer,' he said, 'you'll know that there's always something to fuss about if you like to fuss. There's nothing in it really; the pound's going up. Besides, it doesn't matter what you tell Fleur, so long as you tell her something.'

'She's intelligent, sir,' said Michael.

Soames was taken aback. He could not deny the fact, and answered:

'Well, national affairs are too remote; you can't expect a woman to be interested in them.'

'Quite a lot of women are.'

'Blue-stockings.'

'No, sir; they nearly all wear "nude".'

'H'm! Those! As to interest in national affairs – put a tax on stockings, and see what happens!'

Michael grinned.

'I'll suggest it, sir.'

'If you expect,' said Soames, 'that people – women or not – are going to put themselves out of the way for any scheme like this – this Foggartism of yours, you'll be very much disappointed.'

'So everybody tells me. It's just because I don't like cold water at home as well as abroad, that I've given up worrying Fleur.'

'Well, if you take my advice, you'll take up something practical – the state of the traffic, or penny postage. Drop pessimism; people who talk at large like that, never get trusted in this country. In any case you'll have to say you knew about her visits to that young man.'

'Certainly, sir, wife and husband are one. But you don't really mean to let them make a circus of it in Court?'

Soames was silent. He did not *mean* them to; but what if they did?

'I can't tell,' he said, at last. 'The fellow's a Scotchman. What did you go hitting him on the nose for?'

'He gave me a thick ear first. I know it was an excellent opportunity for turning the other cheek, but I didn't think of it in time.'

'You must have called him something.'

'Only a dirty dog. As you know, he suggested a low motive for my speech.'

Soames stared. In his opinion this young man was taking himself much too seriously.

'Your speech! You've got to get it out of your mind,' he said, 'that anything you can say or do will make any difference.'

'Then what's the good of my being in Parliament?'

'Well, you're in the same boat with everybody else. The Country's like a tree; you can keep it in order, but you can't go taking it up by the roots to look at them.'

Michael looked at him, impressed.

'In public matters,' said Soames, 'the thing is to keep a level head, and do no more than you're obliged.'

'And what's to govern one's view of necessity?'

'Common sense. One can't have everything.'

And rising, he began scrutinising the Goya.

'Are you going to buy another Goya, sir?'

'No; if I buy any more pictures, I shall go back to the English School.'

'Patriotism?'

Soames gave him a sharp look.

'There's no patriotism,' he said, 'in fussing. And another thing you've got to remember is that foreigners like to hear that we've got troubles. It doesn't do to discuss our affairs out loud.'

Michael took these sayings to bed with him. He remembered, when he came out of the war, thinking: 'If there's another war, nothing will induce me to go.' But now, if one were to come, he knew he *would* be going again. So Old Forsyte thought he was just 'fussing'! Was he? Was Foggartism a phlizz? Ought he to come to heel, and take up the state of the traffic? Was everything unreal? Surely not his love for Fleur? Anyway he felt hungry for her lying there. And Wilfrid back, too! To risk his happiness with her for the sake of – what? *Punch* had taken a snap at him this week, grinning and groping at a surrounding fog. Old England, like Old Forsyte, had no use for theories. Self-conscious national efforts were just pomposity. Pompous! He? The thought was terribly disturbing. He got out of bed and went to the window. Foggy! In fog all were shadows; and he the merest shadow of them all, an unpractical politician, taking things to heart! One! Two! Big Ben! How many hearts had he turned to water! How many dreams spoiled, with his measured resonance! Line up with the top-dressers, and leave the Country to suck its silver spoon!

Part III

Chapter One

'Circuses'

*I*n his early boyhood Soames had been given to the circus. He had outgrown it; 'Circuses' were now to him little short of an abomination. Jubilees and Pageants, that recurrent decimal, the Lord Mayor, Earl's Court, Olympia, Wembley – he disliked them all. He could not stand a lot of people with their mouths open. Dressing up was to him a symptom of weak-mindedness, and the collective excitement of a crowd an extravagance which offended his reticent individualism. Though not deeply versed in history, he had an idea, too, that nations who went in for 'circuses' were decadent. Queen Victoria's funeral, indeed, had impressed him – there had been a feeling in the air that day; but ever since, things had gone from bad to worse. They made everything into a 'circus' now! A man couldn't commit a murder without the whole paper-reading population – himself included – looking over each other's shoulders; and as to these football matches, and rodeos – they interfered with the traffic and the normal course of conversation; people were so crazy about them!

Of course, 'circuses' had their use. They kept the people quiet. Violence by proxy, for instance, was obviously a political principle of some value. It was difficult to gape and shed blood at the same time; the more people stood in rows by day to see others being hurt, the less trouble would they take to hurt others themselves, and the sounder Soames could sleep by night. Still, sensation-hunting had become a disease, in his opinion, and no one was being inoculated for it, so far as he could see!

As the weeks went on and the cases before it in the List went off, the 'circus' they were proposing to make of his daughter appeared to him more and more monstrous. He had an instinctive distrust of Scotchmen – they called themselves Scotsmen nowadays, as if it helped their character! – they never let go, and he could not approve in other people a quality native to himself. Besides, 'Scotchmen' were so – so exuberant – always either dour or else hearty – extravagant chaps! Towards the middle of March, with the case in the list for the following week, he took an extreme step and entered the Lobby of the House of Commons. He had spoken to no one of his determination to make this last effort, for it seemed to him that all – Annette, Michael, Fleur herself – had done their best to spoil the chance of settlement.

Having sent in his card, he waited a long while in that lofty purlieu. 'Lobbying', he knew the phrase, but had never realised the waste of time involved in it. The statues consoled him somewhat. Sir Stafford Northcote – a steady chap; at old Forsyte dinner-parties in the 'eighties his character had been as much a standby as the saddle of mutton. He found even 'that fellow Gladstone' bearable in stucco, or whatever it was up there. You might dislike, but you couldn't sneeze at him, as at some of these modern chaps. He was sunk in coma before Lord Granville when at last he heard the words:

'Sir Alexander MacGown,' and saw a square man with a ruddy face, stiff black hair, and clipped moustache, coming between the railings, with a card in his hand.

'Mr Forsyte?'

'Yes. Can we go anywhere that's not quite so public?'

The 'Scotchman' nodded, and led him down a corridor to a small room.

'Well?'

Soames smoothed his hat. 'This affair', he said, 'can't be any more agreeable to you than it is to me.'

'Are you the individual who was good enough to apply the word "traitress" to the lady I'm engaged to?'

'That is so.'

'Then I don't see how you have the impudence to come and speak to me.'

Soames bit his lips.

'I spoke under the provocation of hearing your fiancée call my daughter a snob, in her own house. Do you want this petty affair made public?'

'If you think that you and your daughter can get away with calling the lady I'm going to marry "a snake", "a traitress", "an immoral person", you're more mistaken that you ever were in your life. An unqualified apology that her Counsel can announce in Court is your only way out.'

'That you won't get; mutual regret is another thing. As to the question of damages—'

'Damn the damages!' said MacGown violently. And there was that in Soames which applauded.

'Well,' he said, 'I'm sorry for you and her.'

'What the devil do you mean, sir?'

'You will know by the end of next week, unless you revise your views in between. If it comes into Court, we shall justify.'

The 'Scotchman' went so red that for a moment Soames was really afraid he would have an apoplectic fit.

'You'd better look out what you say in Court.'

'We pay no attention to bullies in Court.'

MacGown clenched his fists.

'Yes,' said Soames, 'it's a pity I'm not your age. Good evening!'

He passed the fellow and went out. He had noted his way in this 'rabbit warren', and was soon back among the passionless statues. Well! He had turned the last stone and could do no more, except make that overbearing fellow and his young woman sorry they'd ever been born. He came out into the chilly mist of Westminster. Pride and temper! Sooner than admit themselves in the wrong, people would turn themselves into an expensive 'circus' for the gaping and the sneers, the japing and the jeers of half the town! To vindicate her 'honour', that 'Scotchman' would have his young woman's past dragged out! And fairly faced by the question whether to drag it out or not, Soames stood still. If he didn't, she might get a verdict; if he did, and didn't convince the jury, the damages would be shockingly increased. They might run into thousands. He felt the need of definite decision. One had been drifting in the belief that the thing wouldn't come into Court! Four o'clock! Not too late, perhaps, to see Sir James Foskisson. He would telephone to very young Nicholas to arrange a conference at once, and if Michael was at South Square, he would take him down to it . . .

In his study, Michael had been staring with lugubrious relish at Aubrey Greene's cartoon of himself in a Society paper. On one leg, like Guy – or was it Slingsby? – in the Edward Lear 'Nonsense' book, he was depicted crying in a wilderness where a sardonic smile was rising on the horizon. Out of his mouth the word 'Foggartism' wreathed like the smoke of a cigar. Above a hole in the middle distance, a meercat's body supported the upturned face and applauding forepaws of Mr Blythe. The thing was devastating in treatment and design – not unkind, merely killing. Michael's face had been endowed with a sort of after-dinner rapture, as if he were enjoying the sound of his own voice. Ridicule! Not even a personal friend, an artist, could see that the wilderness was at least as deserving of ridicule as the pelican! The cartoon seemed to write the word futility large across his page. It recalled to him Fleur's words at the outset: 'And by the time the Tories go out you'll have your licence.' She was a born realist! From the first she had foreseen for him the position of an eccentric, picturesquely beating a little private drum! A dashed good cartoon! And no one could appreciate it so deeply as its victim. But why did every one smile at Foggartism? Why? Because among a people who naturally walked, it leaped like a grasshopper; to a nation that felt its way in fog, it seemed a will-o'-the-wisp. Yes, he was a fool for his pains! And – just then, Soames arrived.

'I've been to see that Scotchman,' he said. 'He means to take it into Court.'

'Oh! Not really, sir! I always thought you'd keep it out.'

'Only an unqualified apology will do that. Fleur can't give it; she's in the right. Can you come down with me now and see Sir James Foskisson?'

They set out in a taxi for the Temple.

The chambers of very young Nicholas Forsyte were in Paper

Buildings. Chinny, mild and nearly forty, he succeeded within ten minutes in presenting to them every possible doubt.

'He seems to enjoy the prospect of getting tonked,' murmured Michael while they were going over to Sir James.

'A poor thing,' Soames responded; 'but careful. Foskisson must attend to the case himself.'

After those necessary minutes during which the celebrated K.C. was regathering from very young Nicholas what it was all about, they were ushered into the presence of one with a large head garnished by small grey whiskers, and really obvious brains. Since selecting him, Soames had been keeping his eye on the great advocate; had watched him veiling his appeals to a jury with an air of scrupulous equity; very few – he was convinced – and those not on juries, could see Sir James Foskisson coming round a corner. Soames had specially remarked his success in cases concerned with morals or nationality – no one so apt at getting a co-respondent, a German, a Russian, or anybody at all bad, non-suited! At close quarters his whiskers seemed to give him an intensive respectability – difficult to imagine him dancing, gambling, or in bed. In spite of his practice, too, he enjoyed the reputation of being thorough; he might be relied on to know more than half the facts of any case by the time he went into Court, and to pick up the rest as he went along – or at least not to show that he hadn't. Very young Nicholas, knowing all the facts, had seemed quite unable to see what line could possibly be taken. Sir James, on the other hand, appeared to know only just enough. Sliding his light eyes from Soames to Michael, he retailed them, and said: 'Eminently a case for an amicable settlement.'

'Indeed!' said Soames.

Something in his voice seemed to bring Sir James to attention.

'Have you attempted that?'

'I have gone to the limit.'

'Excuse me, Mr Forsyte, but what do you regard as the limit?'

'Fifteen hundred pounds, and a mutual expression of regret. They'd accept the money, but they ask for an unqualified apology.'

The great lawyer rested his chin. 'Have you tried the unqualified apology without the money?'

'No.'

'I would almost be inclined. MacGown is a very rich man. The shadow and the substance, eh? The expressions in the letters are strong. What do you say, Mr Mont?'

'Not so strong as those she used of my wife.'

Sir James Foskisson looked at very young Nicholas.

'Let me see,' he said, 'those were—?'

'Lion-huntress, and snob,' said Michael, curtly.

Sir James wagged his head precisely as if it were a pair of scales.

'Immoral, snake, traitress, without charm – you think those weaker?'

'They don't make you snigger, sir, the others do. In Society it's the snigger that counts.'

Sir James smiled.

'The jury won't be in Society, Mr Mont.'

'My wife doesn't feel like making an apology, anyway, unless there's an expression of regret on the other side; and I don't see why she should.'

Sir James Foskisson seemed to breathe more freely.

'In that case,' he said, 'we have to consider whether to use the detective's evidence or not. If we do, we shall need to subpoena the hall porter and the servants at Mr – er – Curfew's flat.'

'Exactly,' said Soames; 'that's what we're here to decide.' It was as if he had said: 'The conference is now opened.'

Sir James perused the detective's evidence for five silent minutes.

'If this is confirmed, even partially,' he said, at last, 'we win.'

Michael had gone to the window. The trees in the garden had tiny buds; some pigeons were strutting on the grass below. He heard Soames say:

'I ought to tell you that they've been shadowing my daughter. There's nothing, of course, except some visits to a young American dangerously ill of pneumonia at his hotel.'

'Of which I knew and approved,' said Michael, without turning round.

'Could we call him?'

'I believe he's still at Bournemouth. But he was in love with Miss Ferrar.'

Sir James turned to Soames.

'If there's no question of a settlement, we'd better go for the gloves. Merely to cross-examine as to books and play and clubs, is very inconclusive.'

'Have you read the dark scene in "The Plain Dealer"?' asked Soames; 'and that novel, *Canthar*?'

'All very well, Mr Forsyte, but impossible to say what a jury would make of impersonal evidence like that.'

Michael had come back to his seat.

'I've a horror,' he said, 'of dragging in Miss Ferrar's private life.'

'No doubt. But do you want me to win the case?'

'Not that way. Can't we go into Court, say nothing, and pay up?'

Sir James Foskisson smiled and looked at Soames. 'Really,' he seemed to say, 'why did you bring me this young man?'

Soames, however, had been pursuing his own thoughts.

'There's too much risk about that flat; if we failed there, it might be a matter of twenty thousand pounds. Besides, they would certainly call my daughter. I want to prevent that at all costs. I thought you could turn the whole thing into an indictment of modern morality.'

Sir James Foskisson moved in his chair, and the pupils of his light-blue eyes became as pinpoints. He nodded almost imperceptibly three times, precisely as if he had seen the Holy Ghost.

'When shall we be reached?' he said to very young Nicholas.

'Probably next Thursday – Mr Justice Brane.'

'Very well. I'll see you again on Monday. Good evening.' And he sank back into an immobility, which neither Soames nor Michael felt equal to disturbing.

They went away silent – very young Nicholas tarrying in conversation with Sir James's devil.

Turning at the Temple station, Michael murmured:

'It was just as if he'd said: "Some stunt!" wasn't it? I'm looking in at *The Outpost*, sir. If you're going back to Fleur, will you tell her?'

Soames nodded. There it was! He had to do everything that was painful.

Chapter Two

'Not Going To Have It'

*I*n the office of *The Outpost* Mr Blythe had just been in conversation with one of those great business men who make such deep impression on all to whom they voice their views in strict confidence. If Sir Thomas Lockit did not precisely monopolise the control of manufacture in Great Britain, he, like others, caused almost anyone to think so – his knowledge was so positive and his emphasis so cold. In his view the Country must resume the position held before the Great War. It all hinged on coal – a question of this seven hours a day; and they were 'not going to have it'. A shilling, perhaps two shillings, off the cost of coal. They were 'not going to have' Europe doing without British produce. Very few people knew Sir Thomas Lockit's mind; but nearly all who did were extraordinarily gratified.

Mr Blythe, however, was biting his finger, and spitting out the result.

'Who was that fellow with the grey moustache?' asked Michael.

'Lockit. He's "not going to have it".'

'Oh!' said Michael, in some surprise.

'One sees more and more, Mont, that the really dangerous people are not the politicians, who want things with public passion – that is, mildly, slowly; but the big business men, who want things with private passion, strenuously, quickly. They know their own minds; and if we don't look out they'll wreck the country.'

'What are they up to now?' said Michael.

'Nothing for the moment; but it's brewing. One sees in Lockit the futility of willpower. He's not going to have what it's entirely out of his power to prevent. He'd like to break Labour and make it work like a nigger from sheer necessity. Before that we shall be having civil war. Some of the Labour people, of course, are just as bad – they want to break everybody. It's a bee nuisance. If we're all to be plunged into industrial struggles again, how are we to get on with Foggartism?'

'I've been thinking about the Country,' said Michael. 'Aren't we beating the air, Blythe? Is it any good telling a man who's lost a lung, that what he wants is a new one?'

Mr Blythe puffed out one cheek.

'Yes,' he said, 'the Country had a hundred very settled years – Waterloo to the War – to get into its present state; it's got its line of life so fixed and its habits so settled that nobody – neither editors, politicians, nor business men – can think except in terms of its bloated town industrialism. The Country's got beyond the point of balance in that hundred settled years, and it'll want fifty settled years to get back to that point again. The real trouble is that we're not going to get fifty settled years. Some bee thing or other – war with Turkey or Russia, trouble in India, civil ructions, to say nothing of another general flare-up – may knock the bottom out of any settled plans any time. We've struck a disturbed patch of history, and we know it in our bones, and live from hand to mouth, according.'

'Well, then!' said Michael, glumly, thinking of what the Minister had said to him at Lippinghall

Mr Blythe puffed out the other cheek.

'No backsliding, young man! In Foggartism we have the best goods we can see before us, and we must bee well deliver them, as best we can. We've outgrown all the old hats.'

'Have you seen Aubrey Greene's cartoon?'

'I have.'

'Good – isn't it? But what I really came in to tell you, is that this beastly libel case of ours will be on next week.'

Mr Blythe's ears moved.

'I'm sorry for that. Win or lose – nothing's worse for public life than private ructions. You're not going to have it, are you?'

'We can't help it. But our defence is to be confined to an attack on the new morality.'

'One can't attack what isn't,' said Mr Blythe.

'D'you mean to say,' said Michael, grinning, 'that you haven't noticed the new morality?'

'Certainly not. Formulate it if you can.'

'"Don't be stupid, don't be dull."'

Mr Blythe grunted. 'The old morality used to be: "Behave like a gentleman".'

'Yes! But in modern thought there ain't no sich an animal.'

'There are fragments lying about; they reconstructed Neanderthal man from half a skull.'

'A word that's laughed at can't be used, Blythe.'

'Ah!' said Mr Blythe. 'The chief failings of your generation, young Mont, are sensitiveness to ridicule, and terror of being behind the times. It's bee weakminded.'

Michael grinned.

'I know it. Come down to the House. Parsham's Electrification Bill is due. We may get some lights on Unemployment.'

Having parted from Mr Blythe in the Lobby, Michael came on his father walking down a corridor with a short bright old man in a trim grey beard.

'Ah! Michael, we've been seeking you. Marquess, my hopeful son! The marquess wants to interest you in electricity.'

Michael removed his hat.

'Will you come to the reading-room, sir?'

This, as he knew, was Marjorie Ferrar's grandfather, and might be useful. In a remote corner of a room lighted so that nobody could see anyone else reading, they sat down in triangular formation.

'You know about electricity, Mr Mont?' said the marquess.

'No, sir, except that more of it would be desirable in this room.'

'Everywhere, Mr Mont. I've read about your Foggartism; if you'll allow me to say so, it's quite possibly the policy of the future; but nothing will be done with it till you've electrified the country. I should like you to start by supporting this Bill of Parsham's.'

And, with an engaging distinction of syllable, the old peer proceeded to darken Michael's mind.

'I see, sir,' said Michael, at last. 'This Bill ought to add considerably to Unemployment.'

'Temporarily.'

'I wonder if I ought to take on any more temporary trouble. I'm finding it difficult enough to interest people in the future as it is – they seem to think the present so important.'

Sir Lawrence whinnied.

'You must give him time and pamphlets, Marquess. But, my dear fellow, while your Foggartism is confined to the stable, you'll want a second horse.'

'I've been advised already to take up the state of the traffic or penny postage. And, by the way, sir, that case of ours is coming into Court, next week.'

Sir Lawrence's loose eyebrow shot up:

'Oh!' he said. 'Do you remember, Marquess – your granddaughter and my daughter-in-law? I came to you about it.'

'Something to do with lions? A libel, was it?' said the old peer. 'My aunt—'

While Michael was trying to decide whether this was an ejaculation or the beginning of a reminiscence, his father broke in:

'Ah! yes, an interesting case that, Marquess – it's all in Betty Montecourt's Memoirs.'

'Libels', resumed the marquess, 'had flavour in those days. The words complained of were: "Her crinoline covers her considerable obliquity".'

'If anything's to be done to save scandal,' muttered Michael, 'it must be done now. We're at a deadlock.'

'Could *you* put in a word, sir?' said Sir Lawrence.

The marquess's beard quivered.

'I see from the papers that my granddaughter is marrying a man called MacGown, a Member of this House. Is he about?'

'Probably,' said Michael. 'But I had a row with him. I think, sir, there would be more chance with her.'

The marquess rose. 'I'll ask her to breakfast. I dislike publicity. Well, I hope you'll vote for this Bill, Mr Mont, and think over the question of electrifying the Country. We want young men interested. I'm going to the Peers' Gallery, now. Good-bye!'

When briskly he had gone, Michael said to his father: 'If he's not going to have it, I wish he'd ask Fleur to breakfast too. There are two parties to this quarrel.'

Chapter Three

Soames Drives Home

*S*oames in the meantime was seated with one of those parties in her 'parlour'. She had listened in silence, but with a stubborn and resentful face. What did he know of the loneliness and frustration she had been feeling? Could he tell that the thrown stone had starred her mirrored image of herself; that the words 'snob', and 'lion-huntress', had entered her very soul? He could not understand the spiritual injury she had received, the sudden deprivation of that self-importance, and hope of rising, necessary to all. Concerned by the expression on her face, preoccupied with the practical aspects of the 'circus' before them, and desperately involved in thoughts of how to keep her out of it as much as possible, Soames was reduced to the closeness of a fish.

'You'll be sitting in front, next to me,' he said. 'I shouldn't wear anything too bright. Would you like your mother there, too?'

Fleur shrugged her shoulders.

'Just so,' said Soames. 'But if she wants to come, she'd better, perhaps. Brane is not a joking judge, thank goodness. Have you ever been in a Court?'

'No.'

'The great thing is to keep still, and pay no attention to anything. They'll all be behind you, except the jury – and there's nothing in them really. If you look at them, don't smile!'

'Why? Aren't they safe, Dad?'

Soames put the levity aside.

'I should wear a small hat. Michael must sit on your left. Have you got over that – er – not telling each other things?'

'Yes.'

'I shouldn't begin it again. He's very fond of you.'

Fleur nodded.

'Is there anything you want to tell *me*? You know I – I worry about you.'

Fleur got up and sat on the arm of his chair; he had at once a feeling of assuagement.

'I really don't care now. The harm's done. I only hope *she'll* have a bad time.'

Soames, who had the same hope, was somewhat shocked by its expression.

He took leave of her soon after and got into his car for the dark drive back to Mapledurham.

The spring evening was cold and he had the windows up. At first he thought of very little; and then of still less. He had passed a tiring afternoon, and was glad of the slight smell of stephanotis provided by Annette. The road was too familiar to rouse his thoughts, beyond wonder at the lot of people there always seemed to be in the world between six and seven. He dozed his way into the new cut, woke, and dozed again. What was this – Slough? Before going to Marlborough he had been at school there with young Nicholas and St John Hayman, and after his time, some other young Forsytes. Nearly sixty years ago! He remembered his first day – a brand-new little boy in a brand-new little top-hat, with a playbox stored by his mother with things to eat, and blessed with the words: 'There, Summy dear, that'll make you popular.' He had reckoned on having command of that corruption for some weeks; but no sooner had he produced a bit of it, than they had taken the box, and suggested to him that it would be a good thing to eat the lot. In twenty-two minutes twenty-two boys had materially increased their weight, and he himself, in handing out the contents, had been obliged to eat less than a twenty-third. They had left him one packet of biscuits, and those had caraway seeds, for which he had constitutionally no passion whatever. Afterwards three other new boys had complained that he was a fool for having it all eaten up like that, instead of saving it for them, and he had been obliged to sit on their heads one by one. His popularity had lasted twenty-two minutes, and, so far as he knew, had never come back. He had been against Communism ever since.

Bounding a little on the cushioned seat, he remembered poignantly his own cousin St John Hayman pushing him into a gorse-bush and holding him there for an appreciable minute. Horrid little brutes, boys! For a moment he felt quite grateful to Michael for trying to get them out of England. And yet—! He had some pleasant memories even of boys. There was his collection of butterflies – he had sold two Red Admirals in poor condition to a boy for one-and-three-pence. To be a boy again – h'm – and shoot peas at passengers in a train that couldn't stop, and drink cherry brandy going home, and win a prize by reciting two hundred lines of 'The Lady of the Lake' better than 'Cherry-Tart' Burroughes – Um? What had become of 'Cherry-Tart' Burroughes, who had so much money at school that his father went bankrupt! 'Cherry-Tart' Burroughes!

The loom of Slough faded. One was in rank country now, and he ground the handle of the window to get a little fresh air. A smell of trees and grass came in. Boys out of England! They had funny accents in those great places overseas. Well, they had funny accents here, too. The accent had been all right at Slough – if it wasn't a boy got lammed. He remembered the first time his father and mother – James and Emily – came down; very genteel (before the word was flyblown), all whiskers and crinoline; the beastly boys had made personal remarks which had hurt him! Get 'em out of England! But in those days there had been nowhere for boys to go. He took a long breath of the wayside air. They said England was changed, spoiled, some even said 'done for'. Bosh! It still smelt the same! His great uncle 'Superior Dosset's' brother Simon had gone as a boy to Bermuda at the beginning of the last century, and had he been heard of since? Not he. Young Jon Forsyte and his mother – his own first, unfaithful, still not quite forgotten wife – had gone to the States – would they be heard of again? He hoped not. England! Some day, when he had time and the car was free, he would go and poke round on the border of Dorset and Devon where the Forsytes came from. There was nothing there – he understood, and he wouldn't care to let anybody know of his going; but the earth must be some sort of colour, and there would be a graveyard, and – ha! Maidenhead! These sprawling villas and hotels and gramophones spoiled the river. Funny that Fleur had never been very fond of the river; too slow and wet, perhaps – everything was quick and dry now, like America. But had they such a river as the Thames anywhere out of England? Not they! Nothing that ran green and clear and weedy, where you could sit in a punt and watch the cows, and those big elms, and the poplars. Nothing that was safe and quiet, where you called your soul your own and thought of Constable and Mason and Walker.

His car bumped something slightly, and came to a stand. That fellow Riggs was always bumping something! He looked out. The chauffeur had got down and was examining his mudguard.

'What was that?' said Soames.

'I think it was a pig, sir.'

'Where?'

'Shall I drive on, or see?'

Soames looked round. There seemed no habitations in sight.

'Better see.'

The chauffeur disappeared behind the car. Soames remained seated. He had never had any pigs. They said the pig was a clean animal. People didn't treat pigs properly. It was very quiet! No cars on the road; in the silence the wind was talking a little in the hedgerow. He noticed some stars.

'It is a pig, sir; he's breathing.'

'Oh!' said Soames. If a cat had nine, how many lives had a pig? He remembered his father James's only riddle: 'If a herring and a half cost three-a'pence, what's the price of a gridiron?' When still very small, he had perceived that it was unanswerable.

'Where is he?' he said.

'In the ditch, sir.'

A pig was property, but if in the ditch, nobody would notice it till after he was home. 'Drive on,' he said: 'No! Wait.' And, opening the near door, he got out. After all, the pig was in distress. 'Show me,' he said, and moved in the tail-light of his car to where the chauffeur stood pointing. There, in the shallow ditch, was a dark object emitting cavernous low sounds, as of a man asleep in a Club chair.

'It must belong to one of them cottages we passed a bit back,' said the chauffeur.

Soames looked at the pig.

'Anything broken?'

'No, sir; the mudguard's all right. I fancy it copped him pretty fair.'

'In the pig, I meant.'

The chauffeur touched the pig with his boot. It squealed, and Soames quivered. Someone would hear! Just like that fellow, drawing attention to it – no gumption whatever! But how, without touching, did you find out whether anything was broken in the pig? He moved a step and saw the pig's eyes; and a sort of fellow-feeling stirred in him. What if it had a broken leg! Again the chauffeur touched it with his foot. The pig uttered a lamentable noise, and, upheaving its bulk, squealing and grunting, trotted off. Soames hastily resumed his seat. 'Drive on!' he said. Pigs! They never thought of anything but themselves; and cottagers were just as bad – very unpleasant about cars. And he wasn't sure they weren't right – tearing great things! The pig's eye seemed looking at him again from where his feet were resting. Should he keep some, now that he had those meadows on the other side of the river? Eat one's own bacon, cure one's own hams! After all, there was something in it – clean pigs, properly fed! That book of old Foggart said one must grow more food in England, and be independent if there were another war. He sniffed. Smell of baking – Reading, already! They still grew biscuits in England! Foreign countries growing his food – something unpleasant about living on sufferance like that! After all, English meat and English wheat – as for a potato, you couldn't get one fit to eat in Italy, or France. And now they wanted to trade with Russia again! Those Bolshevists hated England. Eat their wheat and eggs, use their tallow and skins? *Infra dig*, he called it! The car swerved and he was jerked against the side cushions. The village church! – that fellow Riggs was always shying at something. Pretty little old affair, too, with its squat spire and its lichen – couldn't see that out of England – graves, old names, yew-trees. And that reminded him: One would have to be buried, some day. Here, perhaps. Nothing flowery! Just his name, 'Soames Forsyte', standing out on rough stone, like that grave he had sat on at Highgate; no need to put 'Here lies' – of course he'd lie! As to a cross, he didn't know. Probably they'd put one, whatever he wished. He'd like to be in a corner, though, away from people – with an apple-tree or something, over him. The less they remembered him, the better. Except Fleur – and she would have other things to think of!

The car turned down the last low hill to the level of the river. He caught a glimpse of it flowing dark between the poplars, like the soul of England, running hidden. The car rolled into the drive, and stopped before the door. He shouldn't tell Annette yet about this case coming into Court – she wouldn't feel as he did – she had no nerves!

Chapter Four

Catechism

*M*arjorie Ferrar's marriage was fixed for the day of the Easter Recess; her honeymoon to Lugano; her trousseau with Clothilde; her residence in Eaton Square; her pin-money at two thousand a year; and her affections on nobody. When she received a telephone message: Would she come to breakfast at Shropshire House? she was surprised. What could be the matter with the old boy?

At five minutes past nine, however, on the following day she entered the ancestral precincts, having left almost all powder and pigment on her dressing-table. Was he going to disapprove of her marriage? Or to give her some of her grandmother's lace, which was only fit to be in a museum?

The marquess was reading the paper in front of an electric fire. He bent on her his bright, shrewd glance.

'Well, Marjorie? Shall we sit down, or do you like to breakfast standing? There's porridge, scrambled eggs, fish – ah! and grapefruit – very considerate of them! Pour out the coffee, will you?'

'What'll you have, Grandfather?'

'Thank you, I'll roam about and peck a bit. So you're going to be married. Is that fortunate?'

'People say so.'

'He's in Parliament, I see. Do you think you could interest him in this Electricity Bill of Parsham's?'

'Oh! yes. He's dead keen on electricity.'

'Sensible man. He's got Works, I suppose. Are they electrified?'

'I expect so.'

The marquess gave her another glance.

'You know nothing about it,' he said. 'But you're looking very charming. What's this I hear of a libel?'

She might have known! Grandfather was too frightfully spry! He missed nothing!

'It wouldn't interest you, dear.'

'I disagree. My father and *old* Sir Lawrence Mont were great friends. Why do you want to wash linen in Court?'

'I don't.'

'Are you the plaintiff?'

'Yes.'

'What do you complain of?'

'They've said things about me.'

'Who?'

'Fleur Mont and her father.'

'Ah! the relation of the tea-man. What have they said?'

'That I haven't a moral about me.'

'Well, have you?'

'As much as most people.'

'Anything else?'

'That I'm a snake of the first water.'

'I don't like that. What made them say so?'

'Only that I was heard calling her a snob; and so she is.'

The marquess, who had resigned a finished grapefruit, placed his foot on a chair, his elbow on his knee, his chin on his hand, and said:

'No divinity hedges our Order in these days, Marjorie; but we still stand for something. It's a mistake to forget that.'

She sat very still. Everybody respected grandfather; even her father, to whom he did not speak. But to be told that she stood for something was really too dull for anything! All very well for grandfather at his age, and with his lack of temptations! Besides, *she* had no handle to her name, owing to the vaunted nature of British institutions. Even if she felt that – by Lord Charles out of Lady Ursula – she ought not to be dictated to, she had never put on frills – had always liked to be thought a mere Bohemian. And, after all, she did stand – for not being stuffy, and not being dull.

'Well, Grandfather, I tried to make it up, but she wouldn't. Coffee?'

'Yes, coffee. But tell me, are you happy about yourself?'

Marjorie Ferrar handed him the cup. 'No. Who is?'

'A hit,' said the marquess. 'You're going to be very well off, I hear. That means power. It's worth using well, Marjorie. He's a Scotsman, isn't he? Do you like him?' Again the shrewd bright glance.

'At times.'

'I see. With your hair, you must be careful. Red hair is extraordinarily valuable on occasion. In the Eton and Harrow Match, or for speaking after dinner; but don't let it run away with you after you're married. Where are you going to live?'

'In Eaton Square. There's a Scotch place, too.'

'Have your kitchens electrified. I've had it done here. It saves the cook's temper. I get very equable food. But about this libel. Can't you all say you're sorry – why put money into the lawyers' pockets?'

'She won't, unless I do, and I won't, unless she does.'

The marquess drank off his coffee.

'Then what is there in the way? I dislike publicity, Marjorie. Look at that suit the other day. Anything of this nature in Society, nowadays, is a nail in our coffins.'

'I'll speak to Alec, if you like.'

'Do! Has he red hair?'

'No; black.'

'Ah! What would you like for a wedding-present – lace?'

'Oh! no, please, dear. Nobody's wearing lace.'

With his head on one side, the marquess looked at her. 'I can't get that lace off,' he seemed to say.

'Perhaps you'd like a Colliery. Electrified, it would pay in no time.'

Marjorie Ferrar laughed. 'I know you're hard up, Grandfather; but I'd rather not have a Colliery, thanks. They're so expensive. Just give me your blessing.'

'I wonder,' said the marquess, 'if I could sell blessings? Your uncle Dangerfield has gone in for farming; he's ruining me. If only he'd grow wheat by electricity; it's the only way to make it pay at the present price. Well, if you've finished breakfast, good-bye. I must go to work.'

Marjorie Ferrar, who had indeed begun breakfast, stood up and pressed his hand. He was a dear old boy, if somewhat rapid! . . .

That same evening, in a box at the St Anthony, she had her opportunity, when MacGown was telling her of Soames's visit.

'Oh, dear! Why on earth didn't you settle it, Alec? The whole thing's a bore. I've had my grandfather at me about it.'

'If they'll apologise,' said MacGown, 'I'll settle it tomorrow. But an apology they must make.'

'And what about me? I don't want to stand up to be shot at.'

'There are some things one can't sit down under, Marjorie. Their whole conduct has been infamous.'

Visited by a reckless impulse, she said:

'What d'you suppose I'm really like, Alec?'

MacGown put his hand on her bare arm.

'I don't suppose; I know.'

'Well?'

'Defiant.'

Curious summary! Strangely good in a way – only—!

'You mean that I like to irritate people till they think I'm – what I'm not. But suppose' – her eyes confronted his – 'I really am.'

MacGown's grasp tightened.

'You're not; and I won't have it said.'

'You think this case will whitewash my – defiance?'

'I know what gossip is; and I know it buzzes about you. People who say things are going to be taught, once for all, that they can't.'

Marjorie Ferrar turned her gaze towards the still life on the dropped curtain, laughed and said:

'My dear man, you're dangerously provincial.'

'I know a straight line when I see one.'

'Yes; but there aren't any in London. You'd better hedge, Alec, or you'll be taking a toss over me.'

MacGown said, simply: 'I believe in you more than you believe in yourself.'

She was glad that the curtain rose just then, for she felt confused and rather touched.

Instead of confirming her desire to drop the case, that little talk gave her a feeling that by the case her marriage stood or fell. Alec would know where he was when it was over, and so would she! There would be precious little secret about her and she would either not be married to him, or at least not married under false pretences. Let it rip! It was, however, a terrible bore; especially the preparatory legal catechism she had now to undergo. What effect, for instance, had been produced among her friends and acquaintances by those letters? From the point of view of winning, the question was obviously not without importance. But how was she to tell? Two hostesses had cancelled weekend invitations: a rather prim Countess, and a Canadian millionairess married to a decaying baronet. It had not occurred to her before that this was the reason, but it might have been. Apart from them she would have to say she didn't know, people didn't tell you to your face what they heard or thought of you. They were going to try and make her out a piece of injured innocence! Good Lord! What if she declared her real faith in Court, and left them all in the soup! Her real faith – what was it? Not to let a friend down; not to give a man away; not to funk; to do things differently from other people; to be always on the go; not to be 'stuffy'; not to be dull! The whole thing was topsy-turvy! Well, she must keep her head!

Chapter Five

The Day

On the day of the case Soames rose, in Green Street, with a sort of sick impatience. Why wasn't it the day after!

Renewed interviews with very young Nicholas and Sir James Foskisson had confirmed the idea of defence by attack on modern morality. Foskisson was evidently going to put his heart into that – perhaps he'd suffered from it; and if he was anything like old Bobstay, who had just published his reminiscences at the age of eighty-two, that cat would lose her hair and give herself away. Yesterday afternoon Soames had taken an hour's look at Mr Justice Brane, and been very favourably impressed; the learned judge, though younger than himself – he had often briefed him in other times – looked old fashioned enough now for anything.

Having cleaned his teeth, put in his plate, and brushed his hair, Soames went into the adjoining room and told Annette she would be late. She always looked terribly young and well in bed, and this, though a satisfaction to him, he could never quite forgive. When he was gone, fifteen years hence, perhaps, she would still be under sixty, and might live another twenty years.

Having roused her sufficiently to say: 'You will have plenty of time to be fussy in that Court, Soames,' he went back and looked out of his window. The air smelled of spring – aggravating! He bathed and shaved with care – didn't want to go into the Box with a cut on his chin! – then went back to see that Annette was not putting on anything bright. He found her in pink underclothes.

'I should wear black,' he said. Annette regarded him above her hand-mirror. 'Whom do you want me to fascinate, Soames?'

'These people will bring their friends, I shouldn't wonder; anything conspicuous—'

'Don't be afraid; I shall not try to be younger than my daughter.'

Soames went out again. The French! Well, she had good taste in dress.

After breakfast he went off to Fleur's. Winifred and Imogen would look after Annette – they too were going to the Court – as if there were anything to enjoy about this business!

Spruce in his silk hat, he walked across the Green Park, conning over his evidence. No buds on the trees – a late year; and the Royal Family out of town! Passing the Palace, he thought: 'They're very popular!' He supposed they liked this great Empire group in front of them, all muscle and flesh and large animals! The Albert Memorial, and this – everybody ran them down; but, after all, peace and plenty – nothing modern about them! Emerging into Westminster, he cut his way through a smell of fried fish into the Parliamentary back-water of North Street, and, between its pleasant little houses, gazed steadily at the Wren Church. Never going inside any church except St Paul's, he derived a sort of strength from their outsides – churches were solid and stood back, and didn't seem to care what people thought of them! He felt a little better, rounding into South Square. The Dandie met him in the hall. Though he was not over fond of dogs, the breadth and solidity of this one always affected Soames pleasurably – better than that little Chinese abortion they used to have! This dog was a character – masterful and tenacious – you would get very little out of *him* in a witness-box! Looking up from the dog, he saw Michael and Fleur coming down the stairs. After hurriedly inspecting Michael's brown suit and speckled tie, his eyes came to anchor on his daughter's face. Pale but creamy, nothing modern – thank goodness! – no rouge, salve, powder, or eye-blacking; perfectly made up for her part! In a blue dress, too, very good taste, which must have taken some finding! The desire that she should not feel nervous stilled Soames's private qualms.

'Quite a smell of spring!' he said: 'Shall we start?'

While a cab was being summoned, he tried to put her at ease.

'I had a look at Brane yesterday; he's changed a good deal from

when I used to know him. I was one of the first to give him
briefs.'

'That's bad, isn't it, sir?' said Michael.

'How?'

'He'll be afraid of being thought grateful.'

Flippant, as usual!

'Our judges', he said, 'are a good lot, take them all round.'

'I'm sure they are. Do you know if he ever reads, sir?'

'How d'you mean – reads?'

'Fiction. We don't, in Parliament.'

'Nobody reads novels, except women,' said Soames. And he felt
Fleur's dress. 'You'll want a fur; that's flimsy.'

While she was getting the fur, he said to Michael: 'How did she
sleep?'

'Better than I did, sir.'

'That's a comfort, anyway. Here's the cab. Keep away from that
Scotchman.'

'I see him every day in the House, you know.'

'Ah!' said Soames; 'I forgot. You make nothing of that sort of
thing there, I believe.' And taking his daughter's arm, he led her
forth.

'I wonder if old Blythe will turn up,' he heard Michael say, when
they passed the office of *The Outpost*. It was the first remark made
in the cab, and, calling for no response, it was the last.

The Law Courts had their customary air, and people, in black and
blue, were hurrying into them. 'Beetletrap!' muttered Michael. Soames
rejected the simile with his elbow – for him they were just familiar
echoing space, concealed staircases, stuffy corridors, and the square
enclosures of one voice at a time.

Too early, they went slowly up the stairs. Really, it was weakminded! Here they had come – they and the other side – to get – what?
He was amazed at himself for not having insisted on Fleur's apolo-
gising. Time and again in the case of others, all this had appeared
quite natural – in the case of his own daughter, it now seemed almost
incredibly idiotic. He hurried her on, however, past lingering lawyers'
clerks, witnesses, whatnot. A few low words to an usher, and they

were inside, and sitting down. Very young Nicholas was already in
his place, and Soames so adjusted himself that there would only be
the thickness of Sir James, when he materialised, between them.
Turning to confer, he lived for a cosy moment in the past again, as
might some retired old cricketer taking block once more. Beyond
young Nicholas he quartered the assemblage with his glance. Yes,
people had got wind of it! He knew they would – with that cat
always in the public eye – quite a lot of furbelows up there at the
back, and more coming. He reversed himself abruptly; the Jury were
filing in – special, but a common-looking lot! Why were juries always
common-looking? He had never been on one himself. He glanced at
Fleur. There she sat, and what she was feeling he couldn't tell. As
for young Michael, his ears looked very pointed. And just then he
caught sight of Annette. She'd better not come and sit down here,
after all – the more there were of them in front, the more conspicuous it would be! So he shook his head at her, and waved towards
the back. Ah! She was going! She and Winifred and Imogen would
take up room – all rather broad in the beam; but there were still
gaps up there. And suddenly he saw the plaintiff and her lawyer and
MacGown; very spry they looked, and that insolent cat was smiling!
Careful not to glance in their direction, Soames saw them sit down,
some six feet off. Ah! and here came Counsel – Foskisson and Bullfry
together, thick as thieves. They'd soon be calling each other 'my
friend' now, and cutting each other's throats! He wondered if he
wouldn't have done better after all to have let the other side have
Foskisson, and briefed Bullfry – an ugly-looking customer, broad,
competent and leathery. He and Michael with Fleur between them,
and behind – Foskisson and his junior; Settlewhite and the Scotchman
with 'that cat' between them, and behind – Bullfry and his junior!
Only the Judge wanted now to complete the pattern! And here he
came! Soames gripped Fleur's arm and raised her with himself. Bob!
Down again! One side of Brane's face seemed a little fuller than the
other; Soames wondered if he had toothache, and how it would affect
the proceedings.

And now came the usual 'shivaree' about such and such a case,
and what would be taken next week, and so on. Well! that was over,

and the judge was turning his head this way and that, as if to see where the field was placed. Now Bullfry was up:

'If it please Your Lordship—!'

He was making the usual opening, with the usual flowery description of the plaintiff – granddaughter of a marquess, engaged to a future Prime Minister . . . or so you'd think! . . . prominent in the most brilliant circles, high-spirited, perhaps a thought too high-spirited . . . Baggage! . . . the usual smooth and sub-acid description of the defendant! . . . Rich and ambitious young married lady . . . Impudent beggar! . . . Jury would bear in mind that they were dealing in both cases with members of advanced Society, but they would bear in mind, too, that primary words had primary meanings and consequences, whatever the Society in which they were uttered. H'm! Very sketchy reference to the incident in Fleur's drawing room – minimised, of course – ha! an allusion to himself – man of property and standing – thank you for nothing! Reading the libellous letters now! Effect of them . . . very made-up, all that! . . . Plaintiff obliged to take action . . . Bunkum! 'I shall now call Mrs Ralph Ppynrryn.'

'How do you spell that name, Mr Bullfry?'

'With two p's, two y's, two n's and two r's, my lord.'

'I see.'

Soames looked at the owner of the name. Good-looking woman of the flibberty-gibbet type! He listened to her evidence with close attention. Her account of the incident in Fleur's drawing room seemed substantially correct. She had received the libellous letter two days later; had thought it her duty, as a friend, to inform Miss Ferrar. Should say, as a woman in Society, that this incident and these letters had done Miss Ferrar harm. Had talked it over with a good many people. A public incident. Much feeling excited. Had shown her letter to Mrs Maltese, and been shown one that she had received. Whole matter had become current gossip. H'm!

Bullfry down, and Foskisson up!

Soames adjusted himself. Now to see how the fellow shaped – the manner of a cross-examiner was so important! Well, he had seen worse – the eye, like frozen light, fixed on unoccupied space while the question was being asked, and coming round on to the witness for the answer; the mouth a little open, as if to swallow it; the tongue visible at times on the lower lip, the unoccupied hand clasping something under the gown behind.

'Now, Mrs – er – Ppynrryn. This incident, as my friend has called it, happened at the house of Mrs Mont, did it not? And how did you come there? As a friend. Quite so! And you have nothing against Mrs Mont? No. And you thought it advisable and kind, madam, to show this letter to the plaintiff and to other people – in fact, to foment this little incident to the best of your ability?' Eyes round!

'If a friend of mine received such a letter about me, I should expect her to tell me that the writer was going about abusing me.'

'Even if your friend knew of the provocation and was also a friend of the letter-writer?'

'Yes.'

'Now, madam, wasn't it simply that the sensation of this little quarrel was too precious to be burked? It would have been so easy, wouldn't it, to have torn the letter up and said nothing about it? You don't mean to suggest that it made you think any the worse of Miss Ferrar – you knew her too well, didn't you?'

'Ye-es.'

'Exactly. As a friend of both parties you knew that these expressions were just spleen and not to be taken seriously.'

'I can't say that.'

'Oh! You regarded them as serious? Am I to take it that you thought they touched the ham-bone? In other words, that they were true?'

'Certainly not.'

'Could they do Miss Ferrar any harm if they were palpably untrue?'

'I think they could.'

'Not with you – you were a friend?'

'Not with me.'

'But with other people, who would never have heard of them but for you. In fact, madam, you enjoyed the whole thing. Did you?'

'Enjoyed? No.'

'You regarded it as your duty to spread this letter? Don't you enjoy doing your duty?'

The dry cackle within Soames stopped at his lips.

Foskisson down, and Bullfry up!

'It is, in fact, your experience, Mrs Ppynrryn, as well as that of most of us not so well constituted, perhaps, as my learned friend, that duty is sometimes painful.'

'Yes.'

'Thank you. Mrs Edward Maltese.'

During the examination of this other young woman, who seemed to be dark and solid, Soames tried to estimate the comparative effect produced by Fleur and 'that cat' on the four jurymen whose eyes seemed to stray towards beauty. He had come to no definite conclusion, when Sir James Foskisson rose to cross-examine.

'Tell me, Mrs Maltese, which do you consider the most serious allegation among those complained of?'

'The word "treacherous" in my letter, and the expression "a snake of the first water" in the letter to Mrs Ppynrryn.'

'More serious than the others?'

'Yes.'

'That is where you can help me, madam. The circle you move in is not exactly the plaintiff's, perhaps?'

'Not exactly.'

'Intersecting, um?'

'Yes.'

'Now, in which section, yours or the plaintiff's, would you say the expression "she hasn't a moral about her" would be the more, or shall we say the less, damning?'

'I can't say.'

'I only want your opinion. Do you think your section of Society as advanced as Miss Ferrar's?'

'Perhaps not.'

'It's well known, isn't it, that her circle is very free and easy?'

'I suppose so.'

'Still, *your* section is pretty advanced – I mean, you're not "stuffy"?'

'Not what, Sir James?'

'Stuffy, my lord; it's an expression a good deal used in modern Society.'

'What does it mean?'

'Strait-laced, my lord.'

'I see. Well, he's asking you if you're stuffy?'

'No, my lord. I hope not.'

'You hope not. Go on, Sir James.'

'Not being stuffy, you wouldn't be exactly worried if somebody said to you: "My dear, you haven't a moral about you"?'

'Not if it was said as charmingly as that.'

'Now come, Mrs Maltese, does such an expression, said charmingly or the reverse, convey any blame to you or to your friends?'

'If the reverse, yes.'

'Am I to take it that the conception of morality in your circle is the same as in – my lord's?'

'How is the witness to answer that, Sir James?'

'Well, in your circle are you shocked when your friends are divorced, or when they go off together for a week in Paris, say, or wherever they find convenient?'

'Shocked? Well, I suppose one needn't be shocked by what one wouldn't do oneself.'

'In fact, you're not shocked?'

'I don't know that I'm shocked by anything.'

'That would be being stuffy, wouldn't it?'

'Perhaps.'

'Well, will you tell me then – if that's the state of mind in your circle; and you said, you know, that your circle is less free and easy than the plaintiff's – how it is possible that such words as "she hasn't a moral about her" can have done the plaintiff any harm?'

'The whole world isn't in our circles.'

'No. I suggest that only a very small portion of the world is in your circles. But do you tell me that you or the plaintiff pay any—?'

'How can she tell, Sir James, what the plaintiff pays?'

'That *you*, then, pay any attention to what people outside your circle think?'

Soames moved his head twice. The fellow was doing it well. And his eye caught Fleur's face turned towards the witness; a little smile was curling her lip.

'I don't personally pay much attention even to what anybody *in* my circle thinks.'

'Have you more independence of character than the plaintiff, should you say?'

'I dare say I've got as much.'

'Is she notoriously independent?'

'Yes.'

'Thank you, Mrs Maltese.'

Foskisson down, Bullfry up!

'I call the plaintiff, my lord.'

Soames uncrossed his legs.

Chapter Six

In The Box

*M*arjorie Ferrar stepped into the Box, not exactly nervous, and only just 'made-up'. The papers would record a black costume with chinchilla fur and a black hat. She kissed the air in front of the book, took a deep breath, and turned to Mr Bullfry.

For the last five days she had resented more and more the way this case had taken charge of her. She had initiated it, and it had completely deprived her of initiative. She had, in fact, made the old discovery, that when the machinery of quarrel is once put in motion, much more than pressure of the starting button is required to stop its revolutions. She was feeling that it would serve Alec and the lawyers right if all went wrong.

The voice of Mr Bullfry, carefully adjusted, soothed her. His questions were familiar, and with each answer her confidence increased, her voice sounded clear and pleasant in her ears. And she stood at ease, making her figure as boyish as she could. Her performance, she felt, was interesting to the judge, the jury, and all those people up there, whom she could dimly see. If only 'that little snob' had not been seated, expressionless, between her and her Counsel! When at length Mr Bullfry sat down and Sir James Foskisson got up, she almost succumbed to the longing to powder her nose. Clasping the Box, she resisted it, and while he turned his papers, and hitched his gown, the first tremor of the morning passed down her spine. At least he might look at her when he spoke!

'Have you ever been party to an action before, Miss Ferrar?'

'No.'

'You quite understand, don't you, that you are on your oath?'

'Quite.'

'You have told my friend that you had no animus against Mrs Mont. Look at this marked paragraph in the *Evening Sun* of October 3rd. Did you write that?'

Marjorie Ferrar felt exactly as if she had stepped out of a conservatory into an East wind. Did they know everything, then?

'Yes; I wrote it.'

'It ends thus: "The enterprising little lady is losing no chance of building up her salon on the curiosity which ever surrounds any buccaneering in politics." Is the reference to Mrs Mont?'

'Yes.'

'Not very nice, is it – of a friend?'

'I don't see any harm in it.'

'The sort of thing, in fact, you'd like written about yourself?'

'The sort of thing I should expect if I were doing the same thing.'

'That's not quite an answer, but let me put it like this: The sort of thing your father would like to read about you, is it?'

'My father would never read that column.'

'Then it surprises you to hear that Mrs Mont's father did? Do you write many of these cheery little paragraphs about your friends?'

'Not many.'

'Every now and then, eh? And do they remain your friends?'

'It's not easy in Society to tell who's a friend and who isn't.'

'I quite agree, Miss Ferrar. You have admitted making one or two critical – that was your word, I think – remarks concerning Mrs Mont, in her own house. Do you go to many houses and talk disparagingly of your hostess?'

'No; and in any case I don't expect to be eavesdropped.'

'I see; so long as you're not found out, it's all right, eh? Now, on this first Wednesday in October last, at Mrs Mont's, in speaking to this gentleman, Mr Philip – er – Quinsey, did you use the word "snob" of your hostess?'

'I don't think so.'

'Be careful. You heard the evidence of Mrs Ppynrryn and Mrs Maltese. Mrs Maltese said, you remember, that Mr Forsyte – that is

Mrs Mont's father – said to you on that occasion: "You called my daughter a snob in her own house, madam – be so kind as to withdraw; you are a traitress." Is that a correct version?'

'Probably.'

'Do you suggest that he invented the word "snob"?'

'I suggest he was mistaken.'

'Not a nice word, is it – "snob"? Was there any other reason why he should call you a traitress?'

'My remarks weren't meant for his ears. I don't remember exactly what I said.'

'Well, we shall have Mr Forsyte in the box to refresh your memory as to exactly what you said. But I put it to you that you called her a snob, not once but twice, during that little conversation?'

'I've told you I don't remember; he shouldn't have listened.'

'Very well! So you feel quite happy about having written that paragraph and said nasty things of Mrs Mont behind her back in her own drawing room?'

Marjorie Ferrar grasped the Box till the blood tingled in her palms. His voice was maddening.

'Yet it seems, Miss Ferrar, that you object to others saying nasty things about you in return. Who advised you to bring this action?'

'My father first; and then my fiancé.'

'Sir Alexander MacGown. Does he move in the same circles as you?'

'No; he moves in Parliamentary circles.'

'Exactly; and he wouldn't know, would he, the canons of conduct that rule in your circle?'

'There are no circles so definite as that.'

'Always willing to learn, Miss Ferrar. But tell me, do you know what Sir Alexander's Parliamentary friends think about conduct and morality?'

'I can guess. I don't suppose there's much difference.'

'Are you suggesting, Miss Ferrar, that responsible public men take the same light-hearted view of conduct and morals as you?'

'Aren't you rather assuming, Sir James, that her view *is* light-hearted?'

'As to conduct, my lord, I submit that her answers have shown the very light-hearted view she takes of the obligations incurred by the acceptance of hospitality, for instance. I'm coming to morals now.'

'I think you'd better, before drawing your conclusions. What have public men to do with it?'

'I'm suggesting, my lord, that this lady is making a great to-do about words which a public man, or any ordinary citizen, would have a perfect right to resent, but which she, with her views, has no right whatever to resent.'

'You must prove her views then. Go on!'

Marjorie Ferrar, relaxed for a moment, gathered herself again. Her views!

'Tell me, Miss Ferrar – we all know now the meaning of the word "stuffy" – are public men "stuffier" than you?'

'They may say they are.'

'You think them hypocrites?'

'I don't think anything at all about them.'

'Though you're going to marry one? You are complaining of the words: "She hasn't a moral about her." Have you read this novel *Canthar*?' He was holding up a book.

'I think so.'

'Don't you know?'

'I've skimmed it.'

'Taken off the cream, eh? Read it sufficiently to form an opinion?'

'Yes.'

'Would you agree with the view of it expressed in this letter to a journal? "The book breaks through the British 'stuffiness', which condemns any frank work of art – and a good thing too!" It is a good thing?'

'Yes. I hate Grundyism.'

'"It is undoubtedly Literature." The word is written with a large L. Should you say it was?'

'Literature – yes. Not great literature, perhaps.'

'But it ought to be published?'

'I don't see why not.'

'You know that it is not published in England?'

'Yes.'

'But it ought to be?'

'It isn't everybody's sort of book, of course.'

'Don't evade the question, please. In your opinion ought this novel *Canthar* to be published in England? . . . Take your time, Miss Ferrar.'

The brute lost nothing! Just because she had hesitated a moment trying to see where he was leading her.

'Yes, I think literature should be free.'

'You wouldn't sympathise with its suppression, if it were published?'

'No.'

'You wouldn't approve of the suppression of any book on the ground of mere morals?'

'I can't tell you unless I see the book. People aren't bound to read books, you know.'

'And you think your opinion generally on this subject is that of public men and ordinary citizens?'

'No; I suppose it isn't.'

'But your view would be shared by most of your own associates?'

'I should hope so.'

'A contrary opinion would be "stuffy", wouldn't it?'

'If you like to call it so. It's not my word.'

'What is your word, Miss Ferrar?'

'I think I generally say "ga-ga".'

'Do you know, I'm afraid the Court will require a little elaboration of that.'

'Not for me, Sir James; I'm perfectly familiar with the word; it means "in your dotage".'

'The Bench is omniscient, my lord. Then anyone, Miss Ferrar, who didn't share the opinion of yourself and your associates in the matter of this book would be "ga-ga", that is to say, in his or her dotage?'

'Aesthetically.'

'Ah! I thought we should arrive at that word. You, I suppose, don't connect art with life?'

'No.'

'Don't think it has any effect on life?'

'It oughtn't to.'

'When a man's theme in a book is extreme incontinence, depicted with all due emphasis, that wouldn't have any practical effect on his readers, however young?'

'I can't say about other people, it wouldn't have any effect on me.'

'You are emancipated, in fact.'

'I don't know what you mean by that.'

'Isn't what you are saying about the divorce of art from life the merest claptrap; and don't you know it?'

'I certainly don't.'

'Let me put it another way: Is it possible for those who believe in current morality, to hold your view that art has no effect on life?'

'Quite possible; if they are cultured.'

'Cultured! Do you believe in current morality yourself?'

'I don't know what you call current morality.'

'I will tell you, Miss Ferrar. I should say, for instance, it was current morality that women should not have liaisons before they're married, and should not have them after.'

'What about men?'

'Thank you; I was coming to men. And that men should at least not have them after.'

'I shouldn't say that was *current* morality at all.'

In yielding to that satiric impulse she knew at once she had made a mistake – the judge had turned his face towards her. He was speaking.

'Do I understand you to imply that in your view it is moral for women to have liaisons before marriage, and for men and women to have them after?'

'I think it's current morality, my lord.'

'I'm not asking you about current morality; I'm asking whether in *your* view it is moral?'

'I think many people think it's all right, who don't say it, yet.'

She was conscious of movement throughout the jury; and of a

little flump in the well of the Court. Sir Alexander had dropped his hat. The sound of a nose being loudly blown broke the stillness; the face of Bullfry K.C. was lost to her view. She felt the blood mounting in her cheeks.

'Answer my question, please. Do *you* say it's all right?'

'I – I think it depends.'

'On what?'

'On – on circumstances, environment, temperament; all sorts of things.'

'Would it be all right for you?'

Marjorie Ferrar became very still. 'I can't answer that question, my lord.'

'You mean – you don't want to?'

'I mean I don't know.'

And, with a feeling as if she had withdrawn her foot from a bit of breaking ice, she saw Bullfry's face re-emerge from his handkerchief.

'Very well. Go on, Sir James!'

'Anyway, we may take it, Miss Ferrar, that those of us who say we don't believe in these irregularities are hypocrites in your view?'

'Why can't you be fair?'

He was looking at her now; and she didn't like him any the better for it.

'I shall prove myself fair before I've done, Miss Ferrar.'

'You've got your work cut out, haven't you?'

'Believe me, madam, it will be better for you not to indulge in witticism. According to you, there is no harm in a book like *Canthar*?'

'There ought to be none.'

'You mean if we were all as aesthetically cultured – as you.' – Sneering beast! – 'But are we?'

'No.'

'Then there is harm. But you wouldn't mind its being done. I don't propose, my lord, to read from this extremely unpleasant novel. Owing apparently to its unsavoury reputation, a copy of it now costs nearly seven pounds. And I venture to think that is in itself an answer to the plaintiff's contention that "art" so called has no effect on life.

We have gone to the considerable expense of buying copies, and I shall ask that during the luncheon interval the jury may read some dozen marked passages.'

'Have you a copy for me, Sir James?'

'Yes, my lord.'

'And one for Mr Bullfry? . . . If there is any laughter, I shall have the Court cleared. Go on.'

'You know the "Ne Plus Ultra" Play-Producing Society, Miss Ferrar? It exists to produce advanced plays, I believe.'

'Plays – I don't know about "advanced".'

'Russian plays, and the Restoration dramatists?'

'Yes.'

'And you have played in them?'

'Sometimes.'

'Do you remember a play called "The Plain Dealer", by Wycherley, given at a matinee on January 7th last – did you play in that the part of Olivia?'

'Yes.'

'A nice part?'

'A very good part.'

'I said "nice".'

'I don't like the word.'

'Too suggestive of "prunes and prisms", Miss Ferrar? Is it the part of a modest woman?'

'No.'

'Is it, toward the end, extremely immodest? I allude to the dark scene.'

'I don't know about extremely.'

'Anyway, you felt no hesitation about undertaking and playing the part – a little thing like that doesn't worry you?'

'I don't know why it should. If it did, I shouldn't act.'

'You don't act for money?'

'No; for pleasure.'

'Then, of course, you can refuse any part you like?'

'If I did, I shouldn't have any offered me.'

'Don't quibble, please. You took the part of Olivia not for money but for pleasure. You enjoyed playing it?'

'Pretty well.'

'I'm afraid I shall have to ask the jury, my lord, to run their eyes over the dark scene in "The Plain Dealer".'

'Are you saying, Sir James, that a woman who plays an immoral part is not moral – that would asperse a great many excellent reputations.'

'No, my lord; I'm saying that here is a young lady so jealous of her good name in the eyes of the world, that she brings a libel action because someone has said in a private letter that she "hasn't a moral about her". And at the same time she is reading and approving books like this *Canthar*, playing parts like that of Olivia in "The Plain Dealer", and, as I submit, living in a section of Society that really doesn't know the meaning of the word morals, that looks upon morals, in fact, rather as we look upon measles. It's my contention, my lord, that the saying in my client's letter: "She hasn't a moral about her", is rather a compliment to the plaintiff than otherwise.'

'Do you mean that it was intended as a compliment?'

'No, no, my lord.'

'Well, you want the jury to read that scene. You will have a busy luncheon interval, gentlemen. Go on, Sir James.'

'Now, Miss Ferrar – my friend made a point of the fact that you are engaged to a wealthy and highly respected Member of Parliament. How long have you been engaged to him?'

'Six months.'

'You have no secrets from him, I suppose?'

'Why should I answer that?'

'Why should she, Sir James?'

'I am quite content to leave it at her reluctance, my lord.'

Sneering brute! As if everybody hadn't secrets from everybody!

'Your engagement was not made public till January, was it?'

'No.'

'May I take it that you were not sure of your own mind till then?'

'If you like.'

'Now, Miss Ferrar, did you bring this action because of your good name? Wasn't it because you were hard up?'

She was conscious again of blood in her cheeks.

'No.'

'*Were* you hard up when you brought it?'

'Yes.'

'Very?'

'Not worse than I have been before.'

'I put it to you that you owed a great deal of money, and were hard pressed.'

'If you like.'

'I'm glad you've admitted that, Miss Ferrar; otherwise I should have had to prove it. And you didn't bring this action with a view to paying some of your debts?'

'No.'

'Did you in early January become aware that you were not likely to get any sum in settlement of this suit?'

'I believe I was told that an offer was withdrawn.'

'And do you know why?'

'Yes; because Mrs Mont wouldn't give the apology I asked for.'

'Exactly! And was it a coincidence that you thereupon made up your mind to marry Sir Alexander MacGown?'

'A coincidence?'

'I mean the announcement of your engagement, you know?'

Brute!

'It had nothing to do with this case.'

'Indeed! Now when you brought this action did you really care one straw whether people thought you moral or not?'

'I brought it chiefly because I was called "a snake".'

'Please answer my question.'

'It isn't so much what *I* cared, as what my friends cared.'

'But their view of morality is much what yours is – thoroughly accommodating?'

'Not my fiancé's.

'Ah! no. He doesn't move in your circle, you said. But the rest of your friends. You're not ashamed of your own accommodating philosophy, are you?'

'No.'

'Then why be ashamed of it for them?'

'How can I tell what *their* philosophy is?'

'How can she, Sir James?'

'As your lordship pleases. Now, Miss Ferrar! You like to stand up for your views, I hope. Let me put your philosophy to you in a nutshell: You believe, don't you, in the full expression of your personality; it would be your duty, wouldn't it, to break through any convention – I don't say law – but any so-called moral convention that cramped you?'

'I never said I had a philosophy.'

'Don't run away from it, please.'

'I'm not in the habit of running away.'

'I'm so glad of that. You believe in being the sole judge of your own conduct?'

'Yes.'

'You're not alone in that view, are you?'

'I shouldn't think so.'

'It's the view, in fact, of what may be called the forward wing of modern Society, isn't it – the wing you belong to, and are proud of belonging to? And in that section of Society – so long as you don't break the actual law – you think and do as you like, eh?'

'One doesn't always act up to one's principles.'

'Quite so. But among your associates, even if you and they don't always act up to it, it *is* a principle, isn't it, to judge for yourselves and go your own ways without regard to convention?'

'More or less.'

'And, living in that circle, with that belief, you have the effrontery to think the words: "She hasn't a moral about her", entitles you to damages?'

Her voice rang out angrily: 'I have morals. They may not be yours, but they may be just as good, perhaps better. I'm not a hypocrite, anyway.'

Again she saw him look at her, there was a gleam in his eyes; and she knew she had made another mistake.

'We'll leave my morals out of the question, Miss Ferrar. But we'll go a little further into what you say are yours. In your own words, it should depend on temperament, circumstances, environment, whether you conform to morality or not?'

She stood silent, biting her lip.

'Answer, please.'

She inclined her head. 'Yes.'

'Very good!' He had paused, turning over his papers, and she drew back in the box. She had lost her temper – had made him lose his; at all costs she must keep her head now! In this moment of search for her head she took in everything – expressions, gestures, even the atmosphere – the curious dramatic emanation from a hundred and more still faces; she noted the one lady juryman, the judge breaking the nib of a quill, with his eyes turned away from it as if looking at something that had run across the well of the Court. Yes, and down there, the lengthening lip of Mr Settlewhite, Michael's face turned up at her with a rueful frown, Fleur Mont's mask with red spots in the cheeks, Alec's clenched hands, and his eyes fixed on her. A sort of comic intensity about it all! If only she were the size of Alice in 'Wonderland', and could take them all in her hands and shake them like a pack of cards – so motionless, there, at her expense! That sarcastic brute had finished fiddling with his papers, and she moved forward again to attention in the Box.

'Now, Miss Ferrar, his lordship put a general question to you which you did not feel able to answer. I am going to put it in a way that will be easier for you. Whether or no it was right for you to have one' – she saw Michael's hand go up to his face – 'have you *in fact* had a – liaison?' And from some tone in his voice, from the look on his face, she could tell for certain that he knew she had.

With her back to the wall, she had not even a wall to her back. Ten, twenty, thirty seconds – judge, jury, that old fox with his hand under the tail of his gown, and his eyes averted! Why did she not spit out the indignant: No! which she had so often rehearsed? Suppose he proved it – as he had said he would prove her debts?

'Take your time, Miss Ferrar. You know what a liaison is, of course.'

Brute! On the verge of denial, she saw Michael lean across, and heard his whisper: 'Stop this!' And then 'that little snob' looked up at her – the scrutiny was knowing and contemptuous: 'Now hear her lie!' it seemed to say. And she answered, quickly: 'I consider your question insulting.'

'Oh! come, Miss Ferrar, after your own words! After what—'

'Well! I shan't answer it.'

A rustle, a whispering in the Court.

'You won't answer it?'

'No.'

'Thank you, Miss Ferrar.' Could a voice be more sarcastic? The brute was sitting down.

Marjorie Ferrar stood defiant, with no ground under her feet. What next? Her counsel was beckoning. She descended from the Box, and, passing her adversaries, resumed her seat next her betrothed How red and still he was! She heard the judge say:

'I shall break for lunch now, Mr Bullfry,' saw him rise and go out, and the jury getting up. The whispering and rustling in the Court swelled to a buzz. She stood up. Mr Settlewhite was speaking to her.

Chapter Seven

'Fed Up'

Guided by him into a room designed to shelter witnesses, Marjorie Ferrar looked at her lawyer.

'Well?'

'An unfortunate refusal, Miss Ferrar – very. I'm afraid the effect on the jury may be fatal. If we can settle it now, I should certainly say we'd better.'

'It's all the same to me.'

'In that case you may take it I shall settle. I'll go and see Sir Alexander and Mr Bullfry at once.'

'How do I get out quietly?'

'Down those stairs. You'll find cabs in Lincoln's Inn Fields. Excuse me,' he made her a grave little bow and stalked away.

Marjorie Ferrar did not take a cab; she walked. If her last answer had been fatal, on the whole she was content. She had told no lies to speak of, had stood up to 'that sarcastic beast', and given him sometimes as good as she had got. Alec! Well, she couldn't help it! He had insisted on her going into Court; she hoped he liked it now she'd been! Buying a newspaper, she went into a restaurant and read a description of herself, accompanied by a photograph. She ate a good lunch, and then continued her walk along Piccadilly. Passing into the Park, she sat down under a tree coming into bud, and drew the smoke of a cigarette quietly into her lungs. The Row was almost deserted. A few persons of little or no consequence occupied a few chairs. A riding mistress was teaching a small boy to trot. Some sparrows and a pigeon alone seemed to take a distant interest in her. The air smelled of spring. She sat some time with the pleasant feeling that nobody in the world knew where she was. Odd, when you thought of it – millions of people every day, leaving their houses, offices, shops, on their way to the next place, were as lost to the world as stones in a pond! Would it be nice to disappear permanently, and taste life incognita? Bertie Curfew was going to Moscow again. Would he take her as secretary, and *bonne amie*? Bertie Curfew – she had only pretended to be tired of him! The thought brought her face to face with the future. Alec! Explanations! It was hardly the word! He had a list of her debts, and had said he would pay them as a wedding-present. But – if there wasn't to be a wedding? Thank God, she had some ready money. The carefully 'laid-up' four-year-old in her father's stable had won yesterday. She had dribbled 'a pony' on at a nice price. She rose and sauntered along, distending her bust – in defiance of the boylike fashion, which, after all, was on the wane – to take in the full of a sweet wind.

Leaving the Park, she came to South Kensington station and bought another paper. It had a full account under the headlines: 'Modern Morality Attacked.' 'Miss Marjorie Ferrar in the Box.' It seemed funny to stand there reading those words among people who were reading the same without knowing her from Eve, except, perhaps, by her clothes. Continuing her progress towards Wren Street, she turned her latchkey in the door, and saw a hat. Waiting for her already! She took her time; and, pale from powder, as though she had gone through much, entered the studio.

MacGown was sitting with his head in his hands. She felt real pity for him – too strong, too square, too vital for that attitude! He raised his face.

· 'Well, Alec!'

'Tell me the truth, Marjorie. I'm in torment.'

She almost envied him the depth of his feeling, however unreasonable after her warnings. But she said, ironically:

'Who was it knew me better than I knew myself?'

In the same dull voice he repeated:

'The truth, Marjorie, the truth!'

But why should she go into the confessional? Was he entitled to

her past? His rights stopped at her future. It was the old business –
men expecting more from women than they could give them. Inequality
of the sexes. Something in that, perhaps, in the old days when women
bore children, and men didn't; but now that women knew all about
sex and only bore children when they wanted to, and not always
even then, why should men be freer?

And she said, slowly: 'In exchange for your adventures I'll tell
you mine.'

'For God's sake don't mock me; I've had hell these last hours.'

His face showed it, and she said with feeling:

'I said you'd be taking a toss over me, Alec. Why on earth did
you insist on my bringing this case? You've had your way, and now
you don't like it.'

'It's true, then?'

'Yes. Why not?'

He uttered a groan, recoiling till his back was against the wall,
as if afraid of being loose in the room.

'Who was he?'

'Oh! no! That I can't possibly tell you. And how many affairs
have you had?'

He paid no attention. He wouldn't! He knew she didn't love him;
and such things only mattered if you loved! Ah! well! His agony was
a tribute to her, after all!

'You're well out of me,' she said, sullenly; and, sitting down, she
lighted a cigarette. A scene! How hateful! Why didn't he go? She'd
rather he'd be violent than deaf and dumb and blind like this.

'Not that American fellow?'

She could not help a laugh.

'Oh! no, poor boy!'

'How long did it last?'

'Nearly a year.'

'My God!'

He had rushed to the door. If only he would open it and go! That
he could feel so violently! That figure by the door was just not mad!
His stuffy passions!

And then he did pull the door open and was gone.

She threw herself at full length on the divan; not from lassitude, exactly, nor despair – from a feeling rather as if nothing mattered. How stupid and pre-war! Why couldn't he, like her, be free, be supple, take life as it came? Passions, prejudices, principles, pity – old-fashioned as the stuffy clothes worn when she was a tot. Well! Good riddance! Fancy living in the same house, sharing the same bed, with a man so full of the primitive that he could 'go off his chump' with jealousy about her! Fancy living with a man who took life so seriously that he couldn't even see himself doing it! Life was a cigarette to be inhaled and thrown away, a dance to be danced out. On with that dance! . . . Yes, but she couldn't let him pay her debts, now, even if he wanted to. Married, she would have repaid him with her body; as it was – no! Oh! why didn't someone die and leave her something? What a bore it all was! And she lay still, listening to the tea-time sounds of a quiet street – taxis rounding the corner from the river; the dog next door barking at the postman; that one-legged man – ex-Service – who came most afternoons and played on a poor fiddle. He expected her shilling – unhappy fellow! – she'd have to get up and give it him. She went to the little side window that looked on to the street, and suddenly recoiled. Francis Wilmot in the doorway with his hand up to the bell! Another scene! No, really! This was too much! There went the bell! No time to say 'Not at home'! Well, let them all come – round her past, like bees round a honey-pot!

'Mr Francis Wilmot.'

He stood there, large as the life he had nearly resigned – a little thinner, that was all.

'Well, Francis,' she said, 'I thought you were "through with that fool business"?'

Francis Wilmot came gravely up and took her hand. 'I sail tomorrow.'

Sail! Well, she could put up with that. He seemed to her just a thin, pale young man with dark hair and eyes and no juices in his system.

'I read the evening papers. I wondered if, perhaps, you'd wish to see me.'

Was he mocking her? But he wore no smile; there was no bitterness in his voice; and, though he was looking at her intently, she could not tell from his face whether he still had any feeling.

'You think I owe you something? I know I treated you very badly.'

He looked rather as if she'd hit him.

'For heaven's sake, Francis, don't say you've come out of chivalry. That'd be too funny.'

'I don't follow you; I just thought, perhaps, you didn't like to answer that question about a love-affair – because of me.'

Marjorie Ferrar broke into hysterical laughter.

'Señor Don Punctilio! Because of you? No, no, my dear!'

Francis Wilmot drew back, and made her a little bow.

'I shouldn't have come,' he said.

She had a sudden return of feeling for that slim unusual presence, with its grace and its dark eyes.

'I'm a free-lance again now, Francis, anyway.'

A long moment went by, and then he made her another little bow. It was a clear withdrawal.

'Then for God's sake,' she said, 'go away! I'm fed up!' And she turned her back on him.

When she looked round, he *had* gone, and that surprised her. He was a new variety, or a dead one, dug up! He didn't know the rudiments of life – old-fashioned, *à faire rire*! And, back at full length on the divan, she brooded. Well, her courage was 'not out'! To-morrow was Bella Magussie's 'At Home', to meet – some idiot. Everybody would be there, and so would she!

Chapter Eight

Fantoches

*W*hen Michael, screwed towards Sir James Foskisson's averted face, heard the words: 'Well, I shan't answer,' he spun round. It was just as if she had said: 'Yes, I have.'

The judge was looking at her, everyone looking at her. Wasn't Bullfry going to help her? No! He was beckoning her out of the Box. Michael half rose, as she passed him. By George! He was sorry for MacGown! There he sat, poor devil! – with everyone getting up all round him, still, and red as a turkey-cock.

Fleur! Michael looked at her face, slightly flushed, her gloved hands clasped in her lap, her eyes fixed on the ground. Had his whisper: 'Stop this!' his little abortive bow, offended her? How could one have helped sympathising with the 'Pet of the Panjoys' in so tight a place! Fleur must see that! The Court was emptying – fine birds, many – he could see her mother and her aunt and cousin, and Old Forsyte, talking with Foskisson. Ah! he had finished; was speaking: 'We can go now.'

They followed him along the corridor, down the stairs, into the air.

'We've time for a snack,' Soames was saying. 'Come in here!'

In one of several kennels without roofs in a celebrated room with a boarded floor, they sat down.

'Three chump chops, sharp,' said Soames, and staring at the cruet-stand, added: 'She's cooked her goose. They'll drop it like a hot potato. I've told Foskisson he can settle, with both sides paying their own costs. It's more than they deserve.'

'He ought never to have asked that question, sir.'

Fleur looked up sharply.

'Really, Michael!'

'Well, darling, we agreed he shouldn't. Why didn't Bullfry help her out, sir?'

'Only too glad to get her out of the Box; the judge would have asked her himself in another minute. It's a complete fiasco, thank God!'

'Then we've won?' said Fleur.

'Unless I'm a Dutchman,' answered Soames.

'I'm not so sure,' muttered Michael.

'I tell you it's all over; Bullfry'll never go on with it.'

'I didn't mean that, sir.'

Fleur said acidly: 'Then what *do* you mean, Michael?'

'I don't think we shall be forgiven, that's all.'

'What for?'

'Well, I dare say I'm all wrong. Sauce, sir?'

'Worcester – yes. This is the only place in London where you can rely on a floury potato. Waiter – three glasses of port, quick!'

After fifteen minutes of concentrated mastication, they returned to the Court.

'Wait here,' said Soames, in the hall; 'I'll go up and find out.'

In that echoing space, where a man's height was so inconsiderable, Fleur and Michael stood, not speaking, for some time.

'She couldn't know that Foskisson had been told not to follow it up, of course,' he said, at last. 'Still, she must have expected the question. She should have told a good one and have done with it. I couldn't help feeling sorry for her.'

'You'd feel sorry for a flea that bit you, Michael. What do you mean by our not being forgiven?'

'Well! The drama was all on her side, and it's drama that counts. Besides, there's her engagement!'

'That'll be broken off.'

'Exactly! And if it is, she'll have sympathy; while if it isn't, he'll have it. Anyway, we shan't. Besides, you know, she stood up for what we all really believe nowadays.'

'Speak for yourself.'

'Well, don't we talk of everyone being free?'

'Yes, but is there any connection between what we say and what we do?'

'No,' said Michael.

And just then Soames returned.

'Well, sir?'

'As I told you, Bullfry caught at it. They've settled. It's a moral victory.'

'Oh! not moral, I hope, sir.'

'It's cost a pretty penny, anyway,' said Soames, looking at Fleur. 'Your mother's quite annoyed – she's no sense of proportion. Very clever the way Foskisson made that woman lose her temper.'

'He lost his, at the end. That's his excuse, I suppose.'

'Well,' said Soames, 'it's all over! Your mother's got the car; we'll take a taxi.'

On the drive back to South Square, taking precisely the same route, there was precisely the same silence.

When a little later Michael went over to the House, he was edified by posters.

'Society Libel Action.'

'Marquess's Granddaughter and K.C.'

'Dramatic Evidence.'

'Modern Morality!'

All over – was it? With publicity – in Michael's opinion – it had but just begun! Morality! What was it – who had it, and what did they do with it? How would he have answered those questions himself? Who could answer them, nowadays, by rote or rule? Not he, or Fleur! They had been identified with the Inquisition, and what was their position, now? False, if not odious! He passed into the House. But, try as he would, he could not fix his attention on the Purity of Food, and passed out again. With a curious longing for his father, he walked rapidly down Whitehall. Drawing blank at 'Snooks' and The Aeroplane, he tried the Parthenaeum as a last resort. Sir Lawrence was in a corner of a forbidden room, reading a life of Lord Palmerston. He looked up at his son.

'Ah! Michael! They don't do justice to old Pam. A man without frills, who worked like a nigger. But we mustn't talk here!' And he pointed to a member who seemed awake. 'Shall we take a turn before the old gentleman over there has a fit? The books here are camouflage; it's really a dormitory.'

He led the way, with Michael retailing the events of the morning.

'Foskisson?' said Sir Lawrence, entering the Green Park. 'He was a nice little chap when I left Winchester. To be professionally in the right is bad for a man's character – counsel, parsons, policemen, they all suffer from it. Judges, High Priests, Arch-Inspectors, aren't so bad – they've suffered from it so long that they've lost consciousness.'

'It was a full house,' said Michael, glumly, 'and the papers have got hold of it.'

'They would.' And Sir Lawrence pointed to the ornamental water. 'These birds', he said, 'remind me of China. By the way, I met your friend Desert yesterday at The Aeroplane – he's more interesting now that he's dropped Poetry for the East. Everybody ought to drop something. I'm too old now, but if I'd dropped baronetcy in time, I could have made quite a good contortionist.'

'What would you recommend for us in the House?' asked Michael, with a grin.

'Postmanship, my dear – carrying on, you know; a certain importance, large bags, dogs to bark at you, no initiative, and conversation on every doorstep. By the way, do you see Desert?'

'I have seen him.'

Sir Lawrence screwed up his eyes.

'The providential,' he said, 'doesn't happen twice.'

Michael coloured; he had not suspected his father of such shrewd observation. Sir Lawrence swung his cane.

'Your man Boddick,' he said, 'has persuaded some of his hens to lay; he's giving us quite good eggs.'

Michael admired his reticence. But somehow that unexpected slanting allusion to a past domestic crisis roused the feeling that for so long now had been curled like a sleepy snake in his chest, that another crisis was brewing and must soon be faced.

'Coming along for tea, sir? Kit had tummy-ache this morning. How's your last book doing? Does old Danby advertise it properly?'

'No,' said Sir Lawrence, 'no; he's keeping his head wonderfully; the book is almost dead.'

'I'm glad I dropped *him*, anyway,' said Michael, with emphasis. 'I suppose, sir, you haven't a tip to give us, now this case is over?'

Sir Lawrence gazed at a bird with a long red bill.

'When victorious,' he said, at last, 'lie doggo. The triumphs of morality are apt to recoil on those who achieve them.'

'That's what I feel, sir. Heaven knows *I* didn't want to achieve one. My father-in-law says my hitting MacGown on the boko really brought it into Court.'

Sir Lawrence whinnied.

'The tax on luxuries. It gets you everywhere. I don't think I will come along, Michael – Old Forsyte's probably there. Your mother has an excellent recipe for child's tummyache; you almost lived on it at one time. I'll telephone it from Mount Street. Goodbye!'

Michael looked after that thin and sprightly figure moving North. Had he troubles of his own? If so, he disguised them wonderfully. Good old Bart! And he turned towards South Square.

Soames was just leaving.

'She's excited,' he said, on the doorstep. 'It's the reaction. Give her a Seidlitz powder tonight. Be careful, too; I shouldn't talk about politics.'

Michael went in. Fleur was at the open window of the drawing room.

'Oh! here you are!' she said. 'Kit's all right again. Take me to the Café Royal tonight, Michael, and if there's anything funny anywhere, for goodness' sake, let's see it. I'm sick of feeling solemn. Oh! And, by the way, Francis Wilmot's coming in to say good-bye. I've had a note. He says he's all right again.'

At the window by her side, Michael sniffed the unaccountable scent of grass. There was a South-West wind, and slanting from over the housetops, sunlight was sprinkling the soil, the buds, the branches. A blackbird sang; a piano-organ round a corner was playing 'Rigoletto'.

Against his own, her shoulder was soft, and to his lips her cheek was warm and creamy . . .

When Francis Wilmot left them that evening after dinner at the Café Royal, Fleur said to Michael:

'Poor Francis! Did you ever see anyone so changed? He might be thirty. I'm glad he's going home to his river and his darkies. What are live oaks? Well! Are we going anywhere?'

Michael cloaked her shoulders.

'"Great Itch", I think; there's no other scream so certain.'

After their scream they came out into a mild night. High up in red and green the bright signs fled along the air: 'Tomber's Tyres for Speed and Safety', 'Milkoh Makes Mothers Merry'. Through Trafalgar Square they went and down Whitehall, all moonlight and Portland stone.

'The night's unreal,' said Fleur. '"*Fantoches*"!'

Michael caught her waist.

'Don't. Suppose some Member saw you!'

'He'd only sympathise. How nice and solid you feel!'

'No! *Fantoches* have no substance.'

'Then give me shadow.'

'The substance is in Bethnal Green.'

Michael dropped his arm.

'That's a strange thought.'

'I have intuitions, Michael.'

'Because I can admire a good woman, can I not love you?'

'*I* shall never be "good"; it isn't in me.'

'Whatever you are's enough for me.'

'Prettily said. The Square looks jolly, tonight! Open the doll's house.'

The hall was dark, with just a glimmer coming through the fanlight. Michael took off her cloak and knelt down. He felt her fingers stir his hair; real fingers, and real all this within his arms; only the soul elusive. Soul?

'*Fantoches*!' came her voice, soft and mocking. 'And so to bed!'

Chapter Nine

Rout at Mrs Magussie's

*T*here are routs social, political, propagandic; and routs like Mrs Magussie's. In one of Anglo-American birth, inexhaustible wealth, unimpeachable widowhood, and catholic taste, the word hostess had found its highest expression. People might die, marry, and be born with impunity so long as they met, preferably in her house, one of the largest in Mayfair. If she called in a doctor, it was to meet another doctor; if she went to church, it was to get Canon Forant to meet Dean Kimble at lunch afterwards. Her cards of invitation had the words: 'To meet' printed on them; and she never put 'me'. She was selfless. Once in a way she had a real rout, because once in a way a personality was available, whose name everybody, from poets to prelates, must know. In her intimate belief people loved to meet anybody sufficiently distinguished; and this was where she succeeded, because almost without exception they did. Her two husbands had 'passed on', having met in their time nearly everybody. They had both been distinguished, and had first met in her house; and she would never have a third, for Society was losing its landmarks, and she was too occupied. People were inclined to smile at mention of Bella Magussie, and yet, how do without one who performed the function of cement? Without her, bishops could not place their cheeks by the jowls of ballet-girls, or Home Secretaries be fertilised by disorderly dramatists. Except in her house, the diggers-up of old civilisations in Beluchistan never encountered the levellers of modern civilisation in London. Nor was there any chance for lights of the Palace to meet those lights of the Halls – Madame

Nemesia and Top Nobby. Nowhere else could a Russian dancer go in to supper with Sir Walter Peddel, M.D.,F.R.S.T.R.,P.M.V.S., 'R. I. P.,' as Michael would add. Even a bowler with the finest collection of ducks' eggs in first-class cricket was not without a chance of wringing the hand of the great Indian economist Sir Banerjee Bath Babore. Mrs Magussie's, in fine, was a house of chief consequence; and her long face, as of the guardian of some first principle, moving above the waters of celebrity, was wrinkled in a great cause. To meet or not to meet? She had answered the question for good and all.

The 'meetee' as Michael always called it for her opening rout in 1925 was the great Italian violinist Luigi Sporza, who had just completed his remarkable tour of the world, having in half the time played more often than any two previous musicians. The prodigious feat had been noted in the Press of all countries with every circumstance – the five violins he had tired out, the invitation he had received to preside over a South American Republic, the special steamer he had chartered to keep an engagement in North America, and his fainting fit in Moscow after the Beethoven and Brahms concertos, the Bach chaconne, and seventeen encores. During the lingering year of his great effort, his fame had been established. As an artist he had been known to a few, as an athlete he was now known to all.

Michael and Fleur, passing up the centre stairway, saw a man 'not 'arf like a bull' – Michael muttered – whose hand people were seizing, one after the other, to move away with a look of pain.

'Only Italy can produce men like that,' Michael said in Fleur's ear. 'Give him the go-by. He'll hurt you.'

But Fleur moved forward.

'Made of sterner stuff,' murmured Michael. It was not the part of his beloved to miss the hand of celebrity, however horny! No portion of her charming face quivered as the great athlete's grip closed on hers, and his eyes, like those of a tired minotaur, traversed her gracefulness with a gleam of interest.

'Hulking brute!' thought Michael, disentangling his own grasp, and drifting with her over shining space. Since yesterday's ordeal and its subsequent spring-running, he had kept his unacceptable misgivings to himself; he did not even know whether, at this rout, she was deliberately putting their position to the test, or merely, without fore-thought, indulging her liking to be in the swim. And what a swim! In that great pillared salon, Members of Parliament, poets, musi-cians, very dry in the smile, as who should say: 'I could have done it better,' or 'Imagine doing that!' peers, physicians, dancers, painters, Labour Leaders, cricketers, lawyers, critics, ladies of fashion, and ladies who 'couldn't bear it' – every mortal person that Michael knew or didn't know, seemed present. He watched Fleur's eyes quartering them, busy as bees beneath the white lids he had kissed last night. He envied her that social curiosity; to live in London without it was like being at the sea without bathing. She was quietly – he could tell – making up her mind whom she wanted to speak to among those she knew, and whom, among those she didn't yet know, she wanted to speak to her. 'I hope to God she's not in for a snubbing,' he thought, and as soon as she was engaged in talk, he slipped towards a pillar. A small voice behind him said: 'Well, young Mont!' Mr Blythe, looking like a Dover sole above Kew Bridge, was squeezed against the same pillar, his eyes goggling timorously above his beard.

'Stick to me!' he said. 'These bees are too bee busy.'

'Were you in Court yesterday?' asked Michael.

'No; one read about it. You did well.'

'She did better.'

'H'm!' said Mr Blythe. 'By the way, the *Evening Sun* was at us again this afternoon. They compared us to kittens playing with their tails. It's time for your second barrel, Mont.'

'I thought – on the agricultural estimates.'

'Good! Governmental purchase and control of wheat. Stress use of the present machinery. No more officials than are absolutely neces-sary.'

'Blythe,' said Michael suddenly, 'where were you born?'

'Lincolnshire.'

'You're English, then?'

'Pure,' said Mr Blythe.

'So am I; so's old Foggart – I looked him up in the stud-book. It's lucky, because we shall certainly be assailed for lack of patri-otism.'

'We *are*,' said Mr Blythe. '"People who can see no good in their own country . . . Birds who foul their own nest . . . Gentry never happy unless running England down in the eyes of the world . . . Calamity-mongers . . . Pessimists . . ." You don't mind that sort of gup, I hope?'

'Unfortunately,' said Michael, 'I do; it hurts me inside. It's so damned unjust. I simply can't bear the idea of England being in a fix.'

Mr Blythe's eyes rolled.

'She's bee well not going to be, if we can help it.'

'If only I amounted to something,' murmured Michael; 'but I always feel as if I could creep into one of my back teeth.'

'Have it crowned. What you want is brass, Mont. And talking of brass: There's your late adversary! *She's* got brass all right. Look at her!'

Michael saw Marjorie Ferrar moving away from the great Italian, in not too much of a sea-green gown, with her red-gold head held high. She came to a stand a small room's length from Fleur, and swept her eyes this way and that. Evidently she had taken up that position in deliberate challenge.

'I must go to Fleur.'

'So must I,' said Mr Blythe, and Michael gave him a grateful look.

And now it would have been so interesting to one less interested than Michael. The long, the tapering nose of Society could be seen to twitch, move delicately upwards, and like the trunk of some wild elephant scenting man, writhe and snout this way and that, catching the whiff of sensation. Lips were smiling and moving closer to ears; eyes turning from that standing figure to the other; little reflective frowns appeared on foreheads, as if, beneath cropped and scented scalps, brains were trying to make choice. And Marjorie Ferrar stood smiling and composed; and Fleur talked and twisted the flower in her hand; and both went on looking their best. So began a battle without sign of war declared, without even seeming recognition of each other's presence. Mr Blythe, indeed, stood pat between the two of them. Bulky and tall, he was an effective screen. But Michael, on the other side of her, could see and grimly follow. The Nose was taking time to apprehend the full of the aroma; the Brain to make its choice. Tide seemed at balance, not moving in or out. And then, with the slow implacability of tides, the water moved away from Fleur and lapped round her rival. Michael chattered, Mr Blythe goggled, using the impersonal pronoun with a sort of passion; Fleur smiled, talked, twisted the flower. And, over there, Marjorie Ferrar seemed to hold a little Court. Did people admire, commiserate, approve of, or sympathise with her? Or did they disapprove of himself and Fleur? Or was it just that the 'Pet of the Panjoys' was always the more sensational figure? Michael watched Fleur growing paler, her smile more nervous, the twitching of the flower spasmodic. And he dared not suggest going; for she would see in it an admission of defeat. But on the faces, turned their way, the expression became more and more informative. Sir James Foskisson had done his job too well; he had slavered his clients with his own self-righteousness. Better the confessed libertine than those who brought her to judgment! And Michael thought: 'Dashed natural, after all! Why didn't the fellow take my tip, and let us pay and look pleasant.'

And just then close to the great Italian he caught sight of a tall young man with his hair brushed back, who was looking at his fingers. By George! It was Bertie Curfew! And there, behind him, waiting for his turn 'to meet', who but MacGown himself! The humour of the gods had run amok! Head in air, soothing his mangled fingers, Bertie Curfew passed them, and strayed into the group around his former flame. Her greeting of him was elaborately casual. But up went the tapering Nose, for here came MacGown! How the fellow had changed – grim, greyish, bitter? The great Italian had met his match for once. And he, too, stepped into that throng.

A queer silence was followed by a burst of speech, and then by dissolution. In twos and threes they trickled off, and there were MacGown and his betrothed standing alone. Michael turned to Fleur.

'Let's go.'

Silence reigned in their homing cab. He had chattered himself out on the field of battle, and must wait for fresh supplies of camouflage. But he slipped his hand along till it found hers, which did not return his pressure. The card he used to play at times of stress – the eleventh baronet – had failed for the last three months; Fleur seemed of late to resent his introduction as a remedy. He followed her into the dining room, sore at heart, bewildered in mind. He had never seen her look so pretty as in that oyster-coloured frock, very straight and simply made, with a swing out above the ankles. She sat down at the narrow dining table, and he seated himself opposite, with the costive feeling of one who cannot find words that will ring true. For social discomfiture he himself didn't care a tinker's curse; but she—!

And, suddenly, she said:

'And you don't mind?'

'For myself – not a bit.'

'Yes, you've still got your Foggartism and your Bethnal Green.'

'If *you* care, Fleur, I care a lot.'

'*If* I care!'

'How – exactly?'

'I'd rather not increase your feeling that I'm a snob.'

'I never had any such feeling.'

'Michael!'

'Hadn't you better say what you mean by the word?'

'You know perfectly well.'

'I know that you appreciate having people about you, and like them to think well of you. That isn't being a snob.'

'Yes; you're very kind, but you don't admire it.'

'I admire *you*.'

'You mean, desire me. You admire Norah Curfew.'

'Norah Curfew! For all I care, she might snuff out tomorrow.'

And from her face he had the feeling that she believed him.

'If it isn't her, it's what she stands for – all that I'm not.'

'I admire a lot in you,' said Michael, fervently; 'your intelligence, your flair; I admire you with Kit and your father; your pluck; and the way you put up with me.'

'No, I admire you much more than you admire me. Only, you see, I'm not capable of devotion.'

'What about Kit?'

'I'm devoted to myself – that's all.'

He reached across the table and touched her hand.

'Morbid, darling.'

'No. I see too clearly to be morbid.'

She was leaning back, and her throat, very white and round, gleamed in the alabaster-shaded light; little choky movements were occurring there.

'Michael, I want you to take me round the world.'

'And leave Kit?'

'He's too young to mind. Besides, my mother would look after him.'

If she had got as far as that, this was a deliberate desire!

'But, your father—'

'He's not really old yet, and he'd have Kit.'

'When we rise in August, perhaps—'

'No, now.'

'It's only five months to wait. We'd have time in the vacation to do a lot of travelling.'

Fleur looked straight at him.

'I knew you cared more for Foggartism now than for me.'

'Be reasonable, Fleur.'

'For five months – with the feeling I've got here!' She put her hand to her breast. 'I've had six months of it already. You don't realise, I suppose, that I'm down and out?'

'But, Fleur, it's all so—'

'Yes, it's always petty to mind being a dead failure, isn't it?'

'But, my child—'

'Oh! If you can't feel it—'

'I can – I felt wild this evening. But all you've got to do is to let them see that you don't care; and they'll come buzzing round again like flies. It would be running away, Fleur.'

'No,' said Fleur, coldly, 'it's not that – I don't try twice for the same prize. Very well, I'll stay and be laughed at.'

Michael got up.

'I know you don't think there's anything to my job. But there is, Fleur, and I've put my hand to it. Oh! don't look like that. Dash it! This is dreadful!'

'I suppose I could go by myself. That would be more thrilling.'

'Absurd! Of course you couldn't! You're seeing blue tonight, old thing. It'll all seem different tomorrow.'

'Tomorrow and tomorrow! No, Michael, mortification has set in, my funeral can take place any day you like!'

Michael's hands went up. She meant what she was saying! To realise, he must remember how much store she had set on her powers as hostess; how she had worked for her collection and shone among it! Her house of cards all pulled about her ears! Cruel! But would going round the world help her? Yes! Her instinct was quite right. He had been round the world himself, nothing else would change her values in quite that way; nothing else would so guarantee oblivion in others and herself! Lippinghall, her father's, the sea for the five months till vacation came – they wouldn't meet her case! She needed what would give her back importance. And yet, how could he go until the vacation? Foggartism – that lean and lonely plant – unwatered and without its only gardener, would wither to its roots, if, indeed, it had any. There was some movement in it now, interest here and there – this Member and that was pecking at it. Private efforts in the same direction were gathering way. And time was going on – Big Ben had called no truce; unemployment swelling, trade dawdling, industrial trouble brewing – brewing, hope losing patience! And what would old Blythe say to his desertion now?

'Give me a week,' he muttered. 'It's not easy. I must think it over.'

Chapter Ten

The New Leaf

When MacGown came up to her, Marjorie Ferrar thought: 'Does he know about Bertie?' Fresh from her triumph over 'that little snob', flustered by the sudden appearance of her past, and confronted with her present, she was not in complete possession of her head. When they had moved away into an empty side room, she faced him.

'Well, Alec, nothing's changed. I still have a past as lurid as it was yesterday. I'm extremely sorry I ever kept it from you. But I did practically tell you, several times; only you wouldn't take it.'

'Because it was hell to me. Tell me everything, Marjorie!'

'You want to revel in it?'

'Tell me everything, and I'll marry you still.'

She shook her head. 'Marry! Oh! no! I don't go out of my depth any more. It was absurd anyway. I never loved you, Alec.'

'Then you loved that – you still—'

'My dear Alec, enough!'

He put his hands to his head, and swayed. And she was touched by genuine compassion.

'I'm awfully sorry, I really am. You've got to cut me out; that's all.'

She had turned to leave him, but the misery in his face stopped her. She had not quite realised.

He was burnt up! He was—! And she said quickly:

'Marry you I won't; but I'd like to pay up, if I could—'

He looked at her.

Quivering all over from that look, she shrugged her shoulders, and walked away. Men of an old fashion! Her own fault for stepping outside the charmed circle that took nothing too seriously. She walked over the shining floor, conscious of many eyes, slipped past her hostess, and soon was in a cab.

She lay awake, thinking. Even without announcement, the return of presents would set London by the ears and bring on her again an avalanche of bills. Five thousand pounds! She got up and rummaged out the list, duplicate of that which Alec had. He might still want to pay them! After all, it was he who had spilled the ink by making her go into Court! But then his eyes came haunting her. Out of the question! And, shivering a little, she got back into bed. Perhaps she would have a brainwave in the morning. She had so many in the night, that she could not sleep. Moscow with Bertie Curfew? The stage? America and the 'movies'? All three? She slept at last, and woke languid and pale. With her letters was one from Shropshire House.

'DEAR MARJORIE,

'If you've nothing better to do, I should like to see you this morning.
'Affectionately,

'SHROPSHIRE.'

What now? She looked at herself in the glass, and decided that she *must* make up a little. At eleven o'clock she was at Shropshire House. The marquess was in his workroom at the top, among a small forest of contraptions. With coat off, he was peering through a magnifying-glass at what looked like nothing.

'Sit down, Marjorie,' he said; 'I'll have done in a minute.'

Except the floor, there seemed nowhere to sit, so she remained standing.

'I thought so,' said the marquess; 'the Italians are wrong.'

He put the spy-glass down, ran his hand through his silvery hair, and drew his ruffled beard into a peak. Then, taking an eyebrow between finger and thumb, he gave it an upward twist, and scratched himself behind one ear.

'They're wrong; there's no reaction whatever.'

Turning towards his granddaughter, he screwed up his eyes till they were bright as pins. 'You've never been up here before. Sit in the window.'

She seated herself on a broad window-ledge covering some sort of battery, with her back to the light.

'So you brought that case, Marjorie?'

'I had to.'

'Now, why?' He was standing with his head a little to one side, his cheeks very pink, and his eyes very shrewd. And she thought: 'After all, I'm his granddaughter. I'll plunge.'

'Common honesty, if you want to know.'

The marquess pouted, as if trying to understand the words.

'I read your evidence,' he said, 'if you mean that.'

'No. I meant that I wanted to find out where I stood.'

'And did you?'

'Very much so.'

'Are you still going to be married?'

Really, he was a spry old boy!

'No.'

'Whose doing? Yours or his?'

'He still says he'll marry me if I tell him everything. But I don't choose to.'

The marquess moved two steps, placed his foot on a box, and assumed his favourite attitude. He had a red silk tie this morning which floated loose; his tweed trousers were of a blue-green, his shirt of a green-blue. He looked wonderfully bright.

'Is there much to tell?'

'A good deal.'

'Well, Marjorie, you know what I said to you.'

'Yes, Grandfather, but I don't quite see it. *I* don't want to stand for anything.'

'Ah! you're an exception in our class – luckily! But it's the exceptions that do the harm.'

'If people took one as any better than themselves, perhaps. But they don't nowadays.'

'Not quite honest, that,' interrupted the marquess; 'what about the feeling in your bones?'

She smiled.

'It's good to mortify oneself, Grandfather.'

'By having a better time than you ought, um? So your marriage is off?'

'Very much so.'

'Are you in debt?'

'Yes.'

'How much do you owe?'

Marjorie Ferrar hesitated. Should she compromise, or blurt it out?

'No heel-taps, Marjorie.'

'Well, then, five thousand about.'

The old peer screwed up his lips, and a melancholy little whistle escaped.

'A good deal of it, of course, is due to my engagement.'

'Your father won a race the other day, I see.'

The old boy knew everything!

'Yes; but I believe it's all gone.'

'It would be,' said the marquess. 'What are you going to do now?'

She had a strong desire to answer: 'What are you?' but restrained it, and said:

'I thought of going on the stage.'

'Well, I suppose that might be suitable. Can you act?'

'I'm not a Duse.'

'Duse?' The marquess shook his head. 'One must go back to Ristori for really great acting. Duse! Very talented, of course, but always the same. So you don't choose to marry him now?' He looked at her intently. 'That, I think, is right. Have you a list of your debts?'

Marjorie Ferrar rummaged in her vanity bag. 'Here it is.'

She could see his nose wrinkling above it, but whether at its scent, or its contents, she could not tell.

'Your grandmother,' he said, 'spent about a fifth of what you seem to on about five times the acreage of clothes. You wear nothing nowadays, and yet it costs all this.'

'The less there is, Grandfather, the better it has to be cut, you know.'

'Have you sent your presents back?'

'I'm having them packed.'

'They must all go,' said the marquess. 'Keep nothing he or anyone else gave you.'

'Of course not.'

'To frank you,' he said, suddenly, 'I should have to sell the Gainsborough.'

'Oh, no!'

Gainsborough's picture of his own grandmother as a little girl — that beautiful thing. She stretched out her hand for the list. Still holding it, he put his foot to the ground, and stood peering at her with his bright, intent old eyes.

'The question is, Marjorie, how far it's possible to strike a bargain with you. Have you a "word" to keep?'

She felt the blood mounting in her cheeks.

'I think so. It depends on what I've got to promise. But, Grandfather, I don't *want* you to sell the Gainsborough.'

'Unfortunately,' said the marquess, 'without doing your uncle Dangerfield in the eye, I've nothing else. It's been my fault, I suppose, for having had expensive children. Other people don't seem to have had them to the same degree.'

She stifled a smile.

'Times are hard,' went on the marquess. 'Land costs money, collieries cost money, Shropshire House costs money; and where's the money? I've got an invention here that ought to make my fortune, but nobody will look at it.'

The poor old boy — at his age! She said with a sigh:

'I really didn't mean to bother you with this, Grandfather. I'll manage somehow.'

The old peer took several somewhat hampered steps, and she noticed that his red slippers were heelless. He halted, a wonderfully bright spot among the contraptions.

'To come back to what we were saying, Marjorie. If your idea of life is simply to have a good time, how can you promise anything?'

'What do you want me to promise?'

He came and stood before her again, short and a little bent.

'You look as if you had stuff in you, too, with your hair. Do you really think you could earn your living?'

'I believe I can; I know a lot of people.'

'If I clear you, will you give me your word to pay ready money in future? Now don't say "Yes", and go out and order yourself a lot of fallals. I want the word of a lady, if you understand what that implies.'

She stood up.

'I suppose you've every right to say that. But I don't want you to clear me if you have to sell the Gainsborough.'

'You must leave that to me. I might manage, perhaps, to scrape it up without. About that promise?'

'Yes; I promise that.'

'Meaning to keep it?'

'Meaning to keep it.'

'Well, that's something.'

'Anything else, Grandfather?'

'I should have liked to ask you not to cheapen our name any more, but I suppose that would be putting the clock back. The spirit of the age is against me.'

Turning from his face, she stood looking out of the window. The spirit of the age! It was all very well, but he didn't understand what it was. Cheapen? Why! she had *raised* the price of the family name; hoicked it out of a dusty cupboard, and made of it current coin. People sat up when they read of her. Did they sit up when they read of Grandfather? But he would never see that! And she murmured:

'All right, dear, I'll be careful. I think I shall go to America.'

His eyes twinkled.

'And start a fashion of marrying American husbands? It's not yet been done, I believe. Get one who's interested in electricity, and bring him over. There are great things for an American to do here. Well, I'll keep this list and work it off somehow. Just one thing, Marjorie:

I'm eighty, and you're – what are you – twenty-five? Don't get through life so fast – you'll be dreadfully bored by the time you're fifty, and there's no greater bore than a bored person. Good-bye!' He held out his hand.

She took a long breath. Free!

And, seizing his hand, she put it to her lips. Oh! He was gazing at it – oh! Had her lips come off? And she hurried out. The old boy! He was a darling to have kept that list! A new leaf! She would go at once to Bertie Curfew and get him to turn it over for her! The expression in his eye last night!

Chapter Eleven

Over The Windmill

*D*uring his period of indecision Michael struck no attitudes, and used practically no words; the thing was too serious. Perhaps Kit would change Fleur's mood, or she would see other disadvantages, such as her father. The complete cessation, however, of any social behaviour on her part – no invitation issued, or received, no function attended, or even discussed, during that rather terrible week, proved that the iron had really seared her spirit. She was not sulky, but she was mum and listless. And she was always watching him, with a wistful expression on her face, and now and then a resentful look, as if she had made up her mind that he was going to refuse. He could consult no one, too, for to any who had not lived through this long episode, Fleur's attitude would seem incomprehensible, even ridiculous. He could not give her away; could not even go to old Blythe, until he had decided. Complicating his mental conflict was the habitual doubt whether he was really essential to Foggartism. If only his head would swell! He had not even the comfort of feeling that a sturdy negative would impress Fleur; she thought his job a stunt, useful to make him conspicuous, but of no real importance to the country. She had the political cynicism of the woman in the street; only what threatened property or Kit would really ruffle her! He knew that his dilemma was comic. The future of England against the present of a young woman socially snubbed! But, after all, only Sir James Foggart and old Blythe so far seriously connected Foggartism with the future of England; and if, now, he went off round the world, even they would lose their faith.

On the last morning of that week, Michael, still in doubt, crossed Westminster Bridge and sought the heart of the Surrey side. It was unfamiliar, and he walked with interest. Here, he remembered, the Bickets had lived; the Bickets who had failed, and apparently were failing in Australia, too. Street after mean street! Breeding-ground of Bickets! Catch them early, catch them often, catch them before they were Bickets, spoiled for the land; make them men and women of property, give them air and give them sun – the most decent folk in the world, give them a chance! Ugly houses, ugly shops, ugly pubs! No, that wouldn't do! Keep Beauty out of it; Beauty never went down in 'the House'! No sentiment went down! At least, only such as was understood – 'British stock', 'Patriotism', 'Empire', 'Moral Fibre'. Thews and productive power – stick to the clichés! He stood listening outside a school to the dull hum of education. The English breed with its pluck and its sense of humour and its patience, all mewed-up in mean streets!

He had a sudden longing for the country. His motorcycle! Since taking his seat in Parliament he had not been on a machine so inclined to bump his dignity. But he would have it out now, and go for a run – it might shake him into a decision!

Fleur was not in, and no lunch ordered. So he ate some ham, and by two o'clock had started.

With spit and bluster he ran out along the road past Chiswick, Slough, and Maidenhead; crossed the river and sputtered towards Reading. At Caversham he crossed again, and ran on to Pangbourne. By the towing path he tipped his machine into some bushes and sat down to smoke a pipe. Quite windless! The river between the bare poplars had a grey, untroubled look; the catkins were forming on the willows. He plucked a twig, and stirred it round the bowl of his pipe before pressing in tobacco. The shaking had done him good; his mind was working freely. The war! One had no hesitations then; but then – one had no Fleur. Besides, that was a clear, a simple issue. But now, beyond this 'to stay or not to stay', Michael seemed seeing the future of his married life. The decision that he made would affect what might last another fifty years. To put your hand to the plough, and at the first request to take it off again! You might be ploughing crooked, and by twilight; but better plough by dim light than no light; a crooked furrow than none at all! Foggartism was the best course he could see, and he must stick to it! The future of England! A blackbird, close by, chuckled. Quite so! But, as old Blythe said, one must stand up to laughter! Oh! Surely in the long run Fleur would see that he couldn't play fast and loose; see that if she wanted him to remain in Parliament – and she did – he must hang on to the line he had taken, however it amused the blackbirds. She wouldn't like him to sink to the nonentity of a turntail. For after all she was his wife, and with his self-respect her own was bound up.

He watched the smoke from his pipe, and the low grey clouds, the white-faced Herefords grazing beyond the river, and a man fishing with a worm. He took up the twig and twirled it, admiring the yellowish-grey velvet of its budding catkins. He felt quiet in the heart, at last, but very sorry. How make up to Fleur? Beside this river, not two miles away, he had courted – queer word – if not won her! And now they had come to this snag. Well, it was up to her now, whether or no they should come to grief on it. And it seemed to him, suddenly, that he would like to tell Old Forsyte . . .

When he heard the splutter of Michael's motorcycle, Soames was engaged in hanging the Fred Walker he had bought at the emporium next to Messrs. Settlewhite and Stark, memorialising his freedom from the worry of that case, and soothing his itch for the British School. Fred Walker! The fellow was old-fashioned; he and Mason had been succeeded by a dozen movements. But – like old fiddles, with the same agreeable glow – there they were, very good curiosities such as would always command a price.

Having detached a Courbet, early and about ripe, he was standing in his shirt-sleeves, with a coil of wire in his hand, when Michael entered.

'Where have you sprung from?' he said, surprised.

'I happened to be passing, sir, on my old bike. I see you've kept your word about the English School.'

Soames attached the wire.

'I shan't be happy,' he said, 'till I've got an old Crome – best of the English landscapists.'

'Awfully rare, isn't he, old Crome?'

'Yes, that's why I want him.'

The smile on Michael's face, as if he were thinking: 'You mean that's why you consider him the best,' was lost on Soames giving the wire a final twist.

'I haven't seen your pictures for a long time, sir. Can I look round?'

Observing him sidelong, Soames remembered his appearance there one summer Sunday, after he had first seen Fleur in that Gallery off Cork Street. Only four years? It seemed an age! The young fellow had worn better than one had hoped; looked a good deal older, too, less flighty; an amiable chap, considering his upbringing, and that war! And suddenly he perceived that Michael was engaged in observing him. Wanted something, no doubt – wouldn't have come down for nothing! He tried to remember when anybody had come to see him without wanting something; but could not. It was natural!

'Are you looking for a picture to go with that Fragonard?' he said. 'There's a Chardin in the corner.'

'No, no, sir; you've been much too generous to us already.'

Generous! How could one be generous to one's only daughter?

'How is Fleur?'

'I wanted to tell you about her. She's feeling awfully restless.'

Soames looked out of the window. The spring was late!

'She oughtn't to be, with that case out of the way.'

'That's just it, sir.'

Soames gimleted the young man's face. 'I don't follow you.'

'We're being cold-shouldered.'

'How? You won.'

'Yes, but you see, people resent moral superiority.'

'What's that? Who—?' Moral superiority – he resented it himself!

'Foskisson, you know; we're tarred with his brush. I told you I was afraid of it. It's the being laughed at Fleur feels so bitterly.'

'Laughed at? Who has the impudence—?'

'To attack modern morality was a good stunt, sir, with the judge and the jury, and anyone professionally pompous; but it makes one ridiculous nowadays in Society, you know, when everybody prides himself on lack of prejudice.'

'Society!'

'Yes, sir; but it's what we live in. *I* don't mind, got used to it over Foggartism; but Fleur's miserable. It's natural, if you think of it – Society's her game.'

'She ought to have more strength of mind,' said Soames. But he was gravely perturbed. First she'd been looked on as a snob, and now there was this!

'What with that German actor hanging himself at Lippinghall,' Michael went on, 'and my Foggartism, and this Ferrar rumpus, our pitch is badly queered. We've had a wretched week of it since the case. Fleur feels so out of her plate, that she wants me to take her round the world.'

A bomb bursting on the dovecote down there could not have been more startling. Round the world! He heard Michael murmuring on:

'She's quite right, too. It might be the very best thing for her; but I simply can't leave my job until the long vacation. I've taken up this thing, and I must stick to it while Parliament's sitting.'

Sitting! As if it were a hen, addling its precious eggs! Round the world!

But Michael ran on:

'It's only today I've quite decided. I should feel like a deserter, and that wouldn't be good for either of us in the long run. But she doesn't know yet.'

For Soames the dovecote was solidifying again, now that he knew Michael was not going to take her away for goodness knew how long!

'Round the world!' he said. 'Why not – er – Pontresina?'

'I think,' answered Michael, slowly, like a doctor diagnosing, 'that she wants something dramatic. Round the world at twenty-three! She feels somehow that she's lost caste.'

'How can she think of leaving that little chap?'

'Yes, that shows it's pretty desperate with her. I wish to goodness I *could* go.'

Soames stared. The young fellow wasn't expecting him to do anything about it, was he? Round the world? A crazy notion!

'I must see her,' he said. 'Can you leave that thing of yours in the garage and come up with me in the car? I'll be ready in twenty minutes. You'll find tea going downstairs.'

Left alone with the Fred Walker still unhung, Soames gazed at his pictures. He saw them with an added clarity, a more penetrating glance, a sort of ache in his heart, as if – Well! A good lot they were, better than he had thought, of late! *She* had gone in for collecting people! And now she'd lost her collection! Poor little thing! All nonsense, of course – as if there were any satisfaction in people! Suppose he took her up that Chardin? It was a good Chardin. Dumetrius had done him over the price, but not too much. And, before Chardin was finished with, he would do Dumetrius. Still – if it would give her any pleasure! He unhooked the picture, and, carrying it under his arm, went downstairs.

Beyond certain allusions to the characteristics of the eleventh baronet, and the regrettable tendencies of the police to compel slow travelling over the new cut constructed to speed up traffic, little was said in the car. They arrived in South Square about six o'clock. Fleur had not been in since lunch; and they sat down uneasily to wait for her. The Dandie, having descended to look for strange legs, had almost immediately ascended again, and the house was very quiet. Michael was continually looking at his watch.

'Where do you think she's got to?' said Soames, at last.

'Haven't an idea, sir; that's the worst of London, it swallows people up.'

He had begun to fidget; Soames, who also wanted to fidget, was thinking of saying: 'Don't!' when from the window Michael cried:

'Here she is!' and went quickly to the door.

Soames sat on, with the Chardin resting against his chair.

They were a long time out there! Minute after minute passed, and still they did not come.

At last Michael reappeared. He looked exceedingly grave.

'She's in her little room upstairs, sir. I'm afraid my decision has upset her awfully. Perhaps you wouldn't mind going up.'

Soames grasped the Chardin.

'Let's see, that's the first door on the left, isn't it?' He mounted slowly, his mind blank, and without waiting for her to answer his mild knock, went in.

Fleur was sitting at the satinwood bureau, with her face buried on her arms. Her hair, again in its more natural 'bob', gleamed lustrously under the light. She seemed unconscious of his entry. This sight of private life affected Soames, unaccustomed to give or receive unde- fended glimpses of self, and he stood, uncertain. Had he the right to surprise her, with her ears muffled like that, and her feelings all upset? He would have gone out and come in again, but he was too concerned. And, moving to her side, he put his finger on her shoulder, and said:

'Tired, my child?'

Her face came round – queer, creased, not like her face; and Soames spoke the phrase of her childhood:

'See what I've brought you!'

He raised the Chardin; she gave it just a glance, and he felt hurt. After all, it was worth some hundreds of pounds! Very pale, she had crossed her arms on her chest, as if shutting herself up. He recog- nised the symptom. A spiritual crisis! The sort of thing his whole life had been passed in regarding as extravagant; like a case of appen- dicitis that will not wait decently.

'Michael,' he said, 'tells me you want him to take you round the world.'

'Well, he can't; so that ends it.'

If she had said: 'Yes, and why can't he?' Soames would have joined the opposition automatically. But her words roused his natural perver- sity. Here she was, and here was her heart's desire – and she wasn't getting it! He put the Chardin down, and took a walk over the soft carpet.

'Tell me,' he said, coming to a halt, 'where do you feel it exactly?'

Fleur laughed: 'In my head, and my eyes, and my ears, and my heart.'

'What business,' muttered Soames, 'have they to look down their confounded noses!' And he set off again across the room. All the modern jackanapes whom from time to time he had been unable to avoid in her house, seemed to have come sniggering round him with lifted eyebrows, like a set of ghosts. The longing to put them in their places – a shallow lot – possessed him at that moment to the exclusion of a greater sanity.

'I – I don't see how *I* can take you,' he said, and stopped short.

What was that he was saying? Who had asked him to take her? Her eyes, widely open, were fixed on him.

'But of course not, Dad!'

Of course not! He didn't know about that!

'I shall get used to being laughed at, in time.' Soames growled.

'I don't see why you should,' he said. 'I suppose people do go round the world.'

Fleur's pallor had gone, now.

'But not you, dear; why, it would bore you stiff! It's very sweet of you, even to think of it; but of course I couldn't let you – at your age!'

'At my age?' said Soames. 'I'm not so very old.'

'No, no, Dad; I'll just dree my weird.'

Soames took another walk, without a sound. Dree her weird, indeed!

'I won't have it,' he ejaculated; 'if people can't behave to you, I – I'll show them!'

She had got up, and was breathing deeply, with her lips parted, and her cheeks very flushed. So she had stood, before her first party, holding out her frock for him to see.

'We'll go,' he said, gruffly. 'Don't make a fuss! That's settled.'

Her arms were round his neck; his nose felt wet. What nonsense! as if—! . . .

He stood unbuttoning his braces that night in the most peculiar state of mind. Going round the world – was he? Preposterous! It had knocked that young fellow over anyway – he was to join them in August wherever they were by that time! Good Lord! It might be China! The thing was fantastic; and Fleur behaving like a kitten! The words of a comic ditty, sung by a clergyman, in his boyhood, kept up a tattoo within him:

'I see Jerusalem and Madagascar,
And North and South Amerikee . . .'

Yes! Indeed! His affairs were in apple-pie order, luckily! There was nothing to do, in Timothy's or Winifred's Trusts – the only two he had on his hands now; but how things would get on without him, he couldn't tell! As to Annette! She wouldn't be sorry, he supposed. There was no one else to care, except Winifred, a little. It was, rather, an intangible presence that troubled his thoughts, about to forsake it for months on end! Still, the cliffs of Dover would be standing, he supposed, and the river still running past his lawn, when he came back, if he ever came back! You picked up all sorts of things out there – microbes, insects, snakes – never knew what you'd run into! Pretty business, steering Fleur clear of all that. And the sightseeing he would have to do! For *she* wouldn't miss anything! Trust her! Going round among a lot of people with their mouths open – he couldn't stand that; but he would have to! H'm! A relief when that young fellow could join them. And yet – to have her to himself; he hadn't, for a long time now. But she would pick up with everybody, of course. He would have to make himself agreeable to Tom, Dick, and Harry. A look at Egypt, then to India, and across to China and Japan, and back through that great sprawling America – God's own country, didn't they call it! She had it all mapped out. Thank goodness, no question of Russia! She hadn't even proposed that – it was all to pieces now, they said! Communism! Who knew what would happen at home before they got back? It seemed to Soames as if England, too, must all go to pieces, if he left it. Well, he'd said he would take her! And she had cried over it. Phew! He threw the window up, and in the Jaeger dressing-gown kept there for stray occasions, leaned into the mild air. No Westminster Square did he seem to see out there, but his own river and its poplars, with the full moon behind them, a bright witness – the quiet beauty he had never put into words, the green tranquillity he had felt for thirty years, and only permitted to seep into the back of his being. He would miss it – the scents, the sighs of the river under the wind, the chuckle down at the weir, the stars. They had stars out there, of course, but not English stars. And the grass – those great places had no grass, he believed! The blossom, too, was late this year – no blossom before they left! Well, the milk was spilled! And that reminded him: The dairyman would be certain to let the cows go out of milk – he was a 'natural', that chap! He would have to warn Annette. Women never seemed to understand that a cow didn't go on giving milk for ever, without being attended to. If he only had a man to rely on in the country, like old Gradman in Town! H'm! Old Gradman's eyes would drop out when he heard this news! Bit of old England there; and wouldn't be left long, now! It would be queer to come back and find old Gradman gone. One – Two – Three – Eleven! That clock! It had kept him awake before now; still – it was a fine old clock! That young fellow was to go on sitting under it. And was there anything in the notions that kept him sitting there, or were they just talk? Well, he was right to stick to his guns, anyway. But five months away from his young wife – great risk in that! 'Youth's a stuff' – Old Shakespeare knew the world. Well! Risk, or no risk, there it was! After all, Fleur had a good head; and young Michael had a good heart. Fleur had a good heart, too; he wouldn't have it said that she hadn't! She would feel leaving the baby when it came to the point. She didn't realise, yet. And Soames felt within him the stir of a curious conflict, between hope that, after all, she might give it up, and apprehension lest she should. Funny – that! His habits, his comfort, his possessions . . . and here he was, flinging them all over the windmill! Absurd! And yet—!

Chapter Twelve

Envoi

*A*way from Fleur five months at least! Soames's astounding conduct had indeed knocked Michael over. And yet, after all, they had come to a crisis in their life together, the more serious because concerned with workaday feelings. Perhaps out there she would become afflicted, like himself, with an enlarged prospect; lose her idea that the world consisted of some five thousand people of advanced tastes, of whom she knew at the outside five hundred. It was she who had pushed him into Parliament, and until he was hoofed therefrom as a failure, their path was surely conjoined along the crest of a large view. In the fortnight before her departure he suffered and kept smiling; wryly thankful that she was behaving 'like a kitten', as her father called it. Her nerves had been on edge ever since the autumn over that wretched case – what more natural than this reaction? At least she felt for him sufficiently to be prodigal of kisses – great consolation to Michael while it lasted. Once or twice he caught her hanging with wet eyes over the eleventh baronet; once found her with a wet face when he awoke in the morning. These indications were a priceless assurance to him that she meant to come back. For there were moments when possibilities balled into a nightmare. Absurd! She was going with her father, that embodiment of care and prudence! Who would have thought Old Forsyte could uproot himself like this? He, too, was leaving a wife, though Michael saw no signs of it. One didn't know much about Old Forsyte's feelings, except that they centred round his daughter, and that he was continually asking questions about labels and insects.

He had bought himself, too, a life-saving waistcoat and one for Fleur. Michael held with him only one important conversation.

'I want you,' Soames said, 'to keep an eye on my wife, and see she doesn't go getting into a mess with the cows. She'll have her mother with her, but women are so funny. You'll find her first-rate with the baby. How will you be off for money?'

'Perfectly all right, sir.'

'Well, if you want some for any good purpose, go to old Gradman in the City; you remember him, perhaps?'

'Yes, and I'm afraid he'll remember me.'

'Never mind; he's a faithful old fellow.' And Michael heard him sigh. 'I'd like you to look in at Green Street, too, now and then. Your aunt-in-law may feel my being away a little. I'll let you have news of Fleur from time to time – now they've got this wireless she'll want to know about the baby. I'm taking plenty of quinine. Fleur says she's a good sailor. There's nothing like champagne for that, I'm told. And, by the way, you know best, but I shouldn't press your notions too far in Parliament; they're easily bored there, I believe. We'll meet you at Vancouver, at the end of August. She'll be tired of travelling by then. She's looking forward to Egypt and Japan, but I don't know. Seems to me it'll be all travelling.'

'Have you plenty of ducks, sir? You'll want them at this time of year in the Red Sea; and I should take a helmet.'

'I've got one,' said Soames; 'they're heavy great things,' and, looking suddenly at Michael, he added:

'I shall look after her, and you'll look after yourself, I hope.'

Michael understood him.

'Yes, sir. And thank you very much. I think it's most frightfully sporting of you.'

'It's to be hoped it'll do her good; and that the little chap won't miss her.'

'Not if I can help it.'

Soames, who was seated in front of 'The White Monkey', seemed to go into a trance. At last he stirred in his chair, and said:

'The war's left everything very unsettled. I suppose people believe in something nowadays, but *I* don't know what it is.'

Michael felt a fearful interest.

'Do you mind telling me, sir, what you believe in yourself?'

'What was good enough for my fathers is good enough for me. They expect too much now; there's no interest taken in being alive.'

'Interest taken in being alive!' The words were singularly comprehensive. Were they the answer to all modern doubt?

The last night, the last kiss came; and the glum journey to the Docks in Soames's car. Michael alone went to see them off! The gloomy dockside, and the grey river; the bustle with baggage, and the crowded tender. An aching business! Even for her, he almost believed – an aching business. And the long desultory minutes on the ship; the initiation of Soames into its cramped, shining, strangely odoured mysteries. The ghastly smile one had to keep on the lips, the inane jokes one had to make. And then that moment, apart, when she pressed her breast to his and gave him a clinging kiss.

'Good-bye, Michael; it's not for very long.'

'Good-bye, darling! Take care of yourself. You shall have all the news I can send you, and don't worry about Kit.'

His teeth were clinched, and her eyes – he saw – were wet! And, then, once more:

'Good-bye!'

'Good-bye!'

Back on the tender, with the strip of grey water opening, spreading, between him and the ship's side, and that high line of faces above the bulwark – Fleur's face under the small fawn hat, her waving hand; and, away to the left, seen out of the tail of his eye, Old Forsyte's face alone – withdrawn so that they might have their parting to themselves – long, chinny, grey-moustached, very motionless; absorbed and lonely, as might be that of some long-distance bird arrived on an unknown shore, and looking back towards the land of its departure. Smaller and smaller they grew, merged in blur, vanished.

For the whole journey back to Westminster, Michael smoked cigarette on cigarette, and read the same sentence over and over in the same journal, and the sentence was:

'Robbery at Highgate, Cat Burglar gets clear away.'

He went straight into the House of Commons. And all the after-noon sat listening and taking in a few words now and then, of a debate on education. What chance – what earthly chance – had his skyscraping in this place, where they still talked with calm disagree-ment, as if England were the England of 1906, and where the verdict on him was: 'Amiable but very foolish young man!' National unity – national movement! No jolly fear! The country wouldn't have it! One was battering at a door which everybody said must be opened, but through which nobody could pass. And a long strip of grey water kept spreading between him and the talkers; the face under the fawn hat confused itself with that of the Member for Wasbaston; the face of Old Forsyte above the bulwark rail appeared suddenly between two Labour Leaders; and the lines of faces faded to a blur on a grey river where gulls were flighting.

Going out, he passed a face that had more reality – MacGown's! Grim! It wasn't the word. No one had got any change out of that affair. *Multum ex parvo! Parvum ex multo!* That was the modern comedy!

Going home to have a look at Kit and send Fleur a wireless, he passed four musicians playing four instruments with a sort of fury. They had able bodies in shabby clothes. 'By Jove!' thought Michael, 'I know that chap's face! surely he was in my Company, in France!' He watched till the cheeks collapsed. Yes! A good man, too! But they had all been good men. By George, they had been wonders! And here they were! And he within an ace of abandoning them! Though everybody had his nostrum, and one perhaps was as good as another, still one could only follow what light one had! And if the Future was unreadable, and Fate grinned, well – let it grin!

How empty the house felt! Tomorrow Kit and the dog were to go down to 'The Shelter' in the car, and it would be still emptier. From room after room he tried to retrieve some sight or scent of Fleur. Too painful! His dressing room, his study were the only places possible – in them he would abide.

He went to the nursery, and opened the door softly. Whiteness and dimity; the dog on his fat silver side, the Magicoal fire burning; the prints on the white walls so carefully selected for the moment when the eleventh baronet should begin to take notice – prints slightly comic, to avoid a moral; the high and shining fender-guard that even Magicoal might not be taken too seriously; the light coming in between bright chintz. A charming room! The nurse, in blue, was standing with her back to the door, and did not see him. And, in his little high chair, the eleventh baronet was at table; on his face, beneath its dark chestnut curls, was a slight frown; and in his tiny hand he held a silver spoon, with which over the bowl before him he was making spasmodic passes.

Michael heard the nurse saying:

'Now that Mother's gone, you must be a little man, Kit, and learn to use your spoon.'

Michael saw his offspring dip at the bowl and throw some of its contents into the air.

'That's not the way at all.'

The eleventh baronet repeated the performance, and looked for applause, with a determined smile.

'Naughty!'

'A – a!' said the eleventh baronet, plopping the spoon. The contents spurted wastefully.

'Oh! you spoiled boy!'

'"England, my England!"' thought Michael, 'as the poet said.'

Interlude

Passers By

I

In Washington, District of Columbia, the 'Fall' sun shone, and all that was not evergreen or stone in Rock Creek Cemetery was glowing. Before the Saint Gaudens statue Soames Forsyte sat on his overcoat, with the marble screen to his back, enjoying the seclusion and a streak of sunlight passaging between the cypresses.

With his daughter and her husband he had been up here already, the afternoon before, and had taken a fancy to the place. Apart from the general attraction of a cemetery, this statue awakened the connoisseur within him. Though not a thing you could acquire, it was undoubtedly a work of art, and produced a very marked effect. He did not remember a statue that made him feel so thoroughly at home. That great greenish bronze figure of seated woman within the hooding folds of her ample cloak seemed to carry him down to the bottom of his own soul. Yesterday, in the presence of Fleur, Michael, and other people, all gaping like himself, he had not so much noted the mood of the thing as its technical excellence, but now, alone, he could enjoy the luxury of his own sensations. Some called it 'Grief', some 'The Adams Memorial'. He didn't know, but in any case there it was, the best thing he had come across in America, the one that gave him the most pleasure, in spite of all the water he had seen at Niagara and those skyscrapers in New York. Three times he had changed his position on that crescent marble seat, varying his sensations every time. From his present position the woman had passed beyond grief. She sat in a frozen acceptance deeper than death itself, very remarkable! There was something about death! He remembered his own father, James, a quarter of an hour after death, as if – as if he had been told at last!

A red-oak leaf fell on to his lapel, another on to his knee; Soames did not brush them off. Easy to sit still in front of that thing! They ought to make America sit there once a week!

He rose, crossed towards the statue, and gingerly touched a fold in the green bronze, as if questioning the possibility of everlasting nothingness.

'Got a sister living in Dallas – married a railroad man down there as a young girl. Why! Texas is a wonderful State. I know my sister laughs at the idea that the climate of Texas isn't about right.'

Soames withdrew his hand from the bronze, and returned to his seat. Two tall thin elderly figures were entering the sanctuary. They moved into the middle and stood silent. Presently one said 'Well!' and they moved out again at the other end. A little stir of wind fluttered some fallen leaves at the base of the statue. Soames shifted along to the extreme left. From there the statue was once more woman – very noble! And he sat motionless in his attitude of a thinker, the lower part of his face buried in his hand.

Considerably browned and distinctly healthy-looking, he was accustomed to regard himself as worn out by his long travel, which, after encircling the world, would end, the day after tomorrow, by embarkation on the *Adelphie*. This three-day run to Washington was the last straw, and he was supporting it very well. The city was pleasing; it had some fine buildings and a great many trees with the tints on; there wasn't the rush of New York, and plenty of houses that people could live in, he should think. Of course the place was full of Americans, but that was unavoidable. He was happy about Fleur too; she had quite got over that unpleasant Ferrar business, seemed on excellent terms with young Michael, and was looking forward to her home and her baby again. There was, indeed, in Soames a sense of culmination and of peace – a feeling of virtue having been its own reward, and beyond all, the thought that he would soon be smelling English grass and seeing again the river flowing past his cows. Annette, even, might be glad to see him – he had bought her a really nice emerald bracelet in New York. To such general satisfaction this statue of 'Grief' was putting the finishing touch.

'Here we are, Anne.'

An English voice, and two young people at the far end – going to chatter, he supposed! He was preparing to rise when he heard the girl say, in a voice American, indeed, but soft and curiously private:

'John, it's terribly great. It makes me sink here.' From the gesture of her hand, Soames saw that it was where the thing had made *him* sink, too.

'Everlasting stillness. It makes me sad, John.'

As the young man's arm slid under hers his face came into view. Quick as thought, half of Soames's face disappeared again into his hand. 'John?' 'Jon' was what she had meant to say. Young Jon Forsyte – not a doubt of it! And this girl, his wife, sister – as he had heard – of that young American Francis Wilmot! What a mischance! He remembered the boy's face perfectly, though he had only seen it in that Gallery off Cork Street, and the pastrycook's after, and once on that grim afternoon when he had gone down to Robin Hill to beg his own divorced first wife to let *her* son marry *his* daughter! Never had he been more pleased to be refused! Never had the fitness of things been better confirmed; and yet, the pain of telling Fleur of that refusal remained in his memory like a still-live ember, red and prickly under the ashes of time. Behind his shadowing hat and screening hand Soames made sure. The young man was standing bare-headed, as if in reverence to the statue. A Forsyte look about him, in spite of too much hair. A poet – he had heard! The face wasn't a bad one; it had what they called charm; the eyes were deep-set, like his grandfather's, old Jolyon's, and the same colour, dark grey; the touch of brightness on his head came from his mother, no doubt; but the chin was a Forsyte's chin. Soames looked at the girl. A fair height, brownish pale, brown hair, dark eyes; pretty trick of the neck, nice way of standing too; very straight, an attractive figure! But how could the young man have taken to her after Fleur? Still, for an American, she looked very natural; a little bit like a nymph, with a kind of privacy about her.

Nothing in America had struck Soames so much as the lack of

privacy. If you wanted to be private you had to disconnect your telephone and get into a bath – otherwise they rang you up just as you
were going to sleep, to ask if you were Mr and Mrs Newberg. The
houses, too, were not divided from each other, nor even from the
roads. In the hotels the rooms all ran into each other, and as likely
as not there'd be a drove of bankers in the hall. Dinner too – nothing
private about that; even if you went out to dinner, it was always the
same: lobster-cocktails, shad, turkey, asparagus, salad, and ice cream;
very good dishes, no doubt, and you put on weight, but nothing
private about them.

Those two were talking; he remembered the young man's voice.

'It's the greatest man-made thing in America, Anne. We haven't
anything so good at home. It makes me hungry – we'll have to go
to Egypt.'

'Your mother would just love that, Jon; and so would I.'

'Come and see it from the other side.'

Soames rose abruptly and left the alcove. Though not recognised,
he was flustered. A ridiculous, even a dangerous encounter. He had
travelled for six months to restore Fleur's peace of mind, and now
that she was tranquil, he would not for the world have her suddenly
upset again by a sight of her first love. He remembered only too well
how a sight of Irene used to upset himself. Yes – and as likely as
not Irene was here too! Well, Washington was a big place. Not much
danger! They were going to Mount Vernon in the afternoon, and
tomorrow morning early were off again! At the top of the cemetery
his taxicab was waiting. One of those other cars must belong to
those two young people; and he glanced at them sidelong. Did there
rise in him some fear, some hope, that in one of them he would see
her whom, in another life, he had seen, day by day, night by night,
waiting for what – it seemed – he could not give her. No! only the
drivers and their voices, their 'Yeahs!' and their 'Yeps!' Americans
no longer said 'Yes', it seemed. And getting into his taxi, he said:

'Hotel *Po*-tomac.'

'Hotel Po-*to*-mac?'

'If you prefer it.'

The driver grinned and shut Soames in . . . The Veterans' Home!

They said the veterans had pretty well died off. Still, they'd have plenty coming on from this last war. Besides, what was space and money to America? They had so much they didn't know what to do with it. Well, he didn't mind that, now that he was leaving. He didn't mind anything. Indeed, he had invited quite a number of Americans to come and see his pictures if they came to England. They had been very kind, very hospitable; he had seen a great many fine pictures too, including some Chinese; and a great many high buildings, and the air was very stimulating. It wouldn't suit him to live here, but it was all very much alive, and a good tonic, for a bit. 'I can't see *her* living here!' he thought suddenly. 'There never was anyone more private.' The cars streamed past him, or stood parked in rows. America was all cars and newspapers! And a sudden thought disturbed him. They put everything into the newspapers over here; what if his name were among the arrivals?

Reaching his hotel, he went at once towards the kiosk in the hall where you could buy newspapers, toothpaste, 'candy' to pull your teeth out – teeth to replace them, he shouldn't be surprised. List of arrivals? Here it was: 'Hotel Potomac: Mr and Mrs Cyrus K. McGunn; the Misses Errick; Mr H. Yellam Roof; Mr Semmes Forsyth; Mr and Mrs Munt.' As large as life, but, fortunately, only half as natural! Forsyth! Munt! They never could get anything right in the papers. 'Semmes!' Unrecognisable, he should hope. And going over to the bureau, he turned the register towards him. Yes! he had written the names quite clearly. Lucky, too, or they'd have got 'em right, by mistake. And then, turning the leaf, he read: 'Mr and Mrs Jolyon Forsyte.' Here! At this hotel – those two! A day before them; yes, and at the very top, dated some days ago: 'Mrs Irene Forsyte.' His mind travelled with incredible swiftness. He must deal with this at once. Where were Fleur and Michael? They had seen the Freer Gallery with him yesterday, and a beautiful little Gallery it was, he had never seen anything better, and the Lincoln Memorial, and that great tower thing which he had refused to go up. This morning they had said they should go to the Corcoran Gallery, where there was a Centenary Exhibition. He had known what that meant. He had seen English centenaries in his time. All the fashionable painters of their day – and the result too melancholy for words! And to the clerk he said:

'Is there a restaurant here where I can get a good lunch?'

'Sure; they cook fine at Filler's.'

'Good! If my daughter and her husband come in, kindly tell them to meet me at Filler's at one o'clock.'

And, going back to the kiosk, he bought some tickets for the opera, so that they should be out in the evening, and in ten minutes was on his way to the Corcoran Gallery. From Filler's they would go straight off to Mount Vernon; they would dine at another hotel before the opera, and tomorrow be off by the first train – he would take no chances. If only he could catch them at the Corcoran!

Arriving, he mechanically bought a catalogue and walked up-stairs. The rooms opened off the gallery and he began at the end room. Ah! there they were, in front of a picture of the setting sun! Sure of them now, but not sure of himself – Fleur was so sharp – Soames glanced at the pictures. Modern stuff, trailing behind those French extravagances Dumetrius had shown him six months ago in London. As he had thought, too, a wholesale lot; might all have been painted by the same hand. He saw Fleur touch Michael's arm and laugh. How pretty she looked! A thousand pities to have her apple-cart upset again! He came up behind them. What? That setting sun was a man's face, was it? Well, you never knew nowadays.

And he said: 'I thought I'd have a look in. We're lunching at Filler's; they tell me it's better than the hotel; and we can go straight on from there to Mount Vernon. I've got some seats for the opera, tonight, too.'

And, conscious of Fleur's secrutiny, he stared at the picture. He did not feel too comfortable.

'Are the older pictures better?' he asked.

'Well, sir, Fleur was just saying – how can anyone go on painting in these days?'

'How do you mean?'

'If you walk through, you'll say the same. Here's a hundred years of it.'

'The best pictures never get into these shows,' said Soames; 'they just take anything they can get. Ryder, Innes, Whistler, Sargent – the Americans have had some great painters.'

'Of course,' said Fleur. 'But do you really want to go round, Dad? I'm frightfully hungry.'

'No,' said Soames; 'after that Saint Gaudens thing I don't feel like it. Let's go and lunch.'

II

*M*ount Vernon! The situation was remarkable! With all that colour on the trees, the grassy cliff, and below it the broad blue Potomac, which, even Soames confessed, was more imposing than the Thames. And the low white house up here, dignified and private, indeed, except for the trippers, almost English, giving him a feeling he had not had since he left home. He could imagine that fellow George Washington being very fond of it. One could have taken to the place oneself. Lord John Russell's old house on the hill at Richmond was something like this, except, of course, for the breadth of river, and the feeling you always had in America and Canada, so far as he had seen, that they were trying to fill the country and not succeeding – such a terrific lot of space, and apparently no time. Fleur was in raptures, and young Michael had remarked that it was 'absolutely topping'. The sun fell warmly on his cheek while he took his last look from the wide porch, before entering the house itself. He should remember this – America had not all been run up yesterday! He passed into the hall and proceeded, mousing, through the lower rooms. Really! They had done it extraordinarily well. Nothing but the good old original stuff, from a century and a half ago, reminding Soames of half-hours spent in the antique shops of

Taunton and Tunbridge Wells. Too much 'George Washington' of course!
George Washington's mug, George Washington's foot-bath, and his letter
to so-and-so, and the lace on his collar, and his sword and his gun and
everything that was his! Still, that was unavoidable! Detached from the
throng, detached even from his daughter, Soames moved – covered, as
in a cloak, by his collector's habit of silent appraisement; he so disliked
his judgments to be confused by uncritical imbecilities. He had reached
the bedroom upstairs where George Washington had died, and was
gazing through the grille, when he heard sounds which almost froze
his blood; the very voices he had listened to that morning before the
Saint Gaudens statue, and with those voices Michael's voice conjoined!
Was Fleur there too? A backward glance relieved him. No! the three
were standing at the head of the main stairs exchanging the remarks
of strangers casually interested in the same thing. He heard Michael
say, 'Jolly good taste in those days.' And Jon Forsyte answering, 'All
hand-made, you see.'

Soames dived for the back stairs, jostled a stout lady, recoiled,
stammering, and hurried on down. If Fleur was not with Michael it
meant that she had got hold of the curator. Take her away, while
those three were still upstairs! That was the thought in his mind. Two
young Englishmen were not likely to exchange names or anything
else, and, if they did, he must get hold of Michael quickly. But how
to get Fleur away? Yes, there she was – talking to the curator in front
of George Washington's flute laid down on George Washington's harpsichord in the music-room! And Soames suffered. Revolting to seem
unwell, still more revolting to pretend to seem! And yet – what else?
He could not go up to her and say: 'I've had enough. Let's go to the
car!' Swallowing violently, he put his hand to his head and went
towards the harpsichord.

'Fleur!' he said, and without pausing to let her take him in, went
on: 'I'm not feeling the thing. I must go to the car.'

The words no doubt were startling, coming from one so undra-
matic.

'Dad! What is it?'

'I don't know,' said Soames; 'giddy. Give me your arm.'

Really dreadful to him – the whole thing! On the way to the car, parked at the entrance, her concern was so embarrassing that he very nearly abandoned his ruse. But he managed to murmur:

'I've been doing too much, I expect; or else it's that cookery. I'll just sit quiet in the car.'

To his great relief she sat down with him, got out her smelling-bottle, and sent the chauffeur to tell Michael. Soames was touched, though incommoded by having to sniff the salts, which were very strong.

'Great fuss about nothing,' he muttered.

'We'd better get home, dear, at once, so that you can lie down.'

In a few minutes Michael came hurrying. He too expressed what seemed to Soames a genuine concern, and the car was started. Soames sat back with his hand in Fleur's, and his mouth and eyes tight closed, feeling perhaps better than he'd ever felt in his life. Before they reached Alexandria he opened his lips to say that he had spoiled their trip for them; they must go home by way of Arlington, and he would stay in the car while they had a look at it. Fleur was for going straight on, but he insisted. Arrived, however, at this other white house, also desirably situated on the slope above the river, he almost had a fit while waiting for them in the car. What if the same idea had occurred to Jon Forsyte and he were suddenly to drive up? It was an intense relief when they came out again, saying that it was nice but not a patch on Mount Vernon: the porch columns were too thick. When the car was again traversing the bright woods Soames opened his eyes for good.

'I'm all right again, now. It was liver, I expect.'

'You ought to have some brandy, Dad. We can get some on a doctor's prescription.'

'Doctor? Nonsense. We'll dine upstairs and I'll get over the waiter; they must have something in the house.'

Dine upstairs! That was a happy thought!

In their sitting room he lay down on the sofa, touched and gratified, for Fleur was plopping up his cushions, shading the light, looking over the top of her book to see how he was. He did not remember when he had felt so definitely that she really did care about him. He even thought: 'I ought to be ill a little, every now and then!' And yet, if he ever complained of feeling ill at home, Annette at once complained of feeling worse!

Close by, in the little salon opposite the stairs, a piano was being played.

'Does that music worry you, dear?'

Into Soames's mind flashed the thought 'Irene!' If it were, and Fleur were to go out to stop it, then, indeed, would fat be in the fire!

'No; I rather like it,' he said, hastily.

'It's a very good touch.'

Irene's touch! He remembered how June used to praise her touch; remembered how he had caught that fellow Bosinney listening to her, in the little drawing room in Montpellier Square, with the wild-cat look on his face, the fellow had; remembered how she used to stop playing when he himself came in – from consideration, or the feeling that it was wasted on him – which? He had never known. He had never known anything! Well – another life! He closed his eyes, and instantly saw Irene in her emerald-green dinner-gown, standing in the Park Lane hall, first feast after their honeymoon, waiting to be cloaked! Why did such pictures come back before closed eyes – pictures without rhyme or reason? Irene brushing her hair – grey now, of course! As he was seventy, she must be nearly sixty-two! How time went! Hair *feuille morte* – old Aunt Juley used to call it with a certain pride in having picked up the expression – and eyes so velvet dark! Ah! but handsome was as handsome did! Still – who could say! Perhaps, if he had known how to express his feelings! If he had understood music! If she hadn't so excited his senses! Perhaps – oh, perhaps your grandmother! No riddling that out! And here – of all places. A tricksy business! Was one never to forget?

Fleur went to pack and dress. Dinner came up. Michael spoke of having met a refreshing young couple at Mount Vernon, 'an Englishman; he said Mount Vernon made him awfully homesick'.

'What was his name, Michael?'

'Name? I didn't ask. Why?'

'Oh! I don't know. I thought you might have.'

Soames breathed again. He had seen her prick her ears. Give it a chance, and her feeling for that boy of Irene's would flare up again. It was in the blood!

'Bright Markland,' said Michael, 'has been gassing over the future of America – he's very happy about it because there are so many farmers still, and people on the land; but he's also been gassing over the future of England – he's very happy about it, and there's hardly anybody on the land.'

'Who's Bright Markland?' muttered Soames.

'Editor of our Scrutator, sir. Never was a better example of optimism, or the science of having things both ways.'

'I'd hoped,' said Soames heavily, 'that seeing these new countries would have made you feel there's something in an old one, after all.'

Michael laughed. 'No need to persuade me of that, sir. But you see I belong to what is called the fortunate class, and so, I believe, do you.'

Soames stared. This young man was getting sarcastic!

'Well,' he said, 'I shall be glad to be home. Are you packed?'

They were; and presently he telephoned for a cab to take them to the opera. So that they might not hang about in the hall, he went down, himself, to see them into it. The incident passed without let or hindrance; and with a deep sigh of relief he resumed his place in the lift, and was restored to his room.

III

He stood there at the window, looking out at the tall houses, the lights, the cars moving below and the clear starry sky. He was really tired now; another day of this, and he would not need to simulate indisposition. A narrow squeak, indeed – a series of them! He wished he were safe home. To be under the same roof with that woman – how very queer! He had not passed a night under the same roof with her since that dreadful day in November '87, when he walked round and round Montpellier Square in such mortal agony, and came to his front door to find young Jolyon there. One lover dead, and the other already on his threshold! That night she had stolen away from his house; never again till this night had the same roof covered them. That music again – soft and teasing! *Was* it she playing? To get away from it, he went into his bedroom and put his things together. He was not long about that, for he had only a suit-case with him. Should he go to bed? To bed, and lie awake? This thing had upset him. If it were she, sitting at that piano, a few yards away, what did she look like now? Seven times – no, eight – he had seen her since that long-ago November night. Twice in her Chelsea flat; then by that fountain in the Bois de Boulogne; at Robin Hill when he delivered his ultimatum to her and young Jolyon; at Queen Victoria's funeral; at Lord's Cricket ground; again at Robin Hill when he went to beg for Fleur; and in the Goupenor Gallery just before she came out here. Each meeting he could remember in every detail, down to the lifting of her gloved hand at the last – the faint smiling of her lips.

And Soames shivered. Too hot – these American rooms! He went back into the sitting room; they had cleared away and brought him the evening paper; no good in that! He could never find anything in the papers over here. At this distance from the past, all this space and all this time – what did he feel about her? Hate? The word was too strong. One didn't hate those who weren't near one. Besides, he had never hated her! Not even when he first knew she was unfaithful. Contempt? No. She had made him ache too much for that. He didn't know what he felt. And he began walking up and down, and once or twice stood at the door and listened, as might a prisoner in his cell. Undignified! And going to the sofa he stretched himself out on it. He would think about his travels. Had he enjoyed them? One long whirl of things, and – water. And yet, all had gone according to programme, except China, to which they had given as wide a berth as possible, owing to its state. The Sphinx and the Taj Mahal, Vancouver Harbour, and the Rocky Mountains, they played a sort of hide-and-seek within him; and now – that strumming; was it She? Strange! You had, it seemed, only just one season of real heat.

Everything else that happened to you was in a way tepid, and perhaps it was as well, or the boiler would burst. His emotions in the years when he first knew her – would he go through them again? Not for the world. And yet! Soames got up. That music was going on and on; but when it stopped, the player – She or not She! – would be no longer visible. Why not walk past that little salon – just walk past, and – and take a glimpse? If it were She, well, probably she'd lost her looks – the beauty that had played such havoc with him? He had noticed the position of the piano; yes – the player would be in profile to him. He opened the door; the music swelled, and he stole forth.

The breadth of Fleur's room, only, separated him from that little open salon opposite the stairs. No one was in the corridor, not even a bell boy. Very likely some American woman after all, possibly that girl – Jon's wife! Yet no – there was something – something in the sound! And holding up the evening paper before him, he moved along. Three pillars, with spaces between them, divided the salon from the corridor, avoiding what Soames so missed in America – the fourth wall. At the first of these pillars he came to a stand. A tall lamp with an orange shade stood by the keyboard, and the light from it fell on the music, on the keys, on the cheek and hair of the player. *She!* Though he had supposed her grey by now, the sight of that hair without a thread in it of the old gold affected him strangely. Curved, soft, shining, it covered her like a silver casque. She was in evening dress, and he could see that her shoulders, neck, and arms were still rounded and beautiful. All her body from the waist was moving lightly to the rhythm of her playing. Her frock was of a greyish heliotrope. Soames stood behind his pillar gazing, his hand over his face, lest she should turn her head. He did not exactly feel – the film of remembrance was unrolled too quickly. From the first sight of her in a Bournemouth drawing room to the last sight of her in the Goupenor Gallery – the long sequence passed him by in its heat and its frost and its bitterness; the long struggle of sense, the long failure of spirit; the long aching passion, and its long schooling into numbness and indifference. The last thing he wanted, standing there, was to speak with her, and yet he could not take his eyes away.

Suddenly she stopped playing; bending forward she closed the music and reached to turn out the lamp. Her face came round in the light, and, cowering back, Soames saw it, still beautiful, perhaps more beautiful, a little worn, so that the eyes looked even darker than of old, larger, softer under the still-dark eyebrows. And once more he had that feeling: 'There sits a woman I have never known.' With a sort of anger he craned back till he could see no longer. Ah! she had had many faults, but the worst of her faults had always been, was still, her infernal mystery! And, stepping silently like a cat, he regained his room.

He felt tired to death now, and, going into his bedroom, undressed hurriedly and got into bed. He wished with all his heart that he were on board, under the British flag. 'I'm old,' he thought suddenly, 'old.' This America was too young for him, so full of energy, bustling about to ends he could not see. Those Eastern places had been different. And yet, after all, he was a mere seventy. His father had lived to be ninety – old Jolyon eighty-five, Timothy a hundred, and so with all the old Forsytes. At seventy *they* weren't playing golf; and yet they were younger, younger anyway than he felt tonight. The sight of that woman had – had—! Old!

'I'm not going back to be old,' he thought. 'If I feel like this again I shall consult someone.' They had some monkey thing nowadays they could inject. He shouldn't try that. Monkeys indeed! Why not pigs or tigers? Hold on somehow another ten or fifteen years! By that time they would have found out where they were in England. That precious capital levy would have been exploded. He would know what he had to leave to Fleur; would see her baby grow into a boy and go to school – public school – even! Eton? No – young Jolyon had been there. Winchester, the Monts' school? Not there either, if he could help it. Harrow was handy; or his own old school – Marlborough? Perhaps he would see him play at Lord's. Another fifteen years before Kit could play at Lord's! Well – something to look forward to, something to hold on for. If you hadn't that, you felt old, and if you *felt* old, you *were* old, and the end soon came. How well that woman had worn! She—! There were his pictures too; take them up more seriously. That Freer Gallery! Leave them to the nation, and your name lived – much comfort in *that*! She! *She* would never die!

A crack of light on the wall close to the door.

'Asleep, Dad?'

So Fleur had remembered to come and have a look at him!

'How are you now, dear?'

'All right; tired. How was the opera?'

'Middling.'

'I've told them to call us at seven. We'll breakfast on the train.'

Her lips touched his forehead. If – if that woman – but never – never once – never of her own accord—!

'Good night,' he said. 'Sleep well!'

The light on the wall narrowed and was gone! Well! He was drowsy now. But, in this house – Shapes – Shapes! Past – present – at the piano – at his bedside – passing – passing by – and there, behind them, the great bronze-hooded woman, with the closed eyes, deep sunk in everlasting – profound – pro—! And from Soames a gentle snore escaped.

The Silver Spoon:

Additional material

How John Galsworthy wrote

*B*etween 1908 and 1923, when John and Ada Galsworthy were not in London, they lived at Wingstone, their house in the country. Located on the outskirts of a very small village called Manaton in Dartmoor, it was where Galsworthy was happiest. The peace and quiet it provided meant that it was also where he did a great deal of his writing.

Here follows an account by Rudolf Sauter, Galsworthy's nephew, which gives us an insight into his uncle's daily life at Wingstone:

I see him, as I first became conscious of him at Wingstone, sitting on the lawn of an evening, a blotter on his knee, a black spaniel and a china inkpot on the grass at his feet and a J-nib in his pen – his hair not yet so silver, but already a little thin at the top, and his face, pickled to a fine old leathery bronze, turned towards the lowering sun. Each time, as the tide of shadows crept to his shoes, as the cool shade climbed his knees and fell across the quiet hands, he would edge his chair bit by bit along the lawn to catch a little more of that life-giving sun which was the very essence of his being – and the spaniel John (known in private life as Chris or by some 98 other nicknames) perceiving that his own especial sun had left him, would get up and move in its wake. I remember my surprise at the simplicity of his materials: typing paper (of a day before typing had become so universal among writers) on to which, later, his writing would be faithfully transcribed by A.G.[1], a cardboard pad balanced on his knee, an ordinary inkpot, and that J pen to which he remained faithful to the end, for he was always impatient of everything which came between his thought and the written word. By that same token he regarded typewritten letters as soulless if convenient embodiments of thought, and confined himself to longhand in the writing of all letters.

I always envied the simplicity of his equipment, compared with my own cumbersome painter's paraphernalia, but it was characteristic of him to mistrust elaboration wherever simplicity was attainable . . . I recall our long rides and walks over the moors, and those whimsical discussions in which he always seemed to hint at so much more than he said – each as much a part of his well-ordered day as the mass of work which he got through without flurry or waste of time. This tidiness and method he always acknowledged to be due to A.G., for he confessed to being rather untidy by nature himself and not temperamentally inclined to regularity.

On one particular ride, in 1915 I think it was, at a time when the 'dot and dash' method of writing was at its zenith, I well remember asking him what he thought the next development in Literature would be; and my surprise when he said he envisaged the 'three-decker' on the horizon again.

I remember, too, a walk with A.G. and Gilbert Murray[2] and him on a certain morning of his birthday, when one of us remarked that the locals would be quite surprised because they had never seen him out in the morning before. For he made it a rule all his life to work regularly from breakfast till lunch whether at home or on travel (never altering this except in the train or aboard ship, which he said always induced in him a blankness of mind, suitable only to the reading of detective stories). The afternoon he would devote to walking or tennis or some other form of exercise, and the time between tea and

[1] Ada Galsworthy
[2] Friend of John Galsworthy, well-connected scholar and intellectual

dinner to revision or correspondence, leaving, at Wingstone, just time for a ride before dinner . . . After dinner he usually read, occasionally aloud, and this was indeed a treat.

Reading-group questions

✦ Discuss the character of Fleur and her growth through the story. Do you like her? How similar is she to her father Soames? Does her husband Michael have a positive influence over her? In what ways does she embrace or rebel against being a Forsyte?

✦ Is family loyalty and honour as important to the younger generation of Forsytes?

✦ How does Soames evolve with age? Do you think his love for Fleur changes him for the better or is it still born of a possessive instinct?

✦ Sensitive, understanding and passionate, or confused and weak-willed – how would you interpret the character of Jon Forsyte? Consider him in comparison to Michael Mont.

✦ The 'roaring twenties' were a time of great social change. Discuss how the attitudes of the younger generation had altered since the First World War from those of their Victorian parents. How well do you think John Galsworthy captures the spirit of the age?

THE FORSYTE SAGA
THE MAN OF PROPERTY

John Galsworthy

'"Soames will have trouble with her; you mark my words."'

London, 1880s: The Forsyte family is gathered – gloves, waistcoats, feathers and frocks – to celebrate the engagement of young June Forstye to an architect, Philip Bosinney. They are intrigued but wary of this stranger in their midst, whom they nickname 'The Buccaneer'. Also present is Soames Forsyte and his beautiful wife Irene – his most prized possession. With that meeting a chain of heart-breaking and tragic events is set in motion that will split the family to its very core . . .

In *The Man of Property*, John Galsworthy's stunning first instalment of *The Forsyte Saga*, the stage is set for one of the most absorbing family dramas ever written.

Since it first appeared in 1906, *The Forsyte Saga* has enthralled generations of readers, and been adapted with huge success for both film and television. These sumptuous new editions of each individual novel include reading-group questions and exciting, exclusive material to introduce them to a whole new audience.

'An immortal achievement . . . it is, at all levels, **readability itself**' *Financial Times*

978 0 7553 4085 9

headline
review

THE FORSYTE SAGA

IN CHANCERY

John Galsworthy

'He had never thought that the sight of this woman whom he once so passionately desired . . . could affect him in this way.'

Separated from his wife Irene, Soames Forsyte has almost accepted that she's never coming back. But he yearns for an heir. When he confronts Irene, the raw wounds of his past passion are exposed and he will do anything to claim back what is his. Then his cousin Jolyon Forsyte moves in to protect Irene and the old family rift splinters into new jealousy, hatred and fear. But this time it runs too deeply for forgiveness . . .

Love, infatuation and dishonour – *In Chancery*, the second episode of John Galsworthy's gripping family drama, sees the Forsytes heartbreakingly divided.

Since it first appeared in 1906, *The Forsyte Saga* has enthralled generations of readers, and been adapted with huge success for both film and television. These sump-tuous new editions of each individual novel include reading-group questions and exciting, exclusive material to introduce them to a whole new audience.

'Such a **cracking good story** . . . compulsive, as well as very **modern and outrageous**' *The Sunday Times*

978 0 7553 4086 6

headline
review

THE FORSYTE SAGA

TO LET

John Galsworthy

'"You know there's a feud between our families?"'

Soames Forsyte has built a good life for himself with his second wife Annette. And he has a new focus and purpose; his beautiful, beloved daughter Fleur. But the sins of the father come flooding back to cast a shadow over his child's future. When Fleur, a vibrant and impetuous young woman, catches the eye of warm-hearted and idealistic Jon Forsyte at a chance meeting, it seems fate is determined to torture them all with the hurts of the past . . .

A new generation of Forsytes break open painful family secrets – *To Let* is a heart-achingly poignant tale of forbidden love.

Since it first appeared in 1906, *The Forsyte Saga* has enthralled generations of readers, and been adapted with huge success for both film and television. These sumptuous new editions of each individual novel include reading-group questions and exciting, exclusive material to introduce them to a whole new audience.

'The satire is sharp, the dialogue, **elegant and witty**, and the characterisation – **dazzling**' *Scotsman*

978 0 7553 4087 3

headline
review

THE FORSYTE SAGA

THE WHITE MONKEY

John Galsworthy

'Tomorrow! Second anniversary of her wedding-day! Still an ache when she thought of what it had not been.'

It's 1922 and Fleur Forsyte is now married to Michael Mont. The young couple throw themselves into the social whirlwind of the roaring twenties and seem to be enjoying life, entertaining friends in their smart Westminster house. But their marriage is haunted by the ghost of a past love affair. However vibrant Fleur appears, those closest to her sense a veiled sadness. Michael, devoted to his wife, but not blind to her faults, is determined to stand by her through anything. But just how much can he really forgive?

The hedonism and confusion of post-war London are beautifully captured in *The White Monkey*, drawing us into a new engrossing chapter for Galsworthy's indomitable Forsytes.

Since it first appeared in 1906, *The Forsyte Saga* has enthralled generations of readers, and been adapted with huge success for both film and television. These sumptuous new editions of each individual novel include reading-group questions and exciting, exclusive material to introduce them to a whole new audience.

'Such a **cracking good story** . . . compulsive, as well as very **modern and outrageous**' *The Sunday Times*

978 0 7553 4088 0

headline
review

THE FORSYTE SAGA

SWAN SONG

John Galsworthy

'When, looking down the row of faces at her canteen table, Fleur saw Jon Forsyte's, it was within her heart as if, in winter, she had met with honeysuckle.'

Jon Forsyte is back. After years living in America, he is thrilled to be home and eager to show off his roots to his new bride Anne. When Fleur Mont, Jon's first love, hears of his arrival, she doesn't know what to feel. She's older now, more worldly, and married too with a young son – looking back can only bring pain. But feelings such as theirs are not easily buried. And when their passion is rekindled, no one can halt the devastating events that follow . . .

Swan Song, the sixth mesmerising instalment of *The Forsyte Saga*, marks the end of an era for the Forsytes, the dramatic culmination of an old family rift that has coloured their lives for decades.

Since it first appeared in 1906, *The Forsyte Saga* has enthralled generations of readers, and been adapted with huge success for both film and television. These sumptuous new editions of each individual novel include reading-group questions and exciting, exclusive material to introduce them to a whole new audience.

'The satire is sharp, the dialogue, **elegant and witty**, and the characterisation – **dazzling**' *Scotsman*

978 0 7553 4090 3

headline
review

THE FORSYTE SAGA
MAID IN WAITING

John Galsworthy

'In this family, the troubles of one were the troubles of all.'

As the 1930s bring dramatic change, so Galsworthy's sweeping family saga turns to the Cherrells, cousins of the Forsytes. Young Dinny Cherrell, seemingly fragile, but strong and determined, is a bright and vivid character who breathes life into all those she encounters. To her, family is everything. So when her brother faces extradition to South America, falsely accused of murder, and her cousin is threatened by her unstable husband, Dinny will do anything she can to shield them from harm.

The heartbreak and scandal continues with another branch of the family – *Maid in Waiting* opens a thrilling new phase in *The Forsyte Saga*.

Since it first appeared in 1906, *The Forsyte Saga* has enthralled generations of readers, and been adapted with huge success for both film and television. These sumptuous new editions of each individual novel include reading-group questions and exciting, exclusive material to introduce them to a whole new audience.

'An immortal achievement . . . it is, at all levels, readability itself' *Financial Times*

978 0 7553 4091 0

headline
review

THE FORSYTE SAGA

FLOWERING WILDERNESS

John Galsworthy

'It was like no other hour she had ever spent, and at the end of it she knew she was in love.'

Dinny Cherrell has been proposed to numerous times. But no one has ever come close to capturing her independent spirit – until she encounters Wilfred Desert. They had met briefly at Fleur Forsyte and Michael Mont's wedding and the spark of attraction felt all those years ago flowers into a deep, all-consuming passion. But Wilfred, made cynical by the war, is a complicated and tortured soul. When his past actions come back to haunt him, and the disapproval of Dinny's family work against them, their love is tested to the very limit . . .

Honour, family loyalty and a heart-wrenching love story – *Flowering Wilderness* is the poignant, utterly engrossing penultimate episode in *The Forsyte Saga*.

Since it first appeared in 1906, *The Forsyte Saga* has enthralled generations of readers, and been adapted with huge success for both film and television. These sumptuous new editions of each individual novel include reading-group questions and exciting, exclusive material to introduce them to a whole new audience.

'Such a cracking good story . . . compulsive, as well as very modern and outrageous' *The Sunday Times*

978 0 7553 4092 7

headline
review